T0007099

A PERFECT FIFTH

What Reviewers Say About Jaycie Morrison's Work

The Found Jar

"It's a book full of unexpected depth and humanity. I really appreciated how Morrison manages to illustrate that trauma does different things to different people. Both MCs have experienced trauma and loss that has made them who they are and her characterizations almost depict the two opposites of possible reactions. Having them fall for each other despite the many things they have to work through makes for a really good read. This is Morrison's first foray into contemporary romance, and I hope this continues. I'd definitely recommend giving this book a go as it brings a different approach to romance than I've personally encountered before in the wlw arena and for that reason alone it's worthwhile giving it a try."—*LGBTQ+ Reader*

"The beach setting and Beck's pure heart help to offset the frustration I felt with Emily and her issues. Beck is an innocent and at times naive young woman who suffered a traumatic brain injury in her teens. Emily writes horror novels and battles nightmares and demons from her past. Beck's kindness and innocence are a balm for Emily's tortured soul. And there are kittens, and they soften some of the harsher scenes. It was interesting seeing the contrast between these two women as their relationship developed. One with a TBI who deals with her disability and tries to face her challenges with a positive attitude versus the other with so much emotional baggage that she can't see past her anger and disgust with herself to allow Beck into her life. Will their friendship develop into the relationship you know they deserve?"—*LezReviewBooks*

Heart's Orders

"I am so enamored with this awesome story! While I was reading this book I got so caught up in the struggles the characters faced—I felt as though I was experiencing all of the angst, confusion and elation right along with them. There is one thing that I know for sure; this story is going to stay with me for quite some time. These strong-willed women are truly unforgettable, and they will capture your heart and attention from the first page."—*Lesbian Review*

"Jaycie Morrison has captured the mood of an era really well in these novels, and the determination of the women who have signed up to the WAC to not only do a good job but to forge a place for themselves in the world. ...The romances are sweet and gentle, the mood is soft focus despite the harsh realities of the time. An excellent follow up in the Love and Courage Series, I look forward to book three."
—*Lesbian Reading Room*

Basic Training of the Heart

"There are some great WWII lesbian romances out there, and you can count *Basic Training of the Heart* among them. It's well worth a read, and I look forward to seeing what's next in this series."—*Lesbian Review–Top 100 Books To Start With*

Visit us at www.boldstrokesbooks.com

By the Author

The Love and Courage Series

Basic Training of the Heart

Heart's Orders

Guarding Hearts

The Found Jar

A Perfect Fifth

A PERFECT FIFTH

by
Jaycie Morrison

2022

A PERFECT FIFTH
© 2022 BY JAYCIE MORRISON. ALL RIGHTS RESERVED.

ISBN 13: 978-1-63679-132-6

THIS TRADE PAPERBACK ORIGINAL IS PUBLISHED BY
BOLD STROKES BOOKS, INC.
P.O. BOX 249
VALLEY FALLS, NY 12185

FIRST EDITION: SEPTEMBER 2022

THIS IS A WORK OF FICTION. NAMES, CHARACTERS, PLACES, AND
INCIDENTS ARE THE PRODUCT OF THE AUTHOR'S IMAGINATION OR
ARE USED FICTITIOUSLY. ANY RESEMBLANCE TO ACTUAL PERSONS,
LIVING OR DEAD, BUSINESS ESTABLISHMENTS, EVENTS, OR LOCALES
IS ENTIRELY COINCIDENTAL.

THIS BOOK, OR PARTS THEREOF, MAY NOT BE REPRODUCED IN ANY
FORM WITHOUT PERMISSION.

CREDITS
EDITOR: BARBARA ANN WRIGHT
PRODUCTION DESIGN: SUSAN RAMUNDO
COVER DESIGN BY TAMMY SEIDICK

Acknowledgments

This is truly my pandemic book, in the sense that it was written while the worst variants emerged, and also because by the time I was working on edits, I had my own bout of COVID. My yearning for travel probably shows the times more than anything, and I offer a huge thanks to my UK friends, Millie and Susan, for their help in removing those creeping "Americanisms" from my British characters. Any errors in that realm are strictly my own. Also thanks to my beta readers, Cindy and Avery, whose sharp eyes and helpful suggestions made this a better book than it otherwise would have been. Julie, I count on your discernment almost as much as I do your friendship. And to the Fearsome Foursome group—Cass, Jeannie, and Suzie— whose ongoing reflections demonstrate that talking about writing can somehow be as inspiring as writing itself. Almost.

My profound appreciation to the entire Bold Strokes team for their diligent efforts in working with those of us who scribble away, hoping to bring stories that will move and comfort and entertain. And an extra dose of gratitude to Barbara, who actually has more than one job and does them all extremely well.

Dedication

To my dear friend Marti—with whom I could always talk "book business." I've felt your loss throughout this past year, but never more than at times like these.

To my mom, whose real, unconditional love helped make me the romance writer I am today. You told me you were ready to go, but I'm still not ready for you to be gone. In my heart we talk every day.

And to my wonderful wife, Sandy, whose love and light never fail. Happy anniversary, Sweetie. Let's have this many more again.

Chapter One

Constance Holston was on her third lap around the deck of the luxurious cruise ship, *Ocean Princess*, when the sounds of piano chords trickled past her ears. She would have bypassed the lounge again, but the rendition of "Son of a Preacher Man," the song she and Nelson had first kissed to at the party just before the year turned to 1969, made her stop. The edgy feeling that had her pacing restlessly was at least partially due to him. In their last brief phone call, Nelson had indicated he'd spent the previous weekend studying at Jillian's during the time Constance had been in New York for a few days of shopping with her mother while her father worked. Her problem wasn't jealousy, exactly. Jillian was her very best friend and had been for practically her whole life. Plus, her woman's intuition told her Jilly had no romantic interest in Nelson, and though she couldn't say with absolute certainty that the opposite was true, it was reassuring to envision them in Jilly's study, where the only electricity between them would be in the glossaries of the coming term's texts.

Sometimes, it was difficult having as her closest confidant a woman who was classically beautiful in the way that only a happy genetic accident or generations of thoughtful breeding could produce. In the case of Jillian Stansfield, it was definitely the latter, as her family lineage rivaled the Royals—as evidenced by her father's Earldom—and had the kind of era-spanning wealth that went with it. Unfairly, it sometimes seemed, the chromosomal stew had also gifted Jillian with a vast, perceptive intelligence which her parents thoroughly indulged with all their extensive resources. Her father had assisted her in creating a lab that the local public school would have envied. When Constance had asked if she wanted to be a scientist, Jillian had fixed her with her blazing blue eyes for a moment before she'd shrugged. "I just want to understand how things work and why. Don't you?"

To this day, Constance couldn't say whether Jillian's remark had planted the seed which led to her love of history, but it was almost a relief to find a direction for herself after watching Jillian's determined march toward her future. At university, Jilly's career direction had shifted to engineering—focusing not only on how things worked but also contributing to making them better—while Constance remained dedicated to learning about famous figures and significant events of the past. It suited her to know how things would turn out in advance. Otherwise, she worried too much. Like now, when thoughts of Nelson at Jillian's incredible home only made her worry about Jilly being on her own.

Some of Constance's other acquaintances thought Jillian Stansfield was a standoffish snob, but Constance believed Jilly's parents had just been so focused on her intellectual development that they'd neglected her emotional needs. The years of training that ensured Jillian's faultless public behavior and impeccable manners meant she never relaxed her cool reserve, except in the familiar company of their little group.

At least she had Clive like Constance had Nelson. Clive was honestly more handsome than Nelson and a fabulous dancer besides. Constance had briefly had her eye on him during their early teens, since he had the kind of wit and charm to attract practically any woman. In spite of being a terrible flirt, he hadn't developed the libertine reputation of his father, and it became clear that Jillian was the one he wanted. Constance was certain the four of them would be friends forever, raising their children in each other's company.

But Clive came and went like the wind, so if Jillian didn't hurry and make the shift from friendship to desire, she might lose him to someone outside of their foursome, and that would ruin everything.

Constance hoped Jilly was merely giving Clive time to sort himself out before letting her romantic intentions show, and given her lack of interest in other men, it seemed she was indeed waiting on him.

But sometimes, her aloof attitude or occasional negative comments about relationships gave Constance the uncomfortable sense that her dearest friend was genuinely not interested in finding love at all. As someone whose favorite reading was historical romance, Constance found it inconceivable that Lady Jillian Stansfield wouldn't long for happiness with a handsome stranger who would save her from her somewhat reclusive existence.

She didn't want to spend the whole cruise fretting, but couldn't shake her impatience for this ship to get back to England. She was keen to start her senior year at Cambridge, see her friends, and especially to be with Nelson, to whom she was now unofficially promised, going steady, exclusive. He was kind, with a gentle wit, and because he'd never rushed or pressured her, they'd gone all the way twice, and she considered that their unofficial engagement.

Sighing, she glanced at her watch, finding it was five minutes after five. The bar remained open throughout the day, but at this point, anyone could feel completely justified in having a drink. Her father was fond of saying it was always five o'clock somewhere, and she wouldn't have been surprised to find him in there, but he and her mother had chosen the early dinner seating, so they were probably getting dressed. She listened as the notes merged into another familiar song, then smiled as she recognized The Beatles' "Happiness is a Warm Gun," softened into an easy listening melody.

Nelson had practically worn out *The White Album* already. This performer definitely had a sense of humor, and Constance decided a cocktail was exactly what she needed. She made her way inside, pausing at the entrance to let her eyes adjust to the dim lighting. The piano was on the far side of the room, away from the bar but surrounded by small tables. She made her way to one, and a waitress promptly appeared. Declining the specialty drink menu, she ordered her usual gin gimlet. When the waitress departed, she turned her attention to the musician.

At first, the scene seemed too contrived to be real. Directly above the keyboard, next to the empty music rack, a cigarette burned in an ashtray beside a tip jar with a few bills already inside. The entertainer's bright yellow paisley tie hung loosely down the front of a white oxford shirt, and a well-formed, clean-shaven face was partially shadowed by a black, stingy brim fedora over collar-length, wavy dark hair. While mentally congratulating the cruise line on finding the perfect stereotype of an itinerant musician, she found herself unable to look away from the sure fingers as they made their way confidently along the keys. Strong hands. Nice arms, judging by the rolled-up sleeves. Something tingly crept up her spine. When it dawned on her that her anatomical assessment was bordering on gawking, Constance lifted her gaze back to the face, finding the entertainer's deep brown eyes appraising her.

Just then, the waitress and her drink made their appearance, giving her time to recover from her blush. The song finished amid a smattering of polite applause, and a low, but clearly female voice said, "Thank you very much. I'm Zara, and I'll be here all week." The accent was American, with a trace of those soft southern vowels that were so appealing. Indicating a stack of small rectangular sheets and two short pencils Constance hadn't noticed before, the woman added, "Please feel free to leave your requests or dedications here, and I'll do my best to get to them all. The waitstaff and I hope you'll enjoy your evening here with us in the Empire Lounge."

The world shifted, and Constance took three quick sips to steady herself. With the burn of gin courage, she risked another look. Right, now she could see the swell of breasts and the full lips. Zara began playing again, this time with a slight lift on the side of her mouth. She knew. Constance stayed for two more drinks, neither of which helped reconcile the lingering sense of attraction she'd felt when she'd thought Zara was a man. As Constance asked for her tab, Zara announced she was taking a short break, and she made her way toward the bar after speaking briefly to the groups and singles at the other tables along the way.

Constance regretted she hadn't left sooner, since she'd have to pass the bar on the way out. As she did, Zara said, "You won."

Normally, Constance would never engage in conversation with a stranger. That sort of temerity had been drilled out of her years ago. But she couldn't resist the obvious question. "Won what?"

"The award for Most Surprised." Zara grinned, and Constance felt her blush returning. "Your face…" Zara trailed off with a chuckle as the bartender placed a glass in front of her. In the light of the bar, her skin had a kind of dusky Mediterranean tone, which only added to her mysterious allure.

Constance tried to steady herself. Gesturing at Zara's outlandish outfit, she said, "I suppose that happens to you regularly since you've chosen to invite it."

Zara didn't seem the least bit put off by the snippy response. "Hey, they hired me as a gimmick, right? Patrons get all the T and A they want from other sources, don't they, Gina?" She nodded toward the waitress, whose skimpy costume Constance hadn't even noticed earlier.

"Bite me, Zara," the woman replied, but there was no anger in her tone.

"Maybe later." Zara winked at Gina as she left with a tray of drinks. Then she turned, her attention intently refocused. "Speaking of which, will I see you then?"

Totally out of her element, Constance was too flustered to have any semblance of nonchalance. "See me when?"

"Later." Zara finished her drink. When she leaned a little closer, there was no hint of alcohol on her breath. "Like I said, I'll be here all week. Won't you?"

"I…I have the early seating. Please excuse me." Constance all but stumbled out, shaken, but suspecting they shared the awareness that later would indeed come.

All through dinner, Constance pondered her experience at the lounge. Zara had clearly been flirting, which must mean she was a lesbian. Perhaps it shouldn't have come as such a shock. The world was only months from a new decade, after all, and a so-called gay pride crusade seemed to be attaching itself to the civil rights movements, with signs and slogans about "coming out." She'd never really cared about the issue before, but now dozens of questions flitted through her mind, to the point that she was barely able to keep up with the conversation at the table. Had a lesbian ever flirted with her before? If so, had she just missed it? She supposed it was likely she'd met other lesbians. Had they intrinsically understood she wasn't interested and avoided her? Was this one acting differently because she'd sensed Constance's initial attraction?

Why hadn't she simply explained that her initial interest was due to the male aspect of Zara's facade, and that was all? Pondering her lack of outrage at Zara's presumptuousness, she'd almost decided to avoid the woman for the rest of the trip when her father spoke.

"Shall we retire to the forward lounge?" he asked one of the other couples, his coincidental reference startling her. "My steward told me there's an entertaining piano player on this run. Quite talented and apparently, can play practically anything." He looked gleefully at her mother. "Shall we try to stump him?"

"Stump her," Constance corrected before she could think better.

"Pardon me?" her father asked, as if surprised by her unexpected entry into the exchange.

With all eyes on her, she had to finish. "I stopped by for a cocktail before dinner and heard the piano player. It's a woman."

"One of the liberated types?" her father asked. She gave a noncommittal shrug, but since it wasn't a flat denial, his lips thinned. "No mercy, then. Agreed?"

Several others at the table were game, but Constance was not among them. If she was going to see the intriguing Zara again, it certainly wasn't going to be in the presence of her parents and a handful of their cronies. As they made their way to the door, she murmured to her mother that she was tired and going to bed. Both were true. But her early evening did nothing to resolve her agitation as her ears echoed with music, and her mind supplied endless images of the activities at the piano. And later, in her dreams, someplace beyond.

Her parents didn't comment about their Empire Lounge experience the next day, though her father's mood was particularly sour. Clearly, his intention to confound Zara had failed, which made Constance curious enough to forget her earlier misgivings. She stopped in the lounge after her afternoon walk, having convinced herself it wasn't "later." She was simply in need of a drink.

Zara's transformation was astounding. The hat and tie were gone, and her soft white blouse was open enough to allow Constance to follow her neckline farther down than she should have wanted.

Zara's hair was styled back, and she wore earrings that occasionally caught the evening's fading light. This look didn't create what she had previously referred to as "T and A," but when combined with her mastery of the instrument, created a powerful kind of femininity.

Moved by the music, which seemed more sentimental but not sappy—with hints of jazz or blues and something almost classical at times—Constance thought again of Jillian and her earlier resolve to turn her from practical pursuits to passion. When Zara stopped to give her usual remarks, Constance noticed there was no sheet music. It was inconceivable that these incredible sounds were flowing strictly from Zara's imagination—or her heart—but such was apparently the case. There was an emotional openness in her competence that was precisely what Constance wanted Jillian to find in herself.

In contrast to the flowing beauty of the melodies, Constance observed Zara's somewhat stiff posture, as if she was striving to keep herself physically contained. This too reminded Constance of Jillian, particularly her manner in unfamiliar or uncomfortable circumstances, such as when attending the occasional public event. The more she thought of it, the more Constance became convinced that something in Zara's musical competence was similar to Jillian's intellectual drive. Not that the two were anything alike. Definitely not in terms of class, and physically, they were nearly opposites. Zara's darker complexion and shapelier form differed dramatically from Jillian's pale, blond, lean figure. But there was something in Zara's amazing command of the piano that reminded Constance of Jillian's single-minded dedication to comprehending, indeed to mastering, the world around her.

At the piano, a woman in a tight, low-cut dress filled out one of the request cards. Zara never stopped playing, though the melody shifted to something simpler as the woman stooped and leaned close. Instead of dropping the card onto the stack, she slid it across the piano bench, her lips moving almost imperceptibly before she tucked the paper under Zara's thigh.

A half grin crossed Zara's face as the woman's fingers lingered for a moment. The implication was clear: this was a more personal proposition than a request. As tawdry as the scene was, Zara appeared to be an example—albeit a dubious one—of occasionally setting aside work in pursuit of pleasure. Perhaps she could give Constance advice on redirecting Jillian's unrelenting quest for achievement into deepening her relationship with Clive?

When Zara took her break, she didn't chat with any of the patrons or stop by the bar. Instead, she disappeared out the lounge door. Constance refused to let her imagination fill in the blanks of what might be going on and left her half-empty drink on the table, along with a smaller tip than usual for Gina. That night, she grappled with conflicting emotions, feeling mildly disgusted and vaguely aroused at the same time. Finally, having convinced herself that regardless of the type of desire Zara indulged in, she could still help with Jilly, Constance decided to return to the Empire Lounge the next night.

She'd prepared any number of censoring remarks about Zara's behavior the previous day, but when Zara stopped to visit during her first break, her casual manner and unaffected charm lulled Constance into cordiality. In her seemingly usual, overly familiar way, Zara teased her on everything from her fashionable outfit, "Wow, that jacket alone would probably have paid my rent," to her choice of drink, "They used to refer to gin as 'Mother's Ruin,' you know." In spite of her flippant tone, the attention lifted Constance's mood, and several of Zara's engaging remarks even made her laugh.

Returning to her performance, Zara examined a request card that had been left on the piano seat. Constance thought she saw a quick flash of relief on her face before she began to play a familiar, tender melody. An older couple got up to dance, and the mood of the evening turned sweeter. Zara's posture relaxed slightly as she obliged them with two more songs, a genuine-looking smile on her face as two other couples joined them. The unexpected romantic twist gave Constance a burst of confidence. It would be okay to befriend Zara, just enough to learn her rationale for indulging in random carnal behavior, and then use that insight to move her increasingly reticent best friend in a similar, though more respectable, direction. If she could help Jilly live her emotions more freely, like Zara did, the outcome would surely lead her into Clive's arms, and all would be well.

Constance moved to the bar at Zara's next intermission. "Am I correct that you start your daily performance at five o'clock?"

"Are you asking when I start because you want to know when I finish? Because I have to warn you, it's past your bedtime," Zara said with a wink.

Her teasing reminded Constance of Clive, which made it feel like the perfect time to put her plan in motion. She winked back. "Actually, I was going to ask if you'd like to walk with me before you start playing. There's something I'd like to chat about." Zara's brows rose, and something about the look in her eyes made Constance quickly inject a dose of honesty. "Not anything…personal. It's about a friend of mine."

"Oh sure," Zara said slowly as a grin spread across her face. "It's always about a 'friend.'"

Constance lifted her chin defensively. "This is someone dear that I'm worried about, and I think you two may have a lot in common, so I was hoping you could help."

"You want to get advice from someone who's not your friend about someone who is?"

Hesitating briefly, Constance admitted, "When you put it that way, it sounds foolish. Never mind." She started away, but Zara's touch on her arm made her pause.

"I get asked for a lot of weird things on these trips, but a consultation like this is a first." Her generally self-assured tone seemed more sincere as she pointed at the bow of the ship. "I'll meet you there at three tomorrow. We can walk for an hour, and then I'll need an hour to get ready for work. Deal?"

Pleased with herself, Constance nodded. "Deal."

❖

Constance thought she was prepared for their walk, but yet another change in Zara's appearance threw her off. Today's look included covering her hair with a scarf and her face with oversized sunglasses, giving her an older, more sophisticated appearance, almost evocative of Jackie Kennedy. By way of explanation, Zara disclosed that when a passenger identified her as a crew member, they'd sometimes ask her to pick up their laundry or watch their child for an hour or two, things that weren't part of her job in any case but especially not when she was off duty.

A slight sting of shame goaded Constance toward indignation. Jillian was always pushing her toward participating in some tiresome altruistic work, saying things like, "To whom much is given, much is expected." Constance had assumed the quote came from Adali Stevenson, or another of those American politicians her friend admired, so she was shocked to learn from Nelson that the phrase had Biblical origins. Still, Zara was an employee on the *Ocean Princess*, and as such, she had an obligation to serve. And those of a certain class—Constance and that of her friends—were within their rights to expect such, given they'd paid for the privilege.

So Constance babbled on nervously, unaccountably apprehensive as she talked about family members or school experiences she never expected Zara to relate to or care about. But Zara listened like she played, drawing out superficial descriptions of various experiences until they had some substance and piecing together random stories until they both had a clearer, and for Constance, a more painful, image of her uncomplicated life.

Zara never said anything critical, but as Constance dressed for the evening, she found herself in uncommon introspection, vacillating between embarrassment and feeling defensive. Did wanting to enjoy the fun and easy times make her life superficial and frivolous? She didn't have talent like Zara or genius like Jillian. Did that mean the mundane, petty scratchings of her life would never come to any real use? Positive she shouldn't share those bewildering doubts with her parents, she longed to speak with Nelson or Clive or even one of her school chums, whose very presence would reestablish the sense of self and the order of things she'd always relied on.

Still, she took her customary table near the piano, noting how Zara was once again able to make herself, and the night's performance, engaging and new. Apparently, she made a point of varying her look by changing trousers and tops and accessories—including ties and hats but no jewelry other than the earrings—which made her appearance something everyone could anticipate. The same was true with her playing. Constance was no music connoisseur, but she never heard Zara play the same piece twice unless a specific song was requested. Recalling the other kind of request she'd witnessed, she decided to start the next conversation by asking Zara about herself, seeking an understanding of how she balanced the vitality of her talent with a personal life, including a relationship. She assumed Zara's flirting and extracurricular activities meant lesbians indulged in such things. But asking personal questions of a virtual stranger was not something she was comfortable with, and she was especially hesitant about leading with such a delicate topic. Perhaps she should start more simply, ask about the playing and how Zara came to acquire such a depth and breadth of musical knowledge.

Pleased with her new plan, Constance had ordered a third drink when a group of men began circling the piano. The volume of their voices rose to uncomfortable proportions, and a significant amount of currency changed hands. Apparently, high-stakes wagering was taking place.

"God, I hate rich people." Gina's outburst was uncharacteristic for the dependable and courteous server, who gestured in the direction of the crowd before placing Constance's drink on the table. "But not as much as Zara does. I don't know the whole story, but she got ripped off real bad by someone with money once, and she's still holding a grudge. So now, she gets even by setting them up and getting some back." As if having forgotten she was talking to a customer, Gina backtracked hastily. "My apologies, Miss Holston. I know the two of you talked, and I'm sure you're aware Zara's never that way with people she likes. Please excuse me."

Cheering—and a few audible groans—rose as Zara began to play, and one man collected what appeared to be a large amount of cash from the others. He thumped Zara on the back before counting out some bills and stuffing them into her tip jar.

While he gloated over his victory, Zara continued the melody, her form more rigid than usual. Constance could only assume she was glad for the extra income rather than feeling as if she was debasing her art, but her body language suggested otherwise. Constance's stomach clenched with conflicting emotions, and she wondered how much of her father's money Zara had taken that first night.

The music stopped, and after a moment when another tune started up, there was more raucous shouting from the spectators. Glad the crowd had shifted and she was unable to see Zara's expression, Constance finished her drink. Before leaving, she asked Gina to let

Zara know she would meet her for their walk again tomorrow. She needed to have her planned conversation about Jillian, and then she'd be home and done with this musician.

Zara was late. Almost forty minutes late. Constance had given up and was walking back to the cabin when she heard her name being called. Zara panted toward her, her casual demeanor replaced by concern. "I'm so sorry. Gina just now gave me your message. After you left so suddenly last night, I thought you'd decided to blow me off."

Constance sighed, thinking the time she'd used to practice her speech had gone to waste. "I wanted to talk about my best friend, Jillian, but I think it's too late."

"Oh yes, your friend." Zara moved closer and took her hand. "Let me make it up to you."

Constance swallowed, caught by the intensity in Zara's dark eyes. "What...how do you mean?"

"Meet me tonight on the stern after I'm finished at the Empire. Two a.m." She took another step, and little shivers climbed Constance's arm from where they were touching.

"I couldn't possibly..." she started, stopping when Zara took her other hand.

"Sure you can. I'll make it worth your while." The grin was back. "And we can talk about your friend for as long as you want."

Even though she heard the skepticism around the word "friend," Constance nodded. Zara gave her hands a squeeze before she let go. "See you then."

Constance skipped the Empire that night, accompanying her parents to the bar they frequented instead. Their alcohol consumption was such that they'd be unlikely to hear her moving around later. Lying in bed, pretending to sleep, she told herself repeatedly that it was her sincere concern for Jillian's happiness that had made her agree to meet Zara on the stern.

She crept quietly from their stateroom, feeling a little thrill at the sight of a shadowy figure standing by the railing. In almost no time, Zara was very close, and the darkness of the hour and vastness of the stars felt like a blanket around them. Constance began to murmur about Jillian, and then somehow, the moment led to one brief but intense kiss.

She had no idea how it happened. Perhaps her curiosity coupled with the sudden, inexplicable desire to experience someone other than Nelson. And Zara's lips were so stunningly enjoyable. But as she ran a hand down Constance's left arm, probably to entwine their fingers, Constance felt a tug on Nelson's ring. It wasn't an engagement band, merely a cheap promise ring with her birthstone. But she hadn't taken it off since he'd given it to her. It had meant everything at the time, until the sensual vitality of Zara's presence had made her forget she had it on.

"I noticed this earlier," Zara said, her lips close to Constance's ear. "Now might be a good time to tell me about it. I don't mind being a first or even an only, but I'm not interested in being part of a cheat."

Constance was already leaning into her, making it harder to clear the fog of *whatever* from what remained of her rational brain. "Oh," she managed. "Well, yes, there's this chap…" The image of Nelson's gentle ways and faithfulness floated into her mind, and shame began to crowd out her earlier wanting.

She felt Zara's smile against her cheek before she put some space between them. "With a pretty woman like you, there often is." In spite of the compliment, her voice was a little flatter.

"I'm sorry, Zara. I wasn't thinking. You just…I…"

Zara's touch on her cheek would have been intimate if it hadn't clearly been a gesture of parting. "It's fine. He's a lucky man." Taking another step back, she added, "So we'll just be friends, okay? Come by the bar tomorrow, and I'll buy you a drink. To celebrate your… intended."

Constance nodded, forcing herself to speak. "Thank you."

After Zara winked and disappeared into the ship, Constance stood for a long time, staring at the churning water of the ship's wake, wondering at the thin veneer of her upbringing so easily laid bare by a piano player with too much morality to do the same to her body.

She stayed away from the Empire after that, but being with her parents and seeing the polite but firm way they interacted with the various ship attendants was oddly satisfying, reinforcing that the world was indeed as she'd been taught, despite the peculiar American perception of equality.

She began a long, impassioned letter to Nelson, wavering between begging for forgiveness and complaining of absolute boredom, before tearing it up. Seeing him in person would make everything better. And it was easier to convince herself nothing had really happened when she ran into Zara again on the last afternoon of the voyage.

Zara's friendly greeting reinforced that notion, and they walked together casually. After a few minutes of frivolous chat, Constance gathered the nerve to put aside her self-absorbed existence and asked if Zara would have any time in London or if she'd be working her way back to the States playing on this ship or another.

Slowing, Zara gave Constance a look she couldn't decipher before remarking that she'd be staying on for a few days and possibly longer. "In fact, do you have any suggestions on cheap lodging in the city center?"

Knowledge of cheap lodging wasn't her strong suit, but Constance tried to give it some thought. Stalling, she said, "When will you know your schedule for sure?"

"Sometime during the week after next." When it came to important personal matters, Zara seemed to retreat to cryptic language. Despite a sense of satisfaction at being consulted, Constance felt confused by her vagueness. Zara pulled her out of the path of another walking group. Leaning in as if whispering some scandalous tidbit, she said, "I'm auditioning for a position at the Royal College of Music."

Constance felt her mouth open slightly, and Zara's eyes darted away from her face. Feeling as if she'd had a hand in some fabulous discovery, she touched Zara's arm, trying not to let the physical contact remind her of that night on the stern. "How absolutely fantastic, Zara. Congratulations. I'm...I'm sure you'll be accepted," she gushed, barely stopping herself from saying she was surprised, which could have been taken quite differently from how she meant it. "But won't the RCM help you with housing?"

"Only if I get in. So in the meantime..."

Her mind was a total blank, but she was desperate to try. "Let me think on it, will you?" At Zara's sigh, she added, "I promise I'll come up with something."

"Sure, no pressure. And listen, if you're awake late tonight—packing or something—come by the lounge after it closes at midnight." The familiar cocky grin creased her attractive face. "I'm giving a concert for my fellow cruise workers."

Constance smiled, relieved to be back on familiar ground. "Attending your performance is definitely something I can do."

The room was packed. Even with the tables stacked against the walls and rows of chairs filling the remaining space, it was standing room only. The piano was in its usual place, but the bench was empty. Constance had never before considered how many people worked on this ship, and judging from the stained or wrinkled uniforms, most appeared to have come directly from their various jobs, though the night before docking had to be a busy time. Fairly certain she was the lone non-crew member in attendance, she was looking about for a place to lean when Gina waved at her from a barstool.

"You can have my seat, Miss Holston. I'll be turning the pages for her." She was holding a sheaf of papers.

Constance thanked her and took the seat without hesitation. "Do you read music?"

"God, no." Gina fanned herself. "Zara told me she'd just nod at the right time. But I think I'm more nervous than she is."

"Is she here yet?"

Gina shook her head. "Probably still fussing with her outfit. She said she's treating this as a dress rehearsal for her audition, playing the same three pieces and everything." An officer in dress whites stepped into the room, and the crowd quieted. "Excuse me. That's my cue," Gina whispered and went up the one narrow aisle.

After a few seconds of silent anticipation, a wave of applause started at the door. People who had seats stood, and for a moment, their bodies blocked the view. Constance leaned forward as Zara turned toward her in a stunning, mid-thigh, sleeveless red sheath dress, with a crisscross of matching lace between her full breasts as the sole adornment, other than the earrings she'd worn on several occasions.

Constance took in an involuntary breath. There was no mistaking Zara's gender now, and she was even more captivating for it. Constance joined in the applause and heard a few people shouting Zara's name as she made her way to the piano. Before sitting, she turned toward the assembled group and bowed. The cheers increased as she arranged her music, positioned Gina, and flexed her fingers over the keys. When she placed her hands in her lap, the crowd began to quiet.

"Thank you all for being here. We'll start our evening with a short, relaxing piece composed by Claude Debussy when he was only in his twenties. 'Arabesque No.1.'"

"Oh, I wanted her to play Clair de Lune," a woman in a housekeeping uniform whispered to her companion. "I bought a recording of it after her last concert, but it doesn't sound as good as Zara's version."

Impressed by the reference to the French composer's most famous piece, Constance wondered how many of these concerts there had been.

"Close your eyes and imagine the lines of plants and flowers, of the shapes of nature," Zara said. "Let the sounds take you to your favorite place and time in the world." As the evocative notes of the melody began, Constance wondered how an audience such as this one would react to the suggestion, but most people were doing as Zara had recommended. As the piece progressed, Constance joined in the exercise, letting her eyelids drop and enjoying the delicacy of the composition. When the last soft note faded away, it seemed everyone in the room had been transported in the way that great music beautifully played could do. The room stirred slowly, and warm applause followed.

"Okay, I can see I need to wake you up." There were moans in reply, and Zara grinned. "I know you could use some rest, but I need you with me on this one, or I may screw up."

A few people chuckled, and someone called out, "You won't."

Zara shook her head ruefully. "I hope you're right. I've been practicing this one every day of our crossing."

"Is this the one that makes you cuss?" Gina asked, her question loud enough for everyone to hear.

"Fuck, yeah," Zara answered, and the whole audience broke into boisterous laughter and applause. Constance knew she should be offended, but she felt like giggling at the naughtiness. Someone should probably tell Zara that this kind of behavior would never be acceptable at the Royal College of Music. Zara held up her hands and the room quieted. "So this is 'La Campanella' by Franz Listz, and it's by far the hardest piano piece I've ever attempted. Listz was a great composer but not particularly kind to struggling musicians."

The melody began softly and slowly, but the tempo quickened immediately. Clearly, Zara hadn't overstated the difficulty as the bright quick notes became almost too fast to distinguish.

Over the years, Constance had often joined her parents in their box at the London Symphony. For her, the event was an opportunity to socialize with other members of society, since she knew virtually nothing about music. Even so, she'd never heard anyone there play like Zara. It wasn't only the speed and dexterity; it was the emotion she put into her performance.

Unlike the way she sat rigidly in the lounge, tonight she was loose-limbed and uninhibited. Her shoulders moved from side to side like a dance, and sometimes she talked to herself or to the keys. She smiled at some of the playful runs, and then her focus became absolute. At times, it didn't seem possible for one person to make so much music. Then, when playing two alternating notes with her right hand on the very high keys, her eyes closed as if in ecstasy.

Listening in a way she never had before, Constance recognized the original refrain come back several times but in such different forms that she couldn't imagine how it was possible. Finally, the piece built to a thunderous conclusion, and after the last two chords, the audience didn't wait for Zara to put her hands in her lap before jumping to their feet. Constance found herself joining in as the applause lasted at least half a minute, accompanied by various whoops, cheers, and calls for more. Beyond impressed, Constance felt like she was in the presence of someone truly exceptional. Like the way she sometimes felt around Jillian, she had nothing to offer by way of competition or comparison. But here, it didn't matter because Zara's music put her in touch with the best of what was deep inside herself, the wide variety of her emotions and especially her ability to love deeply, vigilantly, and with fierce allegiance to those she considered "hers."

Zara rose and bowed, and the cheers turned to laughter as she wiped her brow with mock relief. The crowd had just settled again when the officer in whites reappeared in the doorway. "It's time, folks."

"She promised us three pieces tonight, and that's two," someone protested above the displeased murmurs.

The officer shook his head. "We've had several complaints about the lack of service, and you all know what tomorrow will be like."

"At least play us out, Zara," a different voice called, and someone else said, "Yeah, play us some blues, since that's what we'll all be feeling without you."

Zara tilted her head. "Aw, I'll miss y'all, but if things don't go my way, I'll just see you on the next crossing."

Gina turned to her. "Now I don't know what to wish for." Several people laughed.

Zara hugged her, and Gina started down the aisle as Zara began playing some mournful chords along with scattering high notes that blended perfectly, though they sounded random. The room was less than half-empty when Zara transformed what might have been a last, lingering note into what Constance could only think of as boogie-woogie. The tempo instantly energized those still in the room.

Someone shouted, "Oh yeah!" and several couples began dancing. They danced holding outstretched hands or closer, in almost classical dance poses, but their feet were doing things Constance couldn't follow. Swinging and swaying, pulling in and out of each other's arms, every move seemed to anticipate the next part of the song. Those making their way out of the room turned to watch, some doing their own dance steps, snapping their fingers or nodding and smiling at each other.

Zara was now playing standing up, her face aglow as she watched the dancers between checking her fingers. When the officer waved, she nodded, and the notes transitioned to another verse. But this time, Zara worked the same transition three times in a row. The dancers appeared to know what was happening and adjusted so that when Zara played two last, extended chords while tripping along the high notes again, they dipped and swayed one last time.

Zara and the dancers applauded each other, and several of them returned to give her hugs. The embracing and laughter went on until the officer called out again. As the last stragglers made their way to the exit, Zara gathered her music.

Constance met her at the door. "I've seen people appreciate the piano before, but I don't believe I've ever seen it bring such joy. I find myself rather envious of your ability."

Zara brushed a hand down Constance's arm. "Don't feel bad about the envy. The list of things I've coveted could stretch between London and New York and back again." She turned them toward the crew's quarters. "I think one purpose of music is to give us permission to feel. Often, people are afraid to show what's inside, whether it's joy or sadness or longing or excitement or whatever. They're caught up in the past or dreaming about the future. Music, like our truest emotions, happens in the present. And being a part of that experience for other people makes me feel connected to what they're feeling, you know?"

Constance felt a renewed fondness for Zara and returned the brief touch. "You're not only connected. You're the source."

Zara looked away and shuffled her feet, showing a shyness that seemed quite out of character. "Nah. Just the conduit."

Constance considered her insightful words about music and feelings. It was something very close to what she wanted for Jillian. Constance was a planner, but not so much that she couldn't appreciate serendipity when it happened. Zara needed a place to stay for a few days, and there would be guests she could entertain. Jillian needed to be present, with Clive, and she needed to think less and feel more. Clive needed to show Jilly how lovely romance could be. Perhaps Zara's playing could work its magic on them.

When they stopped at the stairway leading down to the crew quarters, Constance said, "I may have a solution to your lodging problem," When Zara's face brightened, she added, "But I'll need to ask for your discretion regarding our earlier...uh...encounter."

Zara blinked and turned her gaze away. For a second, Constance feared she would sneer at the request. But when she looked back, her expression was completely sober. "You don't need to worry about that, Constance. I don't kiss and tell. I don't tell about much of anything, in case you hadn't noticed. But if you're concerned, I'm sure I can make my own way when we get to London. Really, it's fine. I've been there before, just never to stay."

Constance lifted her chin, feeling supremely confident now. "No. Leave everything to me." She patted Zara's arm and started away, thinking of the ship-to-shore call she needed to make. "I'm betting everything will work out perfectly," she called back over her shoulder before turning to face Zara again, wagging her finger. "And that's the only wagering that will take place. Agreed?" At Zara's self-conscious nod, she smiled. "See you tomorrow."

Chapter Two

Nelson had gotten Constance's ship-to-shore call the night before they were to dock, telling him to meet her an hour later than she'd originally said. Her parents were going on as planned, but she needed to wait for some additional luggage. She assured him that Jillian wouldn't be put out by the slight delay since they would be the first ones to reach her house in any case. Plus, she was bringing a surprise.

The conversation was brief, but her tone had been warm, and Nelson had no reason to think anything was amiss. But when he spotted her making her way down the gangplank while chatting enthusiastically with a long-haired, scruffy looking chap sporting a garish tie over an Oxford shirt and tight black pants—a fedora pulled low on his face—he wondered what she might have gotten into. A porter followed them, his cart loaded with Constance's familiar bags, and Nelson was pleased to note the disheveled lad only carried a bag in each hand.

Good, he thought. Perhaps it was merely polite conversation. But after his wave caught her eye, he had to work to keep his expression neutral when Constance grabbed the fellow's arm and dragged him with her.

When he was younger, Nelson had considered entering the priesthood. There was something appealing about the structure of their community, given that his family had moved eight times before he was twelve. But along with his father's job changes and the housing turnovers that came with them, Nelson found himself in several different congregations with priests whose appeal varied greatly. Thankfully, he'd been able to maintain his friendships with Constance and Jillian and Clive through it all, and eventually, the steady presence of his friends became more of a haven than the ceremonies and rituals of religion.

He'd never lost his faith, though, and prayed daily, attending the college chapel services when he could. After discovering a natural affinity for numbers, it hadn't taken long to come to terms with the fact that his life was destined for a different path, especially given his attraction to Constance.

In fact, this most recent separation had convinced him that she was indeed the woman he wanted to spend the rest of his life with. Now he felt a strange kind of possessiveness, as though the presence of a possible rival made him want to bare his teeth and beat his chest. It was possible this fellow was Jillian's surprise, but that thought made him only marginally less disturbed. It was all but given that Clive, Nelson's best friend, would marry Jillian once he got himself together, and they both finished school. At this point, it was hard to tell which of those would come first, but still....

Nelson was considerably relieved when Constance rushed the last few feet to give him a warm hug and a long, generous kiss. When their lips parted, he told himself that Clive had always managed to keep himself in the picture before, and if it was time for him to pick up his game, so be it. Keeping a jealous hand on Constance's waist, Nelson turned to greet her friend. He blinked, giving a second look when the two of them burst into laughter. While Constance had occupied his attention, the scruffy bloke had turned into an attractive woman. The hat and tie were gone, and glossy dark hair curled above an open-collared shirt. Her full lips curved into a grin.

"You two were clearly made for each other," she said to Constance. "His surprised face is even better than yours."

Clearly, this was some kind of inside joke. They shared a laugh, and Nelson attempted a smile as Constance made the introductions. "Zara, this, obviously, is Nelson Garrick. Nelson, I'd like you to meet Zara Keller, pianist extraordinaire. We're going to help Zara find a place to stay for a few days."

Zara offered a hand, and Nelson shook it as she added, "A cheap place."

Constance looked at him meaningfully. They'd spent a significant portion of their lives in each other's company, so Nelson sensed what was expected. "We're on our way to a friend's house," he said, feeling Constance's arm slip around his waist, confirming he was on the right track. "I think she'd be the one to help with that. Please join us."

Zara's gaze flitted between them before she looked away. "Oh, thanks, but I wouldn't want to intrude. My friend Gina mentioned a couple of places to try." She took a step back. "You two enjoy your weekend. It was great meeting you, Nelson. Take good care of your lady here." She winked at Constance, who abruptly moved as if to follow her.

"Zara, no. You wouldn't be intruding, I promise. And I'm certain Jillian can help with your short-term housing needs."

Hearing the insistence in her voice, Nelson nodded agreeably.

"So you actually have a friend—" Zara cut herself off quickly. "I mean, your friend's name is Jillian?"

Nelson couldn't quite figure out the look Constance gave him or the reason for her blush. She cleared her throat. "Yes, she's the one I mentioned. And there will be lots of company this weekend. I promise, one more won't make the slightest difference."

When Nelson sensed Zara was wavering, he added, "And she has a fabulous cook. You really shouldn't miss the food."

Zara licked her lips in what he suspected was an unconscious reaction. "There wasn't food service for us today. I was just going to grab something on the street."

He wasn't sure who she meant by "us," but Constance took charge, as she often did. "Oh no. You're coming with us. It's settled." After directing the porter to add Zara's bags to the load, Constance kept a hand in Nelson's as they made their way toward his car.

Surreptitiously, Nelson observed that Zara was obviously American, her skin tone deeper than someone who'd taken time to tan on the ship. He wondered if there was some Greek or Italian in her background. Given that she'd come over without prearranged lodging, and the fact that she'd emphasized "cheap" in her request, he wondered if she might be planning to bum her way around the country as so many young Americans seemed to be doing these days. And while he wouldn't expect her to have the bearing or carriage of an English lady, Nelson noted a confident, dynamic manner in her walk and gestures.

"So, Zara, are you in London for business or pleasure?" he asked once they'd settled into his car and began to make their way through the city traffic.

"In my case, what will start as pleasure will turn into business, I hope," she answered from the back seat.

Constance laughed. "Always the woman of mystery." She turned to give Zara a fond look. "She has an audition at the Royal College of Music next week. For a fellowship, did you say?"

"Yes. They refer to it as non-student status. But you're expected to be heavily involved in the RCM 'life,' working with students, accompanying at concerts, that kind of thing."

Nelson nodded affably, concealing an unexpected wave of relief. If Constance was going to take up Jillian's habit of caring for strays, at least this one would be on a short-term basis. He couldn't begin to say why, but he felt something off-putting, something almost intimidating about this woman. Perhaps it was the "cool" that some musicians seemed to have, which he'd often been teased about lacking. But never by Constance, thankfully.

"Splendid. Best of luck, then. We'll all be rooting for you."

Constance patted his arm. "She won't need luck. I've heard her play."

"Don't jinx me, Constance," Zara said, her tone more serious than he would have expected. "My CV isn't at all impressive, and I don't have a degree. I'm a long shot at best, but my teacher still had connections there, and she pulled some strings to get me this audition. I'll take all the luck and support I can get."

"Bosh." Constance waved airily. "They'd have to be stone deaf not to take you."

In the rearview, Nelson saw Zara smile faintly before relaxing. After a few moments, her eyes closed. Clearly, he and Constance needed to have a private talk about her before they sprung her on Jillian. It was one thing to offer a few days' stay to someone who was between opportunities, but Zara had made it sound like her prospects weren't good. Nelson had no desire to become involved in another near eviction, much as they'd had to do when one of Clive's friends had spent the better part of a term sponging off the Stansfields' hospitality while offering nothing but excessive drinking and occasional run-ins with the local constable in return.

Clive had visited regularly at first, bringing Tristan along on an outing or two with Jillian, but apparently, there had been something of a row, resulting in Clive leaving Tristan to his own devices. The whole thing was like a comedy of errors, with both expecting the other to do something until Nelson had finally taken the bull by the horns, talking to both Clive and his chum until the wee hours to make sure the situation was properly sorted out, and Tristan was gone the next day. It wasn't that Lord Stansfield was unable to manage or that Jillian herself was unaware. They were just gracious to a fault, and he didn't want that fault to reoccur.

As he and Constance chatted about her trip and his studies, Nelson kept watch on the back seat. By the time they'd reached the countryside, Zara had made no attempt at conversation and hadn't moved in some time, so he took a chance. Lowering his voice to a near whisper, he asked, "How well do you really know this girl? I'm a bit concerned about putting Jilly on the spot with an unknown quantity."

After a quick glance, Constance leaned toward him. "I don't know much about her background, but I have some sense of her character. And we'll all be there through the weekend at least. If there's a problem, it'll surely show by then."

It had become a tradition for their group to spend a few days together prior to starting a new term. They'd met at other places, but the Stansfield manor, Fullerhill, was by far their favorite. Besides the plentiful and generous accommodations, the estate was magnificent. The grounds were a mix of woods, meadows, marshes, and streams, and they'd spent many happy hours in each other's company while exploring the hundreds of acres. Through the years, someone had brought along a friend or two, and recently, the numbers had increased as their individual circles broadened. For outsiders, the gathering had the appearance of a party, and after a time, there were enough hangers-on that Jillian began submitting a guest list to Barton, the Stansfield's social secretary, to keep from being overwhelmed with company. But for their foursome, it was a reunion of sorts, a time to get reacquainted and catch up on the latest gossip and to renew their places in each other's lives.

Nelson knew what he should say. "Of course. I trust your judgment."

Constance kissed his cheek and put her hand on his leg as they drove the familiar route to Fullerhill. When they neared the boundary, Constance shook Zara gently.

"What?" She startled awake, fists clenched, before focusing on Constance. "Where are we?"

"We're almost to Jillian's. I thought you'd want to see this part of the drive."

"Oh, man. Sorry I flaked out on you." Zara relaxed, yawning as she looked out the window at the passing countryside. "Wow. It's really pretty here."

Constance pointed out the rearing Pegasus perched on a stone pillar. "This is where their holdings begin."

"How much land do they have?"

Constance looked to Nelson. "I believe it's just under a thousand acres," he said. "And it's been in the family for generations. Originally a charter from Henry VIII, I believe." He and Constance took a vicarious pride in the fact that the Stansfields had been able to hold on to their home and property in the face of outrageous taxes and constantly rising maintenance costs. Many of the great manor homes had been taken down or turned into museums, private schools, or even safari parks.

Nelson had once asked Jillian if she found it a burden to inherit such responsibility. She'd set him straight with her typical cool, response: "I think of it as an honor."

He glanced in the rearview mirror as they turned into the drive. Zara's mouth was slightly agape. The manor house was imposing from a distance, and as they rolled slowly up the long driveway, Nelson heard her breathe, "Holy shit."

The three-story Stansfield home was a deep red, with accents of light tan stone on the corners and between the floors. A dozen, evenly spaced ovals of the same lighter stone containing sculpted busts set off the first floor from the second. There was an arched main entrance, and two other archways added symmetry to the house's appearance as they flanked the hexagonal turrets on either end of the structure. Perfectly manicured landscaping across the front gave way to natural plants lining the driveway and the sides of the house. It was most assuredly an imposing building, and Nelson thought it more impressive on the inside. Though his memories were of warm and pleasant times with his friends, it was understandable that someone seeing it for the first time, especially someone unfamiliar with wonderful English manor homes like Fullerhill, would find it overwhelming.

Zara apparently felt that and more as they pulled into what Nelson thought of as his reserved parking spot. Face pressed against the window, she muttered, "Fuck me," while gawking at the house from the back seat of the car.

Nelson swallowed a recrimination. He had been teased often enough about being old-fashioned that he could now admit to it, at least about some things, and that included hearing women curse. He wasn't entirely surprised someone like Zara would express herself so coarsely, but he was determined to remain a gentleman, even to the point of doing the heavy lifting for her and Constance. Taking the luggage from the boot, he heard Constance speaking but couldn't make out the words.

Zara's voice was clearer. "Listen, I'm fine to sleep out here in the car. I've done it before and in worse weather. This place is...uh...it's really not my style, you know?"

Constance's door opened, and she went around to the back, pulling Zara out and walking her a few steps away from the house, chatting animatedly the whole time. Nelson assumed Constance was giving their guest a bit of a pep talk, so he took a load to the door, noting as he returned that Zara was smoothing her clothes and fluffing her hair as Constance was trying to brush some kind of makeup on her. Smiling to himself at the thought of making a silk purse from a sow's ear, he'd just set down the last bag when the door opened, revealing Andrew, who'd been the Stansfields' butler for as long as any of them could remember.

Andrew's familiar gravelly baritone offered a dignified greeting, and Nelson gestured. "The ladies are taking an extra moment."

"Ladies have that prerogative," Andrew commented.

When he bent to retrieve a bag, Nelson stopped him. "Miss Constance and I will sort ourselves out upstairs after we've said hello to our hostess."

"Certainly, sir."

The women made their way to the entrance, Zara giving the car an extra look before Constance pulled her up. "Andrew, it's lovely to see you again. This is our friend Zara's first visit here to Fullerhill."

Zara put out her hand. "Hi. Thanks for having me."

Andrew looked at the offered palm as if he'd never seen one before. Turning to Nelson, he said, "I believe the lady of the house is in the banquet room." Jillian's father wasn't returning until the beginning of the week, making her the ranking family member.

Zara shrugged off Andrew's snub and hoisted her smaller bag as Constance took her arm again, and they started down the hall. If he hadn't been watching, Nelson wouldn't have caught the look that crossed Andrew's elderly face: obvious doubt as to whether or not their newest guest would get herself sorted out as well. She wasn't their first American, but they hadn't had many, and every other one had been either wealthy or intellectual. Nelson got the sense that Zara was neither, which could account for her consternation, though she shared the appropriate reaction to Fullerhill: total and complete awe.

He joined the ladies, taking Constance's other hand, half listening as she pointed out the stunning decor they'd all come to take for granted. Zara's head swiveled as Constance took her past rooms containing comfortable reading nooks and overflowing bookshelves, layered rugs, and deep sofas in patterned fabrics. Trinkets of porcelain and china were spaced among plants, candlesticks, and decorative boxes. Some rooms were decidedly more masculine, with exposed beams and strong colors. One in particular boasted mounted antlers and a bear rug. Above a small table was an ancient shield and two crossed swords.

Nelson preferred the rooms with pastel wallpaper that included antiques from different eras. The walls of the hallway were lined with portraits, and they passed a full suit of armor at one corner. Constance stopped beside a large tapestry, one of Jillian's favorites. It was a copy of the famous "Lady and the Unicorn," presenting the sixth sense, understanding or intuition.

"There's a debate about what those words, *À Mon Seul Désir* are supposed to mean." Constance pointed at the words stitched on the wall hanging a little more than halfway up. "Some say they should be translated as, 'To my only or sole desire.' Others say they mean, 'Love desires only beauty of soul' or even 'To calm passion.'"

Zara seemed impressed. She studied the image of the woman standing before a blue tent, holding a necklace as she reached into a box. "You know," she said after a moment. "There was something a lot like this in my childhood home. Although it was much smaller." She used her hands to indicate the size, which was less than half of what was hanging on the wall at Fullerhill.

"Really?"

Nelson couldn't tell by Constance's tone whether she was intrigued or skeptical.

"Yeah, and the subject matter was entirely different."

"Do tell," Nelson and Constance said together.

"It's an allegorical piece about man's inhumanity to man. About how some will sacrifice their honor even to win something that's ultimately quite meaningless."

Constance was looking at Zara with a slight tilt to her head. "What was the title of this piece?"

Zara seemed pleased they'd gotten to the point. "*Dogs Playing Poker*," she said.

Nelson brought his hand up to his mouth, but it was too late. He burst into laughter, encouraged by the grin spreading over Zara's appealing face. After a few seconds of affected dismay, Constance joined in.

The banquet room was empty, but it was obvious Jillian had been there. In place of the one long table, she had chosen to go with several smaller ones, each seating four to six people. It was a nod to more modern dining, though Nelson suspected she might not have made the change if her father had been present. They made their way to the kitchen, where they were greeted by Mrs. Livingstone, the kitchen manager who'd come to the household as a cook just after Mrs. Stansfield had died.

Escaping her unhappy marriage at the tender age of twenty-three, Pauline Livingstone had clearly recognized a domicile in disarray and a motherless girl in need of guidance. Jillian had been only ten years old, and the newest member of the staff must have felt like a cross between an older sister and a young mother figure. Nelson recalled a period during which Jilly would turn to Mrs. Livingstone for permission to go on any kind of outing, rather than asking her grief-stricken father. Around the same time, Constance had told him that Mrs. Livingstone's opinion of Jillian's clothes and hair and makeup mattered more than that of her peers. Mrs. Livingstone knew her place, but it was apparent her heart went out to the household's only child, and she'd done her best over the years to walk the line between acting as a confidant and advisor and being an employee.

The individuality that developed with time, coupled with Mrs. Livingstone's opinion that dabbling in scientific pursuits wasn't ladylike, had gradually put some distance between them. And though she'd been old enough to disregard Mrs. Livingstone's barely masked condemnation of her chosen field, Jilly had never let that or the difference in their social standing diminish the fondness they had for each other.

"The mistress is out on the terrace," Mrs. Livingstone informed them, her smile giving away her affection for the girl she'd had such a hand in raising.

Zara covered her mouth as if hiding a laugh. "Whose mistress is she?" she whispered to Constance, who gave her a playful shove.

Mrs. Livingstone sniffed her disapproval. Nelson gave her a slight tilt of his head, acknowledging their guest was somewhat uncouth. Constance led the way. They all knew that, next to her lab, the out-of-doors was Jillian's favorite place. On a beautiful day like this, she'd certainly be out tramping through the woods if she hadn't been expecting company. Seated at the outdoor dining area, Jillian's back was to them, and she hadn't turned, indicating her attention was elsewhere.

Constance moved, leaving Zara slightly behind Nelson as she stepped to Jillian's side. "Hello, dearest," she said, touching her shoulder.

Jillian rose, her apparent concentration shifting to delight, and they embraced. "I'm glad you're back," she said. Then, seeing Nelson, she added in a stage whisper, "And I want to know details."

Nelson was rather embarrassed to think that Constance had shared the most recent development in their relationship, but she only laughed and motioned him over.

Kissing him on both cheeks, Jillian said, "I'm thrilled for you two. You know I think you're each wonderful and even more so together." She squeezed his arm, and Nelson felt his self-consciousness fade. He'd struggled with the church's teachings on the matter of sexual intimacy outside the bonds of matrimony, but since it was his sincere intention to marry Constance soon, he found himself able to justify being with her. He was grateful they could have that acknowledgement without Clive, as he would have all kinds of inappropriate, or at least teasing, things to say. In some ways, Clive was like an older, more experienced brother. They all knew the story of how Clive's father had taken him to a prostitute at age fifteen, and how profoundly that experience had shaped his attitude toward women other than Jillian.

Giving Nelson a little shake, Jillian asked, "Where have you been? I've been wanting to get out all morning. I'll have Mrs. Liv pack us a lunch. Get changed at once, and we'll go for a picnic."

He looked to Constance, but she'd gone back for Zara, whose discomfort was obvious as her head was down and her steps hesitant. Oblivious, Constance brought her confidently onto the terrace. "Jillian Stansfield, let me introduce Zara Keller. I met her on the cruise, and she's an absolutely amazing pianist. I'm sure we could persuade her to play for us later, won't you, Zara? Oh, and she's auditioning at the Royal College of Music next week. Isn't that fabulous? Zara, this is my dearest friend, Lady Jillian Stansfield."

Zara's head came up slowly, her eyes finding Jillian's. Jillian's lips parted as if in surprise by the arrival of someone unexpected. Nelson was a bit taken aback; he'd never seen two women look at each other with quite such intensity. If it hadn't been a clear day, and they'd been a man and a woman, he might have expected a thunderclap.

They spoke at the same time, Zara saying, "Do I know you?" while Jillian asked, "Have we met?"

He and Constance chuckled at the coincidence, but Jillian and Zara continued to stare. Zara recovered first. Shaking her head, she murmured, "No. I would have remembered." Then she smiled, holding out her hand as she'd done with Andrew. "Hi. Thank you for having me in your incredible home. Constance assured me it was okay to crash your party. I hope she was right."

To Nelson's amazement, Jillian wobbled a little, reaching for Zara's hand as if to steady herself. "Oh," she said as they touched, as if some kind of spark had startled her. "I'm…" She cleared her throat, and he exchanged a look with Constance. The Jillian they knew didn't falter this way, especially not in social situations. Finally, she blinked a few times and started again. "Certainly. You're welcome here, Ms. Keller."

"Please, call me Zara." They were still holding hands.

"Of course. Zara." She seemed to linger on the name for a few seconds. "Any friend of Constance…"

Zara's smile widened, and Nelson felt Constance shift as if she'd finally become uncomfortable with this curious behavior. Replying as if Jillian hadn't trailed off so oddly, Zara said, "I didn't mean to eavesdrop, but I overheard you mention a picnic. That sounds wonderful if you have room for one more." Taking a half step closer, she added, "I've been cooped up onboard ship for a while, and I don't think I've ever seen anything as lovely"—her gaze swept out across the grounds before returning to rest on Jillian's face—"as what I see here."

At that, Nelson wondered if he should step in, but he wasn't sure if Zara's hesitation was for inuendo or if it was a genuine compliment about the Stansfield estate. A slight blush crept onto Jillian's cheeks, but she steadied herself, finally dropping Zara's hand as she assessed her black dress pants and white shirt. "Well, if you're sure you have your land legs back, sailor, you'll want to put on something more casual before exploring terra firma." Her voice was stronger, and Zara nodded excitedly.

"I can do that," she said, and grabbed her bag, darting from the room like a schoolboy unexpectedly let out of lessons early.

Smiling, Jillian looked to Nelson. "Will it be the four of us, then?"

Relieved that she appeared to be coming back to herself, he turned to Constance. "What do you think, darling?"

Constance yawned dramatically, turning her face into his shirt. "I, for one, am not fit for a day in the woods," she said almost unintelligibly. Straightening, she looked up at him, adding, "I need to unpack, and I'm sure a nap in a bed that isn't moving will make me much more suitable company this evening. What about you?"

He would have been fine with a walk, and he wasn't at all comfortable leaving Jillian alone with Zara, who was still an unknown quantity. Then Constance's hand brushed his rear as she encircled his waist, and he remembered they'd be "napping" in the same bed. He shifted, feeling the first stirrings of arousal. He and Constance had only been together twice, and both times had been somewhat rushed. Thinking of some private time here, he resolved that Jillian could handle herself. After all, he'd seen her manage Clive at his worst. "Yes, uh, I think I'll beg off too, if you don't mind. The drive seems to have taken a bit out of me."

Jillian smiled at them. "I'll tell Mrs. Liv to leave something out for you to snack on before you go up."

She turned toward the kitchen, and Constance followed. Nelson heard her say, "Let me walk with you, Jilly. I need to tell you something."

Chapter Three

Jillian honestly couldn't explain what had come over her. When she'd looked into the eyes of Constance's new friend, something dormant inside her had stirred to life, which was both exhilarating and terrifying at the same time. She'd been almost reassured when the woman had asked if they'd met. At least she wasn't the only one who felt completely off, though she couldn't think how something as routine as a previous encounter would explain this strange upheaval.

She'd taken the offered hand primarily to keep herself from utterly losing her internal balance, which it did, and it didn't. She might have stood there all day, struggling to make small talk while watching the light play over Zara's striking face and enjoying the solid, warming feel of her hand. Normally, she'd be uncomfortable with the touch of a stranger, but she felt an unaccountable ease with Zara. Thank God their eye contact had been broken with that awkward remark about being off the ship. It was a peculiar compliment for one woman to give another, but such talk was familiar enough that Jillian had been able to think of something at least half-witted in reply. And the way Zara had scampered off to change made her think of a younger, less jaded Clive.

Once they were in the kitchen, Jillian wondered if Constance was going to ask about her strange reaction to their guest, but she said, "Zara's rather intriguing, isn't she?"

Relieved, Jillian merely inclined her head and finished giving Mrs. Livingstone instructions for their lunches. It bothered her that

Constance sometimes talked in front of the help as if they weren't there, especially her dear Mrs. Livingstone.

As she'd moved up the ranks from cook to housekeeper, Mrs. Liv's firm grasp on the old ways had been hard to understand at first. Jillian's preference for solitary pursuits might have begun with an education that had been exclusively through private tutors. But the advice and comfort she'd desperately needed after her mother's death were only offered when they were alone; in front of others, Mrs. Livingstone was adamant they maintain their status as employer and employee.

Nowadays, when Constance tried to prod Jillian into attending a social event, she would tease her for being practically monk-like in her devotion to her education, her projects, and the weighty responsibilities that had been thrust upon her as mistress of the manor. But it had been through Mrs. Livingstone's direction that Jillian had developed the backbone that was expected of her. She'd learned to set aside disconcerting emotions—especially her sorrow and guilt—and had become the disciplined Lady Stansfield her new role required. It was true, she occasionally awoke on the verge of tears from a dream she couldn't quite remember, or she'd work to the point of collapse to chase away a yearning which hovered on the edges of her consciousness. In the rare moments between her day-to-day tasks and her schoolwork, she sometimes wondered what kind of future would hold anything of real value. In theory, she understood the gratification of marriage and motherhood, but in her rare, quiet moments, she liked to imagine a much bigger life. But usually, as now, she set those thoughts aside, finding her immediate satisfaction in doing what it took to keep Fullerhill running smoothly. At that, her mind went back to her current duties.

"I assume she needs a place to stay," she remarked. Constance nodded, so she moved toward the door leading to the hallway, thinking she'd speak to Andrew, and that would be the end of it. But as she made to have Zara's room readied, Constance stopped her with a hand on her arm.

"Before you decide, there's something else I need to tell you." She lowered her voice with surprising restraint. "I wouldn't normally disclose this kind of private information about a person I just met, but you need to be informed before you go off alone with her. Or let her stay over." She paused dramatically, and Jillian had the uncharitable thought that Constance was enjoying knowing something she didn't, even if it was only some personal tidbit about someone else. They'd never competed at anything meaningful, but she occasionally got the feeling that Constance was given to moments of resentment. She honestly couldn't imagine why, since Constance was the one who seemed the most at ease with her life, but Jillian crossed her arms, waiting for the revelation.

Constance leaned close and whispered, "Zara's a lesbian."

Right. While she couldn't have said what she was expecting, that certainly wasn't it. "How on earth would you know?" Jillian asked, unable to prevent a blush heating her face.

They stood in the corner of the kitchen while Constance disclosed the details of their meeting and her first impressions. When she got to the part about being with Zara on the stern that night, Jillian held up a hand. "Don't tell me she forced you to—"

"Heavens, no," Constance said emphatically. "I wouldn't have brought her here if that was the case. It was actually the opposite. I...I might have gone on with it, but she stopped and asked about my ring, and when I told her about Nelson, she said she wouldn't be part of a cheat."

Jillian's immediate impression was Constance might be more in need of a confession than Jillian was of a warning. Constance and Nelson had been serious about each other for some time, so for her to act in a way that would threaten progress in their relationship seemed quite out of character. But before she could pursue that line of inquiry, Mrs. Liv reappeared with their lunches. Smiling warmly, she handed Jillian two sacks and went through to the terrace with the rest of the food.

"Have you told Nelson?" Jillian asked once Mrs. Liv was outside. Constance shook her head. "Are you going to?" More shaking. "Then is there anything more to this that worries you?"

"I just want you to be careful, Jilly. There's something about her..."

The rest of Constance's words were lost as footsteps approached. Zara passed without a pause on her way out to the terrace, but Jillian couldn't help thinking she very well might have overheard. The idea of being caught gossiping was bad enough, but it was harder to imagine how this knowledge might affect her interactions with the new guest. What would it be like, being alone with such a woman? She found herself of two minds—the scholar in her was intrigued by something previously unknown, while the daughter of Lord Stansfield felt mildly disturbed by the introduction of someone so disposed to challenge convention.

She and Constance stared at each other for a few seconds until they heard Nelson laughing at something Zara must have said. "It's fine. Go on," Jillian urged, stopping to speak with Andrew before rejoining them outside.

Constance had moved her chair closer to Nelson, and they were sharing bites of their lunch. Zara stood to the far side of the table, peering at the forest and sneaking occasional longing glances at their plates. Jillian took advantage of her distraction to study her again, finding her attire of wide-legged jeans and a T-shirt with a stylized cat on the front delightfully modest. The extra long-sleeve shirt tied around her waist suggested an impressive level of preparedness. Her shoes, however, looked as if they might fall apart at any second.

She hadn't realized Zara was aware of her inspection until she asked, "Do I pass, Your Ladyship?"

Nelson coughed, smothering a laugh, as Zara had put some extra drawl into her words. If there had been any hint of sarcasm, Jillian would have resented what the question implied about her title. But when Zara struck a pose like a runway model, it made them all laugh while also sensitively reminding Jillian that she was a grown woman who was entirely capable of judging if those shoes would hold together. She appreciated subtlety, a rare quality among her acquaintances. In that instant, she decided she might like Zara as a person, though she'd have to think more about the lesbian part.

Walking outside usually helped her solve problems with theories or designs, but she wasn't sure if such would be the case today, since she'd be accompanied by her quandary. Stowing their lunches in her rucksack, she turned back to Zara, handing her the water. "If you agree to carry the flask, you'll do."

Parting from Constance and Nelson, they moved into the trees, beyond sight of the house. Unusually for this time of year, the day was perfect, temperature-wise, and Jillian was pleased Zara easily kept up with her. She was accustomed to walking alone and wondered what possible conversation she might have with this stranger. But judging from Zara's contented expression as she took everything in, she seemed happy to simply walk and appreciate the day. Her casual manner made Jillian relax, and she began talking about the history of the house and about the surrounding acreage.

When Jillian began pointing out the different trees and plants, Zara asked, "Did you plan to become a botanist originally?"

"Am I boring you?"

Zara stopped in her tracks. "God, no. Absolutely not. I'm just amazed you know all this, even though it's not your field."

"I've lived here all my life. I thought it only right I should know what the things around me were called."

"You're a person who likes order." She nodded slowly. "So that makes sense."

Jillian cocked her head slightly. "I should think everyone would understand that order is necessary."

"I'd say it depends on whether that order is self-imposed or dictated by others."

Jillian had been thinking about order in the sense of classification, but she realized Zara was thinking of it more as control. She pondered that for a few seconds before deciding to change the subject. In the wider part of the path, they could walk side by side, and she began talking about the upcoming school term and what she hoped to be working on, watching Zara's face as she did. Her friends had their own plans, and they'd heard it all before, which meant they generally began to glaze over after about three minutes. But every time she hesitated, Zara asked a thoughtful question, encouraging her to go on. It was rather liberating to be in the presence of someone unusually attentive, who had absolutely no reason to curry favor. Unlike the occasional visitor who wanted the use of her name or finances for some scheme or cause, Zara had no use for the former and no apparent inclination toward the latter. It was exhilarating, until Jillian realized her conversation was becoming more of an oration.

Self-conscious, she stopped walking. "I've been talking so much I'm thirsty, and I feel like a complete twattle-basket. Why haven't you told me to quiet down?"

Zara burst out laughing. "You feel like a what?"

Jillian glanced at her. "You know. A chatterbox. A blabbermouth."

Shaking her head, Zara's mirth faded. "You're none of that. I'm interested because you're genuinely interesting." Zara handed her the flask, and Jillian felt her cheeks heat with pleasure. Trying to cover her reaction, she took two quick sips and then watched as Zara drank deeply, a small stream spilling from the side of her mouth. Suppressing an involuntary shiver, Jillian looked away.

"And this is glorious! Fresh air, fresh water." At the unexpected exclamation, Jillian startled. She turned to find Zara looking rueful. "Sorry. When I'm not on the ship, I'm usually stuck in a port city. I only meant it's really nice of you to share this with me."

Once again, Jillian found herself smiling at the frankness. "It's my pleasure. And we're about halfway to our picnic spot, if you can hold out a little longer."

"Sure." Zara grinned. "I'm in your hands."

There was something vaguely affecting about her smile combined with the image she'd suggested, but Jillian brushed it aside as they began walking again, wishing Constance had kept her mouth shut. She hadn't yet had time to process it, but she didn't like for her awareness of Zara's sexual proclivity to make her view everything she said and did through that lens. Zara was obviously enjoying the day, so Jillian decided to act as she would with anyone she didn't know well. "Tell me, where did you grow up?" she asked.

To her surprise, Zara gave a short, bitter sounding laugh. "I spent my childhood in Arkansas. As for where I grew up, that's a different story."

When she didn't say anything more, Jillian glanced over. Confounded by her tight, almost angry expression, she said, "I'm sorry if that was overly personal."

After a few steps more, she was surprised to feel Zara touch her arm. "Hey, I'm the one who should be sorry. Your question was fine. I'd gotten kind of immersed in imagining your life, and I wasn't prepared for a question about mine. I usually have a much more vague answer ready."

Jillian considered that as they wound along the trail that led to the stream. Was a "more vague answer" another way of saying she would lie? About something as basic as her upbringing? As if reading her mind, Zara added, "It's just not a story most people want to hear, so I sanitize it enough to make it suitable for the general public."

She wasn't sure what concerned her more, the idea that she was part of the general public or that Zara's past had been difficult. They walked for a time without speaking, but when they reached the stream, Zara gasped with delight. Seeing it through her eyes, Jillian was reminded again of what a beautiful spot it was. The brook cut deeper here, the surrounding vegetation lush and the trees taller and more majestic.

Zara turned to her eagerly. "Tell me we get to stay here for a while."

Jillian couldn't help but smile at her enthusiasm. "Yes. Unless you're not hungry. We can go on for a bit and then come back if you—"

"I'm starving," Zara said, holding up a hand to her forehead theatrically. "If you don't feed me now, I might faint." She looked around and took a few stumbling steps, lowering herself exaggeratedly onto Jillian's favorite rock.

"Well, we can't have that, can we?" Smiling at the comical antics, Jillian handed over lunch as Zara drank from the flask again before passing it back. Jillian had barely taken a sip before she heard paper ripping, followed by chewing and moaning at the same time.

"Oh my God, this is the best sandwich I've ever had in my life."

Mrs. Livingstone did do wonderful things with bread and meat, but Jillian suspected Zara might not have been joking about being hungry. Sitting on a fallen log a few feet away, she said, "We could have eaten at the house, you know. Taken our walk later."

"Nuh-uh." Zara shook her head and swallowed. "I couldn't have waited another moment to get out in the woods with you." Feeling a blush rising again, Jillian was grateful when Zara gestured at the reeds by the stream. "I guess you never had to come out here and cut a switch for a whipping after you got into trouble for the third time in one day, did you? In fact, I'll bet you've never done one bad thing in your whole life. Am I right?"

Gregory. What had been a blush turned into a chill. Her appetite gone, Jillian set the sandwich on her lap and looked down. "No, you'd lose that bet." She could hear the hollowness in her own voice and apparently, Zara could too.

A warm hand touched her shoulder. "Oh jeez, Jillian, I'm really sorry. That was stupidly presumptuous of me. Everyone's childhood has their rough spots, don't they? Please accept my apology."

Jillian turned and found Zara squatting beside her, much closer than she expected. Their eyes met again, and Zara took her hands. Finding it hard to catch her breath, Jillian was relieved when Zara continued. "I promise, my conversation isn't normally such a complete bull in a china shop."

Looking at their joined hands, Jillian wondered at the pulse, the thrill that pushed through her at Zara's touch. Composing herself, she mused, "I suppose you're customarily very smooth."

Zara grinned. "Very."

"And why do you think your smoothness has deserted you?" Were they flirting? Jillian couldn't imagine so, given she had never grasped the art of it.

Zara's lips compressed into a thin line. "I...uh...I get uptight around rich people like you."

Jillian regretted the loss of her smile. And it seemed like Zara was withholding at least part of her reply. "You get uptight? I'm out here in the woods holding hands with a lesbian. I don't even know how to think about that." Was it Zara's guileless American manner that was making her so uncommonly blunt?

Zara laughed good-naturedly. Letting go, she went back to her rock. "I figured that conversation in the kitchen was Constance telling you, right? I'm not surprised since you're such great friends, and it's good for you to know."

Taking several quick bites of her sandwich, Zara nodded, almost to herself. Jillian expected some further remarks because surely such a personal revelation should come with more. More what, she wasn't sure. It wasn't that she wanted to hear about Zara's sexual exploits, of course, but perhaps some explanation of how she'd gotten to be the bold, fearless person she seemed to be.

Zara merely smiled at her as she finished her sandwich, and Jillian sensed it was up to her to lead the conversation. Zara couldn't know that she was terrible at superficial socializing, much less such an in-depth conversation about something so private. The burden of what she should say felt immense, and she realized her mouth was too dry to taste anything, much less take part in some illuminating discussion of human sexuality. She offered Zara her remaining half sandwich, which was accepted with a nod, and took a long drink from the flask.

"I want you to know," Zara said with a final swallow, "that if being around me makes you the least bit uncomfortable, I already told Nelson I'd sleep in his car tonight. It's cleaner than a lot of places I slept when I was younger, that's for sure." She gathered the paper from her meal into a ball and tossed it neatly into the rucksack.

Filing that piece of information away, Jillian replied, "Nonsense. I've already had Andrew take your things to the south wing. Besides, I've been promised a concert later."

Zara clasped her hands and leaned toward her. "Oh gosh, that sounds like fun. I love concerts. Who's playing?"

Jillian laughed, something she couldn't have imagined doing a minute ago. Zara was actually quite nonthreatening, for the most part. She had an appealing, rather innocent quality at times, but there were also those moments when she exuded raw sensuality. No wonder being around her was confusing.

"Jill." Zara spoke softly, but hearing a more familiar version of her name in that husky voice gave Jillian an odd delight. "I want to tell you something, but I don't want you to take it wrong, okay?" She nodded. "That beautiful laugh goes perfectly with the rest of you. I wondered what it would be like out here, not actually knowing anything about you other than you're Constance's friend. And hell, I don't even know her that well. Then, seeing how you live…well, I was pretty anxious. But today has been great, way better than I expected."

Jillian frowned slightly, uncertain as to Zara's meaning. She opened her mouth to speak, but Zara hurried on. "I mean, you've got this mansion and these servants and all this land and the kind of money that goes with it. I generally wouldn't be comfortable around someone like you, but today has been the nicest day I've had in a long, long time. And I want to thank you for that." She took a breath. "In the same way, it's really important to me that things aren't awkward between us. Whatever else, I'd like to be your friend. So if I do something or say something that makes you feel uneasy, please tell me. Okay?"

Jillian almost laughed again. In her typical American way, Zara was just as direct about wanting to clear the air as Jillian had uncharacteristically been earlier. It was actually rather refreshing to have a conversation without worrying about propriety and decorum. Noting Zara's utterly sincere expression was edging toward worry, she had to agree. And change the subject. "Yes, by all means. Thank you." Jillian stood, shouldering the rucksack. "But we should start back. We'll need time to clean up and change before dinner."

Zara followed without a word. Despite their cordial conversation, there was a prevailing sense of discomfort in the silence, rather than the relaxed atmosphere from before. When they reached the wider part of the trail, Jillian stopped, digging into the rucksack for the treat she'd neglected in her rush to leave. "Besides making excellent sandwiches, Mrs. Livingstone also makes wonderful biscuits." At Zara's odd expression, she added, "That would be 'cookies' to you. May I offer you one as your reward for being such a nice hiking companion?"

Zara's eyes widened, and she nodded. After one tentative nibble, hers disappeared in seconds. She groaned appreciatively, and Jillian dug out a second one. "You had me talking all the way out here," Jillian said, "so I think it's your turn. Tell me about your trip over or about how you got started playing or something." She waved the cookie enticingly.

"Isn't that yours?" Zara asked, her gaze riveted to the treat as she spoke.

"I'm actually not a big fan of sweets. I'd trade it for a Zara Keller story."

She grinned. "You're definitely getting shortchanged on that deal, but sure." They began walking again. "I was four or five years old, in Sunday school. We were singing, 'Jesus Loves Me'—acapella—and the girl next to me was terribly off pitch. There was an old upright in the room, and I went over and played the whole song. With one finger, mind you. But the teacher told my parents, and they asked if I wanted to learn to play the piano. The fact that they gave me a choice let me know this was different from the way I was usually told what to do and probably terribly important. Which is why I said yes. They agreed to five lessons, just to see if I would stick with it, and by some wonderful chance, they took me to Mrs. Minton." Her voice wavered a bit, and Jillian glanced over to find her looking down. "She saved my life more times, and in more ways, than I can count. I could never repay her, but I think being accepted into the Royal College of Music would have made her proud."

Jillian had never been physically demonstrative. She accepted hugs from friends but wasn't comfortable initiating them. Touching made her self-conscious because she was never certain about what response would be appropriate. Constance's hugs were warm and caring, but ever since their teen years, Jillian had become self-conscious, apprehensive that she might not be letting go soon enough. Nelson seemed to be every bit as anxious as she was about not overdoing it, and whenever Clive put an arm around her, she knew he meant it as affection, but it always felt a bit smothering.

The wistful tone in Zara's voice made her want to offer some kind of reassurance. Carefully, she put a hand on her shoulder and squeezed lightly before letting go, surprising herself at the lack of awkwardness. "I'm sure she's proud of you. But if you want to call her after you get accepted, you're welcome to use the phone here."

"That's kind of you, but she died a few years ago. Just before I took up cruising." Zara quickly wiped at her face and straightened. "And look where that led me." She turned and smiled, but there was still pain in her eyes.

"I'm very sorry for your loss," Jillian murmured, hating the inadequacy of those staid words. She'd heard them before. Without thinking, she added, "But I'm glad your journey brought you here."

"Are you?" Zara took a step closer, and Jillian felt that strange internal disturbance again. Her heart rate increased, and she had the odd inclination to take a step closer herself. As Zara's dark gaze swept over her face, she tried to work out why she'd want to do such a thing, but she was having trouble understanding any of it. After a few seconds, when she managed a nod, Zara asked, "Then does that mean I get my cookie?"

The laughter bubbling out of her was at least partly relief, and she swatted Zara's arm playfully. This second touch felt even easier. "I can tell you're incorrigible, but yes."

"That's not the first time I've heard that, but it sounds much nicer in your lovely accent." She took a bite and winked. "Tastes better too."

Jillian shook her head, wondering if Zara played the field. She had probably flirted the same way with Constance, which had led to...

No, she didn't want to think about Zara and Constance kissing, indignant at the very idea. Unsure why, she returned to a safer subject. "The only song I ever learned on the piano was 'Twinkle, Twinkle, Little Star.' But I'm not sure I could play more than the first line now."

"Ah." Zara nodded sagely. "But with that, you've already mastered the perfect fifth."

"The what?"

"A perfect fifth is the name for a certain interval of notes. In that song, there are three and a half steps between the first twinkle and the second twinkle."

Jillian could hear the sounds in her head. "And what makes that so perfect?" She was out of her league on this topic, but Zara's expression showed such concentration that she wanted to hear more.

"In Western culture, the perfect fifth is considered more consonant than any other interval except for unison and the octave." Before she could ask, Zara explained, "Consonance in music refers to sounds that are the most pleasant and sweet, and therefore, acceptable." Rolling her eyes, she added, "Doesn't that sound like our society's unrealistic definition of acceptability, especially for women?"

"That's rather harsh, isn't it?" Jillian generally shied away from such potentially acrimonious, socio-political discussions. Engineering, with its provable outcomes, was much more comfortable. "Is there something inherently wrong with being sweet and pleasant?"

"There is if it's all that's expected of you or if it's the only way to be accepted. Is being sweet and pleasant one of the requirements for being Lady Stansfield?" There was an unexpected bite to her tone.

Jillian struggled with an unexpected rush of emotions: anger, guilt, resentment, shame, and some unaccountable sadness. Too much to feel at once. Best to simply move on. "Mmm. Well, I think we'd best get back."

She'd barely taken two steps before Zara caught her arm. "Look, I'm sorry." When Jillian stopped, she let go, brushing her hand across her mouth as if editing herself. "Really. You've been nothing but gracious and kind to me, and I shouldn't talk to you like that. I just get wound up sometimes. Forgive me?"

"Certainly." Jillian gave her a quick nod. "But we need to keep moving."

Zara kept her head down as they quickened their pace. When the house came into view, she gave a deep, almost theatrical sigh. "Back to this sweet, always pleasant world, I guess."

Jillian had to laugh. "It's not honestly all that bad, is it?"

Constance and Nelson were waving from the terrace. "No, of course not. This world is very nice."

But it's not mine, Jillian could practically hear her thinking. Watching Zara smile and wave back, she didn't comment on her sincerity, but she wished she hadn't rushed them so. Zara's outburst had perplexed her, and she found herself curious about its source. She should have asked more questions earlier in their walk instead of babbling about the house and the grounds and herself. Human behavior wasn't among her primary interests, but asking Zara more about being a lesbian would have given her a chance to learn something new.

Squaring her shoulders, Jillian determined that, even with their wholly different pasts, and distinctly separate futures, there was no reason why they couldn't both enjoy this time in the present. After all, she had the reputation of Fullerhill hospitality to uphold.

Chapter Four

Zara's head spun from being on the receiving end of Jillian Stansfield's amazing smile. Jill had shown her up to her room, waving Andrew off, which had made him frown. He might have simply wanted to do his job, but Zara was willing to bet it was more than that. He'd probably had her pegged as a thief, and once upon a time, he'd have been right.

Ironically, when she found both her bags empty, she thought someone had stolen from her. Jill was a few feet down the hall when Zara called, trying to keep her voice calm. "Uh, hey. My stuff is missing."

"The staff usually unpacks for our guests. Did you check the wardrobe?" She didn't laugh or even lift an eyebrow.

Zara stuttered as Jillian walked back into the room. She was unable to resist breathing in Jill's scent as she passed close on her way to the huge cabinet on the far wall. Upon recognizing her clothes, Zara mumbled, "Oh," like a total dumbass. Then Jill opened the top drawer on the dresser, displaying a wallet and passport neatly placed on top of some canceled letters. Zara rarely let those out of her sight, especially the correspondence from the RCM, but today, she'd gone off into the woods with Jillian Stansfield without so much as a thought to take them along.

"Only first-class passengers get this kind of treatment on the ship," she said, trying to cover her ridiculous blunder.

"We want to make it a very pleasant, first-class experience for everyone who stays here," Jill replied and gave her that smile.

When the door closed a second time, Zara had to resist the urge to go after her, since she'd have to fumble for another lame excuse to keep her around. Instead, she made sure the passport was hers and counted her money, though Andrew and the other people who worked here would be thoroughly screened, and they sure wouldn't need to waste their time on her piddly cash.

This incredible mansion was full of really valuable stuff, like a cross between a museum and a palace. She was reminded of the postcards some of the crew had shown her when they'd taken side trips on an off day. She'd never gone, always claiming she was broke, but even if she'd had enough money, she'd never waste it like that. Because for one thing, there was never enough money. Her life before Mrs. Minton had rescued her—again—had taught her about getting necessities first and then saving for the next time's needs.

Zara was pretty sure people who lived in houses like this wouldn't think that way. Now in her third year of performing for rich folks, she'd learned a few things about them. For one, they operated as if the rules they'd so readily created for everyone else didn't apply to them. They also had every confidence that if they got caught with their pants down or their hand in the cookie jar, their money and the influence that went with it would get them off with a slap on the wrist.

Perhaps that was why they couldn't be trusted to do what was right, much less what they promised. In her experience, the monied class only did what was best for themselves and had no compunctions about screwing everyone else. She'd gotten the feeling Constance was one of those types, though occasional flashes of remorse—or guilt—had crossed her face during their conversations. But Nelson obviously doted on her, which made Zara glad she'd stopped things on the stern that night.

And something in her had obviously thought him trustworthy because it was very unlike her to fall asleep in a stranger's car. Normally, she'd be watching every turn and noting landmarks, making sure she could find her way back. And she'd felt like Dorothy in *The Wizard of Oz* when they'd awakened her. One look at the scenery, and she knew she wasn't in Kansas—or Arkansas—anymore. The drive up to the house was like the beginning of some other movie that she had no part in, like a period romance starring Cary Grant or Katherine

Hepburn, and she seriously hadn't wanted to get out of the car. No way would she ever be welcome—or comfortable—among people who lived in such luxury.

What had helped her get through those first few steps inside the mansion was recalling Mrs. Minton's lessons on how to act in new, overwhelming places. After watching Zara slouch and cringe her way through the public moments of their first trip to the symphony, Mrs. Minton had used the song, "I Whistle a Happy Tune" from *The King and I* to coach eight-year-old Zara on conducting herself with confidence, even when she didn't feel it.

"No one else knows if you're feeling scared or strange unless you act that way. If you show them a self-assured, poised person, they'll believe that's exactly who you are." That approach had served her well, from seedy bars to posh cruise-ship lounges and especially in the piano competitions of her youth. Here, she covered her unease with a brash, undaunted persona, conveying what was expected of a crude, somewhat pushy American. Until one unexpected instant had thrown her completely for a loop.

That woman she'd first seen on the terrace was the most stunning person she'd ever seen. Working among the rich and famous had given her opportunities to observe some pretty nice-looking people, but a lot of them sported the kind of looks that could easily be bought. Clothes, tans, makeup, plastic surgery, that kind of thing. But Jillian Stansfield, standing in the natural light of her terrace in worn corduroy pants and a blue camp shirt, was exquisite in the way of something authentic and pure. Zara was captivated and wanted to spend whatever time it took to find out if that loveliness went deeper than the surface.

Usually content with her own company—especially if there was a piano handy—Zara respected Jill's somewhat detached manner. But there had been moments on their walk when her demeanor hadn't seemed strictly innate, as if part of her desperately wanted to experience a real connection and affinity with someone. If they'd met aboard ship, Zara might have made a pass, but during their walk, she'd felt in Jill her same unwillingness to risk too much. Still, Jill hadn't mentioned a boyfriend, and unlike Constance, she wasn't wearing a ring. She was probably straight, but some women simply were until they weren't.

Jillian was also different in that she seemed to guard herself behind that reserve. Constance was like a puppy. She loved attention, and Zara got the sense she just wanted to play. She gushed when she talked. Jillian was much more restrained, like a pond of impenetrable depth, with only a thin stream of conversation trickling out. And as much as Zara wanted to dive in and explore every inch, she didn't want to be disruptive. While she deeply regretted her outburst about perfection, Jillian's cool tolerance made her wonder how many ripples it would take to unsettle those waters.

Okay, focus, Keller. Jill had said to change for dinner, and Zara knew what that meant from her time on the ship. She opened the wardrobe again, finding her black pants and white shirt missing. Damn. She was certain she'd thrown them in her bag when she'd changed for the hike. She rejected the idea of wearing her red dress before her audition and then not again until her first concert. Or so she hoped. She decided to shower first before picking through her meager choices. Maybe Constance would come by, and Zara could ask her opinion. She'd heard Constance introduce her as someone she'd met onboard instead of saying she was working as the piano player in the lounge six nights a week. That meant she was conscious of Zara's subordinate status and was trying to help her fit in, which was both nice and a less-than-encouraging reminder that she didn't. And wouldn't. Ever.

But surely everyone started by showering and putting on clean underwear, which meant she was even with them for the moment. Upon returning to the bedroom, she found her freshly laundered black pants and shirt hanging in the wardrobe. Yeah, weird, but also really nice. She put on a little makeup and pondered the big decisions. Tie or no tie? Hat or only earrings? She'd just started dressing when she heard someone in the hallway. Zara peeked out right as someone she didn't know was passing.

The woman stopped, giving her a thorough once-over. Her dirty blond hair flipped up just at her shoulders, and she wore a knee-length, color-blocked shift dress with a V-neck. Her pinched mouth oozed money, and by her tone when she spoke, she clearly knew it. "Who are you?"

Zara's shirt was unbuttoned, and her slacks weren't zipped, so she didn't open the door all the way, hoping a pleasant expression would suffice. "I'm Zara. I'm a friend of Constance. And Nelson. And Jillian."

"Obviously, or you wouldn't be here. But you must not be a very good friend, or I would know you too."

This chick needed a taste of her own medicine. "Why?" she asked, lifting her eyebrows appraisingly. "Who are you?"

Hand at her chest as if she was deeply offended, the woman announced, "I am Beatrice Bowden, Constance's best friend since we started at Cambridge."

"Well, it's nice to meet you, Beatrice. I'm sure we'll have a chance to speak more at dinner. But I need to finish..." Zara gestured at herself.

"Mmm." The assessment resumed. "You do realize you look rather like someone's waitstaff?"

So definitely the tie. "Thanks for sharing your opinion." Zara moved to shut the door.

"Just trying to be of help." The voice faded down the hallway.

"Bitch," Zara muttered and went to finish dressing. Not like she wasn't nervous enough. Normally, she didn't care about impressing people with her appearance, but she wanted to make a good impression on behalf of her new acquaintances. Maybe they would let her play some before dinner. It would establish her identity, and she'd focus on popular songs, maybe get people singing like they did in the lounge. Everyone would get more comfortable that way. Zara needed to find Constance. She'd understand. Maybe.

But the first person she saw after almost getting lost on her way downstairs was Nelson. He was wearing a conservative suit but gestured smilingly at her colorful tie as she approached. "No hat tonight?" he asked.

Zara grinned back. "No. But I was told I needed a little distinction from the waitstaff, so..."

Constance's angry voice came from behind her. "Who told you that?"

Zara turned to find Constance wearing a lovely, knee-length, green evening gown. God, she was really underdressed. She'd gone with her collar open and the tie loose but wondered if she would look more formal with it tightened. "Just some woman in the hallway. I was hoping it might be you, so I could ask if this was okay. Oh, and she did say she was your best friend at Cambridge."

Nelson and Constance looked at each other, and said, "Beatrice," at the same time. Zara was relieved their disapproving tone wasn't directed at her.

"Anyway, I wondered if I could play some now. Sing for my supper, so to speak. I was going to ask Jillian if it would be okay, but…" She made a show of looking around.

"It's a funny thing," Constance explained, taking her arm and leading her down the hall as another newly arrived guest stepped up to speak with Nelson. "Our Jilly is usually late to her own gatherings. We'll never know if she secretly likes to make a grand entrance or if she's gotten busy in that lab of hers."

"She mentioned something about her projects when we were walking. Does she work here as well as going to school?"

Nelson joined them. "Jillian works all the time. She's one of the most driven individuals you'll meet. I think if it weren't for those walks in the woods, she'd never take a break. It was nice of you to go with her today."

"No, it was nice of her to take me along. It was a really great…" Zara trailed off as they turned into a large room occupied by a dozen or so very well-dressed people. They appeared to be mostly Jillian's age, with a few older and younger faces here and there.

It's no different from playing in the lounge before the first dinner seating, she told herself, trying to swallow her nerves. Except when she arrived in the lounge, those people knew what she was there for, and most of them would already be having a great time. Here, her appearance had interrupted murmured conversations, and every calculating gaze seemed to find her sorely lacking. Her eyes fell on a shiny black grand piano occupying one side of the room, and her tension eased. She worked her fingers and wrists at her sides.

Constance's raised voice reminded her she wasn't alone. "Everyone, this is our new friend, Zara. I met her coming home on the *Ocean Princess*, and she's a fabulous pianist. She's agreed to play a little for us, so we'll all be sweet, agreed?"

There were a few chuckles before most people resumed their conversations. Some curious glances followed her, and a few more heads turned again at her gasp when she sat at the piano. The majority of her training had been on the fine upright Steinway of Mrs. Minton's, and she'd played on a Fazioli twice at competitions when she was younger, but never a Blüthner. These incredible instruments were world-famous…and incredibly pricey.

Clearing her throat, she wiped her damp palms on her pants. She carefully set the few slips of paper and pencil she'd brought for requests next to the music rack. At least she didn't have to worry about what she would play. She always let the room guide her at events like these, and while the lyrics to "I Whistle a Happy Tune" resonated in her head, she knew to start this crowd with something more classic.

She made no introduction because they wouldn't need one. The first four notes she struck would be immediately recognizable to anyone in this group as Beethoven's Symphony No. 5. She played for almost a minute in classical style until the crowd was lulled into the expectation of hearing the whole, familiar piece. Just at the transition from the last allegro con brio chord to the softer, sweeter segment where the horns would come in—had she been a full symphony orchestra—she began her jazz adaptation, which caused more than a few heads to turn. There was some laughter, and one or two throats cleared with displeasure, but three or four people—obviously jazz fans—moved closer.

Zara nodded at them as she finished a shortened version of the piece. A small smattering of applause followed, and someone asked, "Do you play popular music as well?"

"Sure," Zara said. "Name something you'd like to hear. And sing along if you want."

Someone called out, "'Don't Sleep in the Subway,'" and Zara said, "Good advice," as she began to play.

Those closest to her laughed, and she had growing participation for the next three songs. The mood was growing increasingly festive, and the crowd around her grew. Luckily, there were three or four folks who had really decent voices. Judging from the laughter and applause after they finished "Lady Madonna," she estimated she'd won over more than half the guests to at least grudging acceptance. Constance had stayed close at first, though when Zara glanced around a few minutes later, she was gone. But by then, she was in her element, sure of herself and her place in the room. Now, half listening to new song suggestions, Zara became aware of a swell of other exclamations.

Turning, she saw Jillian had arrived. Attractive as she'd been in her comfortable hiking clothes, she appeared equally at ease in a classic, knee-length, black dress that draped so flawlessly, it must have been custom fitted. Everything about her was composed and perfect, and Zara rose almost automatically, her heart swelling as anyone's would upon coming into the presence of such stunning splendor.

The movement drew Jill's eyes, and she nodded. Returning the acknowledgement, Zara sat, feeling foolish as everyone else in the room surged toward Jill. Aware she needed to be background, she began playing Bill Evans's "Peace Piece," a personal favorite, and focused her thoughts on the music. The vague hope of developing a relationship with Jill, even just friendship, faded like the last dying notes of a song. Lady Stansfield was so far out of her league, it wasn't even worth dreaming about.

"If everyone is ready, we can serve dinner and give Zara a bit of a break," Jillian said a few moments later as the last of the melody caused a break in the conversation. There was another sprinkling of applause, which Zara acknowledged with a wave. She would have been happy to sit there alone and keep playing, maybe grab a sandwich later, but a hand on her arm pulled her to her feet. She turned, expecting to see Constance, but Beatrice, the bitch from the hallway, was staring into her face.

"Why didn't you tell me you were a musician?" she demanded.

"It didn't come up," Zara replied, hoping she didn't sound defensive.

"Do you play somewhere in town?" She gestured around the room. "Clearly, you rent out for parties. What's your rate?"

Zara had automatically slipped some of the business cards Mrs. Minton had made for her into her pocket, though the contact information was no longer valid. She held one out, saying, "I don't know if I'll be available after next week. And you won't be able to reach me at that number, obviously."

Beatrice glanced indifferently at the card and handed it back. "Then this won't help, will it? I'm having some people over in two weeks. But it's a more formal affair. You do have something else to wear, don't you?"

"Hello, Beatrice." Jillian's smooth alto held a slight chill. "I hope Miss Keller will perform more for us later, but let's let her get something to eat first, shall we?"

"I'm just trying to—" Beatrice began, but Jillian cut her off with a firmness Zara hadn't heard from her before.

"Later."

Beatrice's mouth closed. Jillian inclined her head, adding, "I'm sure she'll be very interested in hearing your proposal after dinner." She turned away, and Zara gave a half-smile to Beatrice before following close on her heels.

At the doorway, Jill's hand brushed her back, indicating which way they were going. Even if it was merely a guiding touch, Zara felt it all the way to her toes. She hoped her voice wouldn't catch as she said, "Honestly, I don't care to hear her proposal at any time, but if I'm not accepted at the RCM, I'll need jobs like hers until I can catch the next ship to the States."

"Is that your plan?" Jill asked.

"As far as it goes, yeah."

"And then what?"

Zara shrugged, smiling. "I guess I'll just sail wherever the wind blows me."

They reached the dining room, and Jill touched her again, directing her to a table for four where Constance and Nelson were already seated. "I'll rejoin you in a moment," she said. "I need to make the rounds since I was a bit late."

Nelson nodded, and Constance said, "Hurry back, love."

Zara watched her go. She couldn't help it. When she became aware that her staring was verging on gawking, she turned back to the table. Constance was smiling at her knowingly, and she felt her cheeks grow warm.

Thankfully, Nelson spoke. "Constance wasn't kidding, Zara. You're really good. How long have you been playing?" he asked between sips of soup.

While they ate, she gave them the sanitized version of her musical life before directing the conversation to Nelson's interest in computers. When she felt a warmth in her chest, she knew Jillian was returning. A few seconds after she sat, Mrs. Livingstone appeared with her dishes. They nodded briefly at each other before the older woman disappeared down the hallway.

"Sorry," she said, giving them all a little smile. "What are we talking about?"

"Computers," Constance said with an exaggerated sigh, and they laughed.

Jillian's glance flickered over Zara. "You needn't have waited on me." She signaled another nearly invisible server. "Would you please get Miss Keller some hot soup?"

Looking at her full bowl, Zara tried not to show her surprise. She hadn't intended to be proper, and after her time on the street, she generally ate whatever and whenever food presented itself. "Oh, I'm fine, I just—" She stopped as her bowl was removed, and a fresh one appeared in its place. "Thank you."

"These two know to go ahead without me," Jill explained. "Next time, you do the same, all right?"

Zara blinked, pleased to think about a next time while Constance gossiped about who was and wasn't in attendance. During dessert, Jill turned to Zara again. "I'm sorry I didn't get to hear you play very much." She gestured toward the other room. "Would you mind terribly carrying on some more?"

Zara almost laughed. It was a pleasure to do the one thing that would make her feel like she had a place here. Plus, music was her first love. "I think it's the least I could do to repay this wonderful hospitality." Especially the time spent with you, she wanted to add. But that would likely be embarrassing for Jill, or worse, put tension between them as she'd clumsily done at times on their hike. And it wasn't something she wanted to say in front of Constance and Nelson anyway. "But I'd like to wash first, if you can direct me." She held up her hands. "Don't want to chance getting food particles on your beautiful instrument."

Jill looked at her thoughtfully. "I haven't given you the grand tour yet, have I? We'll have to remedy that, but now is not the time. Let me—"

She started to rise, but Zara waved her back down. "Please. Stay and visit with your friends. If you'll just tell me the way..."

She tried, certainly, but Zara ended up wandering down a long hallway, opening each door in the hope of finding the restroom. In the third room, she heard muffled moaning and stepped away quickly, certain she recognized sounds that had nothing to do with what she was looking for. She was nearly at the end of the hall when Andrew appeared from around the corner.

"Is there something I can help you locate?" he inquired in a chilly tone.

"Oh yes, hi, Andrew. Can you please help me find the restroom?" She hoped to convey a combination of appreciation and need.

Without a word, he indicated for her to follow, turning twice before reaching the hallway she was apparently intended to take. "It's through there, Miss," he said, pointing at a door that was slightly open.

"Thanks so much. And please, call me Zara."

He shook his head slowly, eyes half-closed with disfavor as he stepped back. At that point, she almost would have invited him in to watch if it would help. Instead, she found him waiting for her at a discreet distance when she came out, and he mutely escorted her to the music room where a half dozen people were already waiting.

A man and two women came over to speak to her as she sat at the piano. They were all very nice, and though they gave their names, she couldn't have repeated them on a bet. She did what she'd done onboard the ship, smiled and thanked them and asked what they'd like to hear. Luckily, they were all jazz fans, which gave her the chance to play some tunes she'd learned from Mrs. Minton's records of two great pianists, Lennie Tristano and Duke Pearson, while more people gathered. She was about to shift gears into more sing-alongs when someone tapped her shoulder.

"Do you suppose you could find the time to speak with me now?" Beatrice asked in a tone so haughty, it would have been ridiculous except for the expression on her face. Zara hadn't known that many women in the Biblical sense, but she could certainly tell when one was really pissed off.

"Sure." She stood and turned. "But I'm not sure how much more I can tell you." Beatrice took a breath, but Zara added, "It would be best if you gave me your phone number, and I'll call you when I know my schedule. Then you can tell me more about the kind of event you're having."

She appeared to be considering this suggestion. "Well…" When her eyes darted uneasily to the side, Zara suspected Jillian had entered the room. "All right, then." Beatrice fumbled in her bag, pulling out a gold pen before clearing her throat. "Jilly, darling, would you have something I could write on?"

Zara indicated the request slips she'd brought out of habit. "Oh, here. You can write on one of these."

Jillian made no comment nor did she move. Beatrice scribbled for a few seconds before handing the paper back. She drew herself up. "I'll expect to hear from you."

"Yes, ma'am." Zara put the note into her other pocket. "Thank you for this opportunity."

"Mmm." Beatrice gave Jillian an entirely fake smile and melted into the crowd.

Jillian raised an eyebrow, but before either of them could speak, another man approached. "Am I to understand you're available for parties?" he asked.

"I may be, yes. My schedule is a bit…uncertain right now."

"You can call here at the end of next week, Victor," Jillian said with a more welcoming tone. "We'll know more then."

We? Zara liked the sound of that. "Tell me what to play for you," she said to Jill when he'd gone. "What's your favorite music?"

"What would you guess?" she asked.

"A challenge. Hmm. Well, it has to be classical, since you're a classy lady, but also a deep thinker, which makes me think of Bach. Mozart might be too busy, especially if you're working, and it's a piece you don't know well. You'd want something more like background." Jill leaned forward but didn't comment. "But to relax, I suspect you might be a Vivaldi fan."

Her mouth opened slightly. "I am. How did you—"

"Nearly everyone likes Vivaldi, so it was an easy guess. I didn't bring my orchestra, but I'll try the piano score." Zara played the opening chords of "Spring," just as someone across the room called for help in settling an argument about stress loads.

Jill touched Zara's right hand, and she stopped playing, something she almost never did once she'd started a piece. "Please, not now. I have obligations tonight, and I want to be able to give your performance my full attention."

Zara swallowed. "Well, I'm flattered, but I'm not sure my performance merits your full attention. In this particular case, a little distraction might help. I haven't played this piece in quite a while."

Raising her eyebrow again, Jill asked, "Who is this modest woman, and what has she done with my self-assured guest?"

"Tell me which one you prefer, and I'll let you know," Zara said, before she thought better of it.

"Jillian," the voice called again. It sounded like someone had been enjoying the free-flowing liquid refreshment.

"Please, excuse me."

They'd both looked toward the other speaker, so Zara couldn't see Jill's expression before she turned. Damn her big mouth. Heart sinking, she cursed herself for her overeager comeback. She'd probably blown it. Again.

Chapter Five

That first night, Constance tried not to show interest as she watched them. It was quite obvious that Zara was smitten with Jillian. One didn't have to be a lesbian to be impressed with Jillian or her incredible home. What was unexpected was how much time Jillian gave to Zara, especially since they'd already had their walk in the woods that afternoon. Typically, Jillian made the rounds with her visitors once or twice before settling in with her friends for a good chat. Or if Clive was present, he'd often claim her more quickly on their behalf. Tonight, Jill seemed to be watching out for Zara more than anything else. They all knew she was not one for physical displays, but she'd guided Zara to their table, and Constance had noted she'd touched her hand when she'd started playing one of Jillian's favorite pieces. Perhaps she was trying to establish to their regular guests that Zara was welcome or to demonstrate to Constance that she wasn't uncomfortable with Zara's sexuality. But for Jillian Stansfield to find it necessary to justify anything would be most unusual. And she certainly didn't have anything to prove to Zara Keller.

But some kind of nerves were in play because Jilly was drinking a tad more than normal. She'd had her usual cocktail before dinner but a second glass of wine with the meal, and now she was back to whiskey, which almost never happened these days. During their first year at university, Clive had begun drinking much more than the rest of them, and it felt rather like a "drown your sorrows" usage. He'd been unwilling to talk about what was wrong, but Jillian had tried to show her solidarity by joining him on several occasions, resulting in her becoming disastrously inebriated and Clive feeling tragically guilty. Without any explanation, he'd eventually returned to ordinary social drinking, as had she.

Nelson had speculated that Clive's occasional displays of outlandish behavior were simply a way of getting extra attention from Jillian, but Constance feared such behavior would ultimately have the opposite effect. Jillian might tolerate eccentric behavior in her friends, but Clive's recurrent peculiarities were not the stuff of romance or love. Having found the perfect man in Nelson, Constance had begun envisioning her friend's ideal match: someone who was steady but passionate. Clive was high-strung, and though it was obvious he cared about Jillian, he was marginally indifferent to anything where he wasn't directly involved.

Constance could only hope Clive would realize what he risked losing and would rise to the occasion before Jillian started considering one of the many suitors who lingered wistfully at the fringes of their group. She worried because once Jillian made up her mind about something, there was no turning back.

A change in the music made Constance glance at Zara, noting the familiar glass and slips of paper for requests but no cigarette. It had always looked like a prop anyway, since she'd never seen Zara smoking, and from her regular visits to the ship's lounge, she'd learned Zara mainly consumed sparkling mineral water with lime during her performance. Otherwise, it seemed she didn't drink at all unless she did so in the privacy of her cabin, which could indicate a real problem. But there had never been any sign of a hangover, and during one of their walks, Zara had made a vague reference to "getting way too much of my education in bars," with a sense of regret. Perhaps that comment alone should have made Constance anticipate how the lavish surroundings and the social status of those around her would make her nervous. She was playing less stiffly than she did in the ship's lounge but not quite as relaxed as she'd been with the crew.

At least she was a hit with the music fans among the crowd while the rest pretty much ignored her, carrying on as they normally would. Jillian, in the midst of male-dominated conversation as usual, nevertheless glanced at the piano more than once. Zara's scruples, once she'd learned about Nelson, had been admirable, but Constance began to fret over whether those principles would extend to not taking advantage of their slightly tipsy hostess, who did not wear a ring of any kind. Constance could admit she wasn't terribly cosmopolitan, but she was practically worldly compared to Jillian. She told herself Clive would be here tomorrow, and then her plan of using Zara's playing to inspire the romance between him and Jillian could begin.

Nelson smiled at her, oblivious in the way that nice men frequently were. They'd been dancing to a beautiful waltz someone else had requested when Constance decided to push a little. "What do you think of our entertainer?"

"She's incredibly talented. I've never heard anyone with such a range of musical knowledge."

"Yes, but I meant personally."

He blinked. "Oh. Uh…I suppose she's nice enough. In over her head a bit, I would guess."

She hummed encouragingly. "Quite. Anything else?"

"Well…" Constance could tell he was trying to figure out what she wanted him to say. His gaze swept the room, and he nodded toward the group Jillian was speaking with. The piano melody transitioned to something new, and they both watched as Jillian's head turned in Zara's direction. "Jilly seems to like her."

"Hmm." Constance couldn't bring herself to tell him that was exactly what she was worried about because such a remark wasn't fair to Zara and certainly didn't give Jillian credit for the level head she'd always possessed. Plus, there was the issue of what that concern would reveal about her.

They'd stopped their dance, and he focused on her. "You're not jealous, are you?" Since Constance wasn't sure how to answer, she said nothing. "Sweetie, Jillian can have more than one friend. You'll always be first on her list, and Zara won't be around long. But for now, it won't hurt for her to get to know someone rather…different." He grinned. "And maybe Zara will help her get outside of that lab during the times you're busy with me."

Looking into his warm gaze, she saw the man who deserved her admiration and love. "When did you get to be so wise?"

"Must have been when I started hanging around with you," he replied.

"You've practically known me your whole life, silly."

"So I've had a lot of time to work on it."

She tightened her arms around him, and he kissed her softly but not chastely.

"I'm glad you two already have a room." Jillian's voice came from behind them.

Constance turned, smiling, and held out her arm, inviting Jillian into the circle of their love. She stepped in, and Nelson put his arm around her shoulders. "We've missed you, Jilly," he said.

"I've missed the two of you." She seemed surprisingly comfortable with their closeness as she looked around the room. "How can we get these people to go home so we can talk?"

A small group was gathered around Zara, singing another popular song. "They'll never go home as long as there's entertainment. Have your piano player take a break," Nelson observed.

"I don't consider her my piano player," Jillian said, her tone oddly defensive.

"Obviously," Constance said, laughing. "Since you didn't put out a tip jar for her."

"Tip jar?" Jill looked at them both quizzically.

Constance explained, adding that she thought Zara significantly padded her income with the practice without going into specifics about the wagering.

Jill straightened. "Then I'll need to make an announcement for her." She moved to the middle of the room as Zara finished the current song with a flourish. There were a few cheers among the applause, and as soon as they died down, Jillian spoke. "Everyone, if I may have your attention for a moment." Faces turned toward her. "Thank you all for being here tonight. Please join me in expressing our appreciation for the talents of our special guest tonight, Zara Keller." Applause rose, even from those not near her, and Zara stood, bowing slightly before inclining her head to Jill. When the room quieted, Jillian added, "If you'd like more information about hiring Zara or hearing her play again, there are some slips of paper where you can leave your contact information."

Almost immediately, Jillian had to ask Nelson to bring more paper from the small writing desk in the drawing room down the hall.

Zara dodged around the crowd, and Constance saw her make eye contact with Jillian. *Wow*, she mouthed. *Thank you.*

Jillian inclined her head in that regal way she had before adding a more relaxed smile. Constance pulled at her arm. "Let's disappear for a moment and see if this crowd gets the hint."

Nelson joined them. "Yes. You ladies slip away into the drawing room so things can clear out a bit."

With another glance at the group that waited around the piano, Jillian nodded, and they hurried along the hallway into the smaller, more comfortable room where the fireplace was unlit on this unseasonably warm evening. Jillian turned excitedly once they were settled on the loveseat. "Tell me everything about you and Nelson. I need details."

Seeing Jillian almost girlish in her eagerness made Constance laugh. She knew Jilly was still a virgin, or at least basically so, after she'd talked about her one failed attempt at sex with Clive. He'd been unprepared, and she was inexperienced, apparently making the event both embarrassing and upsetting. "Nelson is incredibly sweet and very patient. That certainly helped. But I knew I wanted us to be together, not just purely for him but for me as well."

Jillian took her hand, which she hadn't expected. "You know, I'm incredibly happy for you both." She gave it a squeeze. "But how did it...feel?"

Constance leaned closer, keeping her voice low. "I was a little scared at first. Especially after what we'd read about...the pain. But we went slow, and he made sure I was ready. You know, physically." She wouldn't have spoken this frankly with anyone else, but she knew how much Jillian needed to hear it.

"And was it like in the books?"

After Jillian's disaster with Clive, Constance had been desperate to give her some encouragement, so she'd loaned her two romance novels to read. Bodice rippers, really, with just enough erotica to give her a sense of what should have happened...in the most romantic of all worlds, at least. For someone more accustomed to reading textbooks and technical journals, it must have been something of a shock. "Such drama," Jillian had commented when she'd handed them back. "Why do these things have to be this complicated?"

Jillian and Nelson thought nothing of tossing about terms like dissipation and tensile strength, which Constance thought sounded much more complicated. But now, she needed to be honest. "I think the first time, I was so nervous that I didn't notice those details, silly as that sounds. I mean, it didn't hurt much, and it made me feel full. But in a good way. I liked the way he moved, slow and smooth, and the pleasure on his face made me enjoy it even more."

Voices in the hall were calling good night and thanking Jillian for a lovely evening. They both waved to people passing the doorway.

"Each time after, it's gotten better and better," Constance practically whispered after the crowd had mostly dispersed. "But you know what a dear Nelson is. He truly cares about how I'm feeling." Giggling, she added, "And he takes direction very well."

Jillian smiled almost sadly. "Clive is too sensitive to take direction about anything without getting upset. I blame his father, but he takes any kind of suggestion as faultfinding."

Her reply was cut short when Zara walked past the doorway, stopped, and looked in. "Hi." They must have looked deeply involved because she didn't enter. "Can I get anybody anything?" she offered.

Jillian held out her glass, and Constance did the same. Normally, they'd get their drinks from the servers, but Nelson had probably let them go for the evening. "Whiskey, please," Jillian requested.

When Zara reached to take Constance's wineglass, she asked, "White or red?"

"The cabernet if there's any left. Otherwise, whatever."

She nodded and disappeared. Before they could resume their conversation, Nelson put his head in. "Only those who are staying the night are still here."

"Fabulous," Jillian said. "Thank you, Nelson."

He bowed. "My pleasure." He looked as if he might say something else, but Constance shook her head slightly, and, bless him, he got the message. "I'll see to what's left of the mob. Come join us whenever. Or I'll be back if I can run these folks up to bed."

Because he was such a dear, and because she'd just been saying how special he'd made things for her—once they'd gotten past his religious objections—Constance rose and kissed him quickly. She loved the way it made him smile. After he'd gone, she wasn't sure how to continue with Jillian, but she felt compelled to say one thing more. "Sweetie, if Clive is the right one, he'll want to please you as well as himself."

"It was my fault, really," Jillian said, her eyes tearing up. "I didn't tell him in advance what I'd decided, and I must have shocked him by coming on so strong. I simply thought men could always… and then he managed, but I could tell he was humiliated about not being ready at first, and it was like he was ashamed rather than—" She cut off abruptly at the sound of footsteps.

Zara tapped on the door frame. "Room service." At the sight of Jillian's distraught expression, she stopped. "I'm sorry. Should I come back later?"

Jillian looked away, and Constance stood and took the drinks. Considering the quiet that had descended on the rest of the house, she asked, "Would you be up to making a little more music? No singing and nothing raucous."

"Of course." Zara nodded and disappeared without another word.

"Listen to me ordering her about. Good Lord. You'd think we were back on the ship."

Jillian had composed herself, becoming Lady Stansfield again. "I'm being a terrible hostess. I should return to my guests." She rose, but Constance put a hand on her arm and eased her back down.

"Finish your drink. You're allowed to give yourself a moment here and there."

They sipped in silence for a few moments. "You're a wonderful person, Constance. I hope you know how much I value our friendship."

Her voice wavered with unusual emotion, and Constance was truly touched. "You know I adore you, and I just want you to be as happy as I am with Nelson."

"I'm sure I will be. Someday." They drank quietly as the notes of something unfamiliar but lovely filtered into the room. Jillian sighed after a few moments. "She's quite gifted. Thank you for bringing her."

Constance nodded, pushing down her concern. "Want to go listen?"

"Yes, let's."

Five or six people remained seated around the piano. Zara's shoulders were slightly hunched as she played slow, somber notes.

Her head was bowed, and her body swayed freely. Jillian watched, her expression as intent as when they'd first met, and Constance resisted the impulse to say something to catch her attention.

As if sensing their presence, Zara altered the melody, and the notes gradually shifted into something less subdued. The music became more emotional, the chord progressions and individual notes exquisitely delicate. The new theme continued for several minutes, and when Constance felt Nelson's hands on her shoulders, his simple touch filled her with the kind of wholeness she hoped her dearest friend would someday find. Clive was known to cut a dashing figure with his roguish good looks, and he could be very engaging. He always made them laugh with tales of his exploits and his ever-changing group of associates. But Constance again wondered if he would ever settle into being the kind of man Jillian needed.

After the last sound faded, a beat of silence passed, as if the small audience was too moved to respond. Then the group applauded with a kind of stunned admiration before stirring as if released from a spell. Zara put her hands in her lap, and the evening began to break up. When the three other couples who were staying over stopped to offer compliments, Zara answered modestly, even blushing at one woman's effusive remarks.

Jillian had moved to stand beside her, smiling brilliantly, almost like a proud mother. Almost. Constance drew closer as Nelson was pressed into sorting out some last-minute sleeping arrangement issue.

"I didn't recognize that last piece," Jillian said when the others were gone. "Who was it?"

Zara's blush deepened. "No one's. I mean, at this point in an evening, I sometimes just play what I'm feeling."

"You write music as well?" Constance asked.

"I never write it down. I just...play."

Nelson returned before either of them could ask. Jillian smiled at him gratefully. "You're a good man, Nelson Garrick. I'll see to it Mrs. Livingstone rewards you with that French toast you're so partial to."

"Done," he agreed.

In the meantime, Zara had taken a carefully rolled cloth from her back pocket and was wiping down the piano keys.

Jillian reached as if to touch her but stopped short. "That's not necessary, Zara. In the morning, Andrew can—"

"I really don't mind," Zara said, without looking around. "This is the most wonderful instrument I've ever played." She gestured at the name above the keyboard. "These instruments were owned by kings and queens and emperors and tsars and sultans, even. Look." With extreme care, she lifted the lid, gesturing for them to come closer. Pointing at a plaque inside, she said, "This shows all the awards and prizes and medals presented to the Blüthner company since the mid-1800s."

Constance couldn't tell if Jillian's pleased expression was for the lesson or in reaction to Zara's excitement. Either way, it was an unusually open response for her, and Constance wished she'd taken the time to reiterate her concern about Zara when it had been just her and Jillian.

Lowering the lid again, Zara straightened, her tone almost formal. "Thank you for giving me the honor of playing it and for allowing me the pleasure of looking after it."

As Jillian murmured, "Of course," Zara finished her work quickly and efficiently before gently closing the fallboard.

Then she turned and met Jillian's eyes. "It shouldn't be an obligation or a chore to care for the beauty in this world. Beautiful things deserve to be nurtured because they enrich our lives just by being."

Based on the way Zara's voice had softened as she looked at Jillian, she wasn't only talking about the piano. Constance wondered if the underlying implication came from seeing Jillian upset earlier. At the sweetness of Zara's reassurance, Jillian smiled shyly, and Constance wasn't surprised when she took the conversation in a different direction, away from the personal and into the philosophical. "Are you saying beauty is its own reward?"

Zara grinned. "Either that or virtue is."

"Mmm," Jillian mused. "So beauty isn't a virtue?"

Constance was stunned when, at that instant, they both turned to her as if seeking her judgment. She waved and took a step back. "Oh no. I'm not refereeing this one. It's too deep for this hour."

Zara looked sheepish. "Yeah, you're right. I tend to get overly talkative after I've played for a while. It's how I wind down, I guess. Gina, my roommate on the ship, fell asleep to my gabbing more than once. I'm sure you're both ready for bed. I'll just—"

To Constance's surprise, Jillian put a hand on Zara's shoulder. "I've half a glass of good whiskey that needn't go to waste. I can chat for another moment."

Nelson reappeared and took Constance's hand. "What time is breakfast?"

"It's your call, my dear. I am in your debt for being pressed into service as my gracious cohost." He and Jillian embraced, and Constance took the moment to give Zara a quick hug.

"Don't keep her too late," she whispered. "She's already had a long night."

Zara nodded. "I promise."

At the stairway, Constance looked back. They were already in animated conversation as they turned into the sitting room.

She couldn't have said why she felt compelled to check on them, hours later, as Nelson snored softly beside her. At first, she'd fallen asleep easily in his arms. Perhaps it was the predicted drop in temperature that roused her. Shivering lightly, she listened to the silence in the house as she made her way downstairs.

In some ways, the scene that greeted her was more intimate than simple physical passion. They lay on either side of the L-shaped sofa with their heads almost touching at the intersecting corner. Jillian's back was to the cushions, and Zara was on her stomach, head on her folded arms. Constance could imagine them getting increasingly comfortable as they spoke, not wanting to give up the conversation but not quite able to stay with it. They might have fallen asleep in mid-sentence, even. There was no reason for her to worry, and no purpose was served in waking them, and yet she did, disregarding their bleary eyes and yawns as she made sure they found their own, separate rooms.

In the morning, there was a note. She sensed both apology and resolve in the tone. Jillian explained that she'd promised Zara another hike, and though she said they'd return after lunch, she'd added they were going to the boundary, which meant they'd be gone most of the day. Constance hadn't expected Jillian to disappear again, and it made her uneasy that Zara was occupying so much of her time.

Though no one knew exactly when Clive might put in an appearance, in the past, Jillian found things to do around the house or in her lab while waiting for him. Today, she was out with someone else, a woman whose charismatic talent and calm self-sufficiency seemed a balance to Jillian's tenacious intelligence and constant striving for achievement. Was that all there was to it?

Constance brooded as the weather continued to deteriorate, getting colder and gloomier by the minute. She wanted to talk about it with Nelson, and yet she really had no sense of what "it" was. Well, she had some sense but no idea how to approach the matter in a way that wouldn't ultimately lead to a revelation she didn't want to give and that he wouldn't want to hear.

Chapter Six

Constance had been in an odd mood all day, and Nelson wasn't sure what to do about it. It was possible she was a bit jealous of Zara being with Jillian again, though he doubted she'd have had any interest in joining them on such a beastly day. Or it could be that she was anxious about Clive's arrival, given she and Jillian were most certainly in discussion about him last night. Nelson was glad they'd had a few minutes to talk, though what Constance had shared was nothing new. In any case, he would have willingly used this time to delve a little deeper into the coming term's texts, but Constance was restless, and her disquiet made it difficult for him to concentrate.

They'd risen late, and after joining the remaining couples for the promised French toast, they'd seen them off with invented farewells from their absent hostess. He had to admit it was unusual for Jillian to neglect her lady-of-the-house duties. She might be holed up in her lab at any point during a visit but could always be counted on to make an appearance and bring her practiced charms to bear on the gathering. As far as Nelson knew, she hadn't been in the lab since their arrival yesterday, which was different too.

Usually, she'd be eager to share her progress on whatever project currently had her attention, and they'd ooh and ahh appropriately. But whatever the case, he was confident that when the school year began, Jillian's focus would be absolute, as it always was. When he suggested that to Constance, she seemed to relax, admitting this term would be the most demanding and important of all their lives. Internships and ultimately job offers would come from their results, and futures would be determined. Though Constance had almost certainly secured a teaching position at her alma mater, a prestigious girls' school, there was still work to be done starting in a few short days.

Eating a light lunch, they talked of the coming year, watching for Jillian's return and Clive's arrival as the afternoon wore on. When Constance went to take a nap, Nelson was able to get some studying done. She'd just rejoined him for tea when Andrew announced, "Master Nyes," and Clive burst into the small kitchen nook with his usual energy.

"Darlings," he cried, dipping Constance dramatically in a faux kiss before clapping Nelson enthusiastically on the back. "Where's my girl? Labbing away, no doubt."

Constance muffled a sigh so he explained, "She's off with a chum that Constance brought along. Exploring the ruins, we suspect."

"Today? Ugh!" Clive was not one to get dirty unless it was on his own terms. "Good thing she cleans up well, eh?" If he was disappointed she wasn't there to greet him, he gave no sign. "And who's the newest victim?"

"Someone I met on our return crossing," Constance said. "A musician who's trying for a position at the Royal College of Music this coming week."

His brow creased slightly. "Musician? Some long-haired classical type, I take it?"

Interesting. They'd never seen Clive display the slightest hint of jealousy regarding anyone Jillian might keep company with. Not that there had been many of those.

Constance apparently decided to have him on a bit more. "Oh yes. Classical but also jazz and modern stuff too. Quite accomplished. Incredibly versatile. Attractive too, in that rather blended American way."

"American?" Clive scoffed, clearly somewhat relieved. "New money, then."

"No money, I'd say," Nelson joined in. This was rather fun.

"She's off exploring the ruins in this beastly drizzle with a poor American musician?"

With perfect timing, they caught sight of Jillian and Zara in the distance. Constance smiled before turning back to Clive. "Mmm. Been gone all day."

Mrs. Livingstone began to set out tea, distracting Clive enough that he didn't seem to notice Jillian and Zara until they were almost close enough to hail. "Oh look," Constance said with pretend surprise, pointing through the terrace window. "Here they are now."

Clive's head turned. Jillian must have dressed Zara with half the old clothes in her father's closet. In addition to his well-worn boots, she sported a thick sweater and canvas coat he'd wear when in his outdoor, Lord of the Manor mode. Topping it off was his weathered rain hat. The overall effect was an odd combination of warmly charming and awkwardly unrefined, and best of all for their purposes, generally masculine. Nelson thought Zara's lovely dark eyes would give her away, especially as they sparkled with vigor and some deeper elation, but they might have one more moment of teasing.

Jillian's attire was much more fitted, but even she looked rather disheveled from their exertions. They walked close enough that an occasional arm swing would touch, sometimes eliciting an extra, playful bump. They were both smiling broadly despite their generally drenched and muddy condition.

Clive opened the terrace door and stepped out, staying under the overhang, and Nelson and Constance joined him. It must have been their movement that made Jillian look up, and when she caught sight of Clive, her face changed to her usual focused expression, and she took an extra step away from Zara. "Clive. Good Lord, you're here already? What time is it?"

Constance waved them up. "Just teatime. You must be famished."

Jillian looked everywhere except at Zara, who gave a slight shake of her head. "No, we're fine," Jillian said. "Obviously, we need to get cleaned up. You go ahead and we'll...each...be along later." It seemed to take an extra effort for her to speak for herself. "I'll be down as soon as I can."

She made to step inside, but Clive was still blocking the doorway. "I'll take a proper greeting first, in spite of all your acquired muck," he said, pulling her close. "And then you must introduce me to your new friend."

He kissed her quickly but firmly. Zara froze until Jillian broke away, and Clive laughed, wiping his mouth. "Rainwater and dirt. Marginally disgusting. Good thing I know that's not your usual taste."

He stepped over and held out his hand to Zara. "The dishonorable Clive Nyes. I'd say pleased to make your acquaintance but the jury's still out on that one for both of us, I suspect."

Zara moved slowly, taking his hand. Nelson imagined that years of playing had probably made her grip firm enough that there was no giveaway there. As Jillian remained mute, Constance filled in the silence. "Clive, this is Zara Keller, the musician I was telling you about."

Their handshake ended, and Clive blinked. "Zara?"

Zara nodded and took off her hat, giving it a shake. As her hair fell out, droplets of water spattered Clive. "Oh, sorry," she said. "And no worries about the confusion. Others have had the same reaction. I'm sure they'll tell you all about it."

She and Clive locked eyes for a few seconds, almost as if exploring something in each other before he turned in bewilderment, and Nelson started to laugh with Constance.

Zara winked at him. "Your face is still the winner, though." She followed Jillian, who was already halfway up the stairs.

Clive brushed the dampness off, and they retreated to the warmth of the kitchen nook again. "And now it's time for tea and explanations," Clive said. He sounded more amused than upset, which was good news all around.

Giving Clive a good ribbing had been fun, but the way Jillian seemed to be growing uncommonly attached to Zara was making Nelson a bit uncomfortable. From their first meeting, the subtle standoffishness that Lady Stansfield demonstrated around new people was practically nonexistent. Constance had told him that Jillian and Zara had stayed up late talking last night, and then they'd gone off for the better part of the day on their second hike, alone.

Of course, Zara wasn't a threat to Clive in any romantic sense, but it troubled Nelson that they knew very little about her. When Constance went to change for dinner, he took the opportunity to speak with Clive and advised him to be more...attentive to Jillian. Rather than crumbling as he sometimes did at the slightest hint of criticism, Clive questioned him about his concern, and Nelson might have said more than was prudent. Clive only nodded thoughtfully and sipped his tea, leaving his food untouched.

Jillian rejoined them first before dinner, looking much more like herself, and Clive had clearly taken their chat to heart. He kissed her hand sweetly and told her how much he'd missed her. He remarked on how much he loved to see her wearing her hair down and flattered her for her choice of dress, a deep blue velvet which featured a low V in the front and a high back, with a cutout at her trim waist.

She began to visibly relax and accepted Clive's offer of a drink, the tone of their conversation familiarly affectionate. Nelson stood when Constance approached with Zara behind her. Constance, wearing a new dress that looked quite chic, was her usual, beautiful self. Zara, apparently wanting to make her best impression on Clive, was in a striking red dress, mid-length and sleeveless, which left no doubt as to her completely feminine attributes, even under the wrap Nelson recognized as one of Constance's.

As he and Clive half stood at the approach of the ladies, Nelson assessed Jillian's reaction. For a few seconds, she regarded Zara, her mouth open slightly and color rising in her cheeks. By the time they were seated, her gaze was on her empty glass. "You both look very nice," she said softly.

Constance gestured. "This is Zara's concert outfit. When I heard she was doing Vivaldi tonight, I convinced her to wear it."

"Bloody *Four Seasons*," Clive groused, clearly working to keep his tone light. "Don't you get tired of people asking you for the same damn things?"

Zara met his eyes almost defiantly. "There's too much variety in music for that to ever happen. And if someone cares enough to ask and is kind enough to listen, I'm always happy to play." She shrugged. "I enjoy it."

"Good for you, then," Clive responded, rising to refill his glass.

"Good for all of us who enjoy your talent," Jillian murmured.

Constance lifted her glass. "Hear, hear."

Zara smiled shyly, and Nelson joined in the toast. And that seemed to be the last comment Clive made directly to Zara for the rest of the evening. He nodded pleasantly at her responses to others' questions but always turned the conversation back to something or someone else, speaking of people they knew or other gatherings they'd attended or even the upcoming school term, a topic he generally avoided. While most female guests found Clive's looks and appealing personality worthy of at least mild flirtation, Zara made no attempt to draw his attention. She merely listened, sipping mineral water while Clive concentrated all of his considerable magnetism on Jillian.

For her part, Jillian seemed more discomforted than usual. Nelson wondered if Zara was the cause, as Jillian looked at her several times despite Clive's attempts to distract her. He'd made sure to sit beside her, motioning Zara to his other side.

He poured himself another whiskey, appearing frustrated when Jillian declined. "Come on, my girl. It'll be like old times," he offered, but she only smiled vaguely and shook her head.

By the end of the meal, he'd finished that one and held another as he pulled out Jill's chair. She took his arm and talked quietly to him as they moved toward the music room. As they sat, he nodded, looking chagrined. She patted his arm, and Nelson felt certain his ego had been soothed for the time being.

But when Zara began to play "Spring," Jillian's attention shifted entirely to her. Clive tried twice to start a conversation, and each time, she shushed him with a finger to her lips. When he got up to mix a fresh drink, Nelson motioned him back down, adding more water than usual to his whiskey in the hope he would get the hint.

Instead, he made a face and went to add more liquor on his own. He mixed the next one himself, and by the time the piece finished, he was approaching what Constance referred to as "sloshy." He made a point of cheering more loudly than any of them, making it sound like relief that it was over.

Possibly in response, Jillian rose and went to Zara, placing a hand on her arm and murmuring something that seemed to please her. By the time Clive reached them, Zara was standing and flexing her fingers as Jillian watched with undisguised admiration.

"Let me help you with that," Clive offered smoothly, putting his drink on top of the piano and taking Zara's hands. "I've been told I've got a good touch." His gaze shifted to Jillian for a second. "By some," he added.

Jillian turned away as Zara freed her hands and rescued Clive's glass before it caused a ring. Wiping off the water spot, she said, "Thanks, but something cool usually does the trick." Handing him his drink, she lifted her own from the coaster on the other side, where it had sat untouched for her performance. It was mostly melted, but the remaining shards of ice clinked as she rolled it between her palms.

Clive's face hardened as he studied her, then glanced at Jillian's retreating form before replying, "Well, you've come to the right place, then."

Nelson saw Jillian's back stiffen. Constance must have seen it too, because she moved toward her. The mood in the room was quickly becoming unpleasant, and Nelson suspected that rejection from two women in such a short time wasn't sitting well with Clive.

Throwing his arm around Clive's shoulder, he said, "Let's go warm things up in the sitting room, old man. Andrew set a fire earlier, and it's cozy in there." He focused on Constance but hoped everyone would get the hint. It wouldn't be the first time they'd all adapted their behavior to keep Clive happy. "Ladies, will you join us?"

"Yes," Constance said. "We'll be there shortly."

No one else spoke as he guided Clive out of the room, but he hoped that would be the case.

Once Clive was settled on the loveseat with a fresh drink, Nelson tried to engage him about his future plans. It was time for him to start his top-level banking classes, but whether he would ever follow in his father's footsteps at Barclays was still very much in doubt. He'd said many times that since Jillian would never need his financial support, he didn't see any reason to do something he cared nothing about. Nelson might have been more sympathetic had Clive ever come up with a viable alternative. Instead, Nelson now suggested she might not need money, but stability was something that all relationships needed.

Clive sneered and said, "Not all. In some cases, it's best you come and go as quickly as possible." His stress on the word *come* made it clear what he was referring to. When Nelson expressed offense on Jillian's behalf, replying she was clearly not that kind of woman, Clive only muttered, "Clearly," and they let it go.

As their conversation died out, Nelson was relieved at the sound of female voices in the hallway. He stood, and Clive followed, somewhat unsteadily. Constance joined him on the loveseat while Zara took the single chair near the doorway, setting her fresh drink on a small writing desk. After a second's hesitation, Jillian moved to the corner across from Clive on the L-shaped couch.

Obviously uncomfortable with the silence, Constance said, "Zara's volunteered to perform one of Vivaldi's seasons each night she's here."

At Clive's frown, Zara added, "Yeah, three more nights of playing the whole orchestra is sure to have me ready for my audition. And by then, you'll be more than ready for me to be out of your hair."

Maybe she wanted to assure Clive that her time here was limited and remind him of her function as entertainment, but Clive rose to his feet, asking, "Three more nights?" while giving her a challenging look. Jillian touched his leg, and his attention slowly shifted back to her. He broke into a smile and said, "My love, I can make music for you right now. Something we can dance to." Nelson didn't think he'd ever heard Clive use such an endearment before, and Jillian seemed to be equally stunned, taking his hand almost automatically when he held it out. Or maybe she intended to keep his mind off whatever threat he might find in Zara's presence.

Pulling her roughly to her feet, Clive slipped an arm around her waist, keeping his drink in his other hand. Humming some fast-paced, tuneless notes, he stepped and swayed with her, bumping awkwardly between the couch and the coffee table. Jillian put a hand on his shoulder and paced backward, moving them into the space in front of the fireplace.

Seemingly encouraged, Clive began to sway more dramatically, making Jillian cling to him to keep her balance. The whole display might have been romantic, but there was something so forced and tense in Jillian's manner.

Nelson glanced at Zara, reading something of his own disapproval in her eyes before she looked away. Laughing, Clive attempted to dip Jillian with the arm he still had around her waist.

"Clive, no," she said, but they were already in motion. Between his unsteadiness and the smoothness of her dress, his grasp slipped, and she fell, tumbling in what seemed like slow-motion toward the fireplace.

The smell of burning hair filled the air. Jillian's piercing scream brought Zara to her feet. Clive pulled Jillian away from the blaze, but it was too late. Flames jumped from the tips of her hair to the back of her dress, catching it alight.

"Oh shite," Clive cried, letting her go as he stepped back,

Constance's screams joined Jillian's. Zara ran toward Jillian with her drink. Petrified with terror, Nelson heard the splash of liquid and the sizzling of fabric. With her free hand, Zara beat on the flames, pulling away burning pieces. "Get scissors, ice, and water. Now!"

Constance hurried to the writing desk. Nelson ran to the music room, found the pitcher of water, and added ice as quickly as his trembling hands would allow. When he returned, burning smells still permeated the room, making him cough. Zara had Jillian sitting on a chair, her back facing outward. Constance was cutting off four or five inches of Jillian's hair while Zara continued to peel away the blackened dress, pieces of which blazed again briefly or stuck to her hand with sickening sputters until she rubbed them against her hip.

Whenever Jillian flinched, Zara soothed her skin with a piece of ice, murmuring softly as the fabric gave way. Jillian still sobbed, but Nelson was grateful her screams had stopped. Only Clive remained motionless, his mouth agape.

As soon as the last of Jillian's burned hair dropped away, Zara took the scissors and cut farther down her dress, giving a shaky sigh of relief when it easily fell away. "Call the medics, you idiot," she snarled at Clive.

"Medics?"

Constance clarified, "Ambulance, Clive. Emergency services."

He fumbled with the phone, speaking in low tones. Zara turned to Nelson. "Could you get a few towels, please? Wet one small one and bring the others dry."

He ran to the hall lavatory, his heart still pounding in his ears. It was all terrible, and he blamed himself for speaking so compellingly to Clive about Zara. Jillian's responsiveness to the music had clearly made Clive feel slighted, and he'd reacted by trying to be exciting for her in his own way. Nelson returned with everything he could find, handing Zara two of the larger towels.

She was speaking soothingly to Jillian. "Let's get you out of that dress and dry you off some more." She nodded to Constance, who took charge of that while Zara laid the smaller, wet towel on Jillian's back.

Nelson turned away to give Jillian privacy, but he heard the anger in her voice when she spoke to Clive. "You are no longer welcome in this house. I want you out, now."

"Jilly, darling, I'm so sorry," he began, but she cut him off.

"Nelson, will you please remove this man from the premises?"

Nelson expected a fight when he took Clive's arm, but Clive seemed sobered by the dreadful events of the last few minutes, and Nelson led him to his car without worrying if he could drive. The look on his face was that of a totally defeated man.

At the car door, he clasped Nelson's arm desperately. "God, will she ever forgive me? I never meant—"

"Of course, you didn't. She just needs time. Once she's recovered, I'm sure she'll call." Nelson wasn't actually sure of any of that, but he could hear sirens in the distance, and Clive needed to be out of the picture when they arrived. He'd had too many run-ins with the local constables over the years.

"Will you let me know how she is?" he asked, starting his car.

Relieved, Nelson said, "I'll ring you as soon as we know anything."

After watching him drive away, Nelson returned to the sitting room. Jillian was seated again, wearing a robe open at the back. Her breathing was still ragged, but she wasn't crying. Zara continued to blot at her burns with the wet towel.

"Constance has gone to pack a bag," Zara said. "Where is the fucking ambulance?" That curse was the only sign of stress she'd shown since the incident began.

"I heard the sirens outside."

Nodding, she said, "Go direct them in, will you?"

When he met Constance in the hall, she leaned into him, an overnight bag in her hand. "Oh God, Nelson. I've never seen anything so awful. Is she terribly hurt, do you think?"

"I don't know. But Emergency is almost here. Go be with her, and then we'll ride together to the hospital."

She moved away reluctantly, her mouth quivering.

Everything was a blur after the ambulance arrived. Jillian was put on a gurney and wheeled out, but she had a firm grip on Zara's right hand as Zara carried the wet towel in her left. Nelson and Constance followed, and he heard Jillian say, "Don't leave me."

Zara looked back, and Nelson urged her to go in the ambulance, indicating they would follow in his car.

He was able to stay close until they hit the outskirts of London. Hesitant to run a red light, he lost the ambulance in traffic. But he knew where they were going, and by the time he'd parked and they'd rushed into the St. Thomas Hospital emergency room, the Stansfield name had gotten Jillian into a private room. They crowded in, finding Zara leaning against the wall at the foot of the bed, the towel still clutched in her left hand. A nurse was attempting to take Jillian's vital signs as she lay on her side.

"Hello, love. It looks like they're taking good care of you already." Constance sounded amazingly calm. She'd joined him in prayer as they'd driven, and Nelson believed it had helped.

Jillian looked over and managed a weak smile. "Thank you for coming."

"To be sure," Nelson assured her. "Our place is with you."

The nurse finished her assessment and turned, apparently annoyed at the crowd. "The doctor will be here in a few moments. Please make room for him."

Zara straightened with some effort. "I'll wait in the hallway."

"No," Jillian said. "I want him to look you over as well."

"I'm fine," Zara protested, but Nelson heard the tremor in her voice and noted her face was pale. He hoped the events of the evening weren't sending her into shock.

"Constance and I can stand where you are, Zara. You take the chair." He pointed to the worn, faux leather seat by the door. "There will be plenty of room for the doctor to see you both."

"Yes, Zara. Please." At Jillian's request, Zara moved. She had just eased into the chair when there was a brisk knock followed by the entrance of a short, thin Asian man.

Glancing at his clipboard, he asked, "Mrs. Stansfield? Burn case?"

"It's Miss. And yes."

"Sorry, Miss. I'm Doctor Han. Let's have a look." As he moved to her, she eased back onto her stomach. "Tell me how this injury occurred?"

After a few beats of silence, Nelson gave as few details as possible while explaining the specifics.

The doctor hummed quietly. "Surprisingly, these are almost entirely first-degree burns, although these around the shoulder may be seconds." He looked around. "Who was treating her after the incident?"

"I was." Zara's voice was low and dull.

"You did well. Were you harmed also?"

When Zara only looked down and shrugged, Jillian spoke up. "Please examine her also, doctor."

He nodded, still speaking to Jillian as he jotted some notes. "I believe, once the area is cleaned, you can be treated with some antibiotic ointment and a mild pain reliever. Since it's late, we'll keep you overnight for observation, but I see no reason why you can't go home in the morning."

Constance sighed with relief, and Jillian thanked the doctor as he moved toward Zara. "Where does it hurt?" he asked her.

When she held up the towel-wrapped hand, he squatted, unwrapping it carefully. Thankfully, he blocked Jillian's view, but Nelson could see the damage. The tips of Zara's fingers were red and blistered, and some areas on her palm were already turning black.

"Oh my God," Constance whispered into his shoulder. Nelson felt a rush of guilt as he recalled how they'd prayed for Jillian. It had never occurred to him to ask God to take care of Zara as well.

The doctor gently replaced the towel before standing. "You'll need to go to the burn unit right away. Some of these are third-degree burns, and you'll need special treatment to heal them properly."

"I can't afford that." Zara gritted her teeth as she pulled her hand back onto her lap. "Can't you just give me some ointment too?"

"Nonsense." Jillian spoke as firmly as they'd heard her since she'd told Clive to leave. "Please send any extra charges to the estate." She raised up, turning her gaze on Zara. "You must take care of your hand, Zara. For your career. For your future. Let me help you. It's the least I can do."

The doctor clearly agreed. "Untreated, these types of burns can lead to bacterial infection, which could develop into sepsis." Zara shuddered and closed her eyes, her head dropping back. The doctor stepped into the hall. "Nurse, we need wheelchair transport to the burn unit ASAP. She may be going into shock."

Another flurry of activity ensued. As Zara was helped into the chair, Jillian said, "Constance, please go with her. Make sure she… make sure everything is all right, won't you?"

Constance nodded. "Of course, Jilly. I'll see to it."

They disappeared down the hall as another nurse came in. "Husband?" she asked Nelson.

The events of the night were wearing on him, and it took a few seconds before he understood. "Oh. Oh no. I'm not her husband, no. I'm just a friend. A longtime, very good friend."

"Would you like to wait in the hall, Mr. Longtime, Very Good Friend, while I treat your not-wife's injuries?" she asked, her voice laced with skepticism.

Jillian giggled. It was the best thing Nelson had heard in hours.

As promised, Jillian was released the next morning. Nelson and Constance had checked on Zara twice, finding her undergoing examinations or being given medication both times. They'd spent the night trying unsuccessfully to find anything remotely resembling comfortable chairs in any of the waiting rooms, and nothing sounded better than a bath and a regular bed. But Jillian refused to leave until she'd seen Zara.

When they arrived at the burn unit, the duty nurse informed them that Zara was getting a debriding treatment on her badly burned left hand, and cries of pain echoed along the hallway. It seemed to take forever as they waited, each wiping tears from their eyes before talking quietly about what might come next while Zara recovered from the ordeal. When Nelson suggested she might benefit from a stay in a rehabilitation center near the hospital, Jillian gave him a look that would have withered stone.

"If it weren't for her, I would be the one suffering from third-degree burns. Or worse. If she needs additional treatment, she'll have it at Fullerhill. I'll bring in whatever medical personnel are necessary."

"But what about school, Jilly?" Constance asked. The upcoming Cambridge schedule had them on campus for eight weeks before having the next six weeks off. "You can't expect your father to care for her while you're gone. There are some very nice facilities elsewhere if you don't like the one nearby."

Jillian blinked. "Oh." In that second, it was clear that she'd completely forgotten about the start of the new year, something absolutely unthinkable for the Jillian Stansfield they knew.

Chapter Seven

They stood in a semicircle around the hospital bed, Jillian and Constance on either side at the head and Nelson at the foot. Zara's eyes were closed, the drug they'd given her for the pain having taken effect, and Jillian's stomach clenched at the way her beautiful warm skin looked so sallow now.

Twice last night, Jillian had awakened in horror-filled panic, with flames crackling in her ear and searing along her flesh, only to hear Zara's voice—*It's over, you're safe now, I've got you, you're going to be okay*—murmuring close to her ear as she cooled her stinging skin with ice and the damp towel. That reassuring promise and the memory of her gentle touch continued to heal her as much as Zara's prompt actions had saved her. Without her, Jillian wouldn't have been dismissed promptly from care, sent away with Tylenol and some soothing ointment for her neck and shoulders.

Before leaving her room, she'd asked for a mirror. At another time, the ragged edges of her shorter hair and the blotchy skin of her face would have made her aghast. But what she saw now was a survivor and a very fortunate one at that.

They were waiting on the burn specialist, who, according to the nurse, generally arrived after treatment to check on the progress of her patient's wounds. Whatever Zara's ultimate prognosis, it was obvious she couldn't possibly heal enough in the next few days to play at the Royal College of Music. That thought had made Jillian want to cry more than any pain she'd felt during her experience, and she couldn't stop thinking of how dramatically Zara's life—and hers—might now change. The worst part of it was knowing how Zara had risked her entire future for someone she barely knew. Was that simply the kind of person she was, or was Zara's sacrifice based on what had transpired between them during their hike to the boundary? How harrowing the difference between that day and the evening that followed:

She awakened that morning with an odd knot of emotion in her belly, trying to identify the source as she dressed for the day. Her father would be returning tomorrow or the next day, so perhaps she was pleased that tonight it would be the four of them, assuming Clive arrived as planned. The previous evening's larger gathering had gone exceptionally well, thanks to Zara.

Zara. When her name entered Jillian's thoughts, the enticing sensation quivered as if being fed. Had Zara's music been in her dreams? Rather than explore that possibility, she pushed herself to return to her hostess duties. They'd be five tonight, not four. This was uncommon but not new, as each of the others had introduced someone else to the group at different times. No one had stuck, though, and Zara's stay would be temporary as well. When Jillian examined that thought, it struck her that she'd miss Zara's company, which was strange because they'd only just met.

But their conversation the previous evening had been full of depth and gravity, much like the talks she used to have with her friends. It had been effortless, challenging, and exhilarating, maybe because Zara seemed completely nonjudgmental. Her questions never gave the impression of finding fault; rather, her intent was merely to know and perhaps, to understand.

Jillian might have been sad thinking about how such occasions with her friends had dwindled away, but Zara had made her laugh several times, and instead, she'd felt...comfortable. How was it possible to feel secure with someone unfamiliar and rather unconventional?

The question made her consider the various emotions Zara appeared to generate. Constance had been excited to introduce her, and Nelson obviously respected her talent. Clive might view Zara as competition rather than a possible conquest. That would be different. At parties, Clive often carried on with any woman who would banter with him for a moment, but Jillian had never felt jealous or possessive of his time. Not like the way she felt about Zara's. She didn't want to share her.

Zara's playing was amazing, but Jillian was affected by more than her aptitude. She wanted to know Zara, and even more remarkable, she wanted Zara to feel the same way about her. She'd preferred to keep herself to herself for years now. And though she was unsettled by Zara at times, her presence seemed to diminish the habitual misgivings Jillian hid around most people, making her feel more open and spontaneous. Zara was their perfect fifth, she thought, wanting to laugh as she recalled Zara's scorn for the concept of pleasantness. She wondered if the strange pull she'd felt from their first meeting would go with Zara when she left for whatever her future might hold.

Recalling that feeling made Jillian wonder if Zara was already up, and she hurried downstairs to see.

A quick glance showed no one in the dining hall, though the bustle coming from the kitchen suggested the morning was well under way. Mrs. Livingstone humored Jillian's morning coffee habit with one pot daily, which sat brewing in the breakfast nook. Jillian was pouring a cup when a slight movement on the terrace caught her eye. Zara.

Jillian had been embarrassed to be awakened by Constance in the middle of the night, though she had no memory of falling asleep in the sitting room. But as they'd stumbled up the stairs, Zara's fingers had trailed lightly across her shoulder as she passed. No words, no sound, just a touch that had made everything inside her tingle with anticipation. Perhaps that was the feeling that had awakened her so early.

Seeing her now reminded Jillian of the deeper topics they'd discussed. Passing a suit of armor had led to a conversation about disguises they'd used to keep their true selves from being seen and why. Zara had talked about her outfits on the ship, the hat and tie and sunglasses—and even her fancy dress—she wore in various combinations as a kind of shield. When Jillian had asked why, she'd said it was to safeguard the music. While Jillian was pondering that, Zara had asked what it was she guarded.

Jillian had thought about that question for nearly a full minute. "I mainly protect myself, though I'm honestly not sure what from," she'd finally answered. "There's so much I could be doing to help others. But I keep finding reasons not to start."

She'd never admitted such a thing before. She'd expected censure and would have almost welcomed it from someone who obviously hadn't had every advantage she'd had. Instead, Zara had taken her hands as she had in the woods and had looked into her eyes with an intensity that was temporarily immobilizing. "I can see more than all this, you know?" She'd glanced at their surroundings before capturing Jillian in her gaze again. "I can see you, Jillian Stansfield. Not your wealth and privilege. But what's on the inside," she'd said. "You are going to do great things. Amazing things. You'll know in your heart when the time is right, and once you begin, there will be no stopping you."

Jillian had never been as deeply moved by such simple words. She hadn't wanted Zara to let go. She'd wanted to believe her, to let Zara's conviction guide her. How they'd come to fall asleep after that talk, she had no idea, but now she was oddly invigorated and ready for the day. Luckily, the look on Zara's face as she turned suggested she was eager as well. As they looked out at the day over coffee and a light breakfast, Zara assured her the weather was no problem, but Jillian had doubts about the suitability of her jeans and long-sleeve shirt. But before offering any alternatives, she told Zara more about their destination.

She had been working on this undertaking off and on since she was old enough to make the walk to the property boundary, where her father had insisted her new hobby take place, far away from any possible view from the house. Prompted by some overly sentimental and doubtlessly shoddy primary school research, she'd engaged Mr. Summerford, their overseer, in recreating a wattle and daub house like a family might have lived in during medieval times. Because she'd never been able to give enough time to finishing the project; parts of the structure regularly collapsed, prompting her uncharitable friends to refer to it as "the ruins."

Zara shifted excitedly. "I can't wait. But I have one request. Will you show me your lab?" Jillian hesitated, not convinced of Zara's enthusiasm. After a few seconds, Zara's face fell as she added, "Or if now isn't a good time, I'll wait."

"Oh no, now is fine. But, Zara, please don't feel like you need to act interested. Really."

Zara studied her for several seconds. "I've had to act differently from how I truly felt at times," she said finally. "At school, when I was younger and a lot of times at work. But I don't do that with people I consider friends. With them, I'm not anything other than what I am, and what I say is real, and I ask the same in return. Okay?"

Jillian swallowed away a tightness in her throat and nodded. Why did those words affect her so? She thought again about Constance and Nelson and Clive. After all the years they'd known each other, had their friendship become automatic? Did they only show each other the side of themselves from childhood and not who they'd become? Not certain of her voice, she motioned for Zara to follow. Once in the lab, Zara's youthful curiosity invigorated her, and they were still talking of projects and processes as they armed themselves with another fine lunch and extra biscuits.

Ignoring the worsening weather, they began the walk. Zara seemed especially impressed by Jillian's work on a portable system that used a single glass panel to harness the processes of evaporation and condensation for water purification. Pleased, Jillian continued her description of the project as they walked, but this time, it was excitement instead of nerves that prompted her. She smiled when Zara shook herself like a dog, grinning as she asked, "Why water? Seems like you live in a pretty wet climate, so it wouldn't be on your mind."

"Before my mother died," Jillian began before faltering. She took a breath. "When I was younger, we used to go to church in Guildworth. One Sunday, a missionary spoke about how she was working to bring water and sanitary conditions to Africa. She showed slides of the people in a particular village. I can still remember those beautiful faces. Then she talked about how many children died from preventable diseases and how when water wasn't available nearby, the collection of it fell disproportionately on women and girls, which in turn affected things like their education or their ability to care for their families. After the service, while my father spoke with the pastor, I made my way to the missionary. I peppered her with questions until my father found me."

Zara grinned. "I can envision that little girl very clearly. She's adorable."

Jillian hoped the drizzle hid her blush. She cleared her throat. "For days afterward, that was all I thought about. How was it some people had to go without something as basic as water? Why wasn't the rest of the world helping?"

Zara stopped walking, and they faced each other. "And that's the woman I see now. The one who's going to figure out a way to make the world a better place." When Jillian began to protest, Zara said, "Okay, maybe not the whole world. But some people's world."

Jillian kept her head down as they began walking again, wishing Zara had taken her hands like she had last night. Finally, she looked up, saying, "And now you must tell me about the little girl in you. What were you like as a baby?"

Zara shrugged, blinking a bit. "I was adopted when I was not quite a year old, so I don't know what to tell you about the baby part."

"Oh." Jillian never knew what one said to such personal information, even though she'd asked. "But that was good for you, wasn't it? Better than…"

"Living in an orphanage or foster home? Oh yeah, for sure." Nodding, Zara added, "I just never got it entirely right, you know? I preferred playing ball with my neighbor boy to dolls and tea sets, which meant the frilly dresses Mom bought would get ruined, and those bows would never stay in my hair." She ran a hand through her loose waves. "School was fine, but it took me a while to find a group where I belonged since I wasn't girly enough for the girls or tough enough for the boys, not then. But once I found music, I always had a place."

Jillian liked imagining young Zara wowing her classmates with her piano prowess. "Did you play in the band at your school?"

"Ah!" Zara held up a correcting finger. "The orchestra. Where we played only classical music."

"Of course." They walked on for a bit before Jillian thought to ask about the other thing Zara had said. "What did you mean about not being tough enough for the boys then? Are you now?"

She didn't answer for a moment, but her face took on a harder expression. "If I have to be."

"Why? May I ask what changed you?" As soon as the words were out, Jillian felt like she was prying. She hoped this was also something Zara was willing to tell.

Zara stopped again but didn't face her. "Look, I like you, Jillian. I absolutely do. And I guess it's only human nature that I want you to like me too. But I gotta wonder why you're asking? Is there a reason you want to know me better? Or do you just want to hear about how the other half lives?"

That hurt. But it wasn't unfair, really. Jillian searched herself for the answer, remembering Zara's sweet, inspiring words. "Last night, you said you could see me. I suppose I don't have your gift of insight, or perhaps you have an advantage because you'd heard about me previously from Constance, and you're here in my...what was it? My sweet, pleasant, acceptable world? But you are quite good at getting me to talk without revealing much about yourself."

The side of Zara's mouth quirked, and Jillian's heart rate increased. She forced herself to go on. "I can't completely explain it, but I feel this...something...." She stopped again, trying to find the right, true words. It seemed terribly significant. "In some strange way, it feels important for me to know you, Zara. Like, I ought to know you. Or I want to know you." God, she was bumbling this horribly, but Zara took a step closer and looked into her eyes.

"But why?" she asked again softly. "Why do you want to know me?"

Jillian couldn't look away. "It's the something." How dreadfully vague. But it was all she could say. Her awkwardness eased immeasurably when Zara's grin turned to a genuine smile.

"The something, huh?" The drizzle was turning into rain, and she pulled the borrowed hat lower over her face. "Well, Your Ladyship, I'll make you a deal. I'll tell you my story while we walk, and we'll talk about the something later. Okay?"

"Done." Jillian nearly stumbled with relief.

As Zara spoke, an experience that might have repeated all too often in families like hers unfolded. At age sixteen, she'd thought she was in love. Not unusual for most teenagers, as Jillian knew hormones tended to guide them, but the problem in Zara's case was that the object of her affection was another girl, Jordan. The good news was that her feelings were reciprocated, but the trouble began when Jordan's father had caught them kissing one night behind the garage. They'd somehow convinced him it was what girls did to "practice" for the real thing. And they'd tried to be more careful after that because both sets of parents were extremely conservative, and without really knowing how to express the reasoning behind it, they'd sensed there would be no acceptance for them at either home.

"We were young. Both of us were feeling so much that we didn't understand, and we only had each other. We were overwhelmed at times."

As Jillian listened to the story of murmured phone conversations; urgent, furtive meetings; and the writing of long, impassioned notes, she wondered, not for the first time, why those kinds of feelings had not been part of her own developmental experiences. No boy—not even Clive—had ever caught her fancy in that way, and the idea of such an attraction to a girl had been beyond consideration. Yes, she'd had schoolgirl crushes on her early teachers and rather stronger feelings for Miss Davies, her physics tutor, but Mrs. Livingstone had told her it was simply overblown admiration. She'd explained it as a common reaction of some girls when in the presence of intelligent, attractive older women and had assured her it would go away if she stopped thinking about it.

For whatever reason, there had been a new tutor for the next semester, and Jillian had pushed her dejection beneath the demands of the new instructor. Being educated at home had limited her options for socializing, though Constance regularly invited her to dances and parties. Thinking of it now, it seemed she'd declined more than she'd accepted. But why? Why had she found satisfaction in her studies and projects instead of wanting to socialize and mix with others of her age?

"Jordan had come over to study, and we really did. For a while. But we were reading *Romeo and Juliet* and…." Zara trailed off, memories of longing and loss in her eyes.

For a few seconds, it was easy to put herself in Jordan's place, with Zara as the stunning Romeo. "'A rose by any other name would smell as sweet,'" she quoted. And Zara grinned again.

"Yeah. I'd blame it all on Shakespeare, but actually, it was my mom's sneaky ways. We got caught again, and we were both almost naked this time, so there was no pretending it was anything other than what it was."

Jillian blinked away the image before it could fully form. "What happened?"

"Screaming, tears, accusations, promises. Jordan's parents came. Ultimately, they sent her away to a special boarding school. Supposedly very strict, religious instruction. I…I never saw her again."

With a quiver of emotion in her voice, Jillian asked, "And you?"

"I was furious. Too upset to say the things I should have said. And too stubborn to pretend I was sorry or consent to my folks' demands. The whole thing accelerated way beyond where it should have, but after a point, there was no going back. I think my dad wanted to let things cool off overnight, but my mom was practically hysterical, shouting about all they'd done for me, that kind of thing. I wasn't helping by smarting off, saying I never asked for their help, that they did it all for selfish reasons, accusing them of trying to be all noble by raising a kid who obviously wasn't theirs." Zara gestured at herself. "They're both very fair-skinned with blue eyes, and we used to get asked all the time if I was a cousin or if they were babysitting someone else's kid." She shrugged. "Anyway, I can't even remember who said it first, but somehow, it turned into me leaving their home for good. Kicked out? Ran away? Whatever, I ended up on the streets that night, and that was pretty much it until after I turned sixteen."

Jillian considered Zara's lovely coloring and intriguing bone structure, wondering what it would feel like not to know your heritage. Her family lineage went back more than five centuries. But it could be a sensitive subject, and she wanted to hear more about Zara's youth. "You were homeless? There in Arizona?"

She grinned. "Arkansas. Yeah, but Evergreen wasn't a big enough town for me to stay under the radar. I wanted to get to a big city, to prove I could make it on my own. God, I was really stupid. I was in my early jazz period, and I thought of Chicago because Mrs. Minton had told me about going to jazz clubs when she'd visited her son. So I hitchhiked. Got lucky with two good rides, but when I hit town, it was a different story."

"How so?" Jillian was fascinated. At age sixteen, she'd been panicked about doing the London Season. Her family name had gotten her in for an assessment, and Barton, who had been her mother's social secretary and now worked for her father, made sure she was invited to all the right places once she'd passed muster from the Chair. The expectations had felt as endless as the parties, both governed by those she didn't care about and peopled by those she had no wish to know. The culmination of the events was the Queen's Ball, no longer presided over by a monarch, but now an event to raise money for charity. If it hadn't been for that, and her father's insistence that her mother would have been crushed if she hadn't attended, Jillian would have refused.

"After dark, the streets were pretty much run by gangs. Oh, not where the public could see, but in the shadows, the alleys, in the places you went when you didn't have any place else. I tried to steer clear, to stay legit and get a job bussing tables or washing dishes, but half the owners were afraid of the cops, and the other half were afraid of the gangs, and since I had no connections with either, I couldn't get on anywhere." She shook her head. "After three days, I was so scared and hungry…if I'd believed there was any chance of reconciliation with my parents, I'd have gone back. Instead, I learned how to watch what people threw in the trash and kept looking for places that might be safe at night."

They were still walking, but Zara's words and the wretchedness in her tone made Jillian slow as she moved a bit closer. "Zara, if this is too hard…you don't have to—"

"No, it's just…I don't ever talk much about it." Their eyes met for the first time in several minutes. "My friend Gina knows some. It's not the kind of story people want to hear by way of introduction or entertainment. No one in polite society wants to acknowledge that world. When you're on the streets, most people look right at you and don't see you. But I've been there, and I'll never not see it. There's a growing population of desperation and despair clinging to the fringe. And it's everywhere."

Jillian caught her breath at the reality of what those words described. While there had been nothing in Zara's tone that seemed to include Jillian in "most people," what Zara described was one of the worlds she'd been avoiding, guarding herself from. Like the way she'd forced herself to put aside those faces from the missionary's slideshow in the midst of opulence and abundance. Nothing in her life would help her relate to what Zara had experienced, and yet her insides tightened. Unconsciously, she put her hand to her chest as if to push away the empathy making her heart hurt. Tears pricked the corner of her eyes, and Zara brushed at her own face. Describing the experience had probably made her relive the emotions as well.

"I'm sorry." Jillian's throat constricted around the words. "I simply don't know what to say."

Zara held up her hands in a gesture of futility. "There's nothing you need to say, Jill. I know it's not easy to hear, and I respect that you're willing to listen. And at least my story has a happy ending. So many don't."

Jillian couldn't have explained why, but she very much wanted to connect with Zara, to let her know that what had happened to her mattered. Not sure what else to do, she took Zara's hand and gave a little tug, indicating they should keep walking. "And I want to know how you got to your happy ending. If you don't mind telling me, that is."

Zara stared at their joined hands for a few seconds as she fell into step. She took a breath. "Would you believe I found the only all-girl gang in the city? Or rather, they found me."

She told how, upon visiting Grant Park, a place frequented by the homeless, she was confronted in the restroom by five women, none of whom looked particularly friendly. They'd challenged her being there, had told her she was poaching on their territory, and had said she had to leave.

"I knew they didn't want to hear my sad story. Much as I wanted to cry or run, it was time to make a stand. After some not-too-polite conversation, they decided I had to fight one of them to earn my right to stay."

Jillian tried to conceal her shock. "You had a physical altercation with another woman?"

"Yeah, and I think they were surprised when I picked the biggest one. I figured she'd either be slow, and I'd have half a chance, or she'd knock me out quick, and I'd be out of my misery."

"And what happened?"

"A combination of both, actually. She was slow, and I got in a few licks. But then she cornered me, and it was over pretty quickly." Zara pointed to one of her teeth along the left side of her jaw toward the back. "She knocked this tooth out. I got it fixed once I got off the streets."

"Oh my God."

"The fact that I let her keep it seemed to seal the deal. They let me join their gang, the Ice Rats, on a temporary basis. They had a bunch of convoluted rules about becoming a full-time member, but it seemed to me that if someone could prove they'd broken all of the ten commandments, that should be enough." Jillian couldn't hide her shock, but Zara merely shrugged. "I know, crazy, huh? But that became their thing. And you know, living on the streets, it was fairly easy to get through most of them. We lied and stole and coveted on a regular basis."

Jillian ran through the list of thou-shalt-nots. "What about killing?"

Zara looked away. "People on the streets do what they have to do."

Her answer was almost brusque, and the set of her jaw told Jillian not to pursue this question. They walked for a while before Zara spoke again. Her voice was low, but Jillian could hear the distress in it. "There was a younger girl, Lindy, who showed up one day. It was obvious she had some mild mental impairment. She was a little slow and kinda innocent, you know? She disappeared at night, but once she started staying around during the day, we put her in charge of watching our stuff while we scavenged." She took a breath. "One day, I came back earlier than usual, and a guy I'd never seen before had Lindy on the ground with his hand over her mouth. It was pretty obvious what was going on, so I grabbed a bottle and hit him on the head. I got her up, and we ran. I don't know for sure that I killed him, but it would have been okay with me if I did." She cleared her throat. "At that point, the Ice Rats made me their leader. I'd already been put in charge of organizing our days. I guess I kinda had a knack for making the most of people's time and skills."

Jillian tried to imagine the genial, gifted woman beside her as the leader of a street gang. Her expression must have given away her consternation because Zara looked at their joined hands and said, "I guess you really got me talking this time. And it's okay if you want to let go now."

"But I don't," Jillian answered quicky. She felt compelled to offer reassurance. "In fact, I want to hold on tighter,"

"Thank you for that." Zara smiled for the first time since the story began, and Jillian gave her hand a squeeze.

As girls, she and Constance had held hands, but it had stopped at some invisible barrier of age which Jillian hadn't understood. But since then, she'd only ever held hands with Clive, though occasionally, there were young women doing the same in cafés and shops. Such blatant displays of affection between women had made her look away, lest she be stirred in some deep place. But this contact with Zåra felt more like a bond than a mere social activity.

"So when do we get to the happy part?" she asked, and Zara laughed.

"Well, no surprise, music helped me get out of that life. Almost ten months later, after I hadn't touched a piano, we were walking through another park—Seneca, I think—and some group had a thing called Pianos in the Park, trying to get people interested in buying one. There was a small upright, and they would offer you a quick lesson, or you could just try your hand. I couldn't resist, but when I sat on the bench, the Ice Rats were all laughing and jeering, thinking it was a joke. I started to play, and there were a few murmurs of disbelief, and then I just…I lost track of time. It might have been ten minutes or half an hour, but when I finally wound down, I saw the whole gang sitting around me in a semicircle, and lots of other people on the perimeter were listening too. They all applauded, and a guy came up with a business card. He was opening a new bar, and he wanted some live entertainment, maybe three days a week to start. When he talked about minimum wage plus tips, I got worried because the only identification I had was an expired student ID from Evergreen High School. Luckily, Illinois has pretty loose labor laws. Either that or I looked old enough to be hired.

"Dora—the one I fought with—decided she should take over the gang in my absence. The Ice Rats spent the next two days obtaining new outfits for me." She cut her eyes at Jillian. "Don't ask. And I was given strict instruction about what to do with the money which, you can guess, was basically give it to the gang. But I didn't care. I was going to get to play again and get paid to do it. And as it turned out, Mickey Meyer was one of the nicest men I've ever known."

By the time she'd described the diminutive M and M, as she came to call him—a kind, sensitive blend of Italian and Jewish—and how he'd taught her bartending to make her useful on her off nights, they were almost to the boundary. Jillian tried to swallow the lump in her throat as Zara explained that whatever else she was doing at the bar, she always offered to sweep up or take out the trash or whatever it took to be the last person out. Then she would sneak back in and hide out in the restroom until Mickey was gone. At first, he'd pretended he didn't notice, but by the time winter came around again, a cot in his office was her regular bed.

Jillian had always understood that the luck of her birth had given her a privileged life. But knowing Zara had experienced such want—not having the basic needs of food and shelter and safety—she could imagine how she must look. In her life, she'd been indulged and entitled and spoiled with everything she'd ever wanted or needed without any effort or obligation on her part. *Why does she want anything to do with me?*

"The Ice Rats gradually drifted away, but anytime I saw one, I gave them whatever money I had," Zara said, apparently unaware of Jillian's fretfulness. "Fortunately for me, Mickey's bar, the Copper Cat Pub, became very popular, with a steady clientele. And since we were also listed in all the tourist magazines, we got a lot of out-of-town traffic from people who wanted a real Chicago experience. It also got the reputation of being a cool place for musicians to come and jam, something I really loved doing. And it just so happened that Mrs. Minton's son brought his mother to the pub when she came to visit him." Zara bit her lip, and Jillian could hear the emotion in her voice. "I'll never forget how it felt to see her again. And I didn't think she was ever going to let go of me when we hugged. I think her son was a little jealous, especially when she spent half the night persuading me to return to Evergreen with her. I'd been with Mickey for almost three years then, so it was a hard decision. But I was tired of the bar life, drinking and partying with the staff until all hours and then sleeping the day away until it was time to do it all again. Mrs. Minton convinced me I could be more. She'd always had that effect on me, making me believe in myself in ways that no one else ever did. She helped me get my GED and made sure I took a few college courses. We had other plans, but they didn't work out." She took a deep breath and looked down. "And my parents didn't want to see me, either."

"Did you ever see Mickey again?" Jillian asked carefully, pleased when Zara brightened.

"Oh yeah. I got him to take a cruise with me last year. A short one, just to Mexico. But we had a blast."

"I'm glad." Thanking Zara for sharing her story felt superficial, so Jillian gave her fingers another squeeze. They crested a small rise and stopped. Their hands slipped apart, signaling an ending. "Here we are."

From here, the layout of the village she'd intended to build was visible, some parts outlined with trenches, some with stakes marking the edges of intended structures. "Oh wow," Zara said, turning enthusiastically. "Tell me about this."

Jillian tried not to sound like a boring history professor, but Zara's attentive expression and responsive questions made her go on much too long. When Zara's stomach growled, they both laughed. Jillian pointed to part of the house that was still standing, and they made their way down. Upon close examination, a portion of the walls and roof were intact enough to offer shelter for lunch. As soon as she'd slipped off the rucksack, Zara stepped up and began unbuttoning Jillian's coat. In spite of her racing pulse, she couldn't move. "What are you doing?" she finally managed.

Zara winked. "Right now, I'm making sure you have something drier to put on when we start off again." She hung the dripping garment on a nail in the wood framing and did the same with her jacket. "You can trust me on this, Jillian. Remember, I survived Chicago winters." She pulled one of the cut tree stumps they used as seats and sat close enough that their shoulders were touching. "Body heat is the best, though."

Jillian tried to recover her composure by unpacking their lunch. Dear Mrs. Livingstone had included two thermoses of hearty, still-warm, stew, along with their sandwiches. Zara groaned in the way she did when enjoying food. "You need to give that woman a raise," she said.

"Her presence has been a true gift to our family, so naturally, we've structured her salary accordingly," Jillian said, hearing her tone change but unable to stop it. "And she'll be cared for whenever she decides to retire, which we hope won't be soon."

Was it a case of nerves that was making her take on her Lady of the Manor persona? She hadn't yet shaken the sensation of Zara's fingers unbuttoning her coat, and she was unaccustomed to sitting this close to another woman, even Constance. But she couldn't bring herself to put any distance from the warmth of Zara's body. Mostly to ease her own tension, she began to explain about Mrs. Livingstone and how they'd become close long after Jillian's mother had died.

Zara looked like she wanted to ask something, but Jillian quickly changed the subject, talking about some of the others on the household staff—like Andrew and Mr. Summerfield—who had always been a part of her life. They'd both finished eating when she noticed the intent expression on Zara's face. "Now you have to tell me what you're thinking."

Zara smiled faintly. "I'm thinking that in some ways, we're about as different as two people can be."

"Yes, that's probably true." Given their recent topics of conversation, "probably" was an understatement. Jillian hadn't wanted Zara to feel badly about the obvious disparities in their lives, but when Zara took her hands, her look suggested that wasn't going to be the problem.

"But you know what they say about opposites."

Jillian did, but when she opened her mouth to speak of the chemical bond, Zara leaned toward her, adding, "Maybe that's the something." The softness of her cheek as it brushed Jillian's was so remarkable, she had to close her eyes. "You're not alone in this, Jill. I feel it too." She was whispering close to Jillian's ear as if telling her a secret meant only for the two of them. "I know it's a lot to ask because we don't really know each other. But I'd very much like to kiss you right now."

Jillian had no memory of anything beyond the first touch of lips and then the next and the next. What possessed her in that moment, she had no idea. Had she said yes or made some other affirming sound? Or did she nod or move slightly in Zara's direction? It didn't seem to matter. Before she knew it, they were standing, bodies pressed as close as clothing would allow, arms wrapped around each other. Had she done that? Had Zara? How was it possible to feel such certainty and be completely unmoored at the same time?

A clap of thunder startled them apart. Jillian would have taken it as an omen of warning, but Zara grinned and said, "I was going to say, 'wow,' but that was much more accurate."

Jillian blinked as a wave of panic swept through her. What in heaven's name was she doing, kissing this woman she barely knew? Kissing a woman at all? "Oh, I can't…We should go," she stuttered, looking away. "I must get back."

After a few seconds, Zara held up Jillian's coat. She'd worked her arms into the sleeves when Zara's hands rested lightly on her shoulders. "It's okay, Jill. You know your way back. I'll be following your lead."

They both knew she wasn't only speaking of returning to Fullerhill. But Jillian was struck by the notion that she would be the one determining what happened next between them. Socially, she usually went along with whatever Constance and Nelson had planned, and her private interactions with Clive weren't much more than sitting close, holding hands, and engaging in relatively chaste kisses, none of which had made her feel anything like the way she just had with Zara. She and Clive had become a couple so gradually, it had been hard to notice the change from their childhood friendship. But he must have overheard her asking Constance about the morality of sex outside of marriage because he'd continued to respect those boundaries, even when she'd tried to cross them. Would Zara be like that? Jillian laughed to herself and shook her head. Two women couldn't get married; therefore, the comparison wasn't valid. And why was she thinking of such a ridiculous idea?

Then, somehow, despite the strained silence between them for the first part of the walk, Zara made her laugh when they took a break for their biscuits by exaggeratedly mimicking British teatime practices. And then, with the same gentle touch on Jillian's arm, she added, "I can't bring myself to apologize, exactly, but I will leave if you'd prefer. I can manage on my own, and the last thing I want is for you to be unhappy I'm here."

Jillian assured her it was fine to stay, telling herself she was motivated by her familial reputation for cordiality and not by the private dread she felt at the idea of Zara out on the streets of London alone. They talked casually while finishing their snack, laughing again when the last biscuit left a smear of chocolate alongside Zara's lip. Jillian intended to simply brush it off with her finger, but as she stepped close enough to do that, Zara's eyes captured her.

"Do you want one last taste of the something?" she teased, and Jillian was very much aware that she did. When Zara had kissed her earlier, she'd been captivated by the feel of her mouth. Now she felt compelled to know how Zara tasted. How else could she understand this strange appetite growing inside her?

She only intended to touch the chocolate with her tongue, but when Zara's lips parted slightly as if inviting her in, she was infused with a sense of power vastly different from the authority it took to run the household. She ran her tongue over Zara's generous mouth, something that struck her as more wanton than anything she'd ever done with Clive. When Zara moaned and leaned into her, Jillian felt more in control than any time since they'd met. Was this how it worked with women? Did they take turns being in charge? She circled her arms around Zara's waist, intending it as merely support, but somehow pulling her closer at the same time. Zara's hands came into her hair, and their kiss became all-consuming. The last thought of her rational mind was to equate this give and take to Newton's third law of motion: every action on her part got a reaction from Zara, and vice versa.

She couldn't have said how much time had passed when Zara pulled away with regret in her eyes. Taking a step away, she took Jillian's hand again. "Jill," she almost gasped before swallowing audibly. "I'd kiss you for the rest of the day and all night if I had the chance, but I know you have obligations, and I don't want you to feel guilty, in any way, about having spent this time with me."

Jillian merely nodded, and they both took a moment to gather themselves before she followed the tug of Zara's hand back down the path. She tried desperately to determine if she'd reached any further insight into this strange yearning, which seemed to rouse her in a way she couldn't ever recall feeling. Even after breaking out of the trees and seeing Fullerhill in the distance, she wanted to stay close to Zara, who grinned every time they made eye contact and occasionally bumped shoulders with her as if they'd won some athletic match. But when she spotted Clive and her friends on the terrace, the familiar coolness flooded back into her veins, and she couldn't bring herself to look at Zara again.

After cleaning up, she was warmed from the shower, but not at all in the same way. When she sat with Clive and Nelson, she found herself easing into the comfort of their familiar routine. Then Zara appeared for dinner in her red dress, and Jillian's mouth went dry as something inside her churned almost uncontrollably. She forced her thoughts away from what she'd learned about the feel and taste of Zara's lips, and with effort, she kept her focus on Clive and his charms…until Zara began playing.

The music and the way Zara moved as she played made her feel like she was soaring into some other world. After it was over, she couldn't resist going to her and thanking her for the beauty she'd shared with them that evening. *Zara reminded her of what she'd said about beauty the night before, and when their gazes locked, Jillian might not have been able to look away if Clive hadn't come over.*

Jillian deliberately put away the memories of the fearful events that happened afterward. All she could reflect on now was what would have happened if Zara hadn't been there. She felt the sting of tears as she questioned how she could possibly abandon Zara to the care of strangers in a place she didn't know.

As if in acknowledgement, Zara moaned softly.

Smoothing her hair away from her forehead, Jillian bent to her ear. "You're going to be all right. I promise."

CHAPTER EIGHT

Stirring, Zara began to flex her wrists and fingers as she always did upon waking. Instantaneous and almost overwhelming pain made her cry out, and remembering where she was, she reached for the call button, wanting to escape into the relief of whatever drug they were giving her. But a warm touch stopped her before she grasped the device.

"Zara, it's Jillian. Can we talk for a moment?"

Moving slightly, she blinked against the light as she searched for the face that had been in every dream since she'd arrived at the hospital. "Jillian Stansfield? Are you really here?" she croaked.

Gorgeous blue eyes shimmered above her, and the touch became a gentle squeeze on Zara's uninjured hand. "Yes, and I'll prove it. Can you feel this?" When Zara nodded, Jill leaned down and kissed her cheek, and there was a smile in her voice when she asked, "How about that?"

"Hmm. I'm not sure. Maybe you should try it again."

When Jill moved toward her face again, Zara turned so their lips met. She tried to keep it chaste, not wanting Jill to experience her nasty sick breath, but the lingering feel of those lips was sorely tempting. At the sound of a nurse's voice just outside, Jill pulled back quickly, offering Zara a sip of water.

After Zara drank, Jillian cleared her throat. "There are two things I need to talk with you about. One will be difficult, but I hope the other will be far easier."

"Difficult first," Zara said without hesitation.

Jill responded in kind. "Your audition at the Royal College of Music is scheduled for tomorrow. Obviously, it won't be possible for you to attend, and even if you could, your injury would prevent any performance from measuring up to your own standards…or theirs." Her voice was level, almost matter-of-fact, in contrast to the agonized protest her words provoked.

Tomorrow? Zara tried to account for the time from the horrible moment she'd seen Clive dip Jillian too close to the fire, but she couldn't do the figuring as Jill continued speaking.

"You'll need to call, to explain the situation and…make other plans. Do you have a contact, a sponsor with whom you could speak?"

Don't kill the messenger, Zara told herself, tamping down her resentment. She was only trying to help. "There's a letter with the information I need in the top drawer of my room at Fullerhill," she said through gritted teeth. At one time, she could have recited it from memory, but her brain was fuzzy with drugs and pain, and the paper swam away from her mental vision as if gradually sinking under water.

"Good," Jillian said briskly. "Constance and Nelson are still at the house. I'll call and have them bring it over right away."

When she didn't reach for the room phone, Zara remembered something else. Trying to sound calm, she asked, "What's the good news?"

"I've spoken with Dr. Bankole. You're healing well enough that she thinks you can be released in a day or so. But obviously, you'll need to continue some of your medication and have lots of therapy to regain the flexibility and movement you'll need to…to…." Jill stuttered to a stop, suggesting she knew more than she wanted to say. The burn specialist seemed to always be in a hurry, leaving quickly after each examination, remaining tight-lipped about her condition. But Zara hadn't been in any condition to ask probing questions. "To play the piano again," Jillian finished, the sounds tight in her throat.

Zara's voice hardened as she kept her eyes on Jill's face. "Does footing the bill give you access to more information than I get as the patient?"

To her credit, Jill didn't flinch. "Standard health care is free in this country, Zara. You're in a private room because I requested it.

And as for your prognosis, I was here the last time your consultant did rounds. You weren't particularly with it, and I asked."

Zara felt a flush of embarrassment creep up her neck. "I'm sorry, Jill. I just felt like there was a 'maybe' in that sentence about me playing again, and I…"

Jill waved her apology away. "Well, that's the point, isn't it? To ensure you can resume the life you want, you'll need the best. People experienced and skilled in this kind of rehabilitation, who can be available to you at any time. So I have a plan. We're going to prepare a room at Fullerhill with all the resources and equipment needed. For the first few weeks, we'll also have a nurse monitor your healing and provide whatever treatments you might need. Two full-time therapists—one physical, one occupational—will be brought in and given room and board as well."

Zara blinked in disbelief. It was too much. "Jill, no."

"Yes, Zara." Jill's voice was even more firm than hers had been. "I want this for you. And for me. Because while I can only imagine how terrible this is for you, please believe me when I say that I…I can't possibly express how horrible I feel about what happened."

The voice in the hall had faded, and Zara reached out her good hand. When Jillian took it, she said, "Listen to me, Jill. None of this is your fault. And I am not your responsibility." Gesturing around the private room with her bandaged left hand, she added, "I get the sense you're making sure I get the very best treatment, and that's more than kind. But I couldn't possibly accept—"

"I also want to move your room next to mine." Jill cut her off, smiling shyly. "Ostensibly, so I can hear you in case you need anything. But also, I want you nearby because…because I realize that I need…I want…to explore the…uh…"

Zara really liked how this beautiful woman could be fiercely determined one moment and adorably shy the next. "The something?" she asked, caressing Jill's fingers lightly with her thumb as her heart lightened with hope. Jill's smile widened and she nodded. "Well, that's the best offer I've had all day."

"Good. Then I'll set everything up as soon as I call home and speak with Constance." As Jill used the room phone, Zara drifted a bit as the conversation went on. It took Jillian's voice by her ear to wake her again. "Zara? My father is home, so I need to go and explain everything to him. I'll be back with your letter this afternoon."

"Okay." She yawned, barely registering anything but the soft feel of Jill's lips on her forehead before all other sounds and sensations faded.

Nothing could make Zara relish the torture of her daily treatment, but a happy little hum played in her heart afterward as she waited for Jill to return. Could they each give themselves over to the possibility that the "something" could actually happen between them? Could Jill truly care for her with anything other than guilt or pity about her injured hand? When she'd first been able to think about it, Zara told herself that her actions when she'd seen the flames had been pure instinct, and she would have done the same for Constance or Nelson or Gina. But during the ambulance ride, when the medical people had taken over Jill's care, their reassuring tones convincing her that Jill truly was going to be all right, Zara could admit to herself that what she felt for Jillian Stansfield was beyond concern for a new friend or a compelling attraction to a beautiful woman.

Jill was an exceptional person. Even in the brief time they'd spent together, her genuine sense of caring served to minimize the wealth and privilege Zara would normally spurn. The way she lit up when she talked about her projects made Zara believe Jill would do important work, make a difference in other peoples' lives. But there had also been rare moments when she'd sensed a sadness and a longing, as if Lady Stansfield had a critical piece missing. The something, Zara thought, smiling inside. That lack might have been what had driven Jill academically and socially until now, but could it be possible she was at a place emotionally where she was ready to let someone help her fill that void?

Hope fluttered inside her, and Zara let her fantasies run wild. She imagined them living in a cozy flat, Jillian working at some fabulous laboratory in town while Zara performed as the pianist for the London symphony. Between her occasional touring engagements, she would accompany Jill abroad to establish whatever amazing device she'd invented to improve the lives of impoverished people, helping one place after another. While Jill educated the adults on the wonders of their new world, Zara would volunteer with the youth, teaching music and all the wonderful awakening of self that came with it, something she'd always wanted to do. She smiled at the image of herself as Mrs. Minton, complete with the flowered print dress and sensible heels. Then, she thought about coming home at night to Jillian Stansfield, to her embrace and her kisses and her bed.

The appeal she'd felt from the moment they'd met was like nothing she'd ever known, and it was intriguing to detect that Jill felt it too. When they'd kissed in the ruins, Zara was certain the intensity of their physical connection had been a surprise to Jill, but it didn't seem unwelcome. At least, not until the thunder had broken them apart, and Jill had been compelled to think about what had just happened. At that point, some women would have insisted she leave or resisted any further interaction between them. But Jill hadn't done either of those. In fact, during those last kisses, tasting of chocolate and rain, Jill had taken the lead in their exploration and in so doing, acted on a passion that Lady Stansfield apparently hadn't known was in her. Zara hadn't ever given over control that easily before, and the very memory of it still took her breath away.

The rest of the walk had felt like they were on their way to possibilities neither of them had imagined, though when they'd arrived back at the house, Zara had felt Jill's detachment return. Clive was a factor she hadn't considered, and even though he clearly intended to stake a claim on Jillian, there was something a little...off about him. She could tell Jill liked her in the red dress, though, and she was glad Constance had talked her into wearing it. Thankfully, they were all too nice to comment about her frequent wobbles on the high heels she so rarely wore.

It's all ruined now, just like... Zara's logical mind tried to rouse itself, but she wasn't ready to go there yet. She wanted to keep dreaming, to envision them in each other's lives, to believe they could give each other contentment and a true measure of happiness.

When the door to her room opened, she sat up eagerly, ready to accept Jill's generous offer. Whatever came of more time spent with her, it would be worthwhile. But the figure that entered was unfamiliar. He wasn't wearing a white coat or scrubs or accompanied by anyone medical, but he carried authority with him like a limitless charge card.

"Zara Keller?" he asked. His tone wasn't accusing, but something about his manner had her already on the defensive.

"Yeah. Who wants to know?" Her reply was all Chicago-street survivor.

There was a split second of dispassionate evaluation before his manner warmed, and he approached her with his hand out. "I'm Douglas Stansfield, Jillian's father."

She saw it, then. The family resemblance was unmistakable, though his hair was graying, and his eyes were a muddier blue. "Oh." She pulled the sheet up before extending her right hand. "Sure. It's a pleasure to meet you, sir."

"No, no," he insisted, adding his other hand, enclosing hers with startling fondness. "The pleasure is mine, Miss Keller. I...we...my whole family owes you a tremendous debt."

The appreciation in his emotion seemed completely authentic. Zara shook her head, trying to find the balance between modesty and acknowledgement. "I'm just so relieved Jillian is okay." She felt Lord Stansfield's appraising gaze again before he glanced at the chair beside her bed. Zara straightened her shoulders. "Would you like to sit down, sir?"

"Thank you." He slowly lowered himself into the chair. "I'm given to understand your injuries are a good deal more severe than my daughter's."

She supposed she should be glad he wasn't going to engage her with small talk that she'd have no idea how to respond to. "The doctor hasn't told me anything recently. I'm not sure what the prognosis is at this point."

He shifted slightly. "Jillian tells me you're a musician, a pianist. There was to be a recital at the Royal College of Music, I believe?"

Her tears came from nowhere. Damn. Where was the anger she'd had all the other times she'd thought about this? She turned her head away but suspected he'd already seen because his voice was softer when he spoke again.

"Let me put your mind at ease about that much, at least. There will be no problem rescheduling your audition at whatever point you're prepared to go forward with it. I've taken the liberty of speaking with Mrs. Hilliard, the director of development, to explain your...ah...

situation. She's been most gracious, and a letter with details will be sent to you at your…er…rehabilitation."

Clearly, strings had been pulled. But just as obviously, there seemed to be some new ones attached. Zara had recovered her composure enough to look him in the eye again. "That's very kind of you, sir. Did Jillian also mention her idea about having me recover there at your home?"

Douglas Stansfield sighed. Whatever was coming next, she evidently wasn't going to like it. "Yes. We've had a rather lengthy conversation about that." Zara bit her lip, trying to keep from smiling. The father-daughter confrontations probably didn't happen often, but when they did, someone would likely come away bloodied. Figuratively, at least. His gaze sharpened. "Were you aware that Jillian was going to forfeit this semester at university to supervise your care?"

Zara's mouth opened slightly, her mind too rattled to respond right away.

He nodded, apparently satisfied. "She said not, but I had to make sure." He reached into his jacket pocket and brought out a folded color brochure. "I sent for this as soon as I was contacted about the incident, thinking it might be Jillian who would need to go." His lip quivered faintly, a show of sentiment she suspected was rather unusual. He held it out to her. "This is some information about the Clinique Valmont, one of the foremost orthopedic rehabilitation centers in Europe. Their history of dealing with injuries like yours dates back to World War I, though of course, the facility itself has gone through several updates."

Zara took the offered information but didn't look at it.

"I want to make it clear," he continued, "that we intend to take full responsibility for all financial costs. It would be our honor to do so."

She didn't even have to glance at the paper to know this was some ritzy place. "That's really kind of you sir, but it's not necessary. I'm sure I can—"

"Actually, it is necessary, Miss Keller, and not solely for your sake. I'm fairly certain an arrangement like this is what it will take to convince my daughter that you are receiving appropriate treatment. Otherwise, I fear she will insist on the reckless and possibly damaging course of caring for you in our home." Zara looked down, hearing the chair creak slightly as Lord Stansfield leaned toward her. "Please understand. This has nothing to do with you and everything to do with Jillian's future. Regardless of her outstanding record to date, missing this semester could well cost her the job, perhaps the very career, she's been working toward for her whole life. I'm sure you wouldn't want that on your conscience."

Zara's mouth had gone dry, so she simply shook her head as she looked at him.

He clasped his hands together before continuing. "I'm aware Jillian has only a few good friends, and I gather you two have become close over the past few days. I'm glad for that, but I fail to understand why this friendship can't resume after your rehabilitation and Jillian's graduation." He sighed. "Then again, I was married for almost thirty years, and I have a daughter, but I can honestly say there are many, many things I don't understand about women."

She would have laughed at that if her heart hadn't felt like it was bleeding. She wanted to be angry at him, to shout that despite his reassurances, she knew this essentially was about her and how he didn't want a poor musician getting chummy with his beautiful daughter in their fabulous mansion. But there didn't seem to be anything insincere about him or certainly in his concern for Jill. He was simply doing what Zara wished her own dad had done, seeing to it that his little girl made smart decisions.

She cleared her throat, not really expecting the giant lump inside to go away. "Assuming I agree, when were you thinking I'd be going to this place?" she asked, still not having looked at the booklet on her lap.

"Tonight," he said. "Dr. Bankole has assured me you'll be fine to travel, with a nurse attending you, obviously."

"Tonight?" Her voice went up of its own volition. "Will I be able to speak with Jillian before I go?"

Another sigh. She wasn't going to like this either. "I just don't think that's wise, Miss Keller. My daughter is still quite distraught about the accident, and I'm afraid she'll view our plan as contrary to what she thinks is best in this situation." Zara started to object to the use of "our plan," but he added, "Read over the material and give it some thought. I'm confident you'll come to agree that this course of action is what's right for both of you. Especially if you are indeed Jillian's friend."

He inclined his head, a gesture that reminded her of Jillian, and stood. Zara swallowed, turning the paper over as she fumbled for the pen on her nightstand. "If I could have your address, sir, I'd like at least to write to her and explain why I…I won't be seeing her for a while."

"Certainly," he said with the graciousness of someone who knew they'd won everything meaningful. "I'm sure she'd appreciate it. But I have to insist that you not mention my role in all this. Doing so would undermine all the good we hope to accomplish. For you and for my daughter."

Zara wished her mind was clearer. It seemed like there was something important she was missing, but she only nodded. In the hours following his departure, she was swept along on a tide of purpose directed, yet again, by the forces of wealth and privilege. A servant she didn't recognize brought her things from Fullerhill, after which a solid, stern woman in nurse's whites directed the collection of her medical necessities and helped her change before pushing her wheelchair down to street level, where a car was waiting. Zara's mind had been busy trying to compose her letter to Jill, and she was at the airport before she even knew where they were going.

Still being pushed along in the chair, she pulled the brochure from her bag and examined it. Montreux, Switzerland. Under other circumstances, she would have been thrilled to go somewhere she hadn't been before, but she couldn't stop the nagging suspicion that she was making a mistake, that Jillian could manage her way around any scholastic issues, and that leaving was sending her the wrong message about them and about her willingness to explore their "something."

As soon as they stopped at a gate, Zara stood to look around for a phone. The no-nonsense nurse stood with her. "Did you need something, Miss?"

"Yeah, I need to make a call. Is there a pay phone nearby?"

She glanced at her watch, frowning. "There's no time for that, I'm afraid. We'll be boarding in a few minutes."

Zara was feeling increasingly desperate, as if Jill was sending her some kind of telepathy to get in touch. "This won't take long if you can direct me. I just need to speak to someone before I go."

"I'm sorry. That won't be possible."

She whirled to insist and almost tripped on the chair, losing her balance. Reaching out, she instinctively used her left hand to catch herself, and though it was wrapped, the contact made her cry out and fall back into the chair, squeezing her eyes shut against the pain. Seconds later, she felt a sharp pinch and looked over to see the woman withdrawing a needle from her arm.

"This medication will help with your discomfort," she said.

Maybe physically, Zara thought as a wave of dizziness overtook her. Sometime later, she was moving again, and then there was a lifting sensation as they became airborne. Zara had only flown once before, but she'd loved it. This time, not so much.

Dear Jillian,

I hope you're okay and working hard, as if I need to suggest something like that to you. Ha ha. Mainly, I wanted you to know I'm getting my rehab at this place in Switzerland. It seemed like the best idea, though I really appreciated your offer of staying at your place. But you have a big life ahead of you, and it's important you finish your schooling and get on with saving the world.

She'd thought this out as much as possible, inexplicably certain that someone else would see this before Jillian ever did, or ever would, if she wasn't careful about what she said. But she deliberately put the word "something" in the first sentence, hoping Jill would see it and know what she meant.

They don't tell me much, and when they do, they mostly talk in French or with some other accent so thick, it's hard for me to understand, but if all goes well, I hope to be able to play something special for you again soon. Until then, I'm keeping my armor polished, and I hope you can do the same.

She slipped in another "something," believing Jill would remember that conversation the way she did and would get her coded message about keeping herself protected.

I'm not sure if you can write to me here, but please try if you want to. I haven't seen any other patients getting mail, which makes me think they must want us to concentrate on getting better or something. I guess I'll see you when I see you, but I trust the world won't be too different or turn too many times before that happens.

She slipped in one more "something," and hoped her message was clear. She still felt the same and would no matter how long it took for her to get out of there, and she trusted Jill would give her another chance when that time came.

With deepest affection,
Zara

She couldn't put anything more meaningful, though there was much more she would have said: *You're not like anyone else I've ever known, and I love that about you. Is it weird that I dream of you nearly every night, and you're in my thoughts every day? I know we just met, but being so far away from you makes me feel like I'm missing something I didn't even know I needed.*

Between the extensive medical evaluations after she'd arrived and their liberal administering of pain pills, which she'd finally began declining, it had been almost a week before she finished her final rewrite on Jillian's letter and mailed it. She resisted the impulse to put on some lipstick and press a kiss to the back of the envelope, mainly because Mr. Stansfield didn't strike her as the type to assume such a thing was strictly innocent. And he'd be right. The most important thing was for Jillian to get her message, period.

Returning to her room, Zara told herself—again—that she could be in much worse places. Her room was semi-private, but no one was currently occupying the other bed, and it had a nice view of a small lake and some distant mountains. She'd spent some time outside each day after lunch, enjoying the afternoon sun, ignoring the increasingly cooler temperatures. The weird thing was, there always seemed to be someone nearby, watching. She didn't know if they did this kind of monitoring with everyone, and she hadn't found any other patients who knew much English. She'd listened to the others when they spoke and was trying to pick up words they repeated. But when the aide arrived to take her to therapy, and Zara tried her newly acquired greeting, the girl laughed and told her in her heavy accent to work on getting better and forget about speaking French.

By the beginning of the third week, she began noticing the way the doctor and the physical therapist looked at each other during her treatment. Thus far, all of her questions about her recovery had been met with vague responses, such as "we must wait and see," or "it's too early to tell," or even, "it all depends on how your body responds." She was repeatedly cautioned about overdoing the exercises on her hand, but it still felt like an overcooked piece of meat hanging off her arm and not the responsive tool that had always functioned so skillfully.

When she contemplated the night of the fire, it was never with regret for what she'd done at that moment. She only wished she'd somehow changed the course of events sooner, perhaps by not challenging Clive for Jillian's affection by showing off at the piano. Maybe then, she wouldn't be waiting every day for a positive sign from her body or from the two people who were working on it.

Between that and waiting to see if Jill would write back, her life felt like it was in suspended animation. There was a television in her room, but all the programs were either in French or German, and no newspapers or magazines were available in English. It was disturbing, being cut off from the real world, so she requested a trip into town.

Dr. Rengel himself stopped by her room to explain that she probably needed another two weeks of healing before such a visit would be advisable. There was still concern for infection, did she understand? Zara told him yes, she could accept that, but admitted she was finding her isolation rather discouraging.

Several days later, she was still moping as she returned from another discouraging treatment. Though the worst of the burn on her palm was healing, it wasn't the soft, pliable flesh that it had been. And she didn't need their metric measuring tools to know her reach wasn't what it had been and was nowhere near what it needed to be for her to play like she used to. She sighed, wondering why she hadn't begged Jillian to write back. Hearing from her would make everything better, unless she wrote to say she was no longer interested in exploring the something between them.

Angry at that thought, she pushed the door to her room open with more force than was necessary and almost ran into someone's backside. For half a second, she thought it was the pleasant older woman who cleaned the room, but then the figure turned and hopped a bit awkwardly onto the bed nearest the door—the one that had been vacant since she'd arrived—holding a magazine. Zara's face must have shown the afternoon's frustrations because the young woman's expression turned grave. She nodded slightly, offering some words in German.

Zara managed a half-smile but answered, "Sorry, I'm American, and I only speak English."

"Oh, wonderful," she answered, her accent noticeable but not too pronounced. "I can practice on you." She was blond and blue-eyed, which made Zara think of Jillian. But she broke into a grin at the thought of being practiced on, and that apparently prompted the young woman to lean toward her and hold out a hand. "My name is Andrea." The way she said it, with the stress on the middle syllable, made it sound exotic. "I'm to be your roommate."

Zara had enjoyed her privacy at first, but now she was very glad for some company. Especially someone who spoke English. "Hi, Andrea. I'm Zara," she said, moving to shake the offered hand. "It's nice to meet you. And maybe you can teach me some German too?"

Andrea nodded. "Of course. Germans are easy."

Zara laughed for what felt like the first time since she'd been injured. "I think you mean, German is easy."

She looked away as if retranslating in her head and then frowned slightly. "All right. But what have I said to make you laugh?"

The door opened, and an aide came in. She spoke in German, and Andrea replied. Turning back to Zara, she said, "Please excuse. I go for my evaluation now."

Zara moved aside when she noticed the wheelchair the aide had brought. Andrea pushed herself off the bed, landing somewhat unsteadily, and Zara realized her left leg was missing below the knee.

Quickly, making sure she didn't stare, she answered the earlier question. "I'll explain the laughing when I know you better."

Andrea's eyes twinkled mischievously. "Good. That I will look forward."

Zara laughed again, enjoying the irregular phrasing. She'd probably sound twice as bad when she started speaking German, but she was much more interested in learning it than she had been a few minutes before. And much more positive about her medical progress. If they became friends, she could ask Andrea to translate the notes in her chart and even help her evaluate the treatments she was getting. Maybe that way, she'd be back to her old self when she saw the blue-eyed blonde of her dreams.

CHAPTER NINE

Constance was so excited, she could barely contain herself. After Nelson's proposal, her happiness had been made complete when Lord Stansfield graciously agreed to let them have their wedding at Fullerhill, and now their special day was almost here. She had such lovely memories of how beautifully the manor had been decorated at Christmases past, and having their wedding between Christmas and New Year's would let them take advantage of both holidays and add to all the celebrating that went with them.

With that settled, there had followed a rush of other planning. Nelson had often teased her by pretending to be crushed under the weight of endless decisions, but it wasn't really that bad. It was true, her grades had suffered this past semester, as shopping and fittings and showers had taken up more and more of her time. And then there was the blasted invitation list.

She hadn't expected that deciding who to invite—or more accurately, who not to invite—would be the hardest part of the whole process. Her mother had managed to secure the assistance of Barton, the Stansfield's social secretary, to help with the process. But of all things, she and Nelson had their fiercest debate over whether or not to ask Zara. In the end, Constance had included her because if it hadn't been for her swift, brave actions, Jillian, her dearest friend and maid of honor, might not be here at all.

Not that Jillian was the same since the accident. She'd always been somewhat remote, but now she was even more withdrawn. After initially making noises about skipping the semester to supervise Zara's recovery, she'd arrived at school a week late. And while her grades were as good as always, she looked to be almost apathetic, without the intense dedication to her work she'd always had. Eventually, Constance had gotten out of her that Zara had disappeared, and only after Jillian had repeatedly asked her father to investigate had he finally uncovered that she had gone to a rehabilitation facility in Switzerland. How Zara could afford such a place, Constance couldn't imagine, but she didn't mention that issue to Jillian.

Over Nelson's objections, Constance sent an invitation to the clinic, with a notation to please forward since it seemed unlikely Zara was still there after all these months. Once it had been returned with a handwritten "Undeliverable" scrawled across the envelope, Nelson had disclosed Lord Stansfield's revelation that two pieces of Jillian's mother's jewelry had come up missing after that horrible day. The implication of Zara's involvement was unstated but obvious, and would certainly answer the question of how she could afford to recuperate in Switzerland.

Constance was saddened that she'd completely misjudged Zara's character. She'd even harbored the notion that Zara might recover enough to play during their reception. But with those developments, she'd booked a quartet through a professional music service and had put her mind on the dozens of other matters she had to attend to.

The second-best thing about their upcoming wedding was that Jillian had finally agreed to see Clive again. When Constance recalled meeting Zara on the crossing to England and how she'd thought the passion in Zara's playing might hasten the romance between Jillian and Clive, it had upset her to think how terribly that plan had gone awry. But she and Nelson had been quite relieved when Jillian and Clive had finally reached some kind of accord because there had been no question Clive would be invited. Constance was certain that with the four of them being together again for the happy occasion of their wedding, things would soon be back to normal.

During Jillian's last fitting, Constance teased that perhaps her nuptials would be next. Typical of her recent behavior, Jillian only smiled thinly and said nothing. Admittedly, much of Constance's time had been taken up with wedding preparations, but she missed their talks. After they finished, she all but dragged Jillian into a nearby coffee shop, hoping to recapture the closeness between them that had somehow slipped away.

"Tell me, how are you feeling, really?" she asked, touching Jillian lightly on her previously injured shoulder once they were seated with their drinks.

If she hadn't been watching closely, she would have missed the flicker of pain passing through Jillian's eyes before she said, "I'm fine, thank you. No ill effects." She sipped her coffee before asking. "Has Nelson gotten closer to finalizing which job offer he'll accept?"

Constance knew this to be another potentially sore subject, but apparently, it was preferable to anything more personal. "He's narrowed it down to three firms. They've all agreed to wait on his decision until after the wedding." Jillian's lips twitched slightly. "What about you?" she asked. "Have you contacted any of the businesses Professor Hampton recommended?"

She and Nelson had discussed how ridiculous it was that Jillian's brilliance could be overlooked by many firms simply because she was a woman. Apparently, most companies expected her to come begging, rather than courting her. She shook her head. "Actually, I've been speaking with someone at VSO."

Constance barely managed to keep her jaw from dropping. The Voluntary Service Overseas group was well-respected for its work with impoverished communities but offered mainly the type of fieldwork that would not normally appeal to someone of Jillian Stansfield's station. Much like the American Peace Corps, many of the posts were in the poorest and most marginalized parts of the world. She saw Jillian watching for her reaction, so she made sure to keep her expression neutral. "What made you think of them?"

When Jillian didn't reply straightaway, Constance wondered if she even had a good answer. Perhaps this was just something to say, and she wanted to be talked out of it. As Constance was running through what might be a reasonable approach to doing that, Jillian said, "It was something Zara said about doing amazing things when the time was right. I think this is that time."

Jillian hadn't mentioned Zara since the first week she'd been back in school. Whether it was because her father had told her about the theft or if she'd been vexed by Zara's rejection of her care, Constance didn't know. But in that second, she heard the way Jillian lingered on Zara's name, as if the feel of it on her tongue was something she'd longed for. Wanting to bring a quick end to that notion, Constance spoke dismissively. "Yes, but you could do amazing things without leaving the country, Jillian."

"We'll see," was all she said before returning to the subject of wedding plans.

Constance was careful to stay away from the subject of Zara for the rest of their conversation.

It was nearly a week before Constance remembered to tell Nelson what Jillian had said about VSO. He was equally shocked and concerned and promised to talk with her about it. They discussed the idea of making a substantial donation to the organization as a thank-you for everything the Stansfields were doing for their wedding, hoping their gift would serve as an alternative to Jillian's good intentions. Constance didn't mention Jillian's brief reference to Zara.

Nelson had met Clive twice for dinner and reported he was taking a much more serious approach to his schooling and to his probable career in the financial sector. He added that Clive's penchant for clever quips and funny stories was completely absent. Instead, he appeared virtually paralyzed by guilt. Fortunately, his role in their ceremony seemed to have strengthened his resolve to not simply acquire Jillian's forgiveness but to regain her favor as well. Constance and Nelson agreed that if anything good had come from that terrible night, this change in Clive was it. As the best man, Clive would be partnered with Jillian for the walk down the aisle, and perhaps he was further encouraged by the idea of doing so at their own wedding in the future.

But for her part, Jillian wasn't responding to any such overtures from Clive or anyone else, for that matter. Somehow, word had gotten out that she and Clive were on the outs, but Nelson reported that despite being asked out by various respectable and some disrespectable lads, Jillian consistently had declined any and all offers.

Constance had always believed that Jillian was holding out for Clive, waiting for him to mature enough to be a respectable candidate for marriage. The niggling worry Constance had concerning Jillian's interest in Zara had ceased when Zara had vanished. And now, she was just as glad the invitation had come back undelivered. It was time for Jillian to get as serious about her future with someone as she'd been about her future career.

The day of the rehearsal dinner was a party for old friends and not only for their gang of four. Nelson's parents had long been acquainted with the Holstons and Lord Stansfield from various school and society functions over the years, and everyone was in the best of spirits.

Everyone except Jillian, who acted almost like a funeral was going to take place rather than a joyous event like a wedding. Nelson knew he shouldn't be thinking of another woman on the day before his marriage, but he wished Jillian would be happy. He'd never known her to be one of those girls who was batty over the mere idea of a wedding, but she might at least be glad for the two of them.

At one time, he might have indulged in the fantasy that Jillian's sadness was because she'd wanted to be with him. After all, she was the one who'd first awakened him sexually, though not by anything deliberate on her part. In his early teens, he'd been aroused merely by sitting beside her, smelling her fresh scent and listening to her calm, cultured voice. Jillian might have noticed something in his manner because that was when she first began sitting next to Clive instead of him. He hadn't taken it badly, especially because Constance had begun paying him extra attention, and now, thank God, they were to be married.

And Clive was behaving with absolute perfection. His parents were the only ones not in attendance, but this didn't seem to affect him like it might have at other times. He was respectful but not fawning to the adults, while reserving his fondest looks for Jillian. There was no question he desperately wanted to make amends, while for her part, Jillian didn't ignore him so much as not even see him. Granted, she was busy with hostess duties, as well as being absorbed, along with Constance, in a myriad of last-minute wedding details, including correcting a mix-up concerning music at the reception.

At lunch, Clive made a lovely speech—ostensibly about Nelson and Constance—about how it took the right woman to make a boy into a man, but Jillian never met his eyes and barely sipped her wine. Of course, none of them made mention of the last time they'd all been together, and they carefully avoided the drawing room with its pleasantly warm fire. While the parents chattered happily into the afternoon, Jillian excused herself and disappeared after a quick visit to the kitchen.

Nelson assumed she'd gone to her lab, but she caught up to him in the hallway a few moments later. After a quick check over her shoulder as if to make sure they were alone, Jillian asked him if Zara was on the guest list. He confirmed her invitation, and Jillian's face had momentarily brightened, but when he explained about the returned envelope, she simply nodded. He didn't mention the missing jewelry, deciding that was her father's story to tell. After Jillian thanked him, Nelson watched her go, admiring the attractive styling she'd done with her shorter hair but cognizant there was a bit of a slump in her normally regal bearing.

Later, when they reconvened for tea, Constance told him that Jillian had invited her to go for a walk. Never as outdoorsy as her friend, Constance had declined, having no interest in getting scratched and dirty while tramping through the woods on the day before she was to be married. When Clive joined them, casting a questioning glance at Jillian's empty place at the table, Nelson told him she'd left.

"I'd have gone with her," Clive said, misery evident on his face. "But she hardly speaks to me."

"I know this is hard for you to hear, old man," Nelson said, "but I think she's still traumatized by the accident."

"It's true," Constance added. "I'm sorry, Clive, but she hasn't been the same since she came home from the hospital."

His head dropped. "I know. But how can I make it better when Jilly won't give me a chance? I know I screwed up, but if that damned American woman hadn't jumped in, I would have figured out what to do."

Nelson said nothing, and after a few seconds, Constance began offering consolation. He hoped she wouldn't mention the possibility of Zara being involved in a theft. Even with her apparent guilt and the extreme improbability that their paths would cross again, Nelson didn't want to give Clive any more reason to dislike her. His anger, on the rare occasions it showed itself, was legendary, and when he couldn't find a target for his fury, he was capable of spending it on an innocent bystander. Nelson just didn't want that person to be Jillian.

Much to Nelson's relief, the ceremony went perfectly, and the joy that filled him when they were announced as, "Mr. and Mrs. Nelson Garrick," was almost beyond description.

Constance gave him a proper kiss once they were out of public view, and before the others joined them, she made it clear their honeymoon would be memorable, though they'd be staying at Fullerhill for the night before leaving for Malta in the morning.

Jillian had graciously given over her bedroom—the largest and, she assured him, the most comfortable—on the second floor. He knew there were dozens of other people staying over as well. He'd worried as Constance kept adding to the list, but Jillian didn't seem to care.

After finishing the obligatory photographs, the wedding party formed a receiving line in the piano room while the banquet hall was being converted from the setting of the ceremony back into a dining area. Their parents wanted to mingle, so Constance stood with Jillian and her two other bridesmaids, while Clive and the groomsmen stood with Nelson. Perhaps it wasn't the best location, considering Jillian's memories of that terrible night probably began there, but it was the natural choice for combining greeting their guests and serving cocktails. Nelson had seen to it that the piano was covered and moved to the rear wall, while Constance made sure to line them up facing away from it.

The line of well-wishers moved quickly. Most of their school chums were availing themselves of the liquor, knowing they'd be able to visit at some other point during the reception, so the wedding party was mainly seeing distant family members they hadn't been able to cull from the invitation list. Meeting the assorted cousins from Constance's family was all very nice, but Nelson was ready to be done with the larger activities and move on to the honeymoon sooner rather than later.

During a lull, he caught a glimpse of a strangely dressed woman making her way down the hall. She must have been leaving because a light-colored topcoat was now covering the old-fashioned flowered dress she wore. A clashing scarf covered her hair, and he saw her hesitate for just a second as she passed, her gaze fixing on the back of the room before skimming over their group, her large, tinted glasses covering much of her face.

Constance noted his scrutiny. "Was that your Aunt Helene? If so, she was sitting on the wrong side."

Nelson squinted. There was something familiar about the woman, but he wasn't sure what. "I thought Mother said Aunt Helene was too senile to come. But maybe she had someone bring her from the care home." As if aware of their attention, the woman scurried away. Nelson smiled at his bride. "Definitely not Aunt Helene. She hasn't moved that fast in sixty years."

Jillian's head turned at their conversation. "Do you mean the lady sitting in the last row? From the way she kept looking at me, I thought she was that odd cousin of yours, Constance. Jenelle? Jenette?"

"No, Jenna was sitting in the row behind the rest of the family."

"Seems you might have a wedding crasher," Clive said, sounding only mildly interested.

"Don't wedding crashers usually come for the food and drink? Odd she'd be leaving now," Nelson commented.

"You know, that scarf reminds me of—" Constance cut herself off, turning to Nelson with eyes wide, as if she'd sensed some folly in what she'd been about to say.

He tried to cover for her, beginning a conversation with Clive about the upcoming meal, but of course, Jillian caught the blunder. "Reminds you of what?" she asked.

Constance wasn't given to lying, but she shifted uncomfortably, clearly not wanting to bring up something unpleasant on today of all days. "Uh, the need to keep one's hair covered, like I did on the cruise."

"Oh." Jillian sounded almost disappointed, and for half a second, Nelson thought she'd gotten away with it. Then Jillian shifted, looking quickly into the hallway. "You kept *your* hair covered?" She'd had her hair done professionally for the wedding, but normally, Constance favored a fashionable mod bob that curled right below her chin.

"Well, actually…" Constance tried to stall, lowering her voice when Jillian tilted her head impatiently. "It was Zara who used to wear a scarf like that. See, she—"

Jillian had already left the line and was moving into the hallway. As she went through the front door, they heard her calling, "Madam! Excuse me, could I speak with you?"

Clive absolutely detested weddings. He'd gotten roped into being a groomsman for schoolmates on several occasions, and he found it a ridiculous waste of time coupled with mediocre food and second-rate alcohol. Beyond that, the frequency of divorce and the amount of infidelity that went on made it unlikely that any of his starry-eyed friends would feel the same amorous devotion in a year or two. In his opinion, love was merely a commodity imposed on gullible young people by jewelry stores and florists. And marriage was even worse, offered by the church as a way to sanction sex and supported by society as endorsement for cohabitation, possibly with some new kitchenware. It was all such a farce.

But looking at Constance and Nelson during the ceremony, he could almost believe they would be the exception. Perhaps because they'd known each other for so long, there couldn't be any surprise bad habits or other undesirable behaviors.

He and Jillian were practically in that same company, except for the secret he kept from her…from all of them, actually. When he'd been young and foolish, he'd nearly revealed the truth, believing his dearest friends would still accept him, no matter what. But something had made him hold his tongue, and eventually, he'd been convinced of their ultimate rejection after observing how Nelson always fell back on his bloody religion to resolve any doubts, and Constance was too concerned about propriety and her place in the social order to allow for a friend who didn't conform to the rules of polite society. Jillian was the only one he truly trusted, and he'd always planned to tell her someday, but now the complication the American woman presented might have changed his timetable.

After Constance had sworn him to secrecy, he'd finally gotten her to reveal what she knew about Zara, and it was worse than he'd feared. He'd originally assumed she had intrigued Jillian with her musical talent, but learning she was a lesbian who made no attempt to hide it struck him with both anxiety and dread. Anxiety because dear Jilly was innocent in many ways, and she would be totally unprepared for the kind of seduction someone like Zara would bring. He'd been an innocent himself once, and he knew how compelling someone else's attraction could be. Especially when that someone was different from anyone he'd ever known, and they'd been offering something he hadn't realized he'd wanted.

The dread was something else, something deeper. He'd always supposed Jillian to be one of those women who were simply not interested in the pleasures of the flesh. She was a person of incredible intellect and unrelenting determination, and Clive had speculated that those two traits had simply squeezed out anything else. Why else would she be satisfied with a boyfriend who made no physical demands other than holding her hand when they were alone together and kissing her sweetly when he arrived and again when he departed? The one time she'd attempted sexual contact, he'd been so surprised, he hadn't been prepared with a suitable fantasy that would allow him to manage, as he'd done with other women. Thankfully, she'd seemed almost as willing as he was to simply forget the whole thing. He'd assumed societal pressures or the expectations of her family responsibilities would someday focus her attention on getting married, and he'd always planned to be there for her when that happened.

Not only did Clive truly care for Jillian, he enjoyed her company more than any of his other female acquaintances. And until the horrible incident last fall, she had given every indication of having similar feelings for him. He'd never felt worse in his life than he had that night, and he'd made a vow to mind his alcohol consumption during these festivities as one way to prove to Jillian that he was a changed man. He'd always been confident that the friendships they had in common, along with their shared class values, would make their matrimonial relationship mutually acceptable, meaning Jillian would be free to work whenever and at whatever she pleased, while he would be likewise free to play at whatever he chose. She'd never given any indication of wanting children, but should it be necessary, he could oblige her.

Seeing her with Zara after their hike, he'd been struck by the impression that Jillian might have developed an interest in someone else, someone who'd awakened feelings in her that he didn't—or couldn't. The thought was not simply objectionable, it was unacceptable. Especially since his parents had recently made two things very clear. One, the type of "friends" he'd been bringing home since puberty were no longer welcome in their home, and two, his marriage to Jillian Stansfield was not only expected, it was absolutely necessary to save the family name.

Apparently, the senior Mr. Nyes's private business dealings had not gone well lately, and now they were bleeding away their savings as Mrs. Nyes had no concept of how to economize. Clive couldn't blame her for that, since the last thing anyone might have expected from a man like his father, who was supposed to be the paragon of monetary integrity, was that he was in trouble at work. Was or could be; Clive hadn't quite gotten the whole story during his father's drunken rambling, and none of this was something that could be brought up around the breakfast table. Clive supposed he must have inherited his father's expertise with monetary matters. He'd been able to pass all his classes with a minimum of effort, though he hated everything about banking, investments, and all the market terminology. But not having the Stansfield fortune at his disposal would mean he'd actually have to find work, and that would be as much of a farce as this whole marriage business. The only thing worse would be a repeat of the kind of shameful act he'd been compelled to implement during his last visit to Fullerhill. Clive Nyes, a common thief. God, no wonder he'd had so much to drink that night.

Watching Jillian rush almost frantically from the reception made his stomach roil. He didn't care if Constance was the bride, he was ready to pinch her little head off. How could she have been so stupid as to mention the crossing, or more specifically, Zara? He could tell she was sorry by her bereft expression, but still.

It might fall even more heavily on him to find a way to win Jillian away from the admittedly attractive American. Lord Stansfield had always looked favorably upon him. Perhaps that was an avenue he could explore.

Chapter Ten

Once outside the front entrance to Fullerhill, Zara tried to double her pace as she headed down the long driveway. She pulled her thin coat closer, wishing Constance had chosen some overly fluffy or constricting designs for her bridesmaid dresses so Jill wouldn't be able to follow her so quickly. She cursed herself for seeking to add to her disguise by wearing such ridiculous shoes as Jill's voice came again, sounding closer. "Please, I only need a moment. And don't be concerned. There's no problem."

She wobbled on the heels, recalling they'd all seen her do that the last time she'd been in this house. That must have been the giveaway. Jill called, "Zara, stop!" with a tone that sounded more like authority than anger.

Might as well give up, she thought, and she did, standing motionless where she was. Slightly breathless, Jill caught up to her as she was removing her scarf and tinted glasses. Zara turned, not meeting her eyes as she spoke. "How did you know it was me?"

"Actually, I didn't. But no one in the wedding party could identify you, and then Constance mentioned how you had worn a scarf on the ship, and I had to…I had to know."

Zara still couldn't quite bring herself to look, but she felt Jill take another step closer.

Apparently unsure about what to do next, Jill's voice took on a teasing tone. "That's rather a different look for you. I'm not sure florals are really your style. And I see you haven't spent any more time on heels lately."

Zara shuffled her feet and grinned, her head still down. "I believe we once talked about the need to protect ourselves by using camouflage. A disguise is no good if it's a look people expect. And I had to wear the scarf because you've seen me in a hat." She brought her gaze to Jill's headwear. "But yours is absolutely stunning."

Self-consciously, Jill touched the side of her head. "Technically, this is called a fascinator."

"I can see why." Her smile widened as Jill lowered her hand and bit her lip. The sudden shyness made her think of Jill's nervous manner when they'd sat close together in the ruins. But when Jill cleared her throat, Zara suspected she'd overstepped again. She was probably going to be asked to leave when what she wanted was to move closer and revive the heat she'd memorized from when they'd kissed.

Trying to preempt the likely request, she asked, "How have you been? Wearing your hair that length really suits you. You look…" When she finally looked into Jill's eyes, her heart felt like it was melting, along with all her reserve. "God, you look beautiful, Jill," she blurted. "I could barely force myself to look at Constance occasionally."

Seeing heat rise in Jill's cheeks at the compliment brought a swirl of pleasure. She had a thousand questions, but waiting for the answers would focus her attention on Jill's mouth, and that was dangerous. No, she needed to keep her wits about her, so after a few seconds with no response, she sighed. "Well, my bag's at the end of your drive. I'm going to dump this outfit before trying to catch a ride to the city."

Jill's voice came back in a rush. "Zara, where have you been? And why didn't you come as yourself? You were invited, and everyone would have been thrilled to see you."

In the long pause that followed, Zara swept her eyes over the house and the grounds around it. She wondered if her uncertainty showed when she chose to respond only to the last question. "I don't think that's true, Jill."

Jill's reply was cut off when someone called her name. Her head turned toward Fullerhill. "Oh, I must—"

"I know. Maid-of-honor duties. But listen, thanks for running me down. It was really great to see you again."

As she started to turn away, Jill reached for her hand. "No, I can't let you go until—" Automatically, Zara jerked away, and Jill seemed to realize what she'd done. "Oh my God, Zara. Did I hurt… Forgive me, I haven't even asked—"

"It's fine," Zara said tersely, curling the hand she'd injured into a fist and drawing it up to her abdomen.

"Are you…have you been able to play again?"

Zara thought she heard tears in Jill's voice. She shook her head, digging the nails of her good hand into her palm. "Not yet."

"Oh." The voice called once more. Jill glanced back before stepping closer again. Her arms lifted for a moment as if offering an embrace. Zara almost reacted to the movement, especially as it carried Jill's scent mixed with some delicious perfume. Fighting the urge to step into her touch and never leave, Zara told herself for the umpteenth time that it couldn't happen because Jill wasn't interested in her that way. Lady Stansfield's life had returned to its orderly arrangement, proceeding as it was meant to, and this, at best, was a gesture borne solely from guilt. Jill had probably forgotten all about their kisses, or if the memory remained, it was only an embarrassment.

Zara stood rooted to the spot until Jill's arms lowered, and her voice dropped to a near whisper. "You don't have to go. Come inside with me and have something to eat. Stay until all of this"—she waved vaguely—"is over, and we can have some time together. Alone."

The offer was so tempting that Zara couldn't hold back a sigh before glancing at the house again. "It's nice of you to ask, but I don't think—"

Jill's hand moved again but not close enough to touch her this time. "Please, Zara. I'm very glad to see you, and we need to talk. There are still things I need to understand."

"Things? Not the something?" She worked to keep her tone light, wondering if the set of her jaw was visible. Before Jill could reply, she asked, "Did you get my letters?"

"You wrote to me?" Jill's voice indicated her surprise.

Zara nodded, her question answered. "Three times."

"Was that to explain why you—" Another voice, maybe Nelson's, called again. Jill didn't even look this time. "You absolutely cannot leave until we finish this conversation." Her voice had the

resolute tone that made Zara's insides steam. Jill taking charge was…
compelling? Provocative? Sexy? "Go get your bag and change, if it
makes you more comfortable. But you're coming with me. It will be
a long afternoon, but by tonight, everyone else will be gone or drunk,
and we can talk. All right?"

Zara slowly unclenched her hand as their eyes met again. She
tried to consider all her options, but all she could see was that fierce
blue. Finally, she gave an awkward half curtsy, which must have
looked so silly in her ridiculous dress that Jill giggled. "As you wish,
Your Ladyship."

"Look who I found," Jill announced to the table as she pulled
Zara by her good hand. "Our perfect fifth."

That made Zara grin, even though she felt terribly self-conscious
about being dressed in the same black pants and white shirt they'd all
seen before, but at least she'd added the festive red wool blazer she'd
bought at the thrift store. Red was definitely her color, according to
the shopgirl, who claimed the outfit made her look quite natty. At
the time, she'd been saddened at the thought of her red dress that
had been ruined the night of the fire, since it was the last thing Mrs.
Minton had bought her. Unconsciously, she tightened her grip on Jill,
and the return squeeze reminded her to focus on this moment, Jill's
smile making her feel like she could take a deep breath for the first
time in months. She tried not to make too much of the fact that Jill had
been smiling ever since she had agreed to stay, telling herself Jill was
probably just happy to have gotten her way. But what Zara wanted,
and what had made her willing to walk into that house again, was the
same hope, the same dream that had sustained her through the pain
and adversity of the last months. She hadn't been able to let go of the
notion that what she'd seen in Jill's eyes was real. That the something
between them was real.

Nelson and Clive rose, and Jill added, "Clive, could you please
go see about getting another chair for Zara?"

His mouth hardened into a straight line, but he said, "Certainly,
my dear," and left.

Zara was glad to have a moment to adjust to his presence. The others were okay, but she'd as soon piss on him as look at him. "Let me add my congratulations to you both," she said, gesturing to the newlyweds. "I wish you every happiness."

They thanked her, but their reactions felt more than a little muted. Constance turned to Jill, her voice somewhat frosty. "We've had to move our first dance until after the salad, since you weren't here."

That undoubtedly explained their attitude. Jill didn't seem fazed at all. "I'm sorry, dear. But thank you for waiting. I'm so looking forward to it."

"Me too," Zara chimed in.

Constance huffed a bit, and Nelson's smile looked pained. Jill raised an eyebrow but was distracted when Clive returned with two of the caterers, who were carrying a chair and an extra place setting. After she directed them to take Zara's bag to the kitchen, everyone shifted to make room. Zara was grateful beyond words when Jill put herself between her and Clive. She could scarcely believe the bastard was here, but his longtime friendship with this group was obviously more important to them than the damage he'd done to her, an outsider. Even the idea that Jill might have been severely injured seemed to have been glossed over. Unable to help herself, she glared at him behind Jill's back, and his eyes simmered with something threatening in return. Good. At least there wouldn't be any pretense of cordiality between them. But she'd have to watch him, knowing she could have defended herself with two hands but uncertain how she'd do with only one.

The mood was a bit strained as they ate their salads. Zara found it strange when no one asked her anything about her injury or her recovery. From the way Jill kept looking at her, she guessed she would have peppered her with dozens of questions if they'd been alone. Likely, she didn't want to distract from Constance and Nelson's special day.

When the music started up, Lord Stansfield rose from the table where the parents were seated to announce, "Mr. and Mrs. Nelson Garrick."

At the sound of his voice, Zara flinched. She didn't think he'd noticed her yet, and she would just as soon go through the evening without any confrontation with him. She was ninety-nine percent sure he'd intercepted her letters to Jill, but she couldn't prove it. And now, on his home ground with all his friends around him, he had too much advantage over any accusation she might make. She was leaning back, trying to put more distance between them, when she felt a hand on her leg.

"Don't worry about anyone else," Jill whispered, apparently aware of her anxiety. "Just know that I'm really glad you're here."

The contact made Zara's breath catch, and she brushed her fingers lightly over Jill's. In that moment, she couldn't have named the song the newlyweds were dancing to, though she knew exactly how to play it. She was totally immersed in Jill's touch, in the nearness of her presence. She'd thought of her so many times but with the increasing certainty they'd never see each other again.

At the clinic, Zara had developed a genuine friendship with her new roommate. But after observing the pace of Andrea's therapy, she'd also became convinced that Lord Stansfield had made some arrangement with her doctor. Had Zara improved enough to return to London for an audition, she and Jillian could have met up again, and he obviously hadn't wanted that. She suspected her doctor had slowed her treatment—not enough to cause permanent harm but enough that her healing wasn't close to finished yet. Andrea had been able to discover that Lord Stansfield had paid the facility in advance through the end of the year, and that a partial refund would be given for unused services. Knowing that, Zara had become impatient to leave, but Andrea had convinced her to wait. She'd said that if they acted like there was something more between them, it would explain them leaving together once Andrea's new prothesis was ready. At the time, Zara supposed it wasn't much sacrifice to her integrity to include enough PDA to be convincing to those ever-watching eyes. After all, Jill hadn't written her back, which meant the something was clearly over. And the reimbursement was enough to get her to London, even after giving Andrea a cut when they went their separate ways.

Once in the UK, Zara had pinched every penny—or pence—but she knew how to manage poverty. She'd been planning to get on the next crossing to America—bussing tables or working in housekeeping this time—but the cruise line had already repositioned the ships for their winter destinations. It took some doing, but she was finally able to access her small savings from the bank in America. After finding a cheap efficiency apartment near the train station, she'd begun looking for work tending bar. Having exhausted every place within walking distance, she was riding the bus one day when she'd seen an ad for the music service she'd signed on with the first time she'd been in London. It was one more painful reminder of what wasn't going to happen, and she'd called to take her name off their list, holding back tears as she dialed the number.

To her surprise, the woman who'd answered reported they'd been trying to reach her, as she was booked to be part of a quartet for the Holston-Garrick reception, which was to be held at Fullerhill Manor. Stunned, Zara had asked the date and then said she wasn't available. After hanging up, she'd made a plan to see Jill from a distance one more time, thinking that would be enough to convince herself that the "something" they'd spoken of was just foolishness.

She'd been wrong. The feelings she had for Jillian had not gone away, and despite her protests when Jill chased her down on the driveway, she was going to do whatever Jill asked of her.

The newlyweds finished their dance to much applause and returned to the table. After the meal, Clive gave his best-man speech, full of jokes and off-color comments, as expected. He ended by heading toward the bar—again—to much laughter as everyone saluted him with champagne. Jill's more serious salute to love and commitment was also as expected, and she sat to more applause and more toasting.

When Constance's father rose to speak, Zara tilted her head, murmuring, "Why, Your Ladyship, I hadn't realized you were such a romantic."

It might have been the champagne's influence, but Jill's eyes sparkled as she replied, "Perhaps we hadn't gotten to that part yet."

Zara searched Jill's face, feeling the same powerful sensation as when they'd first met. Her insides still trembled, but now an additional surge of heat settled between her legs. Unable to hold back, Zara leaned in to whisper, "Then, let me tell you that you were on my mind every single day. Thinking about kissing you again got me through some of my darkest hours."

For a second, she thought everyone in the room was applauding her confession, but then she saw Constance and Nelson kissing and realized she'd missed the acknowledgements from the bride and groom.

What had she been thinking, speaking her innermost thoughts at such an inopportune time? "I'm sorry. I'm distracting you from your friends. I should go." Zara put her napkin on the table and started to stand as someone else began speaking.

Jill gently touched the top of her injured hand. "For the past three months, it's been incredibly difficult to focus on anything—school, my projects, this wedding—because I've been worried about you. Seeing you today, having you here, I can't begin to tell you... Zara, I...all I know is, if you try to leave now, I might make a scene. You know I love these two people, and I'm especially delighted for them, but I'm also ready for this to be over so we can be alone. I promise, it won't be much longer."

Zara blinked. "You would make a scene?"

"Indeed."

"Over me?"

"Mmm."

Jill had gotten quieter now that the diversion of the speeches had ended, and Zara suspected she was concerned their conversation would draw unwanted attention from the rest of the party, especially given the flush of emotion on her face. Maybe they would think it was about the excitement of the wedding. But when Constance shot her a quick frown as she and Nelson went to cut their cake, she wondered if they might have been overheard. But Jill's promise of alone time meant she definitely wasn't going anywhere.

Returning the napkin to her lap, she grinned. "Much as I'd like to see that..."

Jill pinched her leg under the table, and she suppressed a laugh by brushing a hand over her mouth. She pretended to slide away... but didn't.

Watching Constance and Nelson laughing together before feeding each other cake, Zara asked, "Is this what you want for your wedding?" Wanting to be heard over the general racket of anticipation, she'd spoken more loudly than before, and Clive must have overheard as he was returning from the bar.

Jill was already shaking her head, and he seemed to take it the wrong way. Sitting a bit closer, he took her hand and raised it to his lips. "Ours will be much grander, won't it, Jilly? We'll put the royals to shame, eh?"

Jill moved to retrieve her hand, but his grasp held as he leaned to look at Zara as if daring her to say something. Possibly feeling the tension between them, Jill shook her head slightly at Zara, obviously trying to discourage her response. But she replied anyway.

"Well, you've known Lady Stansfield much longer than I have—"

"Bloody well right, I have," Clive interrupted. "We're all but promised, and you're nothing but an evening's entertainment."

"Clive," Jill admonished, but Zara went on, unperturbed.

"Then as such, I would make this observation." Her eyes moved to Jill's and held them. "They're outside on a warm spring day, with only a small gathering of close friends and family. She walks in to the sounds of brook and birds and a slight breeze ruffling the tiny green leaves. There's poetry and readings from their favorite authors. They've written their own vows, and when it's over, everyone settles onto blankets laid out on the ground, and they have a wonderful picnic together. Children run barefoot through the grass, and a small circle of musicians, guitar players and those with handheld percussion play familiar songs, inviting everyone to sing. Some do, and some nap. After dark, there's a bonfire and dancing and howling at the moon. They depart at the stroke of midnight, enjoying an early breakfast at an all-night diner before catching the first flight out the next morning." She gave a low chuckle. "Destination, someplace beautiful and private and a well-kept secret from everyone else."

Clive, seemingly stunned into silence, released Jill's hand as he drained the rest of his drink.

Blinking at Zara, Jill murmured, "And you say I'm a romantic?"

"We definitely hadn't gotten to that part yet," she replied softly, pleased when she heard Jill take a breath.

Snorting with disgust as he put down his glass, Clive's tone was heavy with contempt. "Lady Stansfield would never be satisfied with such a hippie wedding."

"Are you really certain you know what would satisfy her?" Zara asked, staring at him with heat in her gaze, even as she kept her tone cool.

"How dare you?" When Clive began to stand, Jill put a hand on his arm.

"Please, let's remember where we are and why we are here." She brushed her other hand quickly over Zara's leg. "I know neither of you wants to spoil Constance and Nelson's special day."

Nothing was said for several long seconds. Then Clive gripped his empty glass. "I need another drink. Can I get you anything, Jilly darling?"

Jill shook her head. Zara's glass was empty, but she was fine with him not asking her. "I'm sorry," she began once Clive was gone, but Jill merely shook her head again. They watched as Constance and Nelson met up with Clive as they were returning to the table, and after a brief moment of conversation, Nelson went with him into the hallway.

Constance sat back at the table, her expression dour. Zara could only imagine what had been said, but that look made her certain that anything she'd offer in response would be dismissed.

Jill gestured in the direction of the hallway. "Keep that man happy, Constance. He is a gem."

"I intend to," Constance said, scrutinizing Zara until her gaze lifted abruptly, and she beamed. "Lord Stansfield, I can't thank you enough for your gracious hospitality. Today has been everything I ever dreamed of, and more."

Zara's every instinct told her to make some excuse and get away. Instead, she followed Jill, rising to greet the figure behind her as she fisted her damaged hand against her stomach.

Lord Stansfield inclined his head toward Constance. "It's been my pleasure, my dear." When he turned toward Jillian, his expression was unreadable. "I see we have an unexpected guest joining us this evening."

"Father, this is Zara Keller. She was the one who…" Jill hesitated as if not wanting to relive the memory. "Her actions helped with my recovery."

"Yes, I recall you mentioning her." There was a slight twitch around his mouth when he looked at Zara. "How is your injury, Miss Keller?"

Under the circumstances, this innocent act was not exactly what she'd expected from him, but she could play along. "Not quite what I'd hoped it would be at this point, but I'm still working on it. Sir." She knew there was odd stiffness in her reply, especially the last word, which sounded like the forced afterthought it was.

"So you'll be returning to America soon, I take it?"

It was clearly an encouragement to do so, and Jill frowned, speaking before Zara could answer. "Actually, I'm hoping she'll stay for the last few days of my holiday. We have a lot to catch up on, and I need a new pair of eyes on my project."

"Jillian..." Constance began, pausing to gesture for Nelson, who was returning to the table alone after a brief word with one of the groomsmen. With Jill distracted, Zara looked back at Lord Stansfield, seeing the animosity and antagonism she'd missed the first time. He was shaking his head slightly, but his message was clear. It wouldn't be wise for her to stick around.

But before she could comment, a groomsman stood and yelled, "Confetti time!"

Nelson pulled Constance into his arms and swung her around. "That's our cue, Mrs. Garrick. It's time to start on our honeymoon."

Constance was giggling like a little girl as Nelson put her down, and Jill moved to kiss them both. While they indulged in a group hug, Lord Stansfield slid something onto the table next to Zara's plate. "That's a very rare, five-hundred-pound white note," he muttered. "Take it and go."

Zara retrieved the bill and handed it back. "No deal," she said, the recklessness of the gesture giving her a surge of adrenaline. "This time, I'm staying until Jill kicks me out."

She glanced over to see the woman in question smiling tearfully at her friends. "I'm so happy for you both," she heard Jill say.

Zara was prepared for more conflict, but Lord Stansfield turned and walked toward the group. She watched as he slipped the five-hundred-pound note into Nelson's hand, clapping him warmly on the back and giving Constance a brief hug before moving away. All of them were in high spirits, and Zara wondered, not for the first time, what exactly it was he had against her? Her poverty? Her uncertain heritage? Her sexuality? Then she saw Jill watching her, and when their eyes met, Zara joined in the smiles. Just that quickly, none of it mattered.

Constance touched Jill's arm, and it might have been intentional when her voice carried to where Zara stood. "Jilly, darling, please be careful,"

Zara braced for Jill's response, but she merely said, "Yes, I know. You already told me."

Nelson's voice wasn't as strident, but his words seemed almost worse. "Not everything."

Zara wondered what he meant. Jill's face shone as she watched her father make his way along the edge of the room, smiling warmly as he encouraged people at each table to join the queue saying good-bye to the newlyweds. She'd have to tell Jill about Switzerland, or Lord Stansfield would make up something to drive them apart.

She nearly laughed at herself. Why was she worried about that when there wasn't even a together for them? A sudden tide of people moving toward the stairway pushed her along. Losing sight of Jill, she turned away from the throng, making her way to the only place she'd ever belonged in this house. She heard cheers and looked down the hallway, catching a glimpse of the happy couple on their way upstairs, running the gauntlet of well-wishers calling farewell, waving handkerchiefs, and tossing confetti.

She stepped into the room and found the piano against the far wall, still covered. She longed to hear its sweet, rich tones but was unwilling to touch it without two functioning hands. She felt an ache of longing as she wondered if "Spring" would be the last thing she ever played. Her fingers moved instinctively through the opening chords until her left hand twinged when she tried for an octave reach.

After that, she sat on the bench—facing away from the covered keys—hearing the fading sounds of revelry. Most of the guests had probably gone back into the dining hall, and with Nelson occupied, she wondered who would take charge of getting everyone settled for the night. After a moment, two voices came closer: Jillian and Clive.

"Come, Jilly, you know we're meant to be together. We can make our announcement tomorrow after the newlyweds have gone."

Zara wasn't surprised he was making a move now. With the emotion of the wedding, the presence of their friends, good food and liquor, plus a dash of competition, he had to be motivated. She stood but didn't move toward the door, uncertain whether her presence would make things better or worse.

"This is not the time to have this conversation, Clive." He must have protested because she added, "You know I value our friendship, and if you feel the same, you'll honor my wish."

Her voice had more than firmness to it. She sounded unyielding to the point that even Clive apparently knew there was no use in arguing. "When you're ready, I'll be here," he murmured, adding something Zara didn't catch.

"Yes. Good night, Clive."

Zara thought she heard the sound of a wet kiss. Then nothing. After a few more seconds, she took a step toward the doorway. When Jill appeared, neither of them spoke for a few seconds.

Jill moved to stand near her, looking at the piano. "No one has played since you," she said softly, lifting the cover to reveal the Blüthner name on the shining black wood. "Would you like to—"

"No." Zara cut her off as she turned toward the doorway. "I can't. I was just…"

Jill seemed to know she couldn't finish, so she took her good hand again, and they walked toward the stairs. "If you're not too tired, we could visit the lab for a bit, but I'd rather not wear this." She gestured at her bridesmaid's dress. "If you don't mind, I'd like to change clothes first."

Zara grinned. "Do I get to watch?"

Jill slapped playfully at her shoulder. "No, but you can talk to me while I change in the washroom. I want to know what was going on between you and my father."

Zara stopped, trying to keep her expression neutral. "I'll tell you later, but right now, I just want to talk about you."

Jill looked around, waving in the direction of the guests who still lingered. "I can't remember a time when the house has been this crowded," she murmured. "I wish all these people would go away. Or at least go to bed."

"If you need to continue your hostess or maid-of-honor duties," Zara started, but Jill cut her off.

"I'm quite done with this wedding business, and I'm tired of making nice with people with whom I'm barely acquainted. The caterers are staying till midnight, and they can take care of anything that might be needed."

They made their way up the stairs, and Jill took a few minutes to run the pranksters away from the door where Nelson and Constance were staying. It was her room, she reminded Zara, who followed her to the far end of the hallway, passing the room where she had stayed before. Jill opened the door to a smaller bedroom. Other than the full-size bed, there was only one upholstered chair and an end table, along with several bookcases and a small desk. "At least there's a private bath," Jill assured her. "And that's where I'm going."

"And I'll be snooping around out here," Zara answered.

Jill's smile was brief. "This was the room my mother used as an office," she said. "Don't dig too deep, or I can't be responsible for what you might find."

"Fair enough."

Zara hadn't intended to meddle, but the bookcase displayed several pictures of Jillian's childhood, and they were irresistible. Several included an attractive woman who Zara assumed to be Jill's mother. She picked one up, and a photograph hidden on the back side of the frame fell out. This one showed both parents and Jill, along with a boy who looked a few years older. There was no family resemblance, but he stood in the middle, the arms of Jill's smiling parents around him. Jill stood off to the side, her expression showing the same remote detachment Zara had seen a few times during her interactions with those she didn't know well or didn't particularly like. She wondered which was the case here.

"Where did you get that?"

Jill's voice was so sharp, Zara jumped, almost dropping the photo. "Uh, sorry. It fell out from behind there." She pointed to the shelf and turned, intending to make a joke about being nosy, but Jill was pale, and her jaw clenched. Shock or anger? It was hard to tell. "Did you want…" She held the photo out, but Jill turned away. Returning the photo to its hiding place, Zara said, "I apologize. I didn't mean to—"

"I shouldn't be surprised she had his picture in here." It was like Jill was talking to herself, but the despondent tone made Zara want to reach for her. She waited, not sure if such an act would be welcome. Jill turned back, unmistakable pain in her eyes. "Remember when you said I'd never done a bad thing in my life? Well, that's your evidence to the contrary."

Zara thought again about the image, trying to understand. Jill's parents seemed happy, but she didn't. "Who is that boy?" she asked gently.

"He was to be my brother." Jill walked to the chair, sitting as if the weight of those words was too much to carry.

"You don't have to tell me, Jill. I'm here to be with you. But if you want to talk about it—"

"You deserve to know," Jill interrupted. "You were willing to tell me your story, so…" Zara lowered herself to the floor as Jill took a breath, endeavoring to relax her shoulders. She fixed her gaze on the bookshelf. "My mother couldn't have more children after me, but she'd always wanted a boy. My father tried to tell me that girls and boys had different places in their parents' hearts, but I knew I simply wasn't enough for her. When I was almost ten, they began interviewing dozens of boys at two orphanages in London. After several weeks, they brought me to meet the one they'd settled on. Gregory. He was thirteen. I couldn't explain it at the time, but there was something about him I didn't like. He came across as too good to be true, using perfect manners, saying all the right things, quite deferential."

Zara nodded, not certain if Jill saw or not.

"Since I hadn't expressed any concerns, he came home with us. I'd never seen my mother so happy. She doted on him, showering him with presents and affection. I already had more than I'd ever need in terms of material things, so I wasn't envious, and for Gregory, it was paradise. As for the attention, I told myself it was just that he was new, and my turn would come around again."

Jill swallowed, and her eyes closed briefly. Zara sensed she was preparing herself for the hard part, so she scooted closer, wanting to be able to touch her.

"Not having had a sibling before, I wanted to spend time with him, despite my earlier misgivings. If either or both of my parents were around, it was fine. But if we were alone, he…it was a playful pinch or a tug on my hair at first, then an extra hard squeeze when he hugged me good night. I thought perhaps he didn't like me or saw me as competition for affection. But after he'd been here about three months, the facade began to slip. It seemed he…he liked causing pain."

"Oh, Jill," Zara said, her voice heavy with sympathy.

"He began smoking cigarettes. Likely, he had the habit before but had hidden it. My mother fussed in an ineffectual way, and they agreed he would only smoke outside, so he spent a lot of time on the terrace. One day, I saw him throwing rocks at the birds gathered around our feeders. It upset me since I loved hearing their songs and watching them hopping about. I told my father, and he said it was a boy thing, that he'd probably done the same at that age. A few days later, I saw Gregory carrying a box into the woods. I followed him. He made it into a kind of trap and caught one of the gray squirrels." Jill's face reflected her distress, and she shuddered. "I don't know where he got the knife, but I'd never heard anything like the sounds…"

When Zara put a hand gently on Jill's knee, she jumped. "Sorry," Zara said, putting her hand back in her lap. "I want you to know I'm here, and I'm listening."

Jill nodded, looking at her for the first time since she'd started talking. "And I should tell you that, besides my father, no one else knows this story. My friends were barely aware we were bringing someone else into the household, and after the fact, they were told it just didn't work out." She blinked a few times, adding, "I couldn't bring myself to talk about it. Even now, I'd give anything for it to never have happened."

"Tell me as much or as little as you want. But nothing you say will leave this room. You have my word."

Jillian took a deep breath. "Gregory had endeared himself to the household staff, and he was next to perfect in my mother's perception. I needed proof for my parents to believe he would do such terrible things. I brought my camera the next time he went into the woods. He caught another squirrel and wrung its neck. I took a couple of shots from behind to keep myself hidden, so they showed almost nothing. I suppose he must have heard the shutter click, though I didn't realize it at the time. He left the trap out and returned to the house.

"That evening, he came into my room after I was already in bed, something he had never done before. With every step he took toward me, I became more and more afraid. When I protested, he took a pencil from my desk and stabbed it through his own hand, right at the webbing between the thumb and first finger. I started to scream, and he put the other hand over my mouth, threatening that he'd tell my parents I had done it to him because I was jealous. He also told me he knew how to hurt people in ways that didn't leave any marks, and if I followed him again, he would show me that as well." Her eyes met Zara's. "I was terrified but also outraged by the thought that he'd simply continue his activities, and I was incapable of stopping him on my own. I hated that powerless feeling more than anything."

"I can imagine."

Jill's expression softened. "I'm sure you can." She drew herself up. "Anyway, after days of trying, I finally got my father to come with me. I was telling him about the wattle and daub house I wanted to build." Zara warmed at the memory but kept her focus on Jill. "At the time, he was possibly humoring me, but I led him to the area where Gregory had his traps. By then, he had several and a space where he... where he used his knife on the poor creatures. There were remains and dried blood. It was a ghastly scene, and my father was horrified. I cried as I told him the whole story."

Zara nodded again, even as she felt herself wilt inside. Obviously, Lord Stansfield was a hero in Jill's eyes. How would she react to Zara's description of her unsuccessful rehab being arranged by the same man? Could Zara tell her how the letters Jill had never seen were most likely diverted by her father after he'd secretly arranged a great deal of distance between her and his daughter? Would she believe he had offered Zara money this very evening as an inducement to leave?

"There was a terrible row. At first, Gregory denied it all. He kept insisting I was inventing this story because I was resentful and overly possessive of my parents, especially my mother. She kept asking me if I was sure, but luckily, my father had seen enough that he believed me."

Jill's voice began to waver, and Zara touched her knee again. This time, Jill put her hand out, and their fingers entwined. Too late, Zara realized she'd used her injured hand. Jill's thumb slid across her palm, seemingly unmindful of the damage. Zara would have pulled away, but she didn't want Jill to feel disconnected from her. When Jill began to speak again, Zara forced herself to focus on her words.

"When Gregory saw it was two against one, he changed his story. He claimed that he wanted to be a doctor, which meant he needed to understand anatomy. He contended that because his schooling had been so poor, he needed to catch up by doing his own experiments. I'm sure he thought this was a way to keep himself in my mother's good graces, but it had the opposite effect. His tacit admission of guilt damaged their relationship beyond repair because everything he'd ever said or done was now suspect. My father accompanied him to pack his things, but at some point, Gregory had time to write me a note, swearing he would get even with me. He said I'd never see it coming, but he'd make me very sorry one day."

"Did you show it to your parents? Shouldn't you have a bodyguard or something?" Zara wanted to pace, but it was more important to keep hold of Jill's hand. Surprisingly, her gentle touch wasn't hurting at all.

"My mother was distraught, and I didn't want to add to her misery. I think my father blamed himself for not seeing who Gregory was. So, no, I didn't show them the note at first. And then…then I didn't need to." Zara heard the tears in Jill's voice before she saw them in her eyes. "About ten days later, we got a call from the orphanage. Gregory…there was a fight…another boy was seriously injured, and Gregory was killed."

Zara stood, bringing Jill with her. They still held hands, but Jill stood stiffly, staring at the pictures on the bookshelf. "You know that wasn't your fault, don't you?" Zara said softly.

Jill turned to her abruptly. "Wasn't it? If I'd minded my own business…if I hadn't said anything…maybe he would have—"

"Jill, you must know that neither of those choices would have made things turn out all right. If Gregory was alive today, do you think he'd be a better person? I don't know a lot about psychology, but I'm pretty sure that kind of behavior only gets worse."

"Even if that's true, losing him broke my mother's heart. She died less than six months later." The tears spilled over, running down her cheeks.

"Oh, babe," Zara said, pulling Jill into her arms. Within seconds, Jill began to sob, burying her face in Zara's neck. "Don't blame yourself for that either," she murmured, stroking Jill's hair. "In fact, you were protecting her as much as you were protecting yourself. He's the one who hurt her, not you."

"Why doesn't it feel that way?"

At Jill's shudder, Zara pulled her closer. "Because you're a good person. You hurt because a bad thing happened to both of you. To all of you. And because she's gone."

"I didn't…I don't…."

Jill began to sag in her arms, her words turning into hiccupping sounds. Zara walked them backward to the bed. "Here," she said, turning so Jill's back was to the mattress. "It's all right. You've had a long day. You'll feel better after you get some rest." Keeping one arm around her, she pulled the covers down, grateful that Jill had already changed into her sleepwear, cute pajamas that she'd barely had time to notice.

"Promise me you're not leaving," Jill murmured, her arm still around Zara's back. "I couldn't bear it if you disappeared again."

"I'm not going anywhere." She slipped out from under Jill's arm and eased her down, pulling the covers over her. When a frown crossed Jill's lovely face, Zara assured her, "I'll be here when you wake up." She tossed her blazer on the chair and slipped out of her trousers and shirt, surprised to find Jill watching when she looked over. She'd never been shy about her body, but something in Jill's inscrutable expression made her tug at her undershirt as she slipped her bra out from under it. "I didn't plan to stay over, but it won't be the first time this has been my sleepwear."

When Jill didn't answer, Zara lifted an extra blanket from the foot of the bed and wrapped herself in it. "I'll be curled up there on the floor like your faithful dog."

Jill raised onto her elbow. "No, you mustn't. This room always gets terribly cold once they turn the heat off downstairs. I thought you might want to—" She trailed off, her eyes welling with tears again.

"Oh, I see," she said, and turned away, hiding her face in the pillow. "Never mind."

"Hey." Zara moved back to the bed. "You thought I might what? What's wrong, Jill?" She could see Jill's body shaking and put a hand softly on her shoulder. "Talk to me, please."

"After the way you kissed me before, and then you said—" Jill's voice choked into the pillow, and Zara lost the end of the sentence. "But you must think I'm truly a terrible person. You don't even want to—"

Zara rushed to the other side of the bed and climbed in, sliding under the covers but making sure their bodies didn't touch. "You're wrong. I'm sure you don't hear that often, but this time, you're dead wrong." She carefully brushed the hair from Jill's face. "I've never for one moment thought you were a terrible person. Not the first time we met and not now. And there's nothing I want more than to be close to you. I'm sorry if I made you feel otherwise. It's just that…I couldn't simply assume you felt the same."

Jill raised her head, blinking as she cleared her vision. "Will you let me see your hand?" she asked, her voice tight.

It was about the last thing she wanted to do, but Zara understood Jill's unusually emotional state. She was accustomed to showing a composed Lady Stansfield to the world, but having shared her deepest pain, she now needed Zara to do the same. When she held it out, Jill sat up, looking intently at the taut, shiny skin covering most of her palm and the red peeling skin around three of the fingers. "Does it hurt?" she whispered.

"Not all the time."

"Are you still recovering?"

Zara swallowed as she considered the question for a few seconds. "I hope so."

Jill looked at her, eyes full of tears again. She bent forward and softly kissed the injured area. "I'm terribly, terribly sorry, Zara. God, every time I think about that night, I wish—"

As her voice dissolved with grief, Zara lay back and pulled her close, settling Jill's head on her shoulder. "Stop right there. Spending your time wishing to change something in the past is a prison. No one knows that better than I do. At this moment, I have everything I could ever wish for, except if you could possibly feel the same. For now, that's all that matters." She pressed a soft kiss against Jill's forehead. Jill relaxed into her, quiet for a moment. "I never expected that this…having you hold me…would feel so nice."

"It feels nice to me too." Zara worked to quiet her racing pulse. You're only comforting her, she told herself. She needs to sleep.

"Will you talk to me some more?" Jill asked softly. "Just the sound of your voice makes me feel better."

Zara smiled into Jill's hair. She began talking about a night early in her time playing at the Copper Cat, when a customer had brought her a list of five songs he'd wanted her to play. "I'll signal you for each one, okay?" he'd asked, and she'd agreed.

After sitting alone, nervously looking around and drumming his fingers on the table, he was joined by a pretty woman. By the time they got to song three, it was obvious the customer was going to propose, and the list was music with special memories for them.

"When she said yes," Zara said, "he tipped me a hundred bucks." Jill made a little sound and briefly squeezed Zara's waist where her arm rested. "It was the most money I'd ever made at one time. But I'd pay way more than that to be here with you, like this."

There was no reply, other than Jill's deep, steady breathing, and Zara was perfectly satisfied with that.

Chapter Eleven

A lovely warmth made Jill sigh as she stirred. She'd never been so comfortable in this room before, even when using an extra blanket. It was still dark, and her deep sleep had been interrupted by an awareness of something uncommon, apart from the temperature. It was obvious she wasn't on her usual pillow, and then she remembered Zara was with her, and she'd been resting her head on Zara's shoulder before falling asleep. Now her arm was stretched across Zara's body as well. She came fully awake upon realizing the uncommon sensation was coming from the weight of Zara's breast right above her hand. Normally, she would be terribly self-conscious being this close to anyone, let alone in such a personal position, but she couldn't bring herself to move. Apparently, nothing about her experience with Zara was normal. And thus far, she'd been unable to explain it, even to herself.

For as long as she could remember, she'd had a need to understand things, to figure out the why and how. Now, willing herself to think, she breathed in deeply, catching Zara's spicy, musky scent. As she did so, her hand contracted slightly around Zara's breast. She froze, her only thoughts wavering between being mortified at what she'd done and a strange compulsion to do it again.

Zara's breasts were larger than hers, fuller, attractively so. Many times during the past months, when she should have been studying or working out the design of her project, her memory had unhelpfully supplied images of Zara's chest filling out her father's sweater or the way her hips moved in that red dress and always the way her arms and shoulders flexed as she played. Earlier tonight, when Zara had stripped down to her clinging undergarments, Jill had been unable to look away from the shapely line of her hips, and the vision of dark nipples behind the thin material of her undershirt had made her pulse race. *Lush* was the word that had come into her mind, a term she'd previously ascribed strictly to vegetation. She'd never thought of another woman, or another person, for that matter, in such physical terms. But it wasn't only that.

After Zara had disappeared, Jill's world had become very silent—except for the piano music in her dreams—and very cold unless she let thoughts of their kisses warm her. She'd been desperate to see her again, and she'd told herself at first it was to thank her for what she'd done. She owed Zara so much, but she'd finally admitted that wanting to spend time with her again was also to explore whatever was between them.

When her father had finally uncovered Zara's whereabouts and had convinced her Zara was safe and recovering, she'd worked to ignore the rejection she'd felt, striving to fill the emptiness with Constance and Nelson's happiness. At their earnest request, she'd agreed to patch things up with Clive, acknowledging that her anger at his carelessness had been dulled by Zara's continued absence, as had most of her other emotions. But all her indifference had vanished as she'd chased the woman in the floral dress down the driveway, her heart beating as if it had suddenly remembered how. And the same something that had started with their first meeting had flooded her again when Zara had met her eyes and smiled. And when she'd followed her into the house, Jill had felt lighter than she had in months. Their brief touch under the table had made her feel more intoxicated than liquor ever had.

Did that explain why she hadn't removed her hand now, and how her fingers seemed to act of their own accord, carefully exploring where Zara's breast curved? When Zara's breathing changed, and she muttered something Jill couldn't quite make out, her logical mind told her it would be a simple matter to turn over now, to curl herself away from Zara's body. If sleep didn't come, as she suspected it wouldn't, she could spend the time thinking about new ways to design her water project or work out a study schedule for her finals, the type of things that used to occupy her before she'd been overtaken by this strong sense of affinity and almost instant attachment to this woman that lodged more deeply than any friendship she'd known.

She tried to recall if this was the way of it in those romance books Constance had loaned her. Or had her sudden, open boldness merely been an imitation of Zara's? Was that why she'd allowed Zara to kiss her that day in the rain? And why she'd been overtaken by the fierce hunger to kiss her back?

Thinking of those kisses gave her a tingling sensation, and when Zara's head turned toward her, she had to hold herself back from moving in to do it again.

"Hi," Zara said softly. "Don't let me interrupt you."

"Oh, I—"

"And please don't say you're sorry." Zara kissed her softly, and Jill felt her insides stretch, as if everything in her wanted to move closer. "Nothing else has to happen. You're in charge. But just know that being touched by you"—taking Jill's hand, she put it under her shirt at the curve of her waist—"is the stuff of my most wonderful dreams."

Jill gasped at the feel of warm, firm skin, but Zara pressed against her hand, stilling any further exploration, adding, "But if it's not the stuff of yours, then stop now. Please."

She might be in charge, but Jill felt like she balanced on a precipice, afraid of falling but unwilling to turn back. "I haven't…I never…" Why was she unable to complete a sentence?

"I know." Zara stroked her cheek, and the tenderness of it made Jill shiver.

"But what if I do something wrong?" She swallowed, moving up Zara's body ever so slowly as she spoke. Her throat was dry at the exquisite sensation of Zara's muscles quivering lightly at her touch.

"I think the odds of that are very slim. But if you do, I'll let you know." Zara cleared her throat. "That's how it works, you know? You tell me what you like, and I tell you what I like. We take care of each other."

Something inside Jill eased. She'd never thought of physical intimacy in those terms. It had always been presented as something people did *to* each other, not *for* each other. She'd wanted to care for Zara after the fire. Could she now care for her in this way? She reached for Zara's breast again. Her skin felt incredible, supple and delicate and welcoming. Zara made a choked sound, and Jill stopped. "Wrong?"

"Nuh-uh," Zara grunted. "Right. Exactly right."

Emboldened, Jill ran her palm over the hard nipple. When Zara's body tightened, Jill didn't have to ask. She kissed Zara's neck, thinking of chocolate and the rain when she licked at the light tang of sweat. "You taste so good," she whispered, her mouth close to Zara's ear.

"You're making me feel good," Zara whispered back.

The words created a craving, and Jill used her other hand to lift Zara's shirt higher. She'd only intended to give herself better access, but when Zara pulled the shirt over her head and threw it on the floor, the recklessness of the gesture fired something inside her. Almost feverish with want, she straddled Zara's waist, taking both breasts in her hands, kneading them. The pulse between her legs matched the movement of her fingers, and she felt herself rocking against Zara's body. Her eyes closed, and she was ready to give herself completely to the sensation when Zara moaned.

"Oh God, Jill. Please let me touch you."

She hadn't realized that Zara was clutching the sheet as if trying desperately to keep her hands to herself. The excitement waned as anxiety flooded her. She'd been confident, being in charge. Would it feel different to give up that lead? "What…what do you want to do?"

"I want to make you feel as good as you're making me feel." Before Jill knew what was happening, Zara had reversed their positions. She was on her back, with Zara's face inches above hers. "Let me?" She felt Zara's hand touching the top button of her pajama shirt. But she was waiting.

"I don't know," Jill said slowly. "The last time someone touched me there, I didn't like it."

Zara's teeth pulled at her lip. Jill hoped she wasn't angry about being refused. After a moment, Zara said, "What if I go slow, the way you did? And I promise, I'll stop the moment you say so." She pushed a strand of hair away from Jill's face. "Or say no right now if you need to, Jill. I don't ever want to make you feel uncomfortable."

She wasn't uncomfortable, really. Just uncertain. Part of her wanted Zara to touch her, but what if she didn't like it? Or what if she did? What was left of her logic told her there was only one way to find out. "Okay. Yes."

Zara carefully undid the top two buttons on her pajama top, and Jill felt her heart rate increase with each move. When Zara pulled the material back to expose her shoulder before leaning in to kiss along her collarbone, Jill's breath caught, and she had to close her eyes against the exquisite sensation. Zara's fingers smoothed down the center of her chest, undoing the rest of the buttons without exposing any more skin. "Okay?" she asked softly.

Jill wet her lips. "Yes."

"Just okay?" Zara teased.

"Yes. Oh, I mean no, not just." Compose yourself, she thought. "You're…it's nice."

"Let's see if we can do better than nice." Zara began easing her hand up from Jill's waist, very much like she'd done, and Jill felt her nipples tighten with anticipation.

"I thought about you every day," Zara said hoarsely. "But being with you like this is so much more than I expected." The look on her face was sending wisps of excitement into Jill's middle. Or maybe it was the fingers tracing the sides of her chest that was causing her reaction. With her other hand, Zara pulled Jill's pajama shirt back, exposing her completely. Before she could formulate a protest, Zara's head lowered, and her warm lips touched the space between her breasts.

Once, at the first of a dozen parties she'd attended during the London Season, she'd let a boy come close to doing the same thing. Gregory had gone, and her mother had died. She'd been desperate to feel something good, and Allan had been quite persuasive. He'd led her to an unoccupied room and had pressed against her, thrusting his hand under her blouse. They'd almost gotten to this stage when voices in the hall had broken them apart. Through the whole thing, Jill had felt cold and stiff and terribly detached.

Now she felt warm and fluid and eager. As she opened her mouth to say something encouraging, Zara's lips moved to her nipple, sucking gently, and what came out of her mouth was a moan of pleasure. Zara

Jaycie Morrison

made a sound in reply, followed by a flick of her tongue that made Jill clench between her legs.

"Oh, Zara, wait, please."

Zara pulled away, covering her again. "What's wrong?" Her other hand lingered, and Jill was glad, even though she could feel the flush of embarrassment rising.

"I'm sorry, but…" Jill took a breath, working to calm herself. "I need to use the toilet."

"Are you sure that's what it is?" Zara's tone was light. She nuzzled Jill's neck, her mouth open slightly in a smile. "Maybe you're getting excited."

"What do you mean?"

Zara rolled back, pulling Jill beside her. Jill's arm draped across her again, as if it was the most natural thing there was. "Do you feel urgent or just wet?"

"Well, yes, that's why I—" Jill stopped as Zara's question registered. The urgency she felt wasn't the usual necessity for the loo.

Zara turned toward her, placing another soft kiss on her lips. "I'm wet too, Jill. Because being close this way is incredibly arousing. I was hoping you might feel the same."

Jill returned the kiss that quickly became more intense. Zara groaned, and Jill came up for air. "Does that excite you?" she asked.

"Oh, yeah," Zara assured her. "Would you like to know how much?" Without waiting for an answer, she took Jill's hand and placed it at the waistband of her underwear.

And there it was. The ultimate brink. While she didn't question Zara's trustworthiness, fully believing she would do—or not do—anything Jill asked of her, she questioned her own intentions. What would it mean to take the next step? What would it mean if she didn't? How could it all feel so wonderful when everyone she knew said it was wrong? And what should she use as her guide, how she felt or what everyone else thought?

Zara must have sensed her dilemma because she whispered, "Do what makes you happy, Jill. Tonight, tomorrow, and for the rest of your life. If that's being with me now, I couldn't ask for anything more. If it's waiting or moving on to someone else or something else, make the choice that's right for you." She grinned. "It's totally cliché

• 174 •

to say, but I'll still respect you in the morning, as long as I know you're doing what you want, not acting on someone else's vision of your future." She lifted Jill's hand from her stomach and held it. "We both know it can be scary and painful out there, but spending every minute trying to protect yourself doesn't leave you any time to sample the exotic deliciousness of new things and new places." She gathered Jill's fingers and kissed them, adding, "I was nervous to be here the first time, and probably damn stupid to come back, but I wouldn't know what it feels like to lie next to you if I hadn't." Jill smiled, but Zara's tone was earnest. "You've got everything you'll ever need to have a meaningful life. Don't let it go to waste."

A meaningful life. Valuable work, yes. Important contributions, to be sure. But she had never considered it might include living with the passion Zara exhibited or allowing herself to fully experience these kinds of emotions with her. She thought of the time she'd tried for intimacy with Clive, for whom she'd felt genuine, long-term affection. It had been like an experiment, clinical and ultimately unsatisfactory for its failure. Nothing like the excitement, the need, she felt now. Her racing heart wasn't due to the forbidden nature of this moment. It was because she desired Zara and wanted her this way.

She moved her hand to Zara's underwear again. "Take these off," she said, almost not recognizing the huskiness in her own voice. Wordlessly, Zara complied, and when Jill slipped her hand down Zara's abdomen, she sensed heat that matched hers. Her breath caught when she touched soft damp curls, and then Zara's whole body shuddered as her fingers dipped lower, into the wetness Zara had promised was there. She explored carefully, marveling at how easily, how perfectly the slickness accommodated her inquisitive fingers.

When she drew back slightly, fondling a small rise of flesh, Zara's breath burst from her. "Oh God, Jill. That feels so fucking good."

So fucking good. The words stirred her, and she moved a little faster, even as her own breathing rasped in her throat. "Like that?"

"Yes," Zara encouraged softly. "So good," she said again, pressing herself against Jill's fingers. She made another sound, more like a hard sigh. Jill looked up to see Zara's head thrown back, her eyes closed and lips parted. The vision was beyond the dreams she'd pretended not to remember, and she reveled at the thought of Zara at her mercy, calling her name, begging. She pressed her mouth to Zara's breast, the feel and taste of her intensifying her other senses. "Right there," Zara called, her voice rising. "That. Oh fuck, yes, Jill. Jill—" Zara's words broke off as she turned her face into the pillow, muffling a long cry. Jill felt Zara's flesh tightening around her fingers, tasted the tautness of her nipple against her lips. Zara's body stiffened, then shuddered all over as her back lifted slightly off the bed. Jill lifted her head, wanting to see this incredible moment, and to hear Zara's fading sounds more clearly. By some instinct, she slowed her hand, stopping altogether when Zara shuddered again.

It was amazing, the profound awareness of what she'd done to— no, for—Zara. As their mutual breathing slowed, a tiny seed of doubt crept in. After another moment, Jill asked, "Was that…I mean, are you, uh…pleased?"

"Oh yeah." Zara cleared the lethargy from her voice. "Better than pleased." She turned, and their faces were inches apart. "It's been a while, and I don't usually come so quickly. You're as brilliant in bed as you are out of it." Jill felt her face flush. She'd never felt or done anything remotely like this before. Was she very different now or just more herself? Zara's fingers moved through her hair. "More importantly, are you all right?"

"I'm honestly not sure, but I think so." Jill tried to organize her thoughts against the tumult of her feelings. "Was it difficult for you, your first time?"

"Not at all, but I was young and willing." Zara shifted up onto her elbow. "Did it feel wrong to you? Are you sorry?" Studying Jill's face, Zara added, "Would you like me to go?"

It took just a second's hesitation for her to answer, having found the place where her heart and her mind connected with the body next to her. "No."

"No to which of those?" Zara's voice had a smile in it, and Jill touched her mouth.

"No to all of them."

"Does that mean yes to letting me do this?" Zara rested her hand on Jill's pajama bottoms.

"Can I decide as we go?" Jill couldn't admit her nervousness. She'd touched herself before, as was completely natural, but it had been more out of curiosity than need. Was that why she'd found it only vaguely pleasant? What if she failed again, as she had with Clive?

"Yes, of course. Tell me if you like this." Zara cupped her sex through her pajama bottoms. From the fullness of her hand, the touch shifted to one finger.

Jill heard herself whimper, and the finger moved carefully, back and forth against her. Her heart rate accelerated, and she heard herself panting to the motion. She wanted... "More."

Zara grasped her pajama bottoms, as her lips brushed Jill's. "Yes. With these off?"

The moment the last of her clothing was gone, Zara was on top of her, pressing her body between Jill's thighs. After reading Constance's books, Jillian had wondered what it would feel like to be naked with another person, but she'd never thought it would be so smooth and so hot and sensuous. She wrapped her arms around Zara's strong back and kissed her hard.

"I've never wanted anyone the way I want you," Zara murmured, breaking the kiss and pushing herself against Jill's center. "Tell me what you like."

"I..." Jill had been about to say she didn't really know what she liked, but that wouldn't be true. She knew now. "I like you. The way being with you makes me feel."

Zara shifted to the side, her fingers trailing up Jill's thighs, teasing her way toward her center. Her lips brushed Jill's neck. "I'm glad."

The anticipation of Zara's touch was almost painful, but when her hand came to rest between Jill's legs, she was unable to control the lift of her hips. The difference without clothes was astounding, and it was exactly the more she'd wanted. Zara touched her slowly, delicately, until Jill's body began to move with insistence. She wasn't sure what she was seeking, but she was certain Zara knew. Everything seemed elevated by this unexplored level of trust. Jill put her arms around Zara's neck, letting the pleasure ripple through every nerve. "Don't stop."

"I won't. Ever." Zara leaned down and kissed Jill's breast, sealing the promise with such tenderness that Jill felt an inevitable force gathering inside her. She moaned at the graze of teeth on her nipple, and her belly tensed. "Shh." Zara lifted her mouth, her tone half-serious. "You have company nearby."

Jill pulled Zara's head to her breast again, thrusting against the movements of her fingers. Zara's warm tongue flicked, and Jill stuttered, "It's…I'm…" The tense heat that had been building inside exploded into sparks and ecstasy. She heard herself cry out, and then Zara's mouth was on hers, taking in her fading exultation until there was only their breathing and her heartbeat.

Zara settled beside her, kissing her shoulder as she pulled the covers back up over them. "Okay, babe?"

"Why don't they tell you the truth?" Jill asked hoarsely.

"About what?" Zara sounded genuinely perplexed.

Jill had to gather herself to explain. "About how this feels," she said.

Zara laughed quietly. "I guess they're afraid that's all we'd want to do."

"They may be right," Jill said softly, turning to press herself against Zara's body.

❖

"Jill." Zara's voice was a whisper.

"Mmm." She was too comfortable to come fully awake, but Zara's voice made her stir. With that, Jill's awareness grew. They were both still naked, and she'd been sleeping with her leg thrown over Zara's body. Either of those things would have been terribly awkward previously, but at this moment she felt profound contentment, tempered with what she now knew was arousal. Zara's arm was around her, and the way her hand moved softly up and down Jill's back made her want to be closer…if that was even possible.

"Babe, I think people are moving around outside."

"Mmm." Personally, Jill had no intention of moving until she absolutely had to. Although…she rolled her hips slightly, finding the sensation of pressure against Zara's leg very compelling.

"Maybe we should put our pajamas on?"

"Maybe you should first let me…" Jill rolled upon her, fully mounting Zara's thigh. She'd never felt so loose and wanton, and the wetness she'd become aware of last night made every movement more stimulating. All she wanted was this, this pleasure and the look on Zara's face as she fondled her breasts.

"God, Jill, do you have any idea how fucking sexy you are?"

Jill moaned, the spiraling intensity of her body's need and Zara's words making her thrust faster. Zara sat up, nipping at Jill's breasts and pulled at her hips, increasing the pressure until Jill began making little breathy cries in time to each lunge. "Zara...I...Oh...Oh..."

Zara tightened her thigh, pushing it up into Jill's center. Jill strained against her until her cries became a wail of gratification. Collapsing onto Zara's chest, she lay panting while Zara held her close.

"Does it...does it just keep getting better?" Jill managed after a few seconds.

"I hope so."

The smile in Zara's voice was followed immediately by a sharp rapping on the door and the worried quality in Mrs. Livingstone's words. "M'lady, are you all right? May I come in?"

Jillian answered the second question first because it seemed the more urgent to her. "No!"

Unfortunately, Mrs. Livingstone clearly heard it as the reply she'd feared—that something was terribly wrong—and she threw the door open. Jill kicked as she rolled off Zara, grabbing for the covers at the same time, and dumping Zara unceremoniously out of the bed and onto her bare ass.

"Mother of God," Mrs. Livingstone exclaimed, crossing herself before turning away.

Zara's response—"Jesus fucking Christ"—was clearly based on a kind of suffering that had nothing to do with religion. Jill had barely found her pajamas when Constance's head poked into the doorway Mrs. Livingstone had vacated. In spite of the hand that quickly covered her mouth, Jillian heard her shocked gasp. She ran for the washroom, slamming the door.

Chapter Twelve

It felt as if someone else was starring in Clive's worst nightmare. It was mere luck he'd never been caught in such a compromising position himself. He could taste the fear that drove so much of his behavior as he avoided looking at anyone directly, in case they saw either his commiseration or his dread. He felt truly bad for Jillian and was even able to produce some sympathy for the scruffy American musician.

Planning to participate in the foolishness of seeing Constance and Nelson off, he'd been dressing when he'd heard the sounds of commotion in the hallway. It was a bit earlier than he'd expected, and he'd opened the door to see Constance supporting Mrs. Livingstone, who was clutching at her chest as if she was about to have a heart attack. Worried for the sweet older woman, he moved toward them, thinking to help get her inside the room where Jillian was staying.

Glancing inside, he saw Zara pulling on a T-shirt with one hand as she pulled up her underwear with the other. Sweeping his gaze across the disheveled bed, he wondered about Jill's absence until he noted the closed door to the loo. He swallowed hard, suspecting his fear of losing her might now be realized. But when Zara called softly to Jillian and there was no response, the thought crossed Clive's mind that Lady Stansfield might well spend the rest of the morning in there. Or possibly the rest of the holiday.

Zara was just stepping into her pants when Lord Stansfield arrived. Clive didn't need to make out the words of the conversation that followed to know Mrs. Livingstone was describing the scene she'd encountered. He was almost glad he couldn't see Douglas Stansfield's face as he pushed past him into the room, but he clearly heard the words directed at Zara.

"You fucking pervert."

Mrs. Livingstone gasped, and Constance began walking her down the hallway, calling for Nelson as she went. Clive positioned himself on the rear of the open door where he could see but not be easily seen. Jill's father was holding Zara by the T-shirt front with one hand, the other clenched by his side. "I knew this would happen if we let American scum like you into this house."

Boldly, Zara looked up into his face. "You may think I'm a pervert, but I know you're a liar."

He drew his hand back to strike her, and she made no move to protect herself, though her eyes flicked again to the closed WC door. Clive could practically feel the hope draining out of her. Jillian clearly wasn't going to defend her, and he imagined Zara might almost be wishing Lord Stansfield could deliver a blow that would knock some sense into her. He knew the feeling. He'd had one or two bedmates who'd given him reason to wish for better judgment. As more people were gathering outside their rooms, making it clear that the humiliation and shame that would mark Zara's departure was going to be widely watched, the absolute silence from the washroom had to be much worse.

Nelson rushed up the hall, entering the room without even a glance in Clive's direction. Stopping behind Douglas, Nelson sounded only slightly less calm than usual when he spoke. "Lord Stansfield, no. It's not worth it." He carefully put a hand on Jill's father's shoulder, and Zara's glare shifted to his face. Her brow furrowed when he added, "She's not worth it."

Coming from a decent man like Nelson, Clive could imagine how profoundly that condemnation must hurt, but he couldn't see Zara's expression as she looked away. Lord Stansfield's hand must have loosened because she bent and grabbed her Oxford shirt, pulling it on without buttoning it before covering it with her wool blazer. She appeared to catch sight of something under the bed and took a step toward it.

"Just a minute, you," Lord Stansfield said, his voice only slightly less enraged. "Nelson, get the piece of luggage I left in the hallway. And watch her for a moment."

Nelson hefted a small carryall onto the bed while Lord Stansfield moved out of Clive's line of sight. Zara cocked her head at the sight of her bag, but Nelson's gaze was fixed on the floor. "Look," she said. "There's nothing in there but the dress I wore to the wedding and a few pounds. Neither of them is going to do me any good now." When Nelson made no reply, she added, "I'm going to get my shoes. They're practically new, and I'm not leaving without them." Nelson had just met her eyes when the sound of a fist pounding on wood made them both jump.

"Jillian," Lord Stansfield called from outside the washroom. "Come out here this instant." After a long pause, the door opened a crack. "I want you to see what kind of person you've chosen to... consort with."

When the door opened a little farther, he seized her arm and pulled. Jillian was now in her pajamas, and Clive could see she'd been crying, but her father didn't seem to notice or care. Dragging her to the bed, he jerked open the case. Clive shifted his position enough to see the delicately woven gold chain of a necklace nestled on the floral dress, along with a pendant made up of a sparkling blue stone surrounded by diamonds. Something else glittered beside it, but he couldn't quite make out what it was.

"Oh, hell no," Zara said, drawing Jill's scrutiny to her for the first time since she'd reentered the room.

Jill's expression turned cold, and her voice was a harsh whisper. "How could you?"

Zara's jaw dropped, and it must have been pure shock that kept her from answering.

Nelson spoke. "This isn't the first time, Jilly. Your father told me some things were missing the last time she was here, but we decided to keep it from you rather than upset you further."

"That is complete and total bullshit." Zara's voice was shaking, but Clive knew it wasn't from guilt. "Jill, use your head. You had them take this bag to the kitchen right when I first came back in, remember?" She seemed to gather herself, then whispered her next words, even though the room was too close for it to help. "When would I have done this? We've been together since I got here." She stopped to glare at Lord Stansfield. "Someone who wanted me to take the fall did this. And let me tell you who—"

"I think we've heard enough of this nonsense." Lord Stansfield's voice brooked no more interruption as he gestured at Nelson, and they each took one of Zara's arms. Towering over her, he snarled, "For the sake of what's left of my daughter's reputation, I'm not going to call the police this time. But if I ever see you near this house or her again, I'll make sure you're sent away for a long, long time."

"You tried that once, and it didn't work." Zara jerked free and turned. "Jill, listen—" she tried, but the lavatory door was closing again.

Clearly, Jillian's initial sense of outrage kept her from considering that the discovery of jewelry in Zara's bag might have been contrived. Clive had to admit the whole scene couldn't have played out better if they'd scripted it…other than the seduction which had clearly taken place earlier. Even that was no surprise to him, having observed Jillian's delight at Zara's return. He'd obviously delayed his proposal too long, but Jillian's rejection still stung, so when Lord Stansfield had approached him to express his concerns about the musician, he'd had no qualms suggesting theft as a way to ensure Zara's luster would dim in Jill's eyes. Better yet, when Lord Stansfield indicated he believed Zara had already done something similar, Clive knew he was absolutely off the hook for the two antique rings he'd stolen during Zara's previous visit. He'd felt like a total cad doing so, but the money from them had paid off several bills, freeing his family from collectors for another month, at least. At the time, he'd rationalized the jewels would be part of his property anyway when he married Jillian. His guilt over the fire had not eased when he'd heard that Zara had disappeared, and it wouldn't have helped to give the jewels back, even if he could do it without giving himself away. Whatever else, he swore to himself he'd do whatever it took to get his family finances sorted out so he'd never have to go through this kind of experience again. And maybe he could to something to help Zara somehow, once the dust had settled.

None of the guests would question the treatment of the pianist after she'd been discovered *in flagrante delicto* with Lord Stansfield's precious daughter, but the morning's real accomplishment came in having Jillian believe that Zara would steal her mother's jewelry.

He watched from his doorway as Zara glanced back one last time before she strode unflinchingly into the hallway, shoes in hand, ignoring the glares and comments from the overnight guests. Clearly not giving a shite about any of them, she began to whistle. At the stairs, she stopped to put on her shoes. Clive followed Nelson and Lord Stansfield, witnessing Zara shove Andrew out of her way when he stood shocked at the front door. Apparently disregarding the cold, she made her way outside with her unbuttoned shirt and blazer flapping in the winter wind. He supposed it was anger and hurt that kept her marching gamely down the long driveway, and he idly wondered if she'd take the time to finish dressing before making her way back to the city.

While she probably wouldn't give a fig for his sympathy, he might admit to a small dose of respect for her comportment during what had to be one of the worst moments of her life. But then, what did he know? Maybe Zara was the type who regularly seduced young ladies, and such an exit was not uncommon. But somehow, he thought not.

In any case, Lord Stansfield then made it clear that poor Jilly would be expected to spend every available moment at Fullerhill for the foreseeable future, eschewing any extra time at the college. There would be no affectionate conversations with Mrs. Livingstone; instead, she'd have to ignore the intrusive stares from their new butler and housekeeper. Andrew had announced his retirement after what he'd termed "the incident." Mrs. Livingstone was staying on, but it was expected that her capacity for long days in the kitchen would be greatly diminished. For Lord Stansfield, these changes provided two of the many emotional swipes he'd taken at Jill since that morning.

Clive remained at Fullerhill throughout the remainder of the holiday, acting as any good friend would. He never once mentioned the scandal and simply kept Jillian company at every opportunity during those first disastrous days, trying hard to keep her spirits up. He even stood up to Douglas on occasion, and Jillian appeared impressed that her father's ire seemed to lessen in the face of his support. Every time he and Jillian were alone, Clive was almost desperate to confess, to tell her how very much he understood exactly what she was going through. But the risk was too great. Jillian was increasingly fragile, and he needed the Stansfield fortune to secure his family's name.

After a solid week of harangues and sermonizing, Jillian's exhaustion and what Clive suspected was an unfamiliar sense of alienation finally reduced her to tears. Lord Stansfield took her breakdown as acquiescence to his demands and finally left her alone. When he heard the ultimatum of marriage as one of those concessions, Clive didn't mind being included that way at all. He believed that in time, Jillian would come to understand it was for the best, as he had. He did wish she didn't seem so numb. Still, with everything falling into place, he could be confident that no further pilfering would be necessary, especially since it was most certain that Zara could no longer act as his convenient scapegoat.

But during the second weekend Jillian was at home, when it was only the two of them, she came out of her lab with a stopwatch. "I need your help," she said, her pensive expression the one she got when a problem was vexing her.

"I'm all yours, love," he replied, pleased to see her showing some life for a change.

Taking his hand, she led him toward the hallway outside the banquet room. "In a minute, I want you to walk with me toward the piano room, like you did on the night of the wedding."

True, she sounded much more like her old self, but as the timepiece began ticking and Jillian disappeared in the direction of her father's room, Clive began feeling a nebulous anxiety. When Jillian returned, Clive could tell she was calculating something in her head. His throat tightened as his sudden worries were confirmed. Jillian Stansfield was going to put her engineering training to use, proving if it was indeed possible for Zara to have stolen those pieces of her mother's jewelry. She'd told Clive twice that there was just one time when she and Zara hadn't been together; she'd lost sight of her in the crowd during the time when Constance and Nelson had made their escape upstairs after the reception. She'd nodded when he made some vague response about the quickness of thieves, and he'd hoped she'd put the whole thing out of her head. Clearly, that was not the case.

When she looked up at him, her focus appeared far away—back to the wedding, he assumed. "I suspected she'd be in the music room," Jillian said. "So I started down this hall, and then you joined me." Taking Clive's arm, she started the stopwatch again.

When he'd seen her moving away from the revelers that night, Clive had gathered himself and followed, taking advantage of their moment alone to make his impromptu offer of marriage, hoping the romanticism of the day might affect her. Her refusal really hadn't come as a surprise. Jillian wasn't a sentimental woman. Or so he'd thought.

Following the debacle of the morning after, when Lord Stansfield had insisted she marry upon finishing her degree this coming spring, Clive was certain he was the obvious choice, even though there had been nothing specified in that regard. Jillian had been almost listless until now, and he probably could have taken her to the altar without a murmur of protest. Clive chafed, aware that was precisely what he should have done, especially if this unexpected investigation derailed his plans.

Still, he accompanied her until they reached the doorway of the room. That night, Jillian had dismissed him there, but after she'd entered, he'd heard part of the conversation. The warmth in her tone had made it obvious she was speaking to Zara, and he'd turned away, bile in his throat. But now, as he relived those moments, he wished his injured pride hadn't gotten the better of him. In trying to get Zara out of the picture, he'd hurt Jilly, and that had never been his intention.

Jillian watched a few more seconds tick off the stopwatch before stopping it. "Zara was already here," she said, "and since she didn't come in behind us, the only other way in was from the other hallway. That's twice as long as the route we just took." She looked up at Clive, her eyes shining with elation. "There is absolutely no way she had time to steal those pieces, stash them in her bag, and make it here before we did."

As much as his conscience urged him to amend the role he'd taken on, Clive deemed his part was written in stone. He tried to suggest alternatives—there'd been an accomplice—or that Zara had committed the theft immediately after the wedding and put it in her bag later, but Jillian was having none of it. Pacing the wide hallway, she said, "Zara was trying to tell me who she suspected, but I didn't listen. I couldn't think beyond what I was seeing. I couldn't think beyond what I was feeling." She turned to him with her lip quivering. She was on the verge of tears again. "Do you think there's any chance I'll hear from her again?"

He thought it was about as likely as if he were to be named next in line to the throne, but he smiled knowingly. "I'm sure you will, Jilly darling. She'd be a fool not to contact you again."

In his head, he was counting on her being exactly that much of a fool.

Everyone complimented her on her tan and suggested that marriage agreed with her. And it truly did. Though setting up the flat with Nelson made her aware that their tastes were sometimes at odds, often on the most peculiar things, like which cabinet would be best for the dishes. She was glad her mother was often there to tip the scales. But on evenings with just the two of them, when Nelson complimented her cooking or let himself be convinced to go out for Chinese before they settled in to study, Constance was genuinely happy.

Everything about their honeymoon would have been perfect as well, except that they'd spent the first two days grappling with the scene from the scandalous morning at Fullerhill. She knew it might take Nelson months to get over the shock of Jillian Stansfield being bedded by another woman, especially one of questionable breeding like Zara. As much as she might have secretly understood what had happened, Constance couldn't admit to any kind of open-mindedness. She couldn't possibly explain to Nelson why she found it tolerable to imagine a woman being with another woman as opposed to the revulsion of thinking of a man with another man.

Nelson insisted they visit at Fullerhill immediately upon their return, stating that his mind wouldn't rest until they saw for themselves that things were okay. Shortly after their arrival, Constance took Jillian aside, beginning her solemn conversation by reminding her that she'd cautioned her about Zara.

"Yes, I know," Jillian replied. Constance was certain she'd never seen her so miserable. "But she didn't take those jewels. I'm certain of it. Someone set her up." The anguish in her voice and the despair on her face was enough to turn the long lecture Constance had planned into a gentle comfort. "Well, even if that's true, it's over now. That's the main thing, isn't it?"

"I suppose." Jillian's tone was still subdued, and Constance noted she'd attempted to cover up the dark circles under her eyes with more makeup than usual. "Has Clive been here the whole time we've been gone?" she asked, thinking to get into a more comfortable topic. "Yes. He's been quite helpful with Father." Constance cocked her head curiously, and Jillian's gaze moved anxiously past her face, her eyes filling with tears. "Clive's presence seems to calm him." She turned away, fumbling in the pocket of her skirt for her handkerchief. "He expects we'll marry."

Jillian spoke that last bit into the cloth, muting her words. "What, dearest?" Constance asked, chancing a touch on Jillian's arm.

Nodding as if it was shock in Constance's question rather than a lack of hearing, Jillian clenched her fists. "Father was beyond upset. He said some terrible things, and I...I couldn't think of how to explain...." Jillian trailed off. Constance kept her expression neutral. "Ultimately, he announced he wouldn't support my finishing school unless I agreed to marry after graduation. I don't think he even cares who it is."

"Other than Zara," Constance offered with a smirk. She watched a surprising show of emotions cross Jillian's face: heartache, uneasiness, and longing. Then, Jillian shrugged, obviously trying to shake it off. "Clive is familiar, so I think both he and my father assumed it would be him."

"But how wonderful." Constance moved around to face Jillian again. "Darling, that's exactly what we always dreamed. The four of us, coupled and together always." When Jillian gave her a weak smile, Constance took her hand. "Come on. Let's rejoin our men. I want to make sure Nelson knows the good news."

Clive appeared a little later, and the three of them worked hard to make the visit feel like a happy reunion between old friends. But as she and Nelson began the drive back to their flat, Nelson couldn't stop talking about how lucky Jillian was that Clive hadn't abandoned her. In fact, Clive had told him how he'd accompanied Jillian upon her return to Cambridge, and how whispers and barely muted slurs had followed her everywhere. She and Nelson agreed that gossip, especially when it featured the disgrace of a previously admired individual, apparently traveled faster than the speed of sound. But school had always been Jill's sanctuary, Constance knew, and the loss of that refuge must have hurt her almost as much as the rest of it.

Thinking of Cambridge brought Constance to her other problem: she was falling further and further behind in her own schoolwork. She'd been given extensions last term after explaining about her upcoming marriage, and those were now coming due, along with her current assignments. None of the work was beyond her capability; it was just that there were a limited number of hours in a day. When Nelson declared they were going to alternate weekends at Fullerhill with Clive, at least until it was clear Jillian had gotten herself together, Constance saw no room for objections. She tried to see it as a chance to get caught up on the easier assignments, at least.

On their first weekend visit, Constance asked Jillian if they could sit together. "If you need to be in your lab, I can read there."

"I'm not working on anything at the moment," Jillian said, her tone so unemotional that Constance blinked. Jillian was always working on something, even if it was simply recreating experiments from her textbooks. "Let's sit in the study," she suggested.

Sit was exactly what Jillian did. She had a book open, but whenever Constance glanced over, she saw Jill's head turned toward the window. After half an hour of accomplishing next to nothing except being aware of Jillian's distraction, Constance closed her notebook with a sigh. "Would you like to go for a walk?" she asked.

Jillian startled as if she'd forgotten Constance was there. "Oh. I…no, I don't think so. But thank you for the offer."

"Jillian." Constance tried to sound sympathetic. "You've got to get a grip on yourself. Nothing you're doing is going to change what happened or bring her back."

"Would you loan me the money to hire a private detective?" The question was so sudden and unexpected that Constance had to choke back the laugh springing to her lips. "Father has put me on a strict allowance," Jillian explained, apparently unaware of her reaction. "But it won't be forever. You know I'll pay you back."

Constance worked to keep her tone gentle. "Jilly, dearest, even if I thought that was a good idea, which I don't, I couldn't give you money without talking to Nelson. And I guarantee he wouldn't approve either."

She watched as Jillian nodded slightly. "I almost didn't ask. But I hoped…since you knew her before—"

"And I wish I'd never brought her to this house," Constance said, raising her voice without meaning to.

"If you hadn't, I might not be here now," Jillian said, her manner still composed. When Constance lowered her gaze, Jillian added, "And you don't know her like I do."

"Obviously."

For a moment, they simply stared at each other. Then Constance began to giggle. Jillian held out for a few more seconds before joining in, and their laughter grew. Falling into each other's arms, they held on through the last of their mirth. Wiping at her eyes with one hand, Jillian whispered, "I just feel so terrible about everything. If I could only see her again…"

"If you do, I don't want to know about it," Constance answered. Jillian nodded again and, by unspoken agreement, they returned to their books.

Jillian sighed as she looked out the window of the taxi. The day seemed even drearier than the one before. She'd spent another mandatory weekend at Fullerhill without trying to show her dejection at the irony of it all. Home was where she'd "gotten into trouble," as she'd heard Mrs. Livingstone refer to it, and Lord Stansfield was rarely present during these short visits. However, Clive or Constance and Nelson were there each time, and she was conscious that every conversation during the time spent together was overly merry and obviously focused on returning her to "normal." What none of them could know was she had an ulterior motive for returning regularly. Despite the circumstances of their parting, Fullerhill was the only place where Zara could conceivably contact her. Not that she expected it, but...

For weeks, she'd replayed all the events of the wedding night, trying and failing to omit the impassioned hours in Zara's arms. She remembered every single touch and every word they'd said to each other, but above all, the stricken sound of Zara's voice the morning after, saying, "When would I have done this?" echoed in her head.

If her training as an engineer had taught her anything, it was how to follow a sequence of actions to a conclusion. When she'd finally had her wits about her enough to do so, the truth was as obvious as the low-hanging clouds of the late afternoon. Zara was innocent of taking anything...except what Jill's guilt circled back to over and over. Zara had stolen into her consciousness and altered her self-image irrevocably. And even if she could discount what they'd experienced together physically, she would never be able to justify her deplorable behavior afterward. The simple fact was that she was a coward, afraid to go outside of her comfortable world, scared to become more than who and what she already was, and terrified of her feelings for Zara.

At first, she tried to blame her inability to reason out these facts at the time on the shock of being so abruptly intruded upon. Never before had Mrs. Livingstone barged into her room with almost no warning. Her father's temper when he'd dragged her out of the lavatory, the clamor of voices in the hall, and Nelson's unexpected presence had kept her from thinking clearly. She'd recognized her mother's jewelry, and knowing of Zara's past on the streets, it had seemed feasible at the time. Besides, she'd never imagined that her father would make such an accusation without solid proof.

But as the days passed and the silence of Zara's absence from her life descended once again, Jillian had to admit to herself that it wasn't shock which had mired her thinking—it was shame. The hours they'd spent in each other's arms had been so private and so intimate, she hadn't been emotionally prepared for everyone in her world to know that she'd been with Zara. But once she'd recovered from the traumas of that morning, she'd been driven to discover her father's inexplicable falsehood by her heart's certainty that the same woman who had given herself freely would not be someone who stole from her.

Zara had every right to feel betrayed and angry. After all, she'd risked her future to save Jillian from the fire, but Jillian hadn't had the fortitude to stand up for her in the presence of her father and her friends. She clung to the notion that Zara would call or write to vent those justified emotions, and in her sleepless hours, Jillian played out fantasies of those conversations and Zara's eventual forgiveness. But now she was returning to school again without any word, precisely like all the weeks before. She supposed she needed to come to terms with the reality that there wouldn't be any contact, though she couldn't entirely quash the little bit of hope that sparked with each day's post or any phone call.

The taxi slowed, drawing her attention to the reflection of red and blue lights flashing off the remnants of the morning rain. "Has there been an accident?" Jillian asked the driver.

"Not sure, miss. Let me try another route."

"If you'll get me a few blocks closer, I'll walk the rest of the way to the station." She had plenty of time to catch the last train to Cambridge, and stretching her legs between the long taxi ride and the train ride to come was appealing, even in the nasty weather.

The driver nodded and turned down a nearby, somewhat run-down residential avenue. Older apartment buildings lined one side of the street opposite small, closely spaced homes. The taxi inched up behind the increasing traffic, reaching a policeman who was directing cars left and right. As the driver leaned out to speak to him, Jillian cracked her window and caught the hint of smoke in the air. Over on the sidewalk, a small group of people stood listening as someone spoke urgently to a fireman. When the fireman began to reply, the woman turned her head slightly, and Jillian caught a glimpse of her face. For a few seconds, she couldn't breathe.

"Stop! Let me out here."

"The officer said it was likely a gas explosion, miss. Are you sure?"

"Yes. Here, please." She handed the driver a bill and grabbed her bag. Mingling into the crowd, Jillian moved close enough to hear, keeping her umbrella tilted low, shielding her face.

"I understand that, sir, but this lady needs to get in out of the weather," Zara was saying as she pointed at an elderly woman in a wheelchair who pulled a blanket closer around her shoulders. "And I promise you, if you put water on this building, there are going to be lots of folks with damaged possessions. These windows leak like a sieve."

"We're waiting on word from our incident commander," the fireman replied. "I can't tell you anything more until then."

"Could you please communicate—"

The fireman turned at a squawk from his walkie-talkie. A moment later, he touched his finger to his helmet. "We're all clear. You folks can go in now."

"Come on, Mrs. Donnelly."

Zara's mouth clenched as she grabbed the handles of the wheelchair, and Jillian suspected her injured hand was still bothering her. A small stream of people moved with them toward the building, several of them speaking words of thanks or patting Zara's shoulder as they passed. She acknowledged them with a few words or a shy grin, never once looking Jill's way. Jillian followed slowly until Zara pushed the chair across the threshold of the ground floor, opening the door of the apartment labeled 1A. Stepping aside to let the remaining residents pass, Jillian could see into the small, sparse living room from her angle.

"Megan should be by in less than an hour," the old woman was saying. She sighed and shifted the covering from her shoulders. "Thank you for the use of your blanket, Zara luv. You're an angel."

"Gotta take care of my favorite neighbor, don't I?"

The warm sound of Zara's voice made Jill's insides quiver.

"Go on with you," Donnelly laughed, waving her away. "And get yourself a little nip in your tea to take off the chill of this evening's adventure." Zara's answering chuckle died as she closed the door and crossed the hallway, unlocking the door labeled 1B. When she hesitated, turning her head slightly, Jillian slipped into the shadows. Once she heard the sound of the door closing, she let out a breath, memorizing the building's address, 24 Eversholt St.

Checking her watch, she hurried along the short walk to the station. Once inside, she found a pay phone and rummaged in her purse for the small notebook she always carried. Flipping until she found the most recent page, she dialed one of the phone numbers she'd jotted down after days of research on burn treatments at the Cambridge medical library. Shortly after, she called a second number. She'd spoken with both the acupuncturist and the massage therapist before, so the conversations were brief. In both cases, she gave the newly discovered address and apartment number, prompted them on their cover story, and verified they had her own location for billing. Before hanging up, she reminded the massage therapist to include a treatment with MEBO, the botanical paste that Dr. Bankole had mentioned when Jillian had cornered her at St. Thomas a week ago while trying to find where Zara might have gone. Though the Moist Exposed Burn Ointment was regularly used in Asia and the Middle East for the treatment of partial-thickness burns, Dr. Bankole had cautioned her that the exact working mechanisms of the ointment had not been studied. Still, she'd admitted, results were often good, and many Western physicians had adopted it. With her promise of a generous pledge to the burn unit, Jillian had gained Dr. Bankole's agreement to confirm that Zara was part of a study on post-release burn patients, should the question arise.

Jillian barely made her train, but she smiled as she sat back in her seat, blessing the fates or whatever gods that had given her another chance to make things right with Zara.

Chapter Thirteen

Jillian forced herself to wait six weeks. It was torture, but the weekly progress reports on Zara's treatments helped strengthen her resolve. She could only hope the positive assessments were genuine and not merely a way to solicit her continued patronage. But both women clinicians had come highly recommended, and she bided her time.

It had given Jillian great pleasure to imagine Zara's surprise when the therapist first appeared. But as she'd suspected, Zara was desperate to improve the functionality of her hand enough that she wouldn't question anything beyond the initial introduction. The acupuncturist added that Zara's mood seemed much improved over the last fortnight, which she attributed to her physical recuperation. When the massage therapist reported that Zara had found work, which meant their sessions would have to be changed to nights or weekends, Jillian assured her she'd be compensated for any irregular hours.

Finally, her self-imposed timeline concluded, and her fervent anticipation made it impossible to wait any longer. She left Fullerhill early Sunday and had the taxi drop her off at the same place as before. It took several seconds before she gathered the courage to knock on 1B. When there was no answer, Jillian had never felt so deflated. Out of desperation, she knocked on 1A, but there was no reply there either. She turned back into the weak afternoon sunlight and glanced up and down the block. In the distance, a wheelchair rolled toward her, a dark-haired figure pushing it steadily. Jillian's heart thudded, and she returned to the street, ducking between two parked cars.

Mrs. Donnelly was laughing as Zara pretended fatigue, puffing and panting up the slight incline before turning at the sidewalk leading to their building. "I think we're both suffering the effects of the new bakery by the park," she was saying. "Too many more of those eclairs, and you'll be replacing me with a muscled stud who'll be sure to get you home before Megan arrives."

Jillian told herself to move now, before they disappeared into the building. Zara was turning toward her footsteps when she found the nerve to speak. "May I help?"

At the sound of her voice, Zara froze. Mrs. Donnelly peered around, looking into Jillian's face. "Why, thank you, dear."

Swallowing, Zara said, "Good God, Jill. What the hell are you doing here?"

"Zara!" Mrs. Donnelly scolded, but Jillian said, "Let's get this nice lady inside. Then we can talk. All right?" She hoped she sounded calmer than she felt. Zara's greeting certainly wasn't welcoming.

After a moment's hesitation, Zara nodded. As they rolled Mrs. Donnelly toward her apartment, the building became shadowed by the coming evening. "You should offer your pretty friend some tea before she goes on her way," the older woman suggested.

A car door slammed, and a young voice called, "Wait up, Gran." Mrs. Donnelly's face lit up. "Megan," she said excitedly, as a cute young woman dressed in a bright blue miniskirt over leggings— probably due to her grandmother's sense of modesty—and a plum-colored, oversized sweatshirt, ran up behind them. Megan gave Zara a cursory hug before taking over the wheelchair. "See you on Friday," she called, and they disappeared into the building.

Zara stood rooted to the spot, staring down.

"Would you?" Jillian asked finally.

"Would I what?" Zara had apparently found something fascinating on the pavement.

"Would you give me a cup of tea before you send me on my way?"

She glanced at the door labelled 1B. "No. It's…I mean, my place is really small, and I don't think you'd be comfortable. Unless you've been robbed again, I'm sure you have enough money left to buy yourself a cup of tea when you get to wherever you're going."

Jillian flinched at the rebuke but knew she had it coming. "Please, Zara," she said softly, moving closer as two people walked past them toward the stairway. "I'll only take a little of your time. Then I'll go if that's what you want."

Zara took a slow breath in through her nose as if smelling the air between them. In anticipation of just this moment, Jillian had put on the perfume from the night of the wedding, an expensive fragrance she hadn't worn since. She saw Zara swallow and knew she remembered it. Being this close again made Jillian relive the feeling of promise she hadn't felt since that night, and she almost vibrated with anticipation.

Zara abruptly unlocked the door and stepped inside, turning on a stark overhead light. Her gaze swept over Jillian's face for the briefest moment before she bowed slightly, sweeping her arm out. "Come in, Your Ladyship."

Ignoring the resentment in Zara's tone, Jillian moved past, scanning the place intently. A small scarred table and two chairs stood near the kitchen, and a ratty oversized chair and ottoman were at the window, with a scratched end table alongside. Opposite them on the side wall was an ancient upright.

"You have a piano," Jillian gasped, turning back to Zara with a smile.

Zara shrugged. "It's on loan from Mrs. Donnelly. We developed a barter arrangement. I check on her before her granddaughter gets here, take her for walks when it's nice outside, that sort of thing."

"So you're playing again?"

Zara stepped up to a small stove without answering. "Did you want tea? Or I have coffee if you'd prefer."

"I'll have whatever you're having," Jillian answered automatically, having noted washroom fixtures through the only other doorway. "Where is the bedroom?"

Zara gave a dry laugh. "You're looking at it. Bedroom, living room, and den, all in one. That's what makes it efficient." She gestured at the wall beyond the kitchen area. "The bed comes down from there."

Jillian now saw the strap on what she'd thought was some kind of wall unit. Thinking of Zara sleeping this close caused a sudden flow of images, the two of them in that bed, the way her body had responded to the feel of Zara's hands and mouth, how the desire to touch Zara's breasts and taste her skin had overwhelmed any sense of propriety she might have had. She'd been unable to forget any of the things Zara had made her feel.

Now, being in the same space with her again, hearing her voice, and smelling the slightly damp scent of her was making her lightheaded, especially after fearing she'd never see her again. Desperately trying to think of some small talk, she asked, "How long have you been here?"

Zara shrugged. "Since right before the wedding. I'm too old for the street, so after I got back from Switzerland, I stayed at a flophouse until I found something I could afford for a couple of months."

Jillian chewed her lip at the thought of Zara in one of those undesirable places. Dozens of possible responses rushed through her mind, but she knew saying anything about money would be a mistake. She moved toward the kitchen.

"If you'd like to sit down, use that chair." Zara pointed before meeting her eyes for the first time. "The other one wobbles."

Instead of sitting, Jillian took a step toward her. "I'm a bit wobbly at the moment, myself." She dared to reach for Zara's cheek, but she was already turning away again. Her hand came to rest on Zara's shoulder instead.

"What is it that you want, Jill?" she asked tightly, sidestepping so Jill's hand fell away.

"First, I…I want to apologize. I feel terrible about—"

"Oh, hey. No need for that," Zara interrupted, pulling the kettle off the burner. "It was great to have a whole new place to be thrown out of. Took me back to my Chicago days." She looked at Jillian. "Good thing I told you about that so you'd find it easy to believe I'd steal from you."

"I'm terribly sorry, Zara. I just…I didn't know what to do. I panicked, and I'm not the panicky type as a rule." Jillian lowered her gaze. "I know it was spineless of me. At the time, I simply couldn't tolerate all the racket…but now I know I was hiding from the humiliation. And I'm even more ashamed to be confessing that to you."

Zara sighed. "It was an extremely compromising situation. I understand that. I guess I just hoped you'd…"

When she paused, Jillian met her eyes again. "Stand up for you? I should have. I truly, truly regret it, Zara. My father had no right to accuse you that way. And I've come to realize you wouldn't have…I mean, I shouldn't have believed that you—"

"Stole your mother's jewelry? Why not? Or did your heroic father admit to his role in all this?"

"No, he…he hasn't been home when I have. Usually. We haven't spoken much since…"

"Since he explained to your guests about the atrocious seduction forced upon you by some degenerate after you had too much to drink at the wedding?"

"That's not—"

"Not the story good Mrs. Livingstone told the rest of the help? Or what dear Mr. Andrew made of the appalling scene early that morning? I'm sure that's what I heard Nelson saying as he was escorting me to the front door."

Jillian hated being put on the defensive. If only Zara would let her finish. "Whatever any of them said or thought, I'm sure their sole intent was to protect me."

Zara snorted. "Oh, and rightly so, princess. Keeping your perfect world intact is the most important thing there is. Nothing could be worse than being found out to be a lesbian. Nothing except having your first affair with a poor American of doubtful parentage and no means—"

"Stop it, Zara." Jillian hoped the pain in her voice wasn't obvious. "You don't understand."

"Yeah, I don't. I don't understand why you're here. I don't understand what you want from me."

Jillian drew herself up. "I want us to try again. I…it was by the merest chance I happened to see you at all, but it made me think that perhaps we're meant to…" She took a breath before turning away. She couldn't face Zara while admitting all her failings. "I failed miserably before, and I still don't know how to do this, Zara. I don't have the slightest idea of how to live like you do, open and unfettered and honest. My whole life has been about doing what was expected, performing my duties, being at the top of my class. I've been trained to please others, but I've never wanted to be close to someone before…before you. I know I have incredible privilege, but the expectations that come with it can be terribly binding. I want very much to be of some use in the world, and I want to be free to feel—" Jillian stopped, trying to swallow her nerves. "I don't know how to tell you…how to…"

She trailed off, hopelessly at a loss about how to say what was in her heart. At the gentle touch of Zara's fingers on her arm, she gathered herself. "I don't know how to be the person I need to be in order to be with you. But I want to try, if you'll let me."

Zara turned her so they were facing each other. Jillian's hopes fell at her stern expression. "You say that now, Jill, and it sounds good. You probably believe it at this moment. But let me tell you what all that really means. It means your life will truly change. You could lose your relationship with your father or your friends. You might not get your dream job. And people may talk about you behind your back or even to your face."

"Some of that already happened when I returned to school," Jillian said softly.

"I'm sorry, but it's good you got an idea of what it's like being on the outside, constantly facing rejection and contempt. Because I'm not going to pretend to be anything other than what I am, and I'm not going to be with anyone who doesn't live like that too. If I'm with someone, I may not make out with her in public, but I'm not going to say we're just friends, either. I want to be able to smile when we look at each other and not have to hide what our smiles mean. I get that I'm asking a lot. But that's what it will take for me. If that sounds like more than you can do, I'm going to ask you to leave now." Zara looked away, her next words softer. "I care for you, Jill. You've been on my mind ever since…well, ever since we met. And I'll never forget the night we spent together. But I won't live a false life, not even if I'd get to be with you. Nothing and no one is worth sacrificing my real self."

Jillian took in the shape of her, thinner than before, it seemed, but still extremely alluring. She thought about what Zara was asking and wondered if she had it in her to be that fearless. Clive had been wonderful during these last hard weeks, and she loved him like a brother. Shouldn't that be enough? Why would she take such a risk when she could go, pretend this meeting never happened, and return to her life of ease and acceptability? She could simply continue to support the therapy for Zara's healing, which would surely fulfill any obligation she might have had.

As if knowing her thoughts, Zara's head dropped slightly, her voice hardening. "And don't do anything out of pity, okay? I've been getting post-burn therapy from St. Thomas, and it's really helping. You don't owe me anything. But you need to figure out what you owe yourself." She turned back into the tiny kitchen. "Let me get your tea."

As pleased as Jillian was to hear the reference to treatments, that wasn't the issue at hand. She tried to imagine what it would be like to be in a relationship with Zara. With no other experience in romance, she had nothing to compare. She just knew she'd never been with anyone who made her feel alive like Zara did, both emotionally and physically. Along with their one night of incredible passion, they'd had such wonderfully deep conversations. Zara was such an intent listener. It felt as if they were the only two people in the world when Jillian talked about her plans, her ideas, and her dreams, and she could hear in Zara's declarations that she believed in them too. She made Jillian feel strong, like she could take on the real world and come out unscathed.

Zara made her laugh without being cruel and made her want to cry when she'd revealed the hardships she'd endured. And the way they'd been with each other the night of the wedding had made her feel all the things that she'd heard in songs and had read about in poems and in the books Constance had loaned her. While she might not know everything about being with Zara, she knew all too well what it was like to be without her. Her world became barren and tiresome, her heart hurting in a seemingly irreparable way.

That thought alone drove her into the kitchen, where she pressed herself lightly against Zara's back. The little sound Zara made gave her the courage to say what she'd been thinking ever since she'd seen her through the taxi window. "I want to spend time with you again. I want to be with you like we were at Fullerhill that night. I'll do whatever it takes." Zara didn't move away, so Jillian slipped her arms around her, linking her hands under Zara's breasts. "Please," she whispered in her ear. "I think about you all the time. My work is suffering, but I can't bring myself to care. Nothing has been right since…I've never missed anyone like I've missed—"

Before she could finish, Zara turned in her arms and covered her mouth in a kiss that was almost fierce. After a second of shock, Jillian matched her passion for passion. When she felt Zara's hands come into her hair, her arms automatically tightened, and her own need to touch Zara everywhere heightened. She ran her hands up Zara's back, letting loose the want she'd been holding back. Leaning away just enough to get her fingers on the buttons of Zara's shirt, she barely restrained a cry when Zara's mouth left hers.

"Okay, yeah," Zara panted. "I've been given second chances in my life, so you get one too. I'm going to trust that you really want this, and we'll agree that if something isn't working for either of us, we'll say so. Okay?"

"Yes, of course," Jillian answered automatically, trying to resist the urge to rub herself against Zara's leg. She'd always loved the sound of Zara's voice, but at this moment, she wished she'd quit talking and kiss her again.

"But if you fuck me over again, that's it."

She grew still at the sudden harshness, blinking when Zara's hand on her chin brought her face back into focus. "And there's one other thing I need to tell you."

Jillian suppressed a sigh. It was entirely fair for Zara to set her terms. "Go ahead."

"We're going to date first." Zara took in a deep breath and eased herself a half step back.

"Date...first?" Jillian's brain wasn't fully reengaged yet.

"Yes." Zara separated from her completely, and Jillian held back a whimper. "Before we, uh, before we're intimate again, we're going to go out in public. Like, have dinner together or go to a movie. The way people do when they're interested in each other."

"Oh. I see." Jillian tried hard to keep the frustration out of her voice.

Zara touched Jillian's cheek, her voice gentle. "Don't misunderstand me, Jill. I'm already interested in you. Any time we had together, just the two of us, I never wanted it to end. Not only the sex, but the hikes, the conversations, all of it. And once upon a time, I'd be taking you to bed right now. But it's not like you're some woman giving me a good line in a bar. You're...this is different. Besides, I'm done with that kind of life." She stared at her palm, and Jillian was pleased to note the healing taking place. The flesh seemed less red and more flexible. "I'm seeing a lot of things differently, as if those dreams I once thought were mine might have been someone else's." She looked up, her expression softening. "That's why I'm asking you for more, for a real relationship. And why I think it's best we take some time to make sure this is what you want. What we both want."

Jillian nodded solemnly before allowing a tiny smile to cross her lips. "You want me to court you, is that it?"

When Zara grinned back, the first smile since she'd arrived, Jillian knew everything was going to work out. "I want us to court each other."

Jillian thought she'd understood the concept of dating, but now she wasn't sure if she'd been misinformed or if Zara just had her own approach. Or perhaps it was because they were both women. In any case, she quickly learned there would be frequent negotiations, which Jillian came to believe was a healthy thing for two people trying to work out a complicated relationship in the modern world.

It began that next Sunday, after Zara agreed to see her again. Certain she could find a way to be released from her "every weekend at home" expectation, Jillian wanted to arrive on Friday evening.

"Friday night isn't good for me," Zara replied laconically. "I won't be home until late."

"Why not?" Jillian asked, genuinely curious. When Zara looked as if she was going to say it was none of her business, she added, "I don't like losing any of the little time we have."

"Yeah, well, I took this job on Friday nights before there was any 'we.' The owner is taking a chance on me, and I wouldn't feel right canceling on him."

"And what will you be doing so late on Friday night?" Jillian asked with a tease in her tone, hoping Zara would answer.

"Barback or runner to start with, hoping to work up to bartending again. Stuff like that."

Although her reply sounded evasive, it might have been because she was describing a working-class job. "So if I came to see you, I could get a free drink?" She moved closer, envisioning Zara behind the bar in a club. She imagined distracting her, being the object of her attention while others waited. Similar fantasies had begun to occupy a lot of her time.

"You don't want to be seen in this place, m'lady." Zara teased back, wagging her finger. "It's a dive."

"Perhaps that's exactly the place to work on my new persona: Jillian Stansfield, dive-visiting dyke."

Zara burst into laughter, putting her arms around Jill's shoulders. "Where did you hear that lovely term?"

"Oh, it was one of many expressions I heard upon my return to school." Somehow, feeling Zara's touch minimized the terrible indignity of those moments.

Zara looked at her with an expression she couldn't decipher. "You're something else, you know?" Zara said, a long very sweet kiss forestalling any reply. She would have done anything after that kiss, so when Zara said, "Come Saturday around noon. After a few weeks, we'll reexamine our schedule. Okay?" Jillian had simply nodded.

Once she was on her way to Cambridge, Jillian began to wonder where she would stay on Saturday nights. Zara's neighborhood didn't seem like it had any decent hotels, but since they wouldn't be sleeping together...

Giving herself a mental shake, Jillian told herself that Zara would have things figured out by next weekend. *Next weekend* echoed in her mind, and she felt excited and settled at the same time. Pulling out her notes for the next day's class, she realized it was the first time she'd been willing to give school more than a passing thought since the spring term had started. Simply knowing Zara was back in her life gave her enough peace of mind to get her through the coming week.

When Jillian arrived promptly at noon the following Saturday, Zara answered the door with a piece of paper in hand. "Did I interrupt your correspondence?" Jillian teased.

Zara folded the paper and put it in her hip pocket. "This is my list of things I'd like for us to do together. And today's map is on the back."

Jillian was confounded. "Was I supposed to do that too?"

Zara shook her head. "Here's my plan. One of us will choose our activity, and the other will be in charge of dining. Then next week, we'll switch. I get a head start because I need to be more financially selective about our outings."

Intrigued, Jillian asked, "Where are we going?"

Zara grabbed her jacket from a hook behind the door and took Jillian's hand. "It's a surprise. Come on."

The simple touch made Jillian long for something more, but she schooled her expression. It was one of those damp, windy days, and she was wearing a heavy, all-weather coat and scarf with matching hat and gloves. Zara's black leather jacket gave her a dangerous air that Jillian found quite appealing, but it didn't look very substantial. "Zara, you'll need more than that jacket to keep you warm," she protested.

Zara winked. "I was hoping to find someone who'd like the job. Think I'll find any takers?"

The wink assured that she was teasing, so Jillian answered in the same manner. "I'll keep an eye out for a likely candidate." At Zara's laugh, she felt like she'd won a prize.

They walked to the nearby tube station and rode for almost half an hour, including one change of trains. After disembarking, Zara referred to her paper, and they began walking again. "You know," Jillian said, glancing around a bit uneasily at the narrow street, "I really haven't spent much time in London proper. There were cultural events when I was younger and some events during the Season, and later, the occasional party Constance dragged me to, but recently, it's only been to the train station and back."

"I've found London to be a fantastic city," Zara replied. "Odd as it sounds, it feels like home." She smiled. "Or maybe I was getting tired of cruising and needed a place to anchor for a while."

Jillian eyed her wistfully. "And there's no other reason you stayed?"

"Hmm. Let me think." Jillian stepped toward her, and Zara backed away, laughing. "Well, there's no shortage of things to do and see, and it's got every kind of food you can imagine."

Her gaze fixed on the restaurant facing them, and Jillian asked, "Have you had lunch? Do we have time for a bite before…before whatever comes next?"

"We've got plenty of time. And no, I was too excited to eat before you got here. But you get to decide about dining today." Zara grinned at her, and Jillian felt the flip of her heart that had been missing every day she'd been alone. She looked ahead to the next eatery.

"This looks new. Would you like to try some barbecue?"

"Barbeque is my favorite."

Zara looked a little chilled, so Jillian asked for a table inside.

"Tell me about school," Zara said after they were seated. "You don't have much longer, do you? What comes next?"

Jillian grimaced. "Only a few more months, yes. And I honestly don't know what comes next. The men in my class are being recruited left and right, but I'm something of an oddity, apparently." She started to mention the possibility of joining the Voluntary Service Overseas when Zara leaned toward her, speaking in a low, purposeful tone.

"You're not odd, Jill," she insisted. "You're incredibly special."

Blushing at the warmth in Zara's voice, Jillian lost her train of thought. Zara had a way of sounding sweet and sincere at the same time, and it never failed to move her. It occurred to Jillian that she didn't have to fight the familiar urge to take her hand, and when Zara's fingers intertwined with hers, she thought her smile was the most beautiful thing she'd seen all day. Was this how it felt to date someone you cared about?

When the waitress approached with menus, Jillian made to pull away, but Zara held fast. "Be brave," she whispered.

Jillian couldn't bring herself to look up, but the woman's tone was pleasant when she asked, "Something to drink?"

Zara ordered tea, and Jillian mumbled that she wanted the same. Once she'd gone, Zara gave her hand a squeeze. "She doesn't care, you know. It's really okay."

Jillian tried to indicate her agreement, but she was relieved when Zara loosened her grip. She took advantage of the moment to put a napkin in her lap, missing the touch but still tense from being so public. "I'm sorry I'm not more—"

Zara cut her off. "You did fine, Jill. We're taking baby steps here, okay?" Jillian managed a nod, and Zara added, "When I push, you can pull back if you need to. But know, I'm going to keep pushing."

"I can't decide if that's reassuring or terrifying," Jillian admitted.

Zara leaned forward again. "Just be honest, babe. That's all I ask."

The affection of the unexpected endearment made Jillian wish for more nerve.

After they'd eaten, the waitress smiled and wished them a good day when she brought the check. Jillian left her a huge tip.

They began walking again, Zara checking the numbers on doorways as they went. She pulled Jillian to a stop in front of another nondescript restaurant. "We're here," she exclaimed, almost gleefully.

"We're where?" Jillian asked.

Zara pointed across the street. Jillian squinted above two parked lorries to read the sign on the shop. "Hoxton Street Monster Supplies?" she asked.

"Yeah. One of my customers last night mentioned it. She said it was the bee's knees."

"Did she?" Jillian raised an eyebrow. "And what else did you get from this woman?"

"Well…" Zara struck a thoughtful pose. "She did have to explain that pissed means drunk. In the US, it means angry, see. Also, that 'spend a penny' is a polite way of saying you're going to the toilet."

"And?"

"Are you jealous, Lady Stansfield?" Zara's grin was as charming as ever, but her question gave Jillian pause.

"I don't know. I don't think I've ever been jealous before so I'm not sure what it's like."

"Well, let me put your mind at ease. This lady was upwards of sixty and missing a noticeable tooth. Not exactly my type, although she was a decent tipper."

"And what is your type? Besides the tipping part."

Zara indicated the store across the street. "My type would stride bravely into a monster supply store and willingly peruse the witches' brew or possibly even sample a toadstool biscuit."

Jillian waved her hand airily. "Done." They crossed the street arm in arm, and an hour later, Jillian was wiping tears of laughter from her eyes as Zara swung the shopping bag they'd accumulated. "You and those petrified mice. I don't know when I've had such fun." It was true. She had fun with Zara because she could relax and be herself. Especially the self she wanted to be. Everything felt new and exuberant and safe.

"You were enormously generous to buy me cubed earwax," Zara said, grinning as she dug a finger around in her ear before offering it to Jill.

Laughing, Jill pulled the packet from their bag and read the fine print on the back. "Clotted cream fudge doesn't sound nearly as monstrous, does it?" Contemplating the storefront again, she said, "I love that their profits go to the Ministry of Stories. Some of those writings were quite exceptional."

Zara nodded, her expression intense. "That's another reason I wanted to bring you here. Because I know you care about people who just need a chance."

Jillian felt her heart clench. Was Zara the only person who knew that about her? Was that why she needed to be with her? "Thank you for that too," she said quietly.

Zara leaned forward and kissed her softly on the lips. A whistle sounded from one of the passing truck drivers, and Zara pulled back as if watching for her reaction. Jillian was astonished to realize she wasn't the least bit concerned about the whistle or the people on the street. She wanted the feel of Zara's mouth and the taste of her lips again. She stepped closer and kissed Zara back, less softly and less slowly. "Can we go back to your place now?" she asked when Zara moaned faintly.

"What about dinner?" Zara asked, her voice husky.

"How do you feel about takeaway?"

"If you mean takeout, I'm very much in favor of that."

Because Zara couldn't decide, they ended up with a wide sampling of Indian food, including chicken makhani, rogan josh, samosas, aloo gobi, and naan. Since it wouldn't all fit on Zara's tiny kitchen table, they rotated the food from the nearest counter until they were both too full for anything else, even cubed earwax.

"This is my favorite now," Zara said, holding her stomach. If she suspected Jillian had bought larger servings for her to eat during the week to come, she didn't say anything as they put the food away. After a moment of silence, she remarked, "I'm sorry I don't have a TV. Or a radio."

"What do you normally do after dinner?" Jillian was genuinely curious.

"I read if I find a copy of the paper someone threw away. Or Mrs. Donnelly invites me over to watch TV."

Jillian looked at the piano. "Do you play?"

Zara swallowed and stared at her hands. "I…I've started doing some developmental exercises. Nothing musical, only stretching and warm-up-type basics."

"How does it feel?" Jillian asked gently.

Zara didn't answer right away, but Jillian would have waited all night. "Like I borrowed a hand from someone else, and that person didn't know how to play," Zara said finally. "So I'm having to teach them." She looked up, meeting Jill's eyes. "I'll never be the performer I was. No Royal College of Music for me. But you know what? I'm actually okay with that. I just want to be able to jam again like I did in Chicago. Maybe back up a band who plays for fun and get a little extra income. I want to feel a connection with other musicians, you know? Being a solo act is fine because I'm in control of the whole show, but sometimes, the best sounds happen spontaneously when I click with someone else." She gave a slow smile. "I guess romance is like that too, huh?"

"I haven't the faintest idea," Jillian said seriously. "But I'd like to find out."

Chapter Fourteen

She'd given a lot of thought to their sleeping arrangements. When Jillian came out of the bathroom in the same penguin pajamas she'd worn—briefly—on their night together, Zara murmured, "Not fair," and Jill smiled knowingly. Zara gestured toward the bed she'd pulled down and tidied during Jill's preparations. Jillian worried at her lip shyly before staring at the extra pillow and blanket that Zara had set on the overstuffed chair.

"You can't mean to sleep there." Jill pointed.

"I've done it before," Zara said casually.

"When you had company?" Jill asked, raising an eyebrow.

"No, before I got the new mattress on the pull-down bed. The one that came with the place was disgusting, but the landlord wouldn't replace it. I didn't want to spend the money, but these days, I'm a little pickier about my sleeping conditions. After I dragged the old mattress out, I slept here for a week before I got the new one delivered. I'll be fine."

"Why don't I take the chair?"

"Because you're my guest, and I insist you take the bed." When Jillian opened her mouth to protest, Zara shook her head. "Please, Jill."

Jillian sighed and climbed into the bed. "I don't suppose it would do any good to state the obvious? That we could both sleep here?"

"We're dating, remember? Not sleeping together right now."

"I'll try my best not to seduce you," Jill purred, her sultry tone implying just the opposite.

Zara closed her eyes against the surge of desire. "You may have that kind of self-discipline, Lady Stansfield, but I don't. Get some rest. I'm taking you out for breakfast before you catch your train."

Over the next several dates, they learned a lot about each other. Jill had gloried in their visit to the London Mithraeum, an amazing reconstruction of the ancient Roman temple dedicated to the God Mithras. She could have spent hours perusing the fantastic number of artifacts dating back nearly 2,000 years, but once Zara learned that the mysterious cult was male only, she scowled through the rest of their visit.

"How many more centuries will we have to put up with that kind of shit?" she asked.

For their next outing, they visited the Twinings flagship store. Jill teased Zara that she needed to be educated on proper English teas. For her part, Zara would have sampled all the free offerings and left, but after a moment, they were led to a private room where Jill had booked a two-hour masterclass called Women in Tea History. Zara was so delighted by the stories of history and innovation that she didn't object when Jill bought a personalized Pick & Mix box containing each of their favorites to keep at the flat.

Touched by the idea of Jillian arranging the class as a balance for her disappointment from the male focus of the previous week's outing, Zara became more convinced that the thoughtful gesture underscored the genuine goodness of Jill's nature.

Jill had begun arriving with one or two newspapers, and they spent their evenings talking about a wide variety of topics, sometimes facing each other across the small kitchen table, sometimes lying close together on the overstuffed chair. Once they'd gone through the news, Zara took great pleasure in reading the classifieds. When Jill asked why, she said it had started with job searches, but gradually, she'd taken an interest in everything from lost pets to wedding announcements to obituaries. Sometimes, she'd read particularly entertaining items aloud, offering sympathy or editorial comments, and Jill seemed to like seeing other people's lives through Zara's perspective.

Jill seemed increasingly comfortable with touching in public too, often taking Zara's hand in spite of the occasional glare or slur called from a passing car. When they dined out, she'd begun sitting next to Zara rather than across from her. They didn't often kiss around others only because it was becoming increasingly hard to stop. During the time they spent in Zara's small apartment, when Jill innocently— maybe—ran her tongue over her lips while they caught up on the past week, or when she let her eyes drift over Zara's body in that way she had, it took every ounce of willpower not to pull down the bed and forget about this dating stuff. She had to keep reminding herself of the reasons for taking it slow.

It had been a long time since she'd gotten beyond the surface with anyone and maybe longer since somebody had taken the trouble to know her. Except for Gina, most of the crew had only been nodding acquaintances, and her occasional fling with a passenger was just that, infrequent and brief.

She'd spoken with Mickey Meyer the last time she'd been in the States, but there wasn't anyone else who really got her. She thought Jill might, and she truly appreciated gaining insight into how Jill's mind worked and how she viewed the world, even when it was different from Zara's way of seeing things. The problem was, she could feel herself getting in deeper with each passing week, and that was trouble. She caught herself awaiting Jill's knock each weekend, feeling a combination of relief and elation at the sound. And after she was gone on Sunday nights, Zara waited to change the sheets, unable to stop herself from falling into the space where Jill had slept, reveling in her scent.

The more time they spent together, the more difficult it was to keep Jill at a distance, especially during the moments when Jill's feelings for her were so clearly the same. While Zara's heart wanted to believe things could actually work out between them, her mind assured her that the day would come when things would get fucked-up. They always did. And when that happened, it was going to hurt like hell. She kept convincing herself that she could keep it light and enjoy the ride, even though she should be working more hours, saving money, and making plans to return to America. But those things were hard to do when she spent the weekends strolling around London with a beautiful, brilliant woman on her arm.

That Saturday was already living up to the prediction that it would be the coldest day of the year, and temperatures were to continue dropping into the night. The heat in Zara's building was pitiful, and she was already wearing an extra layer under her heavy sweater. She hoped Jill would be all right with the project she had in mind for the day but knew that she would go ahead with it in any case.

When Jill arrived with a bag in hand, Zara gave her a look. "Is that lunch?"

"No, but it should go with us when we eat." She pulled out a beautiful scarf that featured alternating wide maroon stripes with smaller bands of black and white and looped it around Zara's neck. "A gift from the Department of Engineering at Cambridge." She pointed to the King's College crest at the bottom. "It looks wonderful on you."

Zara fingered the fine wool wrap. "This is really nice Jill, but you don't need to buy me things to make me want to be with you."

Jill waved her hand dismissively. "I know that, silly. But it's terribly cold out, and I knew you didn't have a scarf. Or gloves." Jill held out a heavyweight, waterproof pair, similar to hers. "I can't have you freezing to death while we're tromping around the city."

Zara couldn't bring herself to tell Jill that she'd already handed over three sets of scarves and gloves to homeless kids she encountered when coming home late at night. She bought replacements at the thrift store, never spending enough to feel bad about giving them away to someone whose life was much harder than hers. Especially now that her life had Jillian Stansfield in it. She took in a breath. "No hat?" she asked, holding back a smile.

Jill laughed and reached into the bag again, producing a black knit hat with the same King's College crest on it. "People will either take you for a student or a tourist."

"That figures, since I'm neither," Zara said, pulling the warm beanie low on her head. She wavered for a moment before throwing her arms around Jill's neck. "Thanks, babe."

Jill held her close. "You're welcome. And I promise, I won't buy another thing today except the taxi fare."

"What taxi fare?" Zara asked, pulling away.

"It's too cold for the tube today. And I have another surprise." She held out two slips of paper. "I got us tickets to the ballet."

"Jill—" Zara began, but Jill cut her off, taking her hands.

"Please, humor me this once." At Zara's frown, she added, "We can take the tube for the rest of the month."

"It's not that. I…I thought we'd do something a little different today."

"Oh?" Encouraged that Jill didn't seem terribly put out—yet—Zara gestured at the table behind her. It was covered with standing tubes with pointy tips. On each of their chairs was a hollowed-out metal piece that resembled a gun with the insides missing. "What is all this?"

"It's caulk. For the windows. From the way the f-ing cold blows in, I'd guess they haven't been sealed since London was bombed, so this should really help. I'd thought maybe we could practice in here and see. If it does, we could do Mrs. Donnelly's and then…see how far we can go with what we've got."

Jill cast another glance toward the materials. "I don't have the slightest idea how—"

"Yeah, I figured that, but it's easy. I haven't started yet, so I could show you." Zara cleared her throat. "But if you'd rather not, we can go to the ballet, and I can start on this tomorrow after you go. It's just that tonight is supposed to be very cold."

"Yes, well…"

Zara waited, holding her breath, as Jill looked once more at the tickets in her hand.

"Do you think Mrs. Donnelly would like to go to the ballet?"

Zara didn't think she'd ever seen her elderly neighbor so excited. And Megan had never been to the ballet, which meant she was doubly thrilled. Once they'd gone, Zara set about teaching Jill the fine art of caulking. It was no surprise that Jillian Stansfield was a quick study, and they finished the two apartments in less than an hour. "Where to now?" Jill asked, her tone eager.

Zara pointed at apartment 1D. "Mr. Davies is pretty much an old sourpuss. He wanted nothing to do with our tenants' council, so he may slam the door in my face, but I'm willing to risk it if you are."

"As it happens, old sourpusses are my specialty."

Zara grinned. Only Jill made her feel this way. Warm and sure and wanting, all at the same time. Unbidden, the words, *I love you*, popped into her head. Shit. Instead, she said, "Then let's go for it."

As she'd expected, Mr. Davies took one look at her and started with, "I already told you, Keller, I'm not signing any—" When his gaze shifted to Jill, he stopped abruptly, giving Zara time to explain their errand. He asked them to wait, and when he returned, Zara was sure he had combed his hair and put on a clean shirt.

Apartment 2A housed a single mom with two children, both under the age of five. The boy, the older of the two, greeted Zara with an enthusiastic hug. But after he saw Jill, Zara seemed to vanish from his consciousness. Before they left, Jill had cut her cashmere scarf in two, giving each child a new warm wrap.

By the time they took a break for lunch, Zara's apartment felt warmer. "It's working!" Jill's smile was brilliant.

"Maybe. Or maybe we're warmer from all our activity."

Jill studied her. "It's not like you to be negative. What's wrong? Am I not caulking correctly?"

"You are caulking spectacularly." Zara squeezed Jill's hand as she took the caulk gun. "And you had old Mr. Sourpuss eating out of your hand. I should have hired some landed gentry to get him to sign our complaint form."

Jill laughed. "I'll bet there'd be dozens of applications for such a position."

Zara couldn't answer for a moment because there was a strange tightness in her throat. She took Jill's face in her hands. "Do you have any idea how fucking beautiful you are right now?"

"Zara, I..." A flush was on her cheeks. "I think this is our best date yet. Thank you for giving me the chance to do something useful."

They kissed, and it was different, as if their lips were having a conversation, saying all the things Zara had no intention of uttering out loud. When she forced herself to stop, it was hard to catch her breath. "Listen, I'm going to use Mrs. Donnelly's phone and call the pizza place down the street. What do you like on yours?"

"Pineapple and extra anchovies?"

Zara brought her hand to her mouth, trying to hide her horrified expression. Jill kept a straight face for a few seconds before breaking into laughter as Zara looked around the room as if seeking a solution to a very difficult problem.

"Give a girl a caulk gun, and she thinks she's a comedian," Zara muttered as she went to the door, the sound of Jill's laughter following her.

They devoured the pizza and returned to caulking. It was fully dark when their supplies ran out, and by then, only four apartments were unsealed. Zara was worn out, the late hours at the bar and shopping early for the caulk catching up with her, but Jill seemed energized.

"Where do we get more of this?" she asked, pointing to the empty tube in her caulk gun.

"We don't. We've expended our budget of time and expenses. We're done."

Jill blinked. "But the job isn't complete."

"It's as complete as it's going to get," Zara said, washing her hands. "It's late, and we've done all we can do for now."

"What if we—"

Zara cut her off. "Jill, I'm glad you enjoyed yourself, but we're calling it a night, okay?

Clearing her throat, clearly trying to be delicate, Jillian said, "Zara, I'd be happy to contribute funds—"

"I didn't ask you for money, did I?" Zara snapped. "You rich types think that's all it takes to get your way. Well, it doesn't always work like that. Money won't open the stores that are already closed, and money won't create more time and energy to get the job done. I'm telling you, there's nothing more to do tonight because we're fucking finished. Get it?"

Jill drew herself up. "Frankly, no. I don't get it. I've never known you to be harsh or heartless like this. But since you've clearly decided to be both, I'm going to get cleaned up. And afterward, I expect you to tell me what happened."

Zara was at the sink, very deliberately cleaning the caulk guns. Her tone was casual. "What happened when?"

"What happened to you that shaped this attitude about letting someone help you. About money."

"Maybe it comes naturally when no one does, and you don't have any."

"Those answers would probably satisfy a casual acquaintance, but I want to know the whole story." Zara opened her mouth, but before she could object, Jill added, "And I want the whole story because I want the whole Zara."

Zara closed her mouth.

She prepared herself during Jillian's time in the shower, but when they finally got the chance to talk, the sweet reassurance of Jill's arms and the sorrow in her eyes made Zara come undone. As she told the story of Mrs. Minton's death and what had happened afterward, she cried like she hadn't in years—maybe ever.

Jill didn't ask a single question, just gradually closed the distance Zara had set between them until she was holding her and softly stroking her hair. When Zara finished, Jillian only said, "This isn't the weather for you to sleep by the window. Come lie with me."

Too emotionally drained to resist, Zara moved to the bed. When Jill pulled her close, she gave in to the comfort, certain that nothing would ever feel as good. When she woke sometime later with Jill's hands on her, she knew she was wrong.

"Tell me if you want me to stop," Jill whispered. "I've been lying here trying to resist, but I need to touch you so badly."

"Forgive me for being such a shit earlier," Zara said, brushing the hair from Jill's face. It was time to put her cards on the table. "I'm afraid of how I feel about you, and my mind tells me I should push you away."

Jill gave a short laugh and lay back down on her side. "Aren't we a pair? I've been trying to deny my feelings ever since you walked onto my terrace." She touched Zara's cheek. "But you've changed me, you know? Not only like this, but in how I see the world. In spite of myself, I'm growing into the life I feel I'm supposed to have."

Zara couldn't bring herself to ask if she was included in that life. "You've found your courage."

"Not entirely," Jill said, and the sudden sadness in her tone made Zara turn to her.

"Don't be hard on yourself. The kind of change you're making can't happen overnight."

"Zara, I—" Jill began, but Zara put a finger on her lips.

"Not now. Enough talk. I'm tired of resisting too." She rested a hand on Jill's abdomen, loving the sound of Jill's breath catching. "Tell me what you want."

"I want you." Jill turned them so she was on top.

Jill, especially in this commanding, demanding position, was unlike any woman Zara had known, and that alone turned her on. She tried to keep her voice steady, willing to go wherever this would lead. "Then have me, Lady Stansfield."

❖

Zara had bought more caulk, and they smiled at each other as they finished their project from last weekend. As they worked, Zara casually mentioned they had a new employee at the bar, one who'd jumped at the chance to work Friday nights.

"Does this mean you'd like to see more of me?" Jillian teased.

"More of you and more often," Zara said. She couldn't bring herself to admit how crazy it made her to think about what it was like for Jill at her home, where she imagined everyone was pushing her toward a wedding. The very thought of her being greeted by Clive with a kiss, sitting beside him at dinner, allowing him to hold her hand, made Zara grind her teeth.

If she believed this was just a dalliance, and that marriage to Clive—or any man—was what Jillian really needed, she would have already given her up. But Jill was coming into her own, seeing the potential for her place in the bigger world. And being with Jill made Zara a better person, more willing to believe in possibilities for herself and them. They were good together, and she found herself ready to take another step toward acknowledging they were a couple.

"I'll see what I can do about that," Jillian said. Zara liked the smile that accompanied her statement.

She made it a point to get cleaned up first, so when Jill got out of her shower, Zara was already dressed in her only suit. It had a somewhat masculine cut, but for tonight, it would be perfect. Jill raised her eyebrows. "What's on for the evening?"

Grinning, Zara said, "We're going dancing."

"Oh, Zara, no. We can't."

"I thought you trusted me,"

"I do, but—"

Zara took both her hands. "No buts. It'll be fine. I promise."

Jill searched her eyes. After a few seconds, she sighed. "What should I wear?"

"Something you can move in, whatever makes you feel like you're ready to have fun."

"So I could wear trousers too?"

"Anything you want."

Zara waited patiently while Jill changed clothes three times. Finally, she settled on a red, puff-sleeve blazer dress with three rows of two buttons each down the front. It hit her at mid-thigh, and she wore medium-height, strappy, black heels. Zara gave a low whistle. Then she made a show of searching the apartment, opening cabinets and lifting the cushions on the big chair.

After a minute, Jill asked, "What are you looking for?"

"You look absolutely amazing, babe. I'm gonna need a big stick to beat them off you." Jill laughed, but Zara kept her tone earnest. "Stay close to me, okay? And don't eat or drink anything unless I give it to you."

"What kind of place are you taking me?"

Zara's face relaxed. "Our kind of place." A horn honked outside. "There's our taxi. Let's go."

Heads turned when they walked in. Jillian tightened her hold on Zara's arm. She'd never felt comfortable in social gatherings, and Zara's warnings had made her even more nervous.

"Let's get a drink," Zara said, and Jillian eyed the crowd as they moved toward the bar. Almost everyone else was in jeans and T-shirts, with a few in trousers and button-down shirts.

"It's all women in here," she whispered.

Zara laughed. "Yep. This is a lesbian bar."

Jillian was astonished. "I had no idea they had such things."

Zara nodded, keeping an arm around Jillian's waist. "There are bars for the men too. Sometimes we mix, and that's fun. But I thought we'd start here."

"How many are there?"

"Here in London or around the world?" Zara grinned.

Before Jill could answer, they reached the bar, and the woman ahead of them turned quickly with two drinks in hand. When she looked up and saw them, she stopped short to avoid a collision, spilling half of one drink and most of the other onto the floor.

"Oi! You toffs just cost me a day's pay in liquor." She focused on Zara. "Get stuffed, will you?"

Jillian felt Zara tense and saw her clench her fists. She took a half step forward. "I expect we're as desperate for a drink as you are. Please, let us buy your round when we get ours."

The woman shifted her gaze to Jillian. "At least someone around here has some manners. Yeah, love. Two whiskeys, if you please. And the pint is mine as well." She deftly combined her spilled drinks and, putting one glass back, grabbed the waiting beer. "We're at that table by the window." She indicated the direction with her head.

"Lovely," Jillian said. "We'll bring the fresh ones right over."

Zara was staring, but Jillian saw an opening at the bar and stepped into it. "Three whiskeys, please," she shouted to the bartender before turning back. "What will you have?"

"Carling."

The bartender began pouring. "You're pretty smooth for a toff," Zara said, and Jillian grinned.

"You said we're here to have fun, so I thought it best we not get into an argument less than a minute after arriving."

Zara rolled her eyes, but once they'd carried the new drinks and their own to the table, they were invited to sit. The place was crowded enough that Zara gave her a thumbs-up.

The woman from the bar introduced herself as Susan. "And this is my lovely Tracy," she said, kissing the cheek of the woman with her.

"I'm Michelle," Zara said quickly. "And this is Sarah. Cheers." She picked up her beer, and they all joined her. The music changed to something a bit slower, and Zara grabbed Jillian's hand. "We're going to dance. Okay if we come sit with you after?" Susan nodded.

On the dance floor, Jillian asked, "Why did you give them false names?"

"Would you prefer I introduced you as Lady Stansfield?" Zara asked, pulling Jillian against her.

For a moment, the headiness of feeling Zara move against her in public took Jillian's breath. "So this is what happens at these places," she finally managed. "You might get into a fight, you might make some friends, or you might get so excited dancing together that you leave before your second drink."

Zara grinned and put her lips to Jillian's ear. "You're a very quick study, Sarah."

Jillian slid her hands down Zara's back and cupped her firm arse. "Tell me why you brought me here, Michelle."

Zara took in a shaky breath. "For all the reasons you said and to show you another part of the world that you didn't know about. There's a community like this almost anywhere you go, and you can be a part of it if you want to."

"I can, or we can?" Jillian asked.

"I think that's up to you. I just wanted you to know there's more than one option for society."

"And what if I only want a society of one?"

Zara kissed her. They kissed until the next song came on, and when Jillian felt someone jostle her for the second time, she said, "Should we rejoin our friends at the table?"

For the most part, the music was too loud for conversation, but it was nice to have a place to sit.

"How long have you two been together?" Susan yelled.

Jillian stiffened. It hadn't occurred to her that Zara might have another purpose in bringing her here. Did she expect Jillian to define their relationship in some way that they hadn't previously? Was this a way of pressuring her into making a commitment?

"A little less than a year," Zara replied quickly, and Jillian's tension eased. Zara wasn't like that, and she knew it.

The two across from them nodded at each other. "We thought it must be something like that," Tracy said. "Young love and all."

"How about you?" Zara was clearly trying to shift the focus.

"Forever." Susan grinned at Tracy. "Six years."

Jillian heard the word forever echoing in her mind. A measure of time like that had never meant anything but an abstraction. But there was something especially sweet about the way Susan and Tracey smiled at each other, and her mind unexpectedly accepted the idea of stretching time into forever with another person. Forever with Zara? Could that be possible?

"You know what they say." Tracy winked, apparently reading Jillian's expression as doubtful. "Time in lesbian relationships is like dog years. One equals seven."

Susan laughed, and Jillian turned to Zara. "Does it feel like seven years to you?"

"Is there a safe way to answer that question?" Zara asked.

Jillian joined in the laughter, feeling much more like herself than she ever had at a gathering like this. Although, she corrected herself, there had never been an outing quite like this before. As if to prove her point, Zara's lips were against her ear. "I'd take seven years with you. Or maybe seven hundred."

An hour later, they were in a cab on the way back to Zara's apartment. Two friends of Susan and Tracy had joined them, and it had been fun until one of the new arrivals had gotten smashed enough that she began hitting on Jillian. "You're the best-looking bird in this whole shire," she'd slurred.

At first, Zara had let the compliment go, but when the woman put a hand on Jillian's thigh, she'd leaned toward her. "That's private property, mate," Zara had said in the basest accent Jillian had ever heard from her.

When they got home, they squeezed in to Zara's tiny shower to wash off the smoke and fell into bed. The sky was gray with a hint of dawn when Jillian awoke to find Zara leaning on one elbow, studying her.

"What is it?" Jillian asked. "Was I snoring?"

Zara shook her head. "You are the best-looking bird in the whole shire," she said. "What are you doing with me?"

"I'm learning. I'm growing." Jillian stopped, hearing the words, *I'm falling in love*, in her head. "And I'm having my honor defended by someone I…" There it was again. The moment to say more. Jillian swallowed. "By someone I rather like."

"So we're in rather like, are we?"

Zara was so funny when she imitated proper English. Jillian laughed. "I think we are, yes."

❖

They were beginning their third month when Lord Stansfield's presence at Fullerhill spoiled Jill's arrival. She'd only planned to put in a quick appearance Friday afternoon, but her father sat her down and began scolding her about her failure to begin planning her wedding. Jill was barely able to keep herself from throwing questions at him about Zara and the supposed theft, but she knew it would only create more animosity between them. She held her tongue until he announced that Clive would be there on Saturday afternoon, and he expected to meet with them to settle some basic matters, such as the date and location of their nuptials.

"But I'm leaving in the morning," Jill stated firmly. Desperate as she was to make sure she and Zara had their time together, she still didn't like lying. "I have a project that needs attention."

He seemed to be just holding his temper. "Jilly, dear, it's time you gave more attention to your personal life and less to your schooling. Constance is doing fine as a married woman, as will you."

"Constance is struggling. Her grades are slipping, and she's exhausted. Establishing their new home and being a wife to Nelson and going to school at the same time is taxing." Jill made sure to keep her tone pleasant. "Couldn't we talk about all this after I graduate? I don't care about having a June wedding. In fact, I'd prefer the fall."

She stayed still in the face of her father's scrutiny, knowing the slightest twitch could give her away. After what seemed like hours, he sighed. "Very well. If that's truly what you want."

Jill couldn't quite bring herself to hug him, but she squeezed his arm. "It is. Thank you, Father."

In spite of her success at getting a temporary reprieve, she left the house much earlier on Saturday, needing to escape the critical eyes of the staff. All the way into town, she wrestled with how to tell Zara about her father's demands for her future. Zara had been sweet and funny and caring through their dating days, but there had been an underlying element of withholding in her manner that Jillian knew was entirely her fault. Though she never said, it was apparent that Zara hadn't truly believed Jillian was fully committed to her. Recently, though, with the return of their intimate connection, they were well into rebuilding a solid foundation of trust. The relationship was growing into more than Jill had ever dreamed. She had a supportive friend, a delightful companion, and a thoughtful lover, all in the same person. Now it was up to her to confess about Clive and hope they could find a way to work through it.

But when she arrived at the apartment, one of Zara's ties was draped over the doorknob, and Mrs. Donnelly's door was open.

"Come have a cup of tea with me, dearie," the older woman called from her wheelchair as she gestured to a well-worn couch. "Zara will be through with her company in a quarter hour or so."

"She has company?" Jillian asked, sitting hesitatingly.

"Indeed, and more every week, I'd say." Mrs. Donnelly leaned toward Jillian slightly and lowered her voice. "We all think it's just what she needs after the accident, you know?"

Mrs. Donnelly's gentle Irish brogue didn't lessen Jill's shock. "She told you about the accident?"

"Ah, to be sure, she did. Seems unlike her to have been so careless. But those old-style fire grates can be dangerous, it's true."

Careless? Old fire grates? What had Zara told her?

"I knew there was something wrong by the way she kept to herself at first, but she was lured in by my offer of these lovely biscuits, as you must be as well." Mrs. Donnelly pointed to a plate on the table. "And then, once we struck our deal, her damaged hand was an issue while holding the wheelchair for a bit, but she's much better now. Helpers from the hospital, you know. Which explains the company, doesn't it?" she added with a wink. "She told me to keep you occupied if you came early because she doesn't want you getting jealous." Jillian was having trouble catching her breath, but the older woman didn't notice. Smiling, she said, "Our Zara must be a talented instructor, based on the sounds I hear."

Jillian couldn't hear anything for the pounding in her head. Here she was, worried about telling Zara about Clive, and Zara was…what? Instructing other women in how to kiss so as to leave someone weak? Lovemaking techniques that would make a woman willing to change her whole life? She got to her feet unsteadily. "Please, excuse me."

When she walked toward the doorway, Mrs. Donnelly said, "You mustn't bother her just yet, dearie."

Jillian stepped through Mrs. Donnelly's doorway right as the door to 1B opened to reveal a tall, elegant woman kissing Zara on each cheek. "Thank you, my darling," she said, her back to the hallway, her accent vaguely familiar. "It was a marvelous experience, as always."

"Of course, Madame—" Zara began, before seeing Jillian in the hallway. With her guest distracted, Zara winked at her before putting on a surprised face. "Oh, hello, Lady Stansfield. You're a bit early for your lesson today."

Jillian's eyes were riveted on Zara's guest. "Professor Garnier?"

The woman turned somewhat reluctantly from Zara. She inclined her head slightly, studying Jillian. "Stansfield? Ah, yes. Jillian, isn't it?"

"Yes, Madame." Jillian was at a total loss but managed to stammer. "It's…it's nice to see you again."

"And you," Jillian's Mathematical Methods professor from her second year sounded less than sincere, but it was enough. "I must say, you never struck me as the type to take up an instrument, much less the piano."

Piano? Jill's mind cleared. *Zara is giving piano lessons.* She laughed a little. "I'm actually just starting. But they say music and mathematics go well together, so I guess I'll find out."

Zara had been watching with an amused expression. "Come on in." She gestured grandly before adding, "I'll see you next week, Madame Garnier."

"You will indeed," the professor agreed, giving Jillian one more quick look before turning away.

Jillian realized Mrs. Donnelly was in the doorway, apparently having witnessed the whole exchange. "I tried to tell her not to interrupt," she stage-whispered to Zara.

"It's no problem." Zara waved and closed the door. Looking to Jillian, who stood staring at the sheet music on the instrument and the few pieces lying on the bench, she said, "Didn't Mrs. Donnelly explain I was giving a lesson?"

"Not as clearly as she might have, no." Turning to Zara, Jillian began unbuttoning her blouse. Zara watched without changing expression, but Jillian was pleased to see the pulse in her neck from across the room. "She said you had company, and I was not to interrupt or be jealous."

When she finished the last button, she looked up to find Zara grinning at her. "Just a wild guess here, but it seems like you've done both."

"Do you find Professor Garnier attractive?" Jillian demanded, taking hold of Zara's chin.

Zara shrugged. "She's okay, I guess."

Jillian let go and allowed her shirt to fall to the floor. "Is she the most attractive of all your students?"

"That depends," Zara said, standing very still as Jillian reached for the button on her fly.

Jillian stopped, her fingers around the waistband of Zara's trousers. "On what?"

"On if I count you as one of my students or not."

Jillian pulled Zara in. "This is another new feeling for me. But I think…no, I'm sure…that if I ever found you in bed with another woman, I would administer a prodigious new level of suffering on you."

Zara put a gentle hand on the back of Jillian's neck. "Let me tell you about my new feeling. I can give you complete assurance you'll never have to worry about that."

"Pull down the bed," Jillian ordered.

"So we're not going to the museum?" Zara's grin was back.

"Pull down the bed, and we'll talk about it."

"Really?" Zara was reaching for the strap.

"No."

By the time Jillian left for school the next afternoon, Clive was the farthest thing from her mind.

Chapter Fifteen

Constance and Nelson had discussed it on two successive days following their last Friday at Fullerhill: Jillian was clearly returning to her old self, but she also seemed...changed. Nelson had been afraid she'd been going in the direction of bitterness or would become even more uncommunicative, but on their recent visits, Jillian was warm and amiable and increasingly affectionate. Nelson was tremendously relieved, so Constance had to keep her worries to herself. Jillian had been badly hurt and was too down to simply bounce back without a reason, and Constance was afraid she knew exactly what—or more precisely, who—that reason was.

When Nelson brought up the topic again on the third night, Constance felt uncharacteristically snappish. "Just leave it, Nelson. We've done all we can to help Jillian make her way through this. We need to concentrate on our own future." He looked at her like she'd grown a second head but wisely said nothing. She simmered for the rest of the week, and the following Friday evening, she pulled Jillian into the study at the earliest opportunity.

"You've seen her." Constance made sure her tone left no wiggle room, but apparently, Jillian didn't want any. Her smile was brilliant.

"Yes. And the way it happened was almost miraculous." Jillian nattered on about the circumstances until Constance ran out of patience.

"And now?"

"We're...dating," Jillian said, her eyes losing focus.

"Dating?" Constance worked hard to keep her voice down. "You can't date another woman."

"Evidently, you can."

Jillian's composure made Constance wish she'd never brought it up. She cast about for a response. "But why would you? You must know there's no future in it. You're not a lesbian. You're marrying Clive, for heaven's sake." Jillian said nothing, but her mouth took on a stubborn set that Constance hadn't seen in years. "And she doesn't mind seeing you when you're engaged to a man? She told me she wouldn't be part of a cheat." At that, Jillian paled. "Oh, Jilly. You haven't told her?"

"I meant to, the last time we were together, but I…" She stood and began pacing. "You know I think Clive is a wonderful person, but he doesn't make me feel like Zara does."

"Maybe you haven't given him a fair chance. You tried one time. Now that you know what you want, see if he can't come close, at least."

Constance watched as Jillian turned this over in her mind. "It would ruin everything if Zara ever found out," she murmured. "She's only just begun to truly trust me."

"Yes, the waitress friend of hers from the ship said that some rich person had ripped her off or some such thing."

"Do you know the story?"

Constance shook her head. She didn't actually care, but if the telling would help Jillian get through it, she would listen. Jillian sat back beside her. "Zara's parents threw her out of the house at a young age because of…you know…her ways."

Relieved that Jillian wasn't waving a flag for homosexuality, Constance nodded.

"She'd been very close with her piano instructor, Mrs. Minton, who eventually rescued her from being homeless. She took Zara in for several years and became her family. Mrs. Minton's children—a daughter and a son—were grown with lives of their own, and Zara was like a third child for her. Closer, really, since the other two had no interest in music, and Zara was a prodigy. Anyway, in later years, Mrs. Minton developed cancer, and Zara gave up her scholarship to the San Francisco Conservatory of Music to care for her. The son called occasionally, the daughter rarely, but neither came home. One night, Mrs. Minton told Zara she was having her will redone, leaving Zara a substantial sum of money and her house and all its furnishings including—most important to Zara—her Steinway. Zara told her she didn't care about anything but the piano, but Mrs. Minton insisted. She also told her she'd written to a friend at the Royal College of Music, and her recommendation alone was such that Zara was promised a position."

Jillian sighed. "You can probably guess how it ends. After the woman died, the daughter arrived first and acted appreciative while she assessed everything in the house and went through her mother's paperwork. Zara made the mistake of mentioning the new will simply because she wanted to assure the daughter that she just wanted the upright. When the son arrived, Zara remembered how he'd seemed almost jealous when she and Mrs. Minton had reunited in Chicago, so she left the house for a while to give him and his sister time to talk. The police were waiting when she returned, and they arrested her. The daughter accused Zara of mistreating their mother and suggested she was responsible for her death. While she was arranging to defend herself from that charge, they managed to have the new will voided. Zara spent nearly nine months and every cent she'd earned in piano competitions over the years, trying to fight them, but was unsuccessful, except for being found blameless in Mrs. Minton's death. Zara said they sold the house and her beloved instrument for pennies on the dollar, which I assume means less than they were worth, which left her homeless again and broke. She wrote to the RCM and was told the delay had cost her the position. All they would promise her was a tryout, but she'd have to get there on her own. She signed on with the cruise line, and the rest, as they say, is history."

Constance wasn't sure what to say. "What is she doing now?" she finally asked.

"She's giving piano lessons during the day, and she works in a bar at night during the week."

"Lovely," Constance said, not completely under her breath. At Jillian's glare she added, "She's given up on the RCM?"

"She told me that was Mrs. Minton's dream, not hers. I think she may recover enough to play casually, for her own enjoyment. Possibly with other musicians."

"And be supported by her wealthy girlfriend," Constance couldn't help adding.

"It's not like that at all," Jillian insisted, seemingly ignoring Constance's eye roll.

"What does she say about her future?"

"We don't talk about the future. We simply enjoy the time we have." Jillian looked down, biting her lip.

"That's not you, Jilly, and you know it. You have a future. One you've planned for and worked toward. You may be enjoying this now, but it won't last. It can't. Tomorrow will come, and you'll have a job and a husband and your wonderful home to care for. Zara can be a fond memory of this time in your life, but that's all she'll be."

Constance saw the tears before Jillian turned to leave the room. Her voice wavered as she said, "It's not tomorrow yet. Not for me." She hurried away.

Fine, Constance muttered to herself. *Let her cry it out. But what are best friends for if not telling each other the hard truths?* She made her way slowly back to the sitting room.

Nelson looked up from his book and smiled. "Will Jillian be joining us soon?"

She would, Constance knew, because that was the way it had always been and would always be. The four of them, together. They didn't need a fifth wheel or whatever it was that Jillian had called Zara before. She would call Clive tomorrow and make sure.

"So how about it, best man? Engagement party first, bachelor party later, wedding after, correct?" Clive hoped Nelson would rise to the task. He'd been through the marriage business before. Clive had no idea what steps to take. He only knew Constance had called and left a message, insisting he get on with it. When Clive had called Fullerhill, Jillian wasn't there, but Lord Stansfield had told him they should put an announcement in the paper sooner rather than later.

"Did you want any of it at your place?" Nelson asked.

None of them knew he'd moved his parents from the spacious modern flat in Muswell Hill to a much smaller, older spot in Bexley. Feeling like their roles had reversed, Clive had put his father on an allowance after identifying that the source of his financial woes was not work-related but an issue with gambling. Their family funds were finally coming under control now, though his mother had been in a state of shock during the move. But as Clive had begun talking to her about the wedding, she'd perked up considerably.

"I think Fullerhill for all of it," he told Nelson. "Well, except the bachelor party. I'll look into finding someplace in town that's suitable…or inappropriate, I should say."

"Have you started on the guest list?" Nelson asked. His voice held some trepidation, and Clive suspected he was recalling how Constance had insisted on inviting Zara to their wedding. And probably what had happened afterward. Once again, Clive was thankful he'd never told any of them about his preferences. While this marriage would solidify things for him both financially and socially, he occasionally found himself wondering what it would be like to live as brazenly as Zara did. He felt a pang of resentment, unable to imagine what it would be like to awaken with the person he'd bedded the night before.

Breathing in, he told himself this was no time for envy, as he'd vowed to be the best husband he could possibly be, all things considered. It was a good thing Constance had prodded him, since it now dawned on him that he hadn't spoken to Jilly in several weeks.

"No. I suppose we will, once we pick a date."

"You don't have a date yet?" Nelson seemed confounded. "You've got to get on the ball, dear boy. All of this doesn't just happen. If nothing else, Barton will need to start writing invitations before too long. What does Jillian say?"

"Fall."

"What?"

"She apparently wants to marry in the fall. That's all I know. She's been in and out of Fullerhill so quickly for the last few weeks, it's been impossible to meet up for a discussion."

"Yes," Nelson said. "She's been there on a few Friday evenings, but then she goes back to school to work on some project."

Clive pondered this, knowing he'd been lax in finding time to be at Fullerhill. But his reasons, unlike Jillian's, were strictly pleasure-based. His classes had been over weeks ago, and he'd secured a position with Barclays, though in a different division from his father. At that, he'd given himself permission to play a little. He loved Jilly in his own way and fully intended to be true to her, at least until they talked of other options. He'd speculated more than once if she'd tell him about her own inclinations, even with Zara out of the picture. Something niggled at his consciousness. "What project could Jilly be working on this late in the semester? Most of the labs are closed, aren't they? Why wouldn't she be working at home?"

"I don't know," Nelson said. "Constance said her job prospects weren't as good as they should be, especially considering her brilliant mind, so maybe it's something to try to impress a future employer."

"Hmm." Clive decided to put in an appearance at Fullerhill on Friday. "What holidays happen in the fall? Say, in September?"

"Only the equinox comes to mind, on the twenty-third, I believe, but that's not exactly a holiday," Nelson said.

"No, but it's perfect. On the day of equal amounts of light and darkness, equality will be our theme. We'll have a contemporary twist to our wedding." Clive found himself genuinely excited about the whole prospect. He and Jillian would show the world what was possible in a modern relationship.

Nelson enjoyed lunch in town with some of his school friends until Victor asked about Zara, "the piano player from your party," and whether she was free for some bash he was throwing. Nelson called for the check and changed the subject. Thank goodness Victor hadn't been at their wedding. Nelson couldn't imagine what he would say if he knew the other part of the story.

On his way home, Nelson reflected yet again on how unimaginable it had been for Jillian Stansfield to risk her reputation, and that of her storied family, for what could only be described as an inconceivable indiscretion. As he rounded the corner approaching her station, he saw two women half a block ahead holding hands. Good heavens, was he going to be confronted with this aberration everywhere he went? He kept his distance, observing with surprise how none of the passers-by gave the display a second look. Perhaps because the behavior seemed almost playful, rather than overtly sexual.

It was kind of sweet, actually. He didn't want to think of himself as one of those sneering, name-calling lads, so when the women bumped shoulders good-naturedly, Nelson allowed himself a smile. He'd managed to shake the shock of finding Zara in Jillian's bedroom, especially after Clive's announcement of their upcoming wedding. Instead, he'd put Zara in the category of someone whose ability he admired but whose morality was clearly lacking. The same was obviously true of these two.

He caught up to them as they turned to each other. A tender look passed between them, and they shared a quick kiss. Nelson stumbled slightly as unexpected recognition caught him off guard. Jillian. She'd initiated the kiss, while the look on Zara's face was one of pure adoration.

Nelson continued to follow them, his steps automatic, while his mind raced with questions. Should he approach them, and if so, how? His inclination was to grab Jillian and pull her away, but perhaps he should greet them casually, pretending a commonplace encounter between friends. Once in their company, he could quietly offer some admonishment about their behavior.

But more to the point, what was Jillian doing in town with Zara? Hadn't she told her father she was finishing a project at school?

When they turned into his tube station, Nelson paused, giving himself time to make a decision. It was more important to find out what Jillian was doing there. To his knowledge, she'd not been back to Fullerhill since her graduation was all but assured. And once Lord Stansfield had gotten an agreement between Clive and Jillian, he had seemed preoccupied with other matters, so Nelson and Constance hadn't visited in several weeks.

Recalling his recent conversation with Clive, Nelson was filled with distress. How could he possibly explain to Clive what he had just seen? Or more importantly, how could Jillian justify such conduct?

Nelson walked resolutely down to the platform, determined to have a word. The time of day meant the crowd was fairly sparse, but the women were nowhere to be seen. It wasn't until he glanced across the tracks that he realized they were going in the opposite direction. Their way would take them to Kings Cross, which might mean Jillian was returning to Cambridge.

As he watched, a woman with a toddler approached them, and Zara subtly shifted to face her, putting Jillian in a protected position behind her. The woman's face was contorted with revulsion and the occasional word, "shameful...disgusting...perversion," echoed in the underground.

Clearly in reaction to the vicious tone, the toddler began squirming in the woman's arms, and she lowered the child to the ground as Zara put out her hands as if appeasing her. Anyone with sense could have predicted what would happen next, but the screaming woman was clearly senseless, and her child skipped to the tracks. Nelson held his breath.

Jillian took off like a shot, snagging the child by the collar a few feet before the drop-off. Nelson sighed with relief, and a scattering of people applauded. The woman snatched the toddler from Jillian's grasp and stormed off without even a nod of appreciation.

"Poor tot," Nelson heard a man near him say. "He'll have a rough go with such a bitch for a mum."

Someone else murmured in agreement, and when Nelson looked back, Jillian and Zara were embracing. As they broke apart, their eyes met his. Nelson sketched a wave before clapping his hands silently. Jillian inclined her head sheepishly, while Zara simply watched. The signal for an approaching train sounded, and seconds later, they were gone, leaving Nelson to contemplate what he would say in their next conversation.

During the ride home, Nelson couldn't stop thinking about Jillian's heroic behavior. She had always been a bit restrained and was likely to consider all sides of any possibility before taking action. Obviously, a child lurching toward disaster didn't allow for much consideration, but still...he'd never seen Jilly move like that. It was almost as if she had a new, freer body. Nelson wondered, too, about the earlier look of intense devotion on Zara's face. It seemed similar to the way Constance looked at him sometimes. Did it mean the same thing between Jillian and Zara? He sighed, thinking about the wedding plans being made and deliberated, for the first time, if they were doing the right thing for Jilly.

Chapter Sixteen

When Jillian arrived at Fullerhill for the first time in almost six weeks, she was surprised to find Constance, Nelson, and Clive sitting in the drawing room with several different newspapers spread on the table in front of them. She'd called her father from Mrs. Donnelly's apartment the previous morning while Zara was giving a piano lesson, telling him she'd be coming by to speak with him, but she hadn't expected her friends to be there as well.

Zara had noticed she'd been quiet but had only asked if there was something they needed to talk about. Jillian had shaken her head, going over what she was going to say to her father for what seemed like the millionth time. It was time to tell him she would not be marrying Clive, she was dating Zara, and she had a different future in mind from what he expected.

It was cowardly, but since she'd made the decision about her plans, she'd hoped to avoid ever having a conversation with Zara about her engagement by breaking it off today. On the ride to Fullerhill, her anxiety had intensified with each kilometer, but she knew what she was doing was right. She was in love with Zara, and though they hadn't said so, she was certain Zara felt the same.

Constance rose and hugged her, whispering, "Congratulations," before stepping aside. Nelson inclined his head, but he didn't meet her eyes. Jillian couldn't be certain if that meant he'd told everyone about seeing her with Zara or not. When Clive stood and approached her, wearing his most charming smile, she presumed it was the latter.

"Hello, my darling girl. I've missed you terribly." He took Jillian in his arms, holding her with a more lingering embrace than usual. "I was beginning to worry I wouldn't see you until the day of the wedding."

"Yes, well." Jillian cleared her throat. "About that—"

Her father came in, smiling almost as broadly as Clive. "Hello, everyone. I trust I'm not late." Even though it had been a matter of weeks, he looked older and more careworn than when she'd last seen him. She hesitated, knowing the words she'd come to say might add to whatever burden he was carrying. Perhaps she should wait another few days?

After a few seconds of silence, Clive took the lead. "Not at all, sir."

Her father leaned to look at one of the papers, gesturing toward Jillian after he straightened. "Have you seen these yet, my dear? I think Barton did a fine job."

Jillian's stomach roiled. The mention of Barton meant some social occasion was involved. Struggling to keep her composure, she said, "I haven't seen anything. I've only just arrived."

Clive strode to the table and selected a page from *The Guardian*. "Well, take a look, my dear. We're there in black and white."

Jillian skimmed the announcement. "Oh God," she murmured before looking into her father's face. "I told you to wait until fall."

"There's no date on it, Jilly." Constance came up behind her. "That's for you two to decide."

"But it says we're to be married," Jillian sputtered.

"And so we are." Clive beamed. "Right here in front of this good company. And anyone else you want to invite, of course."

"But I can't." Jillian sought out Nelson, trying to hold back tears. "And you know why I can't." Constance gave Nelson a sharp look.

Clive took Jillian's hand, drawing her to him. "Jilly, love. Let's talk about this, just you and me." His voice was warm and soothing as he bent close. "You've been working so hard, and I know you weren't quite prepared for this. But graduation is next week, and we want all our friends to know about our happy event before we part ways with them. Constance and your father and I agreed."

"But I didn't agree," Jillian protested weakly.

"That's only because we haven't seen you. Your school work is finished now. Let's talk details tonight or tomorrow or whenever you want."

Tonight? She was supposed to be with Zara tonight. "Oh, God. I think—" The image of Zara reading the paper, turning to the classifieds as she liked to do, seeing Jillian's name and those words: *The right honorable Lord Douglas Stansfield of Fullerhill Manor is pleased to announce the engagement of his daughter...* "I think I'm going to be ill. Excuse me."

As she rushed from the room, she could hear her father saying, "Don't take it personally, my boy. Women, even the intellectual types like my daughter, have a tendency to get emotional at times like these."

Jillian tried to get away alone, promising, swearing even, to return in time for the celebratory dinner, but when her panic kept her from coming up with a plausible explanation for where she was going or why, her father insisted Clive accompany her. They took his car and rode in silence for almost half the trip.

Finally, Clive began speaking, and Jillian only heard the first few words, "Jilly, this may not feel like what you want right now, but I promise we can make it work." Everything else was drowned out by the screaming in her head. She wanted to cry, she wanted to shout at him to hurry, but instead, she pressed her forehead against the window, praying they'd be in time. She was still working out what she would say to Zara when the sound of his voice stopped. Then she heard her name.

"Jillian?"

"What?"

"Have you heard a word I've said?"

None of this was his fault. He was simply following the expected path, the steps that their lives had prescribed long ago. She was the one who had failed, who hadn't had the nerve to say what it was she truly wanted out of love or even out of life.

"No. I'm sorry, Clive. I'm a bit shaky just now. Not able to concentrate, it seems." She hoped he hadn't been making some heartfelt profession of love. Forcing a slight smile, she turned to him. "Could you say it all again later? Tonight, perhaps?"

He stared as if she'd asked him to recite the *Magna Carta* in the original Latin. "No, I…never mind."

They didn't speak again except for Jillian giving him directions. When they pulled up in front of Zara's building, he said, "I'll wait here."

"Thank you." She squeezed his hand and sprang from the car, running for 1B as if her life depended on it. She rapped on the door with increasing force until the skin on her knuckle split open. Stopping long enough to blot the blood with her handkerchief, she startled when the door across the hallway opened.

Mrs. Donnelly's eyes were red. "She's gone," the old woman said, her voice subdued. "All she said was she'd gotten some bad news and had to leave."

"Oh God." Jillian put her good hand to her throat, trying to restrain her sob.

"She didn't try to sell nothing or pack more than her clothes. Returned my piano and then left me the key, saying to give whatever was left to anyone who needed them."

"Could I…" Jill gestured toward the apartment, fumbling with the key Zara had given her. She didn't finish, unable to risk more in case Mrs. Donnelly said no, but she simply nodded. As Jillian fitted the key into the lock, she tried not to remember the joy of Zara pressing the cool metal of it against her skin, teasing her about not stealing any of her stuff before taking Jill's other hand and pressing it to her chest, twanging some funny, country-sounding line about having stolen her heart.

Jill had laughed and kissed her soundly, but they'd both known Zara was letting her into more than her apartment. She'd handed Jill a list of the times she was scheduled to give lessons, asking her not to be there then, saying how even accomplished people like Professor Garnier were self-conscious about learning something new in front of others.

Jill shook herself slightly. She didn't want to think about Zara and Professor Garnier. She didn't want to think about Zara and anyone else.

"I suppose you should let me have that when you're done," Mrs. Donnelly said, pointing to the key before turning away and closing her door.

Jillian opened the door slowly, feeling as if she was entering a sacred space. But the rooms where love had grown, where she'd taken small steps toward becoming the person she truly wanted to be, were now nothing more than a mausoleum. The warm gloves, along with the scarf and hat bearing the colors of the Department of Engineering at Cambridge were on the small kitchen table. There was no note, but none was needed. The good-bye was everywhere.

She sat, holding the scarf against her cheek, breathing in Zara's lingering scent. At first, the moments that came to her mind were seemingly trivial things: Zara at the stove and the smell of cooking food, the way the bathroom faucet had to be turned just right or it would drip, and how she'd been warmed by the casual greetings from their neighbors in the building. It had been unexpectedly easy to blend their days together once Zara had made it clear that Jill was welcome to stay after finishing her work at Cambridge.

Little by little, she'd learned what it was to have a life with someone. Soon, what woke her in the wee hours of the morning wasn't some vague worry about her future or bothersome concern about an upcoming event at Fullerhill. It was because Zara was home from her job and had turned on the shower, washing off the bar smells of cigarettes and liquor before she came to bed. When Jill had suggested bathing at such a late hour wasn't necessary, Zara was more adamant that it was, and Jill could tell she was going to lose that dispute.

Once Zara climbed into bed, Jill had never mentioned the traces of smoke clinging to her hair or the rare nights when hints of alcohol had lingered on her breath. Instead, she'd feigned sleep until Zara had pressed against her or her arms had come round her, and then the amazing joy of loving someone and being loved by them would fill her and they'd—

A faint tapping on the door made her rise, full of foolish hope. Clive stood at the threshold, seeming to know he shouldn't enter. "I need to get you back to Fullerhill. It's getting dark, and they'll be worried."

"Oh. Yes, I—"

Mrs. Donnelly's door opened, and she eyed the two of them. Focusing on Clive, she said, "Are you the bad news that's costed me my favorite neighbor?"

Clive drew himself up. "I beg your pardon?"

Moving her gaze to Jillian, Mrs. Donnelly added, "I heard that girl crying like her heart was broken. She's a tough one, on the outside, at least. I can't imagine what it would take to hurt her so much. Can you?"

Jill shuddered, wishing for the detachment, the aloofness she used to be able to summon at will, wanting anything to distance herself from this terrible guilt. Instead, she let the truth of her reply cut all the way into her heart. "Yes," she said. "I can."

After Nelson finished the story, Constance simply stared for a time, trying to make sense of it. Oh, she could believe Jilly would rescue a child. But Jillian Stansfield being physically demonstrative in public was almost unbelievable; the idea of her being physically demonstrative with another woman was completely unthinkable. And when Nelson dared to imply the look—and the kiss—Jillian had shared with Zara might denote anything like what the two of them experienced, she'd had to lie down on the couch and close her eyes, not unlike what her mother used to do when she was overwhelmed by the inconceivable. Nelson apologized and excused himself, leaving her with her thoughts.

Hours later, when they finally heard Clive's car, he joined her as they stood anxiously at Fullerhill's entrance. Ever the gentleman, Clive came around and opened Jillian's door, helping her out. He kept an arm around her shoulder, and Constance was encouraged to see her leaning into him with what appeared to be affection. Clive's relief at seeing them looked profound.

"I think Jilly needs some time before dinner," he said. "Constance, will you help get her ready for a lie down?"

Jillian made it to the bedroom with Clive's help, and before he left, he whispered to Constance, "She's had a rough go. I think a night's rest would be the best thing for her. Let's reschedule the dinner for tomorrow night." Constance agreed, and he told her he'd let Nelson and the staff know. "Take care of her," he murmured, giving her a meaningful look, and Constance nodded.

Jillian was practically inert as Constance helped her into a gown while chattering brightly the whole time. When Jillian spoke, her voice was so hoarse with sorrow that Constance almost couldn't make out the two words.

"She's gone."

"Who, dearest? Zara?" Obviously, Constance knew who "she" was, especially after the events Nelson had described. "Are you sure?"

Jillian sniffed, wiping her face. "The neighbor said she only took her clothes and sundries because she—" Something between a hiccup and a sob made her cover her mouth. She closed her eyes for a long moment, as if unable to bear what came next. "She had some bad news." Her expression was full of pain when she opened them. "She loves to read the classifieds so I'm sure…" She trailed off, her gaze on something neither of them could see. Tears spilling over, Jillian leaned into her, lamenting, "It was me. I'm the bad news."

"You're nothing of the kind," Constance asserted. "And what is bad news for one person might be the best thing for another."

"No," Jillian moaned. "She was the best thing. And I was my best when I was with her."

Constance stroked Jillian's hair, sorry for her pain even as she knew the words could not be true. After many minutes, Jillian began to quiet. There was a gentle tap on the door frame, and they both looked up to see Nelson holding a generous pour of brandy. Constance waved him in, and he pressed the glass into Jillian's hand. "Drink this, Jilly darling. It'll help clear your head."

Jillian's wet eyes were almost too sad to look into when she said, "I don't think my head is what needs clearing, Nelson."

"You need time," Constance assured her. "Time and distance from this moment."

Jillian drank, handing the empty glass back to Nelson. She took a deep breath. "Would you think it terrible if I had another?"

He obliged, and she finished that one too. "Have you eaten today?" Constance asked.

"No, and I couldn't possibly," Jillian said. She looked as if she were about to become ill at the very idea.

Constance spoke up quickly. "Well, we haven't either, so I'd like to see if Mrs., uh, if the kitchen can put something together for us. Would you like to put on your robe and sit with us?"

She watched Jillian make an effort to pull herself together. "Yes, of course. Forgive me for keeping you. I just...I couldn't..." She looked around. "Is Clive gone already?"

"Yes. We agreed we'd have our dinner tomorrow night."

Jillian nodded absently. "I know we talked, but I can't even remember the drive home." She looked at them with tears starting again. "Right now, the thought of being here alone is...."

Constance broke in, pulling Jillian to her feet and motioning to Nelson to join in their embrace. "You're not alone, dearest. And you never will be. Come on."

Nelson walked slowly downstairs and glanced through to the terrace. Jillian sat at the table, a notebook in front of her and a cup by her hand. He knew Constance had been up with her until the wee hours, and as much as he was willing to have a turn, he dreaded it as well. What was he to say? What comfort could he offer? But he and Constance had agreed to stay until Clive arrived, and the three of them could make a plan.

The moment he'd witnessed between Jillian and Zara came to mind again. Nelson had appreciated Zara's talent from the first, but more importantly, he'd respected the tremendous sacrifice she'd made for Jillian's welfare the night of the fire. The contrast between that heroic action and stealing from the Stansfields still puzzled him, but no one else could be a suspect. And while Jillian was one of the most moral people he knew, she'd clearly been intimate with the American on more than one occasion, something she'd never done with Clive. Why? Why was she willing to risk so much? Why put her relationship with her father and her friends, her standing in the community, possibly even her entire future at stake? He felt like he was reaching for an understanding just beyond his grasp.

Jillian turned and held out her hand. Nelson sat, noticing most of what had been written on the pad was scratched out. He didn't comment, and they drank their coffee in silence.

"I need to locate the release mechanism," she said after a time, gesturing at her notes. Nelson tilted his head in confusion, and she gave his arm a fond squeeze. "I know I'll never see her again, and I have to find a way to let her go." He nodded very slowly, not wanting to disturb her from this train of thought. "She taught me everything about the heart except how to fix it when it's broken."

"You love her," Nelson said, both jolted and reassured by the awareness of it. After all, love was the greatest commandment. If Constance had been there, she would have teased him about being Mr. Obvious, but Jillian didn't seem to mind.

"Yes," she said simply. "But I was too afraid to tell her so."

Nelson took a breath. "Did she love you?"

"I think so, yes. But perhaps my fear made her afraid to say." Her voice quavered. "And now we'll never know."

They sat a while longer, each lost in their own thoughts. After Constance joined them, the new kitchen girl served breakfast. Jillian took a few mouthfuls before excusing herself, saying she needed to finish some things in her lab. Such normalcy brought a small measure of relief.

Clive arrived right after they finished their meal. He looked rather worse for wear. "Where is she?" he asked, tension in his voice.

"In her lab. Perhaps you should wait a bit," Constance suggested. "She was acting more herself this morning."

"I think I can help her along with that," Clive said. "I'm calling off the wedding."

The clouds made the darkness come earlier than usual for late spring. Nelson switched on a light just as Constance came back into the sitting room. "Did she speak to you?" he asked.

"She only repeated for us to go." The stress of the last twenty-four hours showed on her face, and Nelson was certain he looked equally strained.

"But we can't leave yet. We need to be here when she tells her father. We need to be sure she's be all right."

Clive had gone, not being one for overly emotional scenes, though Nelson had been surprised by the warm embrace he and Jillian had shared at the door. He supposed their friendship would remain intact, despite the awkwardness of a broken engagement.

After the sound of Clive's engine had died away, Jillian had turned to them. As she'd gathered herself to speak, Nelson had the impression that these last twenty-four hours had aged her the most. "I know you both had the best of intentions," she'd said. "But no matter your reasoning, you had no business interfering in my private life. You went along with posting the engagement announcement without my knowledge, assuming you knew what was best, without making the slightest effort to understand." She'd looked away for a moment, the pain and loss so apparent, Nelson had felt the sting of tears. She'd taken a deep breath. "You both knew, from things I'd said or actions you'd observed, how my life had deviated from its predicted path, and perhaps you feared me falling short of everyone's expectations. But I'm an adult. As long as I'm not harming anyone, I should be entitled to live as I choose in whatever way makes...made me happy." Her voice had thickened, almost a whisper by the end. "The happiest I've ever been."

Constance began to cry. "I'm sorry, Jilly. Truly, truly sorry. And you're right. All we can do is beg your forgiveness. Please know, it's only because we love you—"

"Just stop right there. I don't want to hear that just now. I'd like you both to leave, please." She had turned and disappeared up the stairs.

At least she hadn't said she never wanted to see them again. Maybe that was why they'd stayed, both as immobile as part of the furniture at first. A different kitchen girl brought them a light supper. Jillian did not appear. Nelson had begun yawning when Constance went in search of her again, telling him she wasn't surprised to find Jillian in the same bedroom where she'd been caught with Zara. She'd fallen asleep with her head on the small writing desk, surrounded by dozens of wadded pieces of paper. Constance had edged closer, seeing envelopes bearing each of their names under her elbow.

Jillian had muttered something, and Constance had laid a gentle hand on her shoulder. "Jilly, darling. You've fallen asleep." Jillian had stirred, taking a moment to focus. "Whatever are you doing?"

"Oh, I…I was making some notes. Reminders, really. Of all the things I want to tell each of you." She had gathered the envelopes and had tucked them in the drawer. "I've come to realize that I'm truly the one at fault. I should have told my father I wouldn't marry Clive. Especially after Zara and I…At the very least, I should have told Zara what my situation was. I'm sure we could have figured something out." She had sighed, glancing at her watch. "It's late, and you might as well stay. But please be gone in the morning. I need time alone to finalize some plans."

Constance had left her there, telling Nelson how she had seemed more resigned than angry. "It's as if she's seen a course of action. Not what she would have chosen, perhaps, but maybe a way through."

"Does it include still being friends with us, do you think?" Nelson asked.

Constance blinked back tears. "I don't know."

Nelson had never felt as remorseful. Or so powerless.

Chapter Seventeen

Two years later

Why did his dates always want to impress him by going someplace "cool"? To his way of thinking, "cool" would be if they skipped all this bogus getting-to-know-you nonsense, and just went to a nice hotel. Instead, he was sitting in a questionable bar with an even more dubious liquor selection and waiting for Mason to return from a visit with his "friend," who Clive suspected was actually either an ex or a bit on the side. Either way, it was no bother, as he had both of those himself.

Mason's bloke was a drummer in this random band. Clive had been assured they were great. He found such hyperbole rarely lived up to its promises and not only about music. Two guitarists stood tuning on stage. A few notes drifted in from an electric piano that changed to the sound of an organ. Clive scanned the players again. Both the thin, skimpily-dressed bass player with the spikey hair and the tall, tough-looking guitarist—who wore a bandana as a headband—were female. Nothing to see there, he told himself.

A fedora made it impossible to determine who sat at the keyboards that were positioned sideways toward the rear, facing the other musicians rather than the audience. Clive focused on Mason's alluring backside as he continued chatting with the burly chap making adjustments to his various drums and cymbals. When Mason gestured in Clive's direction, the drummer glanced up. Clive nodded, and got the slightest show of acknowledgement before the fellow went back to his business.

A man with a guitar joined the group, running through a series of notes. Clive sighed, wondering how much of the evening would be spent listening to third-rate music from a group of amateurs whose onstage posturing never offset their lack of competence. Generally, the best he could hope for was a pair of tight pants or a bare chest, but apparently, neither would be in evidence here.

"May I get you something?" a smooth male voice asked.

The waiter was tall and slim with a thick mustache. Just his type. Clive couldn't help the smirk edging across his face. "What are you offering?" When the waiter grinned back, Clive elaborated. "Do you have a specialty?"

The waiter leaned closer. "I have several. What are you in the mood for?"

Clive sighed. This kind of suggestive foreplay was at least fun. But Mason could return at any moment, so he played it safe. "Normally, I go for something with a long finish and a nice buzz, but as I'm not alone tonight, it would have to be subtle. And quick."

The waiter's smile faded. "Let me see what we have. I'll check back with you."

Clive gestured perfunctorily. "While you're deciding, I'll have a scotch on the rocks. The Glenlivet, since I assume you don't carry Laphroaig."

A cocked eyebrow, along with a nod, suggested his choice—and the money it implied—might carry some weight. Clive's salary, and the capacity to spend without worry, had a lot to recommend it. The weight of working didn't seem quite as heavy since he'd been able to move his parents to a more desirable part of town, even after his father's retirement. Of course, he'd kept them on a budget. He wasn't made of money, after all.

Mentally cringing at the echo of something his father had said a hundred times, he let his thoughts drift to the lovely bonus he'd gotten after bringing the Stansfield account to his firm.

He hadn't expected someone like Lord Stansfield to hand over his fortune at the first mention, so Clive had taken his time, wooing the old man with frequent visits over the last two years. Their conversations were never about reserves or investments or anything as crass as money. Douglas was obviously lonely, the house big and empty with Jillian gone, and Clive genuinely wanted to be sure the old man was taken care of. It wasn't solely because of guilt over stealing the jewelry or fouling things up for Jillian. He owed her for her friendship over the years and for giving him the courage to be truer to himself. While he hadn't told anyone else about his "tendency," he'd stopped dating women and was more willing to be seen publicly with his man of the moment.

At least in places like this.

The last transfers of the Stansfield assets had taken place last week, but Clive had yet to fulfill Douglas's one personal request. It was highly unlikely that he ever would, but Lord Stansfield had been surprisingly insistent on the matter. Clive had refrained from asking why, but the old man's tone had been sad rather than angry, so he suspected the intention was repentance rather than retribution. Douglas Stansfield had gotten what he'd wanted, after all. Or what he'd thought he wanted.

Constance had said that Zara had probably gone back to America after the cruise lines had returned to their summer crossings, and Clive couldn't imagine trying to track her down in such a large country. He didn't share that information with Lord Stansfield, mostly because he was concerned about the old man's health. But even though he might never locate Zara Keller, he would continue to visit Fullerhill. He'd call in the guise of business while really keeping an eye on what appeared to be a gradual deterioration in Douglas's well-being.

It was harder to keep up with Jillian's adventures. Her position with the VSO kept her constantly on the move. He needed to ask Constance for her current location in case the old man declined further.

Watching the cute waiter make his way to the bar, Clive wondered if his assistant had finished the review on the Stansfield account yet. He needed to remember to ask when he got back to the office.

Mason returned to their table as the drummer sat and pulled the mic close. "Ladies and gents, welcome to the Camden Nest. We're All Out." At a cheer from the audience, the drummer thumped the bass drum. "And we hope you're ready to have a good time."

The first notes of a popular song, "Your Mama Don't Dance," had the crowd on its feet. The thin bass player and the rugged-looking woman sang lead and harmony, with the rest of the band joining in the chorus along with most of the audience. They were quite good, Clive had to admit. The electric keyboard took a solo, but with dancers crowding the stage, he still couldn't see who was playing.

After the song finished to wild applause, the band went directly into "We Won't Get Fooled Again." The piano now sounded like an organ as the haunting introduction soared over the screams of the crowd. The entire band had turned toward the keyboard player, and at a fist in the air, the rest of the band came in together. The drummer took vocals, and he too had a decent voice. The lead guitarist harmonized and played well, though he was no Pete Townsend.

The song finished cleanly, with the keyboard player's fist punctuating the last few chords, and Mason stood and screamed his approval. His face glowed when he sat back down, and he leaned in over the next song, something Clive didn't recognize. "Told you they were fab. Lucas, the drummer, told me it was the piano player what really whipped them into shape. Lucas says she can play anything, and she runs the rehearsals, divides the singing parts, and even conducts them sometimes like you saw." He chuckled. "They call her the band bitch, but hearing the difference in how they sound makes everyone go along. I think she's shacking up with the bass player. Don't know if they're a thing. Who can tell with women, ya know?"

Clive sorted through Mason's typical avalanche of useless information. "The keyboard player is a woman too? They're rather integrated, aren't they?"

"Yeah, and she's American while the other lady guitar player is Polish, I think. No, she's Hungarian. Whatever, they're all bent, just like us, my dear." He eyed Clive with a strangely hopeful expression. "They're going on tour to some of those Communist Bloc countries, supporting all the suppressed gay and lesbian comrades."

A talented American lesbian piano player? What are the odds? Clive shifted in his seat, feeling a tingle of expectation.

Mason's face took on a pouting expression. "You're not ready to go yet, are you?"

A different waiter set down his drink, and Clive thanked him perfunctorily. "Not at all. I'd like to stay at least until the intermission. Especially if you can arrange for me to give my compliments to the band."

Mason nodded enthusiastically and scooted a little closer. "Anything for you."

Two songs later, when the band had eased into "You Wear It Well," Clive asked why there was no microphone in front of the keyboard player. "Zeek doesn't sing," Mason said.

"Zeek?" Clive asked.

"It's a nickname, after her initials, I'm told. They all have stage names except for Lucas. He started the band, so I guess he's always used his real name."

Z as in Zara and K as in Keller? Standing to take off his jacket, Clive stretched to see over the crowd, but it was impossible.

The band ended their set with "Tumbling Dice," by the Rolling Stones. The crowd was still shouting their praise when Lucas said, "Before we take a short break, let me introduce our wonderful musicians. We've got Tiki on bass and Rader on guitar." Each of the women took a bow. "That's Mo on lead and Zeek on keys. I'm Lucas, and we're All Out!"

Clive tried to see more, but only saw the backs of the performers as they left the stage to more applause. "Come to the break room," Mason said, motioning Clive toward the rear of the club. Everyone else was aiming for the bar, so it felt like they were swimming against the tide. When they finally made it to the stained and chipped door marked Employees Only, Mason knocked confidently.

"Fuck off," a woman's voice called from inside.

"Oh," Mason said, turning to Clive with wide eyes. "I forgot to tell you. I might have suggested you'd be willing to give a donation to help with the tour." He knocked again as Clive stared at him, open-mouthed.

"You might have told them *what*?"

The door swung open, revealing the male guitarist holding a half-consumed pint. "What part of fuck off do you not—" He broke off. "Oh, hi Mase."

"Cheers, all."

Despite his annoyance at Mason's presumption, Clive peered at the unfamiliar faces. Perhaps he'd been wrong. "Which one is the piano player?"

The man grinned. "Fancy her, do ya? Too bad, son. She don't play on your team."

"She's gone to the loo." The spikey-haired woman stepped forward, squinting at him. She'd torn the neck off the black T-shirt she was wearing, and it slid off one shoulder. "You from immigration?"

"What? No."

"Zeek's having some trouble with her passport," Mason whispered. Clive had had no idea he was such a groupie. "Where's Lucas?" Mason asked.

"Same," the tall woman said, retying her bandana. "Sometimes, the crowd won't let 'em butt in line."

"And sometimes, he gets up to something else in there," the male guitarist added, sneering.

After a few seconds of awkward silence, another voice said, "What the hell is he doing here?"

Clive turned to see Zara staring at him with an expression of disbelief. In the next second, she paled and took a half step toward him. "Is Jill all right?"

"Oh, yes. Yes, she's fine." As far as I know, he added silently.

Zara swallowed, flexing her fingers as if shaking out some tension. "Then get the fuck out of here." She pushed past him, walking toward the back of the break room. The thin bass player gave Clive a glare before following.

Even with his hunch confirmed, he didn't know how to start. "Zara, I'd like to speak—" He was cut off by the other woman guitarist getting in his face, her frame tall enough to look him in the eye.

"You heard her, mate. Get the fuck out of here." She and the man joined ranks, blocking Clive's view.

"What's all this?" Lucas appeared from behind Mason. Clive's first thought was how much larger he was up close than he looked behind the drum set.

Mason, to his credit, tried to save the situation. "My friend wants to contribute to the tour fund."

Zara's voice echoed clearly. "We don't want his fucking money. We don't want a goddamn thing from him."

Lucas shrugged. "Zeek's the boss." He leaned toward Mason. "We'll be passing the hat later if he wants to toss something in there."

"No way." Zara turned to face them. "And he's out of here, or I don't go back on."

Every band member gaped at her. After a beat, Lucas put a large hand on each of their backs. "Let me walk you out, gents."

Zara yelled something after the door closed, but Clive couldn't make it out. The crowd had reassembled around the stage, shifting restlessly, obviously expecting the band to have already returned. A few people caught sight of Lucas, and whistles and calls followed him.

"Listen," Lucas said. "Zeek never acts the diva. She always says the band comes first. We even replaced our other rhythm guitarist because she'd throw a tantrum, and Zeek said she was bad for morale. So I don't know what you did to her, but there's obviously no going back. Thanks anyway. And Mase, I'll see you around."

They were at the door, and Lucas gave them both a very gentle shove out onto the sidewalk.

Clive racked his brain. There had to be some way he could get Zara to listen. He should have told her he had some news from Jill. Then it dawned on him…maybe he did.

He called Constance from the office the next morning, confirming that Jillian had sent a separate letter for Zara to her address. With her usual skill, Constance made him spill his story about the less-than-pleasant reception he'd gotten.

"And you're surprised?" Constance asked. "There was the fire. And the announcement—"

"Yes, yes." Clive interrupted. "Which brings me to the other reason I'm calling. I thought I might draft you into looking her up the next time." After she agreed, he promised to keep her updated.

He asked his assistant for the Stansfield file. Given Lord Stansfield's ebbing health, Clive needed to familiarize himself with the details of the estate. When Ellis laid the thick file on his desk, he also held out a single page. "I'm sure you'll want to read it yourself, but I've also prepared a summary of the pertinent facts."

"Excellent. Thank you, Ellis. I'll let you know if I have any questions." Clive made a mental note to give the young man a raise.

Thirty minutes later, having washed down two aspirin with a shot of the Laphroaig he kept in his drawer, Clive read the information for a fifth time, hoping against hope something on the page had changed. It hadn't. The Stansfield estate was heavily in debt—worse than his family had been a few years ago—and Fullerhill was already mortgaged to the hilt. Given her abrupt departure to the VSO, he thought it unlikely Jillian knew, and he couldn't imagine Lord Stansfield passing on such information in a letter.

He put his head in his hands, envisioning the upcoming events. Douglas would die, and it would fall to him to tell Jillian that unless she'd happened upon a few million in diamonds or gold while bringing water to the needy, the bank now owned her family home and the majority of land around it. A small portion had been cut out and put into a trust for her, and Clive made a note on the summary sheet to investigate that. Otherwise, Jillian had only the possessions inside the manor, and she would have to sell most of those to have any hope of covering the death taxes.

Clive sent up a cursory prayer to a God he didn't even believe in, asking for Lord Stansfield to hang on until Jillian returned, so father and daughter could have a few good moments before the bad. He added his guilt-ridden thanks that their marriage hadn't gone through, sparing him any personal responsibility for Jillian's finances.

Racking his brain for something positive he could send to Jillian, he drafted a telegram, planning to ask the VSO to send it wherever she might be.

SAW YOUR FRIEND IN A BAND. THEY WILL TOUR. KEEP WATCH WHEREVER YOU ARE. MISS YOU.

CHAPTER EIGHTEEN

A particularly vicious jolt snapped Jillian's head back, rousing her from a very nice daydream. The driver apologized, and she waved it off. One of the aid workers in the refugee camp she'd just left had reminded her so much of Zara, Jillian had stared until she'd almost embarrassed herself. Trying to excuse her overt attention, she'd had László, their Hungarian translator, tell the woman she'd reminded Jillian of a neighbor who'd been a close friend. It had seemed to work, although afterward, the woman had kept her distance.

László had suggested that it was because no one would want Jillian to be sad. Such concern was typical of the deeply decent people who worked under difficult conditions with those who had nothing but what they carried on their backs. It wouldn't have helped either of them to explain that she thought of Zara every day, and that her sadness would never go away.

She was starting her third year of troubleshooting for VSO, installing or inspecting water systems in outlying areas. If it wasn't for her reports and journal, she might have lost count of the countries, cities, villages, compounds, and camps she'd been to. After having lived in one place for her entire life, she had been ready to see more of the world, and the VSO had taken her at her word. They were non-political, so she'd ended up working in some unlikely places, like several satellite countries of the Eastern Bloc. She was glad for the chance to help people but still a bit self-conscious about being treated like a savior by those desperate for clean water, something taken completely for granted in the life she'd left behind.

As a specialist, she was rarely required to stay in the places she worked. Like now, when she was being taken to the city closest to her assignment and given the best possible sleeping arrangements.

In Hungary, a small stream of refugees escaping Yugoslavia had been intercepted by government troops near the border. After setting up her water system at their camp, Jillian was being taken to Dunaújváros, one of the newest cities. The Communist leaders wanted to put their best foot forward to assure the continued participation of the VSO as they attempted to modernize the Eastern Bloc. She'd been in Poland and Czechoslovakia last year, so such efforts weren't new to her.

As she looked out the window, Jillian recalled the time Zara had played for her, not long before things had gone terribly wrong. Jillian had wanted to confess her role in sending the acupuncturist and the physical therapist, but she wasn't sure how to go about it. She'd also wanted to know if Zara might need occupational therapy to complete her healing. Zara had resisted playing with Jill there, insisting that her performance would be nowhere near what it had been.

"I don't care if you play 'Twinkle, Twinkle, Little Star,'" Jillian had said, and Zara had grinned at her in the way that always made her smile back.

"Do you remember the term for those two notes?"

"Of course." Jillian had run a hand through Zara's hair. "From the first time you came into our group of four, I always thought of you as our perfect fifth."

Then Zara had kissed her, gone to the piano, and played that very song. She'd started by going all the way through once, like a beginner, before moving to a slightly more up-tempo, baroque version of the same tune. Next, she'd transitioned to a style like a romantic show tune before going into ragtime. Jillian had been awestruck by her creativity. But as Zara had moved into what would have been a truly classical version, she'd faltered, moving through the same progression twice before abruptly closing the lid and turning away from the piano.

"I can't. I don't have the reach anymore."

"But your playing was wonderful, Zara. You're clever with how you put each of those together and—"

Zara had cut her off. "Don't, Jill. I appreciate you're intending to be kind, but I don't need patronizing." She'd gone into the bathroom, closing the door soundly.

Jillian had given her a moment before knocking softly. The sound of running water might have prevented Zara from hearing her, so she'd slowly opened the door. Zara was standing at the sink, head bowed, splashing water on her face. Jill had moved to stand behind her but didn't touch her, only watched her in the mirror.

"Zara, you have such an incredible gift. Talent too, and you can do things on that instrument no one could teach. I'd like you to consider getting some more help with your mobility."

Zara had shut off the water and reached for a towel, drying her face. "Like what?"

"Occupational therapy with someone who specializes in musicians. I'm sure we can get a referral from one of your previous therapists. Or we could drop by the hospital and ask Dr. Bankole."

Zara had swallowed, and Jillian could see her considering the idea. "I'd rather not go back to the hospital. Those women who worked with me earlier were really good, but I don't know how to get in touch with them."

"I do." Jillian had moved to her purse in the other room, holding up her little notebook. She'd taken a breath, hoping she was doing the right thing. "The same way I got in touch with them before."

Blinking in the way she did when she was trying to work something out, Zara had repeated, "The same way you..." She'd taken a step. "Are you telling me they weren't sent by the hospital?"

"I saw you in the street the night of the gas explosion. Merely by chance, some would say, but I saw it as a sign. I got your address, and I sent those therapists."

Zara had crossed her arms over her chest. "Why?"

Jill had met her gaze. "To try to give you back at least part of what you'd lost on my behalf. And because of the something between us. Which I failed to defend, to my great shame."

"Would you defend it now?"

Jill had shut her eyes, trying to hedge her reply. "I'd like to believe I would."

"So why the cover story? Did you think I wouldn't accept help from you?" Jill had nodded, her eyes still closed. Zara's fingers had traced along her cheek as she'd said, "You're probably right. I can be stubborn sometimes."

"Sometimes?" Jill had whispered, and Zara chuckled, her fingers moving down Jill's neck. That admission had gone well. She probably should have mentioned Clive too. But as Zara's hand had found its way under her shirt, tracing her collarbone, Jill had found herself unable to think clearly.

"Well, thank you," Zara had said in her ear. "I wouldn't be where I am without your help." She'd kissed the same path on Jillian's neck before pulling back. "And thank you for telling me at a time when I was ready to hear it."

Those words had given Jill the excuse she'd needed to put off mentioning her engagement. Zara wasn't ready to hear it, she'd told herself. And Jill had been certain she'd be able to find a way out before needing to say anything, saving them both another difficult conversation.

Now, it was one of those "if only" moments she returned to over and over. But the worst came two days later, when any hope she'd had of reconciling with Zara had vanished with a few simple words. She'd remained at Fullerhill, trying to figure out her next steps. Like so many other bits of what she and Zara had together, it had started as a fluke. She'd been approaching her father's office, ready to tell him about Clive and about Zara, when she'd heard his enthusiastic tone after Barton, his part-time secretary, had called him to the phone. "Who? Oh yes, I see. Wonderful. Yes, we are having a wedding. Yes, and how much of a problem will this short notice be? Oh, good."

Jillian had stopped dead in her tracks, her breath catching, before putting her head in the door. "Who is it, Father?"

Lord Stansfield had smiled as he'd covered the mouthpiece. "The catering company you contacted last week. They want to confirm some information about your ceremony."

She hadn't called anyone. Reaching for the phone, she'd tried to keep her voice steady. "May I speak with them, please?" When he'd passed the receiver, she'd tried to swallow around the dryness in her throat before speaking. "This is Jillian Stansfield."

"But not for long, apparently."

Zara, as she'd guessed. Desperate as she was to find a way to fix what had happened, Jillian couldn't let her father know who was really on the line, or he would sever the connection. "I'd like to speak to you about that."

"Why, when your obliging father has once again provided you a way out? And I'm the stupid one who actually believed we—" When Zara had cut herself off, Jillian had clenched her jaw at the bitterness lingering in the silence. Then Zara had taken a breath. "I've gotten all the information I need, Your Ladyship. You've fucked me over for the last time."

Zara's voice had gone so cold, it had made Jillian bite her lip. She'd focused all her energy on making Zara stay on the line. "Could we meet to discuss it? Because that's something I haven't done. Not really."

Zara had given a dry laugh. "Just keep telling yourself that, babe. Thanks for the ride, and have a nice life."

The line had gone dead. Jillian had gripped the receiver hard enough to turn her knuckles white. She'd wanted to scream, to smash the receiver into bits, to claw at her heart until her chest was bloody. Instead, she'd said, "Thank you for calling. I'll speak with you again soon," even as she had known those last six words would never be more than a wish.

She'd left without another word and had driven herself to the Voluntary Service Overseas office. After spending the better part of a day explaining the details of her water purification device to five different people, she'd been promised placement, assuming she passed the training. She'd returned to Fullerhill long enough to pack and argue with her father over breaking her engagement before moving into a dorm with her new colleagues.

Three months later, she'd put letters to Constance, Nelson, Clive, and her father in the post right before boarding the plane to Johannesburg, where she'd make one more hop to Botswana to meet up with her trainer and mentor, Albert Simmons. They'd traveled to the Central Kalahari Game Reserve to deliver five of her purification devices to a group known as the San people.

Jillian had written to Zara as well, but having no idea where to send it, she'd mailed the letter to Constance, asking her to deliver the message to Zara should the need arise. She'd had no idea what to expect for her first posting, but there were things she'd wanted each of them to know in the event she didn't return. Especially Zara.

"Tomorrow, you come with us to Budapest," László said, bringing Jillian back to the present. "A band is to play. Good English." Jillian tried not to grimace. In the six weeks or so since she'd gotten Clive's telegram, she'd seen four different bands. Three had featured traditional music, which was fine, while the fourth had attempted covers of American rock and roll, which was extremely painful. Especially the lyrics. She had no faith in László's assurance, but she had to get to Budapest anyway. Her schedule included a day to do her laundry and one night in the capital before leaving for East Germany and her next job. "Yes, thank you," she said, forcing a smile. At least László made an effort to be pleasant, unlike some of the other translators, who made no pretense of being anything but guards who happened to speak some English.

A warm shower helped work the knots out of her shoulders, and she found the bed at the hotel in Dunaújváros to be better than most. Thinking of the "good English" band, Jillian slipped into one of her favorite fantasies. Zara, having accepted her explanation and forgiven her, playing just for her again with promise in her eyes of what was to come.

It gave Zara the creeps to be in a communist nation, even when lying in a comfortable bed. After the ferry ride across the channel, they'd driven the van through France, West Germany, and Austria, doing multiple shows along the way, before entering Hungary. The deeper they'd traveled into this country, the more anxious she'd become. She'd never seen so many armed guards in her life, and her passport had been intensely scrutinized at each checkpoint—partly because she was American and partly because it was almost expired, she supposed—and she'd begun to expect the possibility of being detained or expelled at any moment. They'd all suffered through questions about their intentions in this country. Tiki, who still carried a Hungarian passport along with her British Indefinite Leave to Remain card, had gone practically catatonic with fear, even though this tour had been her idea.

"Let us bring inspiration to those who don't enjoy the freedoms we have," she'd urged them. After they'd finally made it to her cousin

Bence's house, she'd collapsed into his arms, carrying on in Hungarian. Zara couldn't understand but could easily imagine their meaning.

Their concert was scheduled for tomorrow night, and she hoped Tiki would be okay by then. Zara had her own experience with not being "okay" during a show: the night Clive had come into the club. As soon as she knew his appearance had nothing to do with Jill, she'd had as much use for him as a fish did for a bicycle. What possible news could he have that she would want to hear? An invitation to their anniversary party? They'd had a baby and were going to name it after her? Her playing had been off for the rest of the night. She'd come in late twice and missed quite a few notes along the way. The audience probably didn't notice, but Tiki did, giving her a look.

Zara knew she had it coming. After all, she was the one who'd stressed about finding the sweet spot between perfection and improvisation, and had lectured about how striving for the former could allow for more of the latter. She'd had neither that night, and she'd known why.

Seeing Clive had made her brood—again—about leaving London. She'd planned to, especially during those first few months when nearly everything in the whole damn city had made her think of Jillian Stansfield. Her anger hadn't lasted long, overtaken by emotional chaos that swung from longing to bewilderment to desolation. The passing years had made the sting of loss a little less sharp unless, like now, the swell of missing Jill washed over her with an unexpected current of heartache.

When the bottom had dropped out of her life after learning of Jillian's engagement, the cruise line wasn't due to resume its Atlantic crossings for another month. She'd have to wait until then to work her way back to America. She hadn't quit her job since Jill had never been to the bar, so at least she was spared any painful memories there. Tiki, her Friday night replacement, had been looking for a new flatmate. So they'd struck a deal, and she'd arrived at the somewhat dilapidated two-bedroom apartment with her small suitcase. Tiki's bass guitar, microphone, stand, and amps took up half of the living room, and when they'd talked about music, the pain in Zara's heart had eased slightly. She'd accompanied Tiki to her next rehearsal just to observe. But music was the lover who'd never let her down, even if she no longer had her whole self to bring to their affair. And playing every day was as good as therapy, for both her hand and her heart.

Now, two years later, All Out had developed a loyal following, solidly booked into both gay and straight clubs. Of course, the straights thought their name only referred to a committed performance. They laughed about it. The band become her family, and being onstage with them fed her soul.

But there wasn't anything feeding her heart and hadn't been since Jillian. She'd tried with Tiki, who she genuinely liked, but there wasn't anything beyond that. And the music. They were still sharing a flat, but Zara was glad it was a two-bedroom. Otherwise, it would be awkward when Tiki occasionally brought someone home after a gig. Zara told herself she'd do the same someday, when the right woman showed up. So far, she hadn't.

Conversation drifted in from outside where Tiki's cousin and his friends were taking turns guarding the van and equipment. Sure, there were places in the UK or in the US where they would need to keep watch on their stuff, but in this case, their most likely enemy was government itself. Zara shivered, and out of habit, curled her once-injured hand against her abdomen.

Bence drove, taking the long way to the venue and giving them a tour of the city. Maybe everything looked better in daylight, but Zara found Budapest to be a charming city, although some places still showed history of the war. Zara sat next to Tiki, holding her hand, reminding her of their purpose in being here and talking about plans once they returned to London. Tiki was a gifted poet, and Zara wanted them to collaborate on some original songs.

They arrived at the small club four hours before the concert, needing to set up and go through a couple of numbers to calm everyone's nerves. Tiki held Zara back from getting out, kissing her softly on the lips once everyone else had gone inside.

"I'm not giving up on collaborating with you in other ways," she said.

"Tiki," Zara began, but Tiki put a finger on her lips.

"Later, we'll talk, Now, we play."

With the ancient electrical wiring in the club, it took an extra hour to get the instruments set so no one would blow a fuse. But the acoustics were fine, and Zara felt the usual buzz of excitement before a show. Playing in front of people never got old, and the band had a wide variety of tunes to satisfy almost any audience. For this show, they'd changed their set list considerably after Tiki had told them country songs were popular among the older crowd. Lucas was a hard-core rocker, but they'd found some songs that were close enough for him. Learning to play country had been a challenge for both Zara and Mo, as one or the other had instrumental solos in every song, but Zara was confident they were ready.

Tiki flirted with the bartender, so everyone else had several drinks before the doors opened. Zara abstained. She never drank before a show, but tonight she might have a few afterward. There was no break room, and the whole band was onstage when the doors opened. Rader gasped as people surged in as if someone was giving away money. In a sense, they were, the band having agreed on no cover charge, so a lack of funds wouldn't prevent anyone from coming. They'd pass the hat before the last song if anyone remembered to do it. In moments, the place was packed to capacity, and a ring of people four-deep stood outside the open doorway.

The murmur of conversation was low compared to similar clubs in the UK, and when Lucas thumped the bass drum, the crowd fell silent. Lucas spoke while Tiki translated. She swayed slightly while speaking, and Zara suspected she might have overindulged in liquid courage.

"Hello, and welcome to the show. We're Very Hot, and we're here to offer an evening of entertainment for all of our Hungarian friends."

There had been some discussion about how to translate the band's name. "Out" was an idiom the Hungarians didn't have. Tiki had told them the Hungarian word *meleg* meant warm but was also slang for homosexual. In a rare piece of choreography, Mo and Rader fanned themselves at Lucas's words, and the audience burst into wild applause, clearly taking the second meaning.

They launched into "Good Hearted Woman," with Lucas singing lead and Rader singing harmony. They played with the pronouns,

Lucas sometimes using he instead of she, and Rader taking the line about the woman loving her in spite of her wicked ways. It was hard to hear the audience reactions over the clapping and yelling. When they did "Take Me Home, Country Roads," they substituted local names for West Virginia, the Blue Ridge Mountains, and Shenandoah River, and the crowd went wild each time. Lucas had to signal for quiet before the next song.

"We're gonna slow things down for this next one, which features your own Katalin Farkas." Tiki, smiling at the use of her real name, waved, and the crowd cheered again. She spoke a few sentences in Hungarian, and the crowd made sounds of approval. Then she gestured at Mo, and the song began with a soft guitar. Tiki had a nice voice, but as she sang, "Help Me Make It Through the Night," she put more emotion than usual into her singing.

At the first chorus, she turned to Zara, moving her shoulders seductively, the words clearly an invitation. Zara grinned, going along with the act, but Tiki's words before they'd left the van made her worry. Tiki sauntered toward her, drawing closer and closer until she was leaning over Zara's keyboard during the repeat of the last verse, giving her, and part of the crowd, a clear view of her full breasts. Singing the last two lines, she cupped Zara's chin, making their eyes meet. The music finished, and Tiki gave her a wink before returning to her usual place.

While the audience roared its approval, Zara fanned herself with her hat, and Tiki blew her a kiss. Inside, her stomach contracted uncomfortably. *Shit.* Flirting had been fun when she'd first joined the band, but after a few weeks, Zara had pulled away, unable to consider even a casual fling. It had been hard on both of them, and she wasn't ready to go through that again.

"Let's pick it up," Zara yelled to Lucas, who nodded. He'd heard both sides of their not-romance. "'Your Mama Don't Dance.'" She pointed at Rader, and they were off.

The song was an easy transition, and if Tiki minded the change of pace, it didn't show. At the break, she yelled something, and contrary to the song title, the crowd began to dance. The energy was incredible, and since they'd agreed to only play one set, they played longer than usual. "Won't Get Fooled Again" had been scratched by the authorities, but Tiki had said that if the Security Enforcement officers weren't there, they should do it as their next-to-last number before ending with a Beatles medley.

Lucas was starting to lose his voice anyway. Tiki began yelling between the pauses in the lyrics, her fist in the air. The crowd quieted to hear her, and Zara realized she was translating the words to the song. Right as they reached the bridge, the power to their instruments and microphones went out.

Lucas's drums continued for a few seconds. Cries went up from the audience, and all hell broke loose as a large group of uniformed men pushed toward the stage. Some audience members ran; others attempted to surround the black-jacketed officers. Tiki screamed, "Oh shit, oh shit," as she was grabbed by a huge man and pulled off her feet.

Zara moved toward her, yelling, "Let her go," but another man grabbed her and threw her roughly to the ground. She curled into a ball to protect herself, but nothing more happened, so she peeked out to see her attacker and two others trying to subdue Lucas. She took advantage of the moment to find Rader, who was trying to hide her tall form behind the big bass amp.

"Let's see if there's a back way out," she called, and Rader nodded.

They kept in a crouch and were nearly off the stage when a hand caught Zara's collar, spinning her around and pinning her arms behind her. Rader grunted and in another second was beside her in the same position. The crowd had cleared out except for small groups on either side of the room who stood silently, watching.

"Call the American embassy," Zara shouted to the blurry forms as she was marched past.

Lucas and Mo began calling, "Call the British embassy." She'd just turned her head to call out again when she caught sight of a face that made the words freeze in her mouth.

Jill? Before Zara could recover from the shock, pain exploded by her ear, and the world vanished.

Chapter Nineteen

It's sedition," Colonel Kardos, a paunchy man with a thick graying mustache said, pounding his fist on the desk for emphasis.

"It's a song," Jillian replied calmly. "Written by sullen spoiled youths of a decaying capitalist society. It has no meaning here...or there, for that matter. It's merely noise."

"If it has no meaning, why did so many come to hear it?"

Jillian was certain Kardos was enjoying the argument, though she suspected he had no personal stake in the outcome, other than using the opportunity to keep her in his office. Having worked with him before, she knew he fancied her, and he took every opportunity to touch her, always longer than necessary. She'd learned to keep her distance and politely refuse his offers of dinner without jeopardizing his goodwill toward her assignment.

She allowed herself a passing appreciation for the two years she'd spent dealing with other officials who valued their power—real or imagined—above all else. Learning how to negotiate those situations had prepared her for this crucial moment. "The forbidden is often intriguing for those of weak minds. Which is why it would be more dangerous to keep them here than it would be to expel them. They would become martyrs to a losing cause, which would only lengthen the struggle. Pointlessly."

The colonel steepled his fingers. Jillian wondered if he was out of ammunition in their mental battle. "But there must be some penalty. To make an example of their misguided ways."

"Of course." They'd reached the bargaining portion of the program. Jillian was certain a group of traveling musicians couldn't offer much in the way of a bribe. "You could confiscate their instruments." She hated to say it, but what else was there? His head cocked slightly. Good, but there needed to be more. "Along with their transportation," she said. Now Kardos was nodding. "And then, since the government wishes them gone…" She paused for a split second in case he wished to argue, then continued as if this had already been agreed upon. "Escort them to the airport and put them on a flight to London."

He grunted, but she could see the wheels turning as he calculated his portion of the profit from the sale of the group's goods. *One more little push.* "The VSO would look favorably on this action since the majority of the group are British citizens."

Colonel Kardos shuffled some paper, and Jillian realized she'd made a tactical error. He hadn't been thinking about nationalities, and now Zara and Tiki, Zara's apparent her new lover, were in danger of becoming separate bargaining chips.

"We'll release the American, but the Hungarian citizen must remain here. For reeducation."

Jillian suppressed a shiver. She had an idea of what that meant. She'd never worked in those camps, but she'd been driven past two of them, and the despair was almost palpable. She thought back to the previous evening. László had saved her a seat at the bar in the crowded club, and her heart had come alive again when she'd realized it was Zara at the piano. Even though her back was to them, Jillian knew Zara's form, her movements, and her expertise. At those first notes, gravity was replaced by that familiar pull, and Jillian wanted to float over and land beside her.

"Good, yes?" László had asked after the first song. Jillian couldn't quite bring herself to look away from Zara, so she'd nodded enthusiastically. During the next song, she began planning to meet Zara after the show. She would send László as an intermediary, setting it up as a semi-official meeting to ensure Zara's presence. She'd almost envisioned the whole thing when the dream had become a nightmare. Jillian had been unable to look away as the sultry-voiced bass player had all but draped herself over Zara during the slow, romantic number. Part of her had wished she could see Zara's face—to judge if the singer's obvious feelings were mutual—but part of her didn't want to know. She told herself she had no right to expect Zara to be available just because she was. But it had pierced her core to be this close, to have found Zara and to feel her joy at being able to do something she loved but be unable to share it.

When the song ended, László whispered in her ear, "This is no good. To act this way is dangerous. They should stop." He'd shaken his head occasionally but had seemed generally satisfied with the band's behavior for the remainder of the evening, until they started a song with Zara's haunting organ chords. "No." He clenched his fist. "This one not approved. Speaks of fighting and revolution. Radical. Bad." He'd looked around, clearly anticipating trouble. During the riot that had ensued, László had kept her safe, but she'd lost sight of Zara until the last moment, when Zara had been shouting about calling the embassy before the police had clubbed her into silence.

Now, Jillian considered how simple it would be to agree, to let them keep the girl and try to get Zara to reconsider their relationship. Simple, but not acceptable. She shook her head. "If you keep one, you keep the problem. Especially her. She speaks your language, which practically guarantees an endless stream of propaganda about her and from her. I believe you would regret it." She gave him a few seconds to contemplate. "Obviously, the decision is entirely yours. But I would think it better to be seen as a high-minded, benevolent member of the community of nations, rather than as one who made an international incident over five unknown and untalented musicians."

She shrugged and stood as if the matter no longer interested her. "VSO's work with the refugees is finished. I hope the matter in your bordering state will be settled soon." She held out a hand. "Thank you for meeting with me."

He took her hand but instead of shaking it, he kissed the air above her knuckles. She forced herself not to shudder. "Will we be seeing you again in our fair land anytime soon?"

Not unless I'm visiting Zara in prison, she thought, carefully withdrawing her hand on the pretense of collecting her handbag. "Unfortunately, I think not. I'll be flying to the German Democratic Republic tomorrow. I was supposed to go today, but I wanted to speak with you before I left, and I knew how busy you would be with all of this." She waved vaguely toward the cellblock where she presumed Zara and the other women had been taken.

"Tomorrow?" he mused. "Good." With some effort, he stood as well, bellowing for his adjunct to come in. "Comrade Stansfield will accompany Corporal László to the airport when the prisoners are released tomorrow morning. To ensure they are put on the first plane to London." The adjunct saluted stiffly, and Kardos turned back to her. "Perhaps you are free for dinner this evening?"

Jillian shook her head, attempting to fix a regretful expression. "Perhaps next time."

The colonel nodded as if this was expected. "Perhaps next time."

László picked her up before dawn in the prison transport, a dark van that stank of fear. Jillian got out when they arrived at the cellblock, but László gestured for her to stay by the open door at the rear. After an impossibly long wait, the door opened, and the big drummer came out with dried blood on a split lip, his clothing disheveled. The male guitar player came close behind, cursing and holding his left elbow.

"Do you speak English?" the drummer asked, and Jillian nodded. It would have been funny if she wasn't so worried about Zara. "They're letting us go?"

"Yes," Jillian said. "To the best of my knowledge, we're going to the airport, and you'll be flown back to London on the first flight."

The guitar player stared. "That's posh English. You with the embassy?"

"No. I'm with VSO."

They stared at her for a moment before gingerly making their way into the van. Jillian waited again, trying to keep her breathing steady. Then Zara was at the door, squinting in the pale morning light and waiting as the tall, rough-looking guitar player limped out behind her. When she stopped and looked at the van, Zara did too. She blinked, rubbed her face, and looked again. Jillian couldn't move, but she managed a smile. Zara said something to the other woman, who stayed at the door as she walked hesitantly toward Jillian.

"It really is you," she said, stopping a few feet away. Her hand lifted slightly for the briefest second before it dropped to her side. "Last night, I thought it was my life passing before my eyes."

"I was surprised to see you too. Last night, I mean." Jillian tried not to be obvious about scrutinizing Zara's condition. Her leather jacket was cut down the arm, but Jill didn't see any blood. Zara's knuckles were raw and bruised, but she seemed okay otherwise.

"You heard the whole show? Or what there was of it?"

Jillian nodded. "Your band is very good." She took a step toward Zara. "And you're as gifted as ever."

"Not quite. But enough. It's fine." Zara said, her gaze never leaving Jillian's face. "You're still wearing your hair short, I see. And it still suits you."

Jillian felt a blush start up her neck. "It's easier since I'm traveling a lot. And yours is longer." God, she wanted to run her hands through the dark waves resting on Zara's back and flowing past her shoulders.

"Yeah, I'm too cheap to pay for a cut. What are you doing here?"

"I've been working with VSO since...for almost three years now."

"Your water project?" Zara asked.

Jillian smiled. "You remember."

"I remember everything, Jill." It could have been said with anger or resentment, but her voice was soft, her expression gentle.

"I do too." As they looked at each other, time seemed to slow in contrast to the wild, hopeful beating of Jillian's heart.

"Zeek," the other woman called. "Tiki's hurt bad." Jillian looked over to see the provocative singer and bass player slumped heavily against the wall. She had a black eye and a cut across her cheek. There was blood on her jeans.

"Excuse me." Zara hurried back, and grief settled in Jillian's stomach like a stone. When Zara's hand had lifted toward her, Jillian thought of the moment on the driveway after Constance and Nelson's wedding. She was flooded with memories of seeing Zara then, when she'd thought it would never happen again, and her excitement had carried over to them being together for the first time. That night had shaken everything she'd thought she'd known about herself. And the feeling of unexpected joy had magnified a hundred times when Jillian had seen her from the window of the taxi, and what she'd wanted in life had changed for good during the months they'd shared in Zara's tiny apartment. But both those times, Zara had been unattached. The way she wrapped a tender arm around the injured woman—Tiki—and the memory of last night's performance made it obvious such was not the case now.

The other guitar player was helping, and they moved very slowly toward the van, giving Jillian time to collect herself. When László came out, carrying a folder, he hurried to help, and the group worked to lift Tiki into the van. Jillian couldn't bring herself to watch. She settled into the passenger's seat, but Zara appeared at the window. The crank to roll it down was missing, and Jillian made a helpless gesture and started to open the door.

Zara waved at her to stop. "The guys say we're going to the airport. Are you going too?" she called. Jillian nodded, and Zara grinned. "Good. We can talk then."

But the first words of conversation came from the big drummer as the rest of the band helped the injured woman to her feet outside the terminal. "Where's our stuff? And why are we being sent out on a plane? Where's the van?"

László, obviously ready to leave before any further confrontation, pushed slips of paper into each person's hand. "Tickets. You go inside now." He bowed slightly to Jillian. "Safe travels, Madam."

As the transport roared away, Jillian moved inside, the men following on her heels as Zara and the other woman helped Tiki, who seemed barely conscious. "Look," Jillian said when they found a less crowded area. "You performed radical songs and"—she broke off to glance at Tiki—"exhibited questionable behavior on stage. I had to bargain to get you freed, and I had nothing else to offer."

"You didn't even fucking consult us," the male guitar player said angrily.

"Did you see visiting hours posted in the prison?" Jillian asked sharply, and the man looked down. "I've spent some time in communist countries, and I believed getting you released would either happen immediately or not at all. If you'd like to go back and see if you can strike a better bargain, be my guest."

Angry at the lack of gratitude, she turned and began walking toward her gate. The drummer grabbed her arm, his grip almost painful. "I don't think you understand, lady. How are we supposed to be a band without instruments? We still have a tour to finish. How are we supposed to get to gigs without a van? Is the VSO picking up the tab for what we've lost?"

Before she could answer, Zara appeared at her side. "Lucas, take your hands off her. This instant." Her tone was low and deadly serious. The drummer gave her a look and breathed out before letting go.

"All right, Zeek. You tell me how we're going to manage as a band with no instruments and no transport."

"How do you think we'd manage in a Hungarian prison? We can always get new instruments. Freedom is something to never take for granted. I would think even one night in a cell would make that obvious to you." Zara turned her gaze to Jillian again. "You owe this lady a huge thank-you, at least."

Lucas grunted something which could have been a thank-you, but their raised voices had drawn the guards' attention. Wishing to avoid anything that might lead to further interactions with Colonel Kardos, Jillian stepped back, excused herself without looking at Zara, and made for the nearest restroom. She finished washing her hands and tipped the attendant when Tiki and the other woman guitar player entered. After propping Tiki against the counter, the tall woman went into a stall while Tiki stared at Jillian.

"Did you need help with something?" Jillian asked.

"You're Jill, yeah?" Tiki's knuckles were nearly white from holding on to the counter, but her voice was firm. "Zara's ex?" Jillian had never thought of herself as an ex, but she nodded. "And I'm betting you sprung us because of her, am I right?"

Jill considered her answer. "I don't know any of you, but I know her, so yes, that's accurate." As Tiki leaned toward her, Jill observed that her pupils were different sizes. "Be sure and see a doctor when you get to England," she advised. "I think you may have a concussion."

"Yeah, and they gave me a lot worse." She shifted painfully. "But I came in here because I've got something to say to you. Leave

Zara alone. She's just getting over what you did to her before, which means you need to keep away, hear me?"

Jillian was too stunned to reply. Was this the demand of a lover or the plea of a friend? Did it matter?

"Concussion or no, I saw the way she looked at you. And you a married woman, for Christ's sake."

Jillian blinked as the toilet flushed, and the other woman came out. "All right, Tiki girl, you've had your say. Let's go before you fall down." Her mouth quirked, and she gave Jillian an apologetic look.

When they were gone, Jillian stood for a moment, staring at the mirror, trying to get her swirling thoughts to quiet. It was only natural for Zara to tell her bandmates about what had happened between them. She'd done the same in letters to her father and friends. But these people, including Zara, believed Jillian had gone through with the wedding. Given what Zara had with her music and this new love, wasn't it better to leave things as they were?

Jillian felt the optimism she'd had earlier draining away, the familiar icy reserve taking its place. Their moments by the van and the way Zara had come to her defense was just Zara being who she'd always been, a good-hearted, compassionate person. It didn't mean there was still hope for their something.

Jillian focused on her pale reflection, her face drained of promise, empty of expectation. Forcing her emotions to settle, she reclaimed the composed and capable person she'd been before she'd known who she was and who she loved and who she'd returned to when that love was gone. Her work was waiting. She gave the attendant another coin before picking up her bag and moving quickly out into the terminal. A small crowd blocked her view of the area where Zara had been. Then someone stepped aside to call for help. Tiki was on the ground, Zara kneeling beside her.

At Jillian's movement, Zara looked up. Meeting her eyes, she signaled with her hand and mouthed, "Wait."

Jillian had always found it hard to admit there were things she couldn't do. But at this moment, she knew she couldn't stay, couldn't wait, couldn't watch Zara care for her new girlfriend. Was it a kind of love to finally and utterly let someone go? Jillian pointed at her watch and shook her head before moving through the terminal as quickly as she could. Zara called her name once, but she didn't look back. *Be happy, Zara. I would give everything if I could have been the one to make you that way.*

The last thing Zara expected to see as she and Rader walked Tiki off the plane was Constance Holston Garrick standing there with a big smile, waving as if she was in a parade. After rubbing her eyes to make sure she wasn't imagining things, Zara realized Nelson was there too, standing to the side and a bit behind.

Constance approached slowly, her face transitioning to worry. "Oh, Zara dearie. Are you all right?"

"Uh." Zara wasn't sure how to answer, but Tiki moaned, and Rader uncharacteristically took over.

"Our friend needs to go to hospital, but we got no way to get her there. We don't have a shilling between us. Fucking commies took everything."

Lucas and Mo joined them, their unkempt appearance making it obvious they were part of the band. Nelson stepped toward them, apparently thinking this was his cue. "Taxis for you gentlemen? And Zara, we can take you and your friends to St. Thomas in our car."

Zara looked around at Lucas and Mo, who were perhaps even more befuddled than she was. "Is this on the level?" Lucas asked.

"Yeah. I mean, I know them, and they're good for their word." She turned back to Constance. "What I don't know is how they came to be here." Another movement caught her attention, and she saw Clive standing by a pole. She decided to ignore him. If he wanted to get news of his wife, he ought to ask her directly.

Constance gestured. "Jillian called Clive to tell him what happened, and he called us and asked if we could help. This seemed like the least we could do." She lightly touched Zara's arm. "I'm so sorry. For everything."

So Jillian and Clive had spoken. How nice. Zara shifted her feet, not sure how to deal with the unexpected appearance of Jillian's friends, not to mention Constance's sincere apology.

When she spoke to Lucas and Mo, her voice was a little shaky. "There's your answer. The same person who got us out of a hellhole in Hungary has arranged for our rides home. Any complaints now?" They both had the grace to look ashamed. "Okay. We'll meet at the bar in two weeks, right? Eight o'clock." They all nodded, and Tiki half raised her hand. "Go, team, go." Her voice was weak and dreamy.

"At least we don't have to wait for our luggage," Mo said cheerfully.

Their laughter led them into a group hug, and then Clive walked Lucas and Mo toward the taxi stand. "May I offer to help?" Nelson said, indicating Tiki.

Zara looked at Rader, seeing the same weariness in her face that she was feeling. Tiki was semi-conscious, and it seemed unlikely Nelson could hurt her any worse than she already was. "That would be great, Nelson. Thanks."

He picked Tiki up as if she weighed less than Constance's purse, which was possible, and they made their way to the exit.

Without the Stansfield name to get them a room in mere minutes, the wait in the emergency room took hours. Zara gritted her teeth, deliberating if it might be time to return to America. Was she back to everything in this town making her think of Jillian? Between the delay on getting her passport renewed and the likely loss of her band, was there a reason to stay?

Constance brought food from the hospital cafeteria, which could have come from the Ritz, as far as Zara and Rader were concerned. They hadn't eaten in almost two days, and the irony of being thirsty enough to drink liters of liquid wasn't lost on her; even something as simple as water brought to mind Jillian and her project. *Damn.*

Nourishment made Rader surprisingly chatty, and she entertained Constance and Nelson with stories of their best and worst shows, giving Zara time to think. Obviously, Jill's influence had gotten them released, and calling on her friends to provide rides was incredibly thoughtful. Just like the Jill she'd known before. And like the first time they'd met, seeing her again had made Zara experience a sizzle of connection. For a few moments, she'd let herself hope Jill had felt it again too. *Stupid.*

Zara had had more than two years to consider what had happened between them, and she often reflected on their last conversation, capable now of recognizing the desperation in Jill's voice instead of only knowing her own deep hurt. This morning, Zara had thought Jill understood the meaning of her request to wait at the airport was so they could talk, maybe even spend more time together when Jill came back through London. But perhaps Jill thought Zara was going to ask her for something else, money being the most likely. She sighed, and Rader turned to her.

"Tiki will be all right, mate. She's tough."

Zara was fine with the misunderstanding. "Yeah, true."

By the time they learned Tiki would stay overnight for tests and observation, all Zara wanted to do was crawl into bed and sleep for a week. Rader volunteered to remain at the hospital, reminding Zara she could sleep anywhere. She had once fallen asleep stretched out across three amps. During practice.

Once they were in Nelson's car, Zara gave him her address, adding, "Once you get me to my flat, I can pay you for the food and drinks. I've got some cash stashed away."

"Not necessary," Nelson said.

"And actually," Constance said, turning to her. "We have to make another stop first." She was speaking carefully, as if there was some delicate object balanced nearby that she didn't want to break.

"Sure," Zara said, unable to suppress a yawn. "Just wake me when we get there." She leaned against the seat. "Just like old times, huh?"

She could hear laughter in Constance's voice when she said, "I was thinking the same thing."

Constance's remark was the last thing she remembered until someone was shaking her. She almost struck out, thinking it was one of those bitches from the prison, but Constance's posh accent was unmistakable. "Zara, we're here."

Their errand must have taken some time because the sounds of city traffic had died down to practically nothing. She got out, stretching and scrubbing at her face. "Sorry, I was really bushed. Just give me a second to—" She cut herself off as she looked past Constance to the building behind her. "What the fuck?" They were parked out front of

Fullerhill, the last place she'd ever expected to be again. She turned to Constance. "When I said like old times, I didn't mean you had to go this far."

"Clive asked us to bring you, Zara. He's been visiting here regularly, and apparently, Lord Stansfield wants to see you."

Zara crossed her arms over her chest. "Well, I don't want to see him, thank you very much." She looked to Nelson. "If you won't take me back to the city, loan me the money for the bus, and I'll go down the road and wait." She narrowed her eyes. "I've done it before, as you well know."

Nelson looked troubled, but he shook his head. "Zara, we're only asking for a few minutes of your time. For Jillian."

Zara blinked, her heart leaping. "Is she here?"

"No," Constance said. "She hasn't been home since she started working for the VSO. But she would want this, I'm sure. For closure. For everyone concerned."

"Closure, huh? And after a few minutes, you'll take me to the city?"

"I'll take you directly to your flat as soon as your meeting with Lord Stansfield is over," Nelson clarified. "You have my word."

Maybe she was delirious. Or maybe since surviving a Hungarian prison, she was up for anything. She didn't want to admit it was most likely the mention of Jill's name. "Sure. A few minutes. But I'm going to need some coffee first."

Outside the kitchen, Mrs. Livingstone still guarded her former territory, and she shrank from Zara as if she was the devil incarnate. Constance took charge, explaining that his Lordship had requested a meeting with her.

"But he's already retired for the evening," Mrs. Livingstone protested.

Clive came from the hallway, assuring the housekeeper Zara's presence was absolutely necessary. Mrs. Livingstone crossed herself and went to make the coffee. Zara wouldn't have been surprised if she'd spit in it but thanked her as nicely as she could. They made their way toward a part of the manor where Zara hadn't been before.

"What's down there?" she asked, hanging back as Constance started along a hallway.

"Lord Stansfield's rooms. His office and the master bedroom suite," Nelson answered. "Weren't you in there when you—" He stopped abruptly, face turning red.

Zara crossed her arms, aware of what he was referring to. "No, I wasn't. Because I didn't."

"She's telling the truth." Clive's words made them all turn toward him. "Lord Stansfield and I wanted to deceive Jillian and make Zara look undesirable by having it appear she had stolen items of her mother's jewelry."

Zara's mouth opened slightly. "You admit it?" She took a step toward him, fists clenched. "You've got some fucking nerve."

"We each had our reasons. Does any of it matter now?" Clive looked directly at Zara for the first time. "But I am very sorry."

"As am I, Zara." Nelson moved closer, holding out his hand. "Please forgive me."

Zara was having a hard time making sense of all this sudden love and understanding. "Sure, fine." She shook Nelson's offered hand. "But could someone explain why I'm suddenly acceptable company when my last visit ended with me being tossed out on my ass?"

"Jillian wrote to each of us before she left," Constance said. "She was able to…to make us all see what was actually important. And we've all missed her so much since then, but I'm not sure what it will take for her to feel good about coming home." She fumbled in her bag. "She wrote to you too, but she didn't know where to send it, so…"

Zara stared at the thick envelope with her name on it. After a few seconds, she tucked it into her jacket pocket. "I'll read it later," she said, pleased her voice didn't give away the way her pulse had jumped.

Constance nodded, and they moved into the sitting room. Lord Stansfield seemed smaller than Zara remembered. He rose unsteadily from a beautifully upholstered wingback chair. His belted burgundy smoking jacket hung loosely over a pair of shapeless black trousers. He didn't move toward her, merely inclined his head at the group before addressing her.

"Thank you for coming, Miss Keller. Clive tells me you had a rather difficult time in your recent travels, and I appreciate you seeing me. Would you like to sit down?"

Zara wasn't ready to give him anything other than a brief shake of her head. "I'm fine, thanks."

After a few seconds of awkward silence, Douglas looked to the group. "Please excuse us for a few moments. Miss Keller will rejoin you shortly."

❖

Zara woke at half-past noon. After tossing and turning for a while, she got up, knowing sleep would be impossible once her mind started working. In spite of her overtiredness last night, she'd hadn't gone right to bed, spending some time mulling over her conversation with Jill's father and contemplating how unexpected it had been to see Jill's group of friends again.

Clive's admission of guilt had been pretty satisfying, and everyone had apologized. Even Lord Stansfield. When he'd moved toward her and taken her hand, the frail coolness of his skin had almost made her recoil. But his words had been warm. "I thought her being involved with you was the worst thing to happen. I was wrong. Please forgive me. And please forgive Jillian for going along with the idea of marrying Clive. She was only doing what she thought would make me happy. That was what we did for each other after her mother passed, until…"

He'd trailed off, coughing, and had pointed to the end table next to his chair. Alongside an empty glass was a piece of paper. It was an Indefinite Leave to Remain form with his name listed as her sponsor. She'd picked it up, nodding at him.

"Complete the information and take it to the American Embassy tomorrow," he'd said, his voice a soft wheeze. "Ask for First Secretary Norris. He's expecting you."

Zara had been stunned. "This is very kind. Thank you, sir."

The coughing had started again, and Zara had grabbed the glass and filled it with water from his bathroom sink. She couldn't help noticing the large number of pill bottles on the counter. He'd managed a few sips before lowering himself into his chair. "I want to see my daughter before I die. There are things I need to tell her."

"I'll do what I can, sir."

He'd nodded, closing his eyes, before whispering, "And make her happy." After a few seconds, when it became clear he'd needed to rest, Zara had left him there. She wasn't sure how to answer his last comment, since making Jill happy wasn't up to her. Not only had Jillian gone along with marrying Clive, the way she'd left so abruptly at the airport had made Zara wonder if she'd hallucinated those moments by the van. In any case, it was apparent Jill didn't want anything more to do with her.

The next morning, she scrounged some cereal, which she ate dry, and had a cup of tea. She was dressing to go out when the phone rang. It was Rader calling to tell her they were still waiting on Tiki's test results, but she was going home to shower and rest. Zara promised to go by the hospital later. She shrugged into her ripped jacket, feeling the crinkle of Jill's letter. She stood motionless, pondering Jill's behavior again. Thinking of visiting the embassy today made her wonder if the embassy in Hungary, or at least the VSO, had asked Jill to intercede on their behalf. If getting them out had simply been a work assignment, that would explain why she'd been nice at the van, then couldn't get away fast enough at the airport. She'd done the job, and that was that.

Feeling the envelope again, Zara reasoned that the letter's contents were probably a "Dear Jane" message, offering a last good-bye. And why not, considering how, in their last conversation, Zara had told her to fuck off. It was a shame she wouldn't be able to fulfill a dying man's last wish, but it seemed obvious she wasn't the one to make Jillian Stansfield happy.

CHAPTER TWENTY

Clive stood to pace just as he had done off and on for the last three hours while awaiting Jillian's phone call. They'd talked the night before when she'd rung to make sure they'd been able to find Zara and her band at the airport.

At the beginning of the call, Jillian's voice had been warm but calm, as usual. They'd been talking every month or so over the years, ever since they'd started being completely honest with each other, and their relationship was better than ever. When he'd gently asked how it had been for her to see Zara again, Jillian had begun crying, heartrending, agonizing sobs made all the more poignant as she'd tried to control herself. By the time she'd managed to finish the story, Clive knew he couldn't mention the way Zara had taken the girl to the hospital or even how she'd gone to Fullerhill and spoken with Douglas.

On a personal level, Clive doubted he'd ever been in love, but he knew Jillian Stansfield better than he knew himself in some ways, and she wouldn't cry that way over someone she didn't care about. Which made him wonder about Zara and how she'd acted rather strangely when she'd rejoined them after her conversation with Douglas, refusing Nelson's offer to drive her home and requesting a taxi instead. Now he wondered if it was a deliberate move on her part to keep them from finding her again. But why?

Earlier this afternoon, he'd had to send another telegram through the VSO, asking Jillian to phone him ASAP. This would be the second difficult conversation of the day, the first one being Mrs. Livingstone's call this morning, her voice tinged with a panic he'd never heard from her before.

"I think his Lordship might be having a heart attack."

"Call an ambulance," Clive had told her. "Have them take him to St. Thomas. I'll meet you there." He'd considered trying to contact Jillian right then but had decided it would be best to see Douglas's condition first. Finding Lord Stansfield in the ICU, Clive's brief visit with him had been enough to send him to the VSO office before going home to wait for Jillian's next call. He didn't want to break this news by telegram. And Lord Stansfield would need to know his daughter was on her way, if only to give the old man a reason to hang on.

Another hour had passed before the phone rang. The connection was terrible, as was often the case in the places Jillian called from, but he knew she heard him when he said, "You need to come home immediately, Jilly. He won't last long."

There was static for a few seconds before she said, "All right. I'll call you when I've arrived."

After another phone call to the Garricks, telling them Jillian was on her way, he'd asked Nelson to keep vigil outside the ICU and had given Constance a different job. "I need you to find the girl Zara brought in. Wait there until Zara comes to visit and then get her address and phone number. We need to be able to find her later if she doesn't agree to our plan now."

"Right," Constance agreed, and Clive knew that if anyone could work the system or walk the floors if necessary, it would be Constance. "Are we going to—"

"We're going to try. But the timing is terrible with Douglas being sick, so I don't know."

They both sighed. "It's got to work, Clive," Constance said, her voice quavering. "For both their sakes."

Jillian didn't get in until late in the evening, but she insisted on going directly to the hospital. Even in the intermittent headlights, Clive could see how drawn her face was.

"How is he?" she asked, and as much as he wanted to ease her into the situation, he knew she needed the truth.

"He's stable at the moment, but the doctors think he's too weak to withstand an operation. It's a matter of days, possibly weeks. But no more than that."

Jillian nodded, apparently not shocked by his assessment. She didn't say anything else, and Clive kept quiet, wanting her to have whatever rest she could. St Thomas was much calmer than it was during the day but not deserted. He'd already made arrangements with an ICU nurse to let Jillian in at whatever hour she might arrive, and the woman was as good as her word. The usual length of visitation was fifteen minutes, but that time came and went while he sat in the waiting room. After almost forty minutes, he heard alarms and saw a flurry of activity as Jillian came through the doors, pale and shaking.

"They're working on him, but…"

Clive rose and took her hand. "Do you want to stay?"

She shook her head. "We…I think we said everything we needed to say. If he's ready to go now, I'm ready to let him."

"Would you like to stay at my flat?" Clive asked softly. "I have a guest room."

"Yes, please. I haven't been sleeping well, and I don't think I can face being at Fullerhill just now." She swayed and he put his arm around her, guiding her to his car.

Once he'd shown her around and put her things in the guest room, she said, "It's strange to be in London again. So much is the same—the sounds, the smells—but it feels different."

"Everything will be better in the morning," Clive told her. "I'll be here to make sure."

Zara walked briskly down the hall, apparently in high spirits. Constance had already enjoyed an enlightening conversation with the young woman in the bed closest to the door, and it was all she could do not to pounce on Zara the moment she came within range. When Zara saw her, Constance detected the slightest hesitation, making her even more disposed to snare her as if she was easily spooked quarry.

"What are you doing here?" Zara had clearly summoned her nerve; her tone sounded almost combative.

"I need to talk to you…alone. But have your visit first," she added graciously. "I'll wait."

Zara looked as if she was considering disputing, then thought better of it. She muttered something which might have been, "Fine," and disappeared into the room.

Constance moved a few steps down the hall, congratulating herself on not listening in, though she desperately wanted to. Nelson was obviously a good influence, but she'd always known that about him.

After less than fifteen minutes, Zara reemerged, a puzzled expression on her face. "I need to make a phone call before we talk. Tiki's getting released today, and she wants Rader to come get her."

"Certainly," Constance said. "There's a phone in the cafeteria downstairs. We can get tea."

"But we share a flat," Zara said through a mouthful of ham sandwich. "Wouldn't it make more sense for me to take her?"

"Well…" Constance leaned forward conspiratorially. "We only spoke for a few minutes, but I got the impression Tiki has developed a fondness for this Rader person."

"Yeah, she said so. And why not, I guess."

"You guess?" Constance wasn't too happy with her equivocation.

"The thing is, when two people in a band get involved, it can wreak havoc on the dynamics of the group, you know?"

"I don't know. But if I understand you correctly, your concern has more to do with the workings of your ensemble than with any feelings you have for Tiki, correct?"

Zara gave her a look. "My feelings for Tiki are solidly in the friend category. And she's aware."

"Based on our little chat, she is, and she isn't," Constance said. "If nothing else, she's quite protective of you, worried about your emotional well-being."

Shaking her head, Zara put down her meal. "She told you that?"

"Mmm. And more importantly for our purposes, she told Jillian that."

Zara paled. "What are you talking about?"

"Apparently, your friend Tiki had a conversation with Jillian in the airport restroom in which she warned Jilly against hurting you again and told her she should leave you alone." Ignoring Zara's open mouth, Constance added, "She gave me to understand her main objection was that Jillian is a married woman. Which, of course, she isn't."

Zara felt like a swarm of bees were flying around in her brain, stinging her here and there. But it wasn't hard to decide which one to swat first. "What do you mean, she isn't?"

"Jillian isn't married, Zara." Constance's voice was surprisingly gentle. "Clive was actually the one who called off the wedding, but Jillian would have if he hadn't."

The buzzing diminished. "But her father said she went along with—"

Constance shook her head. "She went along with the *idea*, just to keep peace in the family until she could work out how to tell everyone she wasn't going through with it. Haven't you read her letter?"

Zara felt in her jacket. The paper rustled. "No, not yet."

"Maybe you should. And then come to Fullerhill this evening for dinner." Constance squeezed her hand. "Lord Stansfield had a heart attack. He's not expected to be with us much longer. Jilly came in last night and she—"

"I'll be there," Zara said. "What time?"

When Zara walked into Fullerhill that evening, still carrying Jillian's letter in her jacket pocket, everything looked different to her: brighter, sweeter, more pleasing. The museum quality of the home was unchanged, but she wasn't looking at that. Instead, she saw young Jillian playing sedately among the precious objects, soaking up the history and the sentimental meaning of everything surrounding her, learning about things but remaining distant from people.

At first, Jillian had said in her letter, she had thought her friends truly understood her, but came to realize they were only playing at it, like a game of make-believe. She hadn't minded because she didn't really understand them either. She knew her own mind as it pertained to her work, but she'd never known her heart. "Not until I met you," Jillian had written.

Until then, Zara had been in suspense, a niggling apprehension of a farewell to come still hovering in her mind. She'd been lying on her back, the letter above her face, just trying to get through it without breaking down. But at that shift, she'd sat upright, knees drawn up, with the letter resting on them.

The next line had felt like the beginning and the end. "I love you." Jillian's perfect handwriting had seemed to blur, and Zara had to set the writing aside until she could be certain her eyes were focusing correctly. When she'd picked the letter up, the words were still there. She'd read them again. "I love you. And my love has grown since the first moment we met. Do you remember what those women in the bar said about dog years? I knew then that I wanted forever with you. But I couldn't bring myself to tell you. Why not? As I've prepared to leave England for what might be forever, I've thought more about that than I have about anything else. Why do I have the nerve to leave forever but lack the courage to stay forever?"

Because I never told you, either. But I love you too. I wanted forever with you. I was even more gutless because I had less to lose. I couldn't let myself believe in us, so I took the cretin's way out the first chance I got, not expecting how much it would hurt. Not knowing it would hurt still.

There was one other page, but Zara had folded the letter back into its envelope. She'd needed time to get her head together for dinner this evening. Part of her hadn't wanted to start reading Jill's words for fear that when she was done, their something would be over for good.

Now, walking down the long hallway, Zara stopped to watch two men she didn't recognize making their way around the various rooms. One carried a calculator, the other a notepad. She was so intent on their activities, she didn't notice Clive and Nelson coming from the kitchen until they were nearly on top of her.

She forgot the apology she'd prepared for leaving so abruptly the night before and gestured toward the other two men. "What's going on?"

Clive took in a breath. "Lord Stansfield transferred his accounts to me—well, to my firm—a few months ago. Only then did I learn that, for all practical purposes, the Bank of England already owns Fullerhill. Lord Stansfield has apparently been trying to raise funds for some time now with no success. He might be able to make another month or two, but the amount of debt is going to catch up with him... uh, with them...sooner than later."

Zara turned to Nelson, seeking confirmation. He nodded sadly. Zara blinked. "But the stuff inside here—"

"Along with the debt," Clive cut her off, "there will also be taxes upon his death. I'm not sure if selling every single thing will clear them."

They stood in silence for a few moments while Zara tried to absorb the news. Finally, she asked, "Does Jill know?"

Clive shook his head. "Not yet. Given her father's condition, I haven't been able to bring myself to tell her." He paused for a few seconds. "We haven't even told her you're here."

Zara assumed they were protecting Jill as they'd always done, guarding her against hurt, or so they thought. "Should I go? I can come another time."

"No, no. Please stay. She and Constance are at St. Thomas. They'll be here for dinner. Unless...." Nelson trailed off, not stating the obvious issue of mortality.

Zara turned to watch the men working. "So what are they doing?"

"Getting an assessment," Nelson answered. "It has to be done before the bank takes possession."

This was going from bad to worse. "When will that happen?"

Clive shrugged. "It could be anywhere from six months to a year. But the process is under way, meaning it's inevitable at this point."

"But..." Zara began, trying to frame her thoughts in an acceptable way. "There must be something left for Jill. I mean, where will she live? And how? I don't imagine working for the VSO pays much more than playing in a band."

Nelson and Clive exchanged glances. After a few seconds of silence, Clive said, "Come for a drive with me, Zara. Please. There's something I want to show you."

Zara couldn't remember the last time he'd called her by name, much less asked her for something as politely. "Uh, okay. Sure."

They took Nelson's sturdy sedan rather than Clive's sports coupe. When she asked where they were going, he simply repeated that he had something to show her. At the main road, they turned the opposite way, driving alongside the Fullerhill property, a way Zara had never gone. She'd never thought of Clive as the type to drive her down a deserted road and beat the shit out of her—or worse—but maybe he'd hired someone else to do it? She should have remembered the apology.

Clive turned off on a rough dirt road, and she tried to calculate the distance they'd driven, but it was almost dark and impossible to find landmarks. They bounced along for another minute or two before he turned sharply, shining his headlights on a small structure. Opening his door, he gestured to her, and she stepped out, looking around anxiously. When she spotted a small rise beyond the building, her breath caught, and she realized exactly where she was. This was the boundary, as Jill had called it, though her friends referred to it as "the ruins." But it wasn't a ruin any longer. She turned back to the building. What had been a collapsing shell was now a complete, cozy-looking home. Modest, or undersized compared to Fullerhill, it had the wattle and daub exterior but was clearly a new construction. It would be perfect for two or perhaps for a small family.

Zara turned to Clive with her mouth open. He smiled. "It's my impression Lord Stansfield spent the last of his ready cash to create this home for Jillian." He sniffed. "And for you, I suppose, if you're so inclined. Apparently, he knew the end was coming for Fullerhill. And perhaps even for himself. This small portion of the estate is strictly in Jillian's name, and as such, is not involved in any of the larger bankruptcy issues."

Zara looked at the tidy home again and considered the new dirt drive carved out of the woods. It was completely unlike the grandeur of Fullerhill and much more like the person she'd seen in the Jillian Stansfield she'd known. "Damn, Clive. This is perfect. Jillian will—"

She tried to swallow around the unexpected lump in her throat. Seeing this place, Zara could easily get lost in her favorite dream of a future with Jill. The one where they were together, living quiet, contented lives. In love. But the Jill who had written the letter Zara was still carrying, professing her love, could have changed in the past years. Was there any chance she still felt the something…for her?

Clive patted her shoulder awkwardly. "Jillian will love it."

"Yeah."

"There's just one thing," he said with a slight frown.

Of course there was. How could she be so gullible as to get lost in her dreams and forget there was always a catch? "What?" she asked, apprehensive that she might be it.

"Jillian's not to know until the reading of the will."

Zara gaped at him. "What? Why not?"

Clive took a breath. "I know it sounds rather conniving, but I sincerely think his Lordship didn't want to risk Jillian selling it off to try to save him. Or to save Fullerhill. He wants this to be hers with no regrets."

Zara thought about it. She wouldn't have pegged Jill's father as an optimist. "Judging by what we talked about the other night, I thought he'd know better. There's no such thing as a world with no regrets." And she should know.

Clive said nothing at first, only indicated they return to the car. As they began the drive back, he cleared his throat. "Speaking of regrets, there are two things I want to tell you, Zara. The first is about the accident with the fire. I…I want you to know I've cut back on my drinking since the night it happened. I'm very much aware my condition at the time doesn't excuse my behavior, but knowing about what your injury meant and thinking about what could have happened to Jillian…it changed me. Ultimately, I called off our wedding because it became obvious to me how much Jillian felt for you, and not standing in your way seemed like the best way to, in some small way, make up for what happened."

Zara flexed her left hand. The accident had changed her too, but she still had her music. In a way, forgiving him could complete her healing. She nodded. "Okay, yeah."

They drove in silence for a few minutes. She wasn't sure if Clive expected something more or if he was preparing himself for saying more.

"I also want you to know how much I respect your...openness... about your life," he said quietly. "Maybe someday, we'll all be able to live that way."

Hearing him say "we" confirmed something she had long suspected. He was gay. But still, she answered cautiously. "We can't wait for someone else to decide we're okay. If we want freedom, we have to live it. Constance and Nelson—"

"Constance and Nelson have decided that since Jillian loves you, they will too. They don't know anyone who loves me." He laughed bitterly. "Hell, I don't know anyone who loves me."

"Jill loves you, Clive. Just in a different way."

"Hmm."

She gave him a playful nudge. "Are you looking for Mr. Right?"

He gave her a sideways look. "I'm fine with Mr. Right Now."

Constance hadn't changed a bit, Jillian thought. Neither time nor marriage nor working part-time nor even Lord Stansfield's illness could alter her ability to chatter in a sweet but mostly meaningless way. Jillian was certain the chitchat was partially to keep her mind off that last thing. Douglas was fading. Not suffering, thank God, but there was a little less of him each time she saw him. It was strange because he'd always been this larger-than-life figure, and for a long time, he'd been her hero. Until he wasn't.

When Clive had given her the news, Jillian had wondered if there would be enough time to reestablish at least forgiveness, if not love, with her father. Their last conversation before she'd left had been more of an argument, ostensibly about her joining the VSO, although they'd both known the real issue had nothing to do with her plans to use her engineering degree on water systems in underdeveloped countries or underserved regions. Since she'd finished at Cambridge, there was nothing for him to hold over her head, so her announcement about not marrying Clive had been met with stony silence. Finally, he'd said, "I don't know what more you could want if not him."

"I've lost what I wanted through my own misdeeds. Perhaps doing something worthwhile can help me compensate for it in the larger scheme of things."

He'd thrown up his hands. "I hope you don't expect me to understand what you mean."

She'd suspected he did, but knew anything more would be wasted breath. She'd needed to move on, to get started with a new life, so she'd kissed his cheek and told him she loved him, not knowing if it might be the last time she would have a chance to do either. Now, she was glad it hadn't been.

ICU notwithstanding, she'd gone in to see her father while intending to speak her mind. She'd told him she knew Zara hadn't stolen her mother's jewels, and he'd admitted his part in the deception. Slightly nonplussed, she'd added that she wasn't going to tolerate the kind of bullying he'd done after Constance and Nelson's wedding ever again. He'd apologized profusely, offering no excuse, only saying he deeply regretted how poorly he'd behaved. At that, she'd sat in the small room where he was being constantly monitored, had taken his hand, and had told him she'd loved Zara and wasn't going to change. She hadn't yet found another person to share her life, but she was quite positive that when she did, it would be another woman.

"I just want you to be happy," he'd said, wheezing faintly. "Are you giving up on her?"

Jillian had almost managed to keep her voice steady when she'd replied, "I think she's given up on me. She's with someone else."

"Is she?" he'd asked, sounding stunned. Then the alarms on one of the devices connected to his chest had starting squealing, and the nurse had rushed in, pushing her out the door.

"Come back tomorrow," the nurse had ordered. "He needs rest now"

Today, he'd wanted to talk about her mother, a subject that had been all but forbidden beyond a superficial mention in the decade-plus since she'd died. "I'm glad you had each other," Jillian had told him.

"You should have someone too," he'd answered.

"Maybe someday," Jillian had said, forcing a smile.

"Maybe sooner." He'd patted her hand and closed his eyes.

Walking out, she and Constance had stopped to get some coffee. Jillian drank a lot of it these days, probably too much, since Mrs. Livingstone was no longer scrutinizing her daily intake. Sometimes, she almost missed that part of her life where everything was supervised and controlled and safe before remembering it was also restrictive, censoring, and unrealistic. Or maybe the reality of it had been somewhere in between.

"My father was talking about my mother," Jillian said once they'd gotten in the car. "Do you still believe they'll see each other in heaven?"

Jillian could admit to herself she had an ulterior motive for asking. She was too tired to make conversation, and she was betting Constance could carry this topic on her own for a while. It wasn't until she felt Constance taking the tilting coffee cup from her hands that she realized she'd fallen asleep.

"I'm so sorry," she apologized.

Constance patted her shoulder. "Don't worry. I know exactly how you feel. When we're in bed and I'm dead tired but can't quite fall asleep, I ask Nelson to tell me about his day."

Jillian couldn't hold back a snort, and in seconds, they were both wiping tears of laughter from their faces. "God, I've missed you," she said.

Constance took her hand. "I've missed you too, dearest. We all have. Please say you'll stay for a little while, at least."

"I'll go by the VSO office tomorrow and ask for a leave of absence," Jillian agreed. "I'm sure there are lots of things I need to take care of here."

"Indeed," Constance murmured, turning in at the driveway.

As they pulled up to the house, Jillian was stirred by an odd feeling of nervous anticipation. Clive and Nelson stood in the open door, arms around each other's shoulders like schoolboy chums. Jillian's happiness felt more genuine than it had in a long time, and a swell of gratitude filled her. How very special it was to have these friends, people she'd known her whole life. Even if they didn't completely understand her, they knew her and she them. The "gang of four" was together again. She wouldn't let herself think about her perfect fifth. Not now.

They shared a group hug and group tears. Then Jillian walked slowly down the hallway, her friends trailing her as she reacquainted herself with her family home. It was still beautiful, but after spending almost three years in poverty and deprivation, it also felt uncomfortably excessive. It would be selfish to burden her friends with her uneasiness, so she kept her smile in place, wondering if any of them would notice the new artificiality in her expression. In the dining room, a round table was set with five places. Her heart gave a little blip until she concluded it was intended to honor her father.

Mrs. Livingstone appeared, and they shared a long hug. When the housekeeper's expression suggested an apology was forthcoming, Jillian shook her head. "It's wonderful to see you. Won't you join us for dinner?" She indicated the extra seat.

Mrs. Livingstone laid a gentle hand on Jillian's cheek. "You can't have forgotten your manners, so I know your asking is meant to be gracious. But come see me later in the kitchen, will you?" Jillian nodded, and Mrs. Livingstone turned to Clive. "Could I see you for a moment, please, sir?"

Clive excused himself and followed her.

"I'll take your things to your room, Jilly," Nelson offered. "And Constance can unpack for you while you finish your tour."

It seemed silly to go on with her inspection since everything seemed the same. "There's no need for you to—" Jillian began, but they waved her off.

"Please, dearest. This is something we want to do for you." Constance gave her a quick kiss on the cheek. "You'll want a moment alone with things here."

Jillian shook her head fondly as they disappeared. She turned toward the terrace, and as she stepped out, her gratitude for the sensitivity of her friends redoubled. They were right. She did need a minute. She needed to revisit her memories here, good and bad. And just breathe.

After a few moments, she looked into the sky, wondering if Zara was seeing the same stars. When she heard movement behind her, she prepared to turn, to make some genial comment about being back in one of her favorite places. But before she could move, a soft voice said, "Hi. Your friends said it was okay to crash your reunion. I hope they were right."

Jillian froze, the familiar words making her breath catch, the unforgettable sounds filling her heart. She turned slowly, finding Zara's eyes. Zara's lips were parted slightly, as if she might say more. Or maybe it was for something else. She would take either. Or both.

Jillian walked to her, steps sure and unwavering. Taking Zara's hand, she said, "They were right. You're always welcome here, Miss Keller."

Zara grinned. "Any friend of Constance's?" she asked. Jill laughed, and they both looked at their joined hands. "There's so much I need to tell you," she whispered.

"And I want to hear it all. But first, there's something I need to show you."

When Zara kissed her, Jill knew she was truly home.

Epilogue

Sleeping on a mattress on the floor reminded Zara of a couple of the flophouses she'd stayed in, not that she'd admit it. And anyway, this mattress was clean and really comfortable. Plus, Jill was next to her, as opposed to some out-of-luck junkie or poor kid running away from an abusive home.

They'd brought a few pieces of furniture from the manor house and the Lady and the Unicorn tapestry. Zara gestured at it, watching Jill walk naked from the shower. "You know that means 'to my only desire.'"

Jill smiled, bending to kiss Zara again. "It does now."

Lord Stansfield's funeral hadn't been the glum event Zara had dreaded. Jill had asked everyone not to wear black, and she had been stunning in a bright green dress, belted at the waist. The reception at the Guildworth church had been lovely, and Lady Stansfield had willingly taken time with all her father's cronies and her more distant acquaintances. When it was all over, though, she'd asked Nelson to take her back to the graveyard. She'd sat on the ground between her parents' graves and had talked to them.

"As if they were there," Nelson had said.

"Do you think she's all right?" Constance had asked worriedly.

"She's just fine," Zara had assured them both. And she was.

Clive had arranged for the National Trust to take over Fullerhill, explaining tearfully to them it was the only way, given the debt and the death taxes. Jillian had hugged him for a long time, whispering in his ear. Then the four of them had met there last evening for one last hurrah. Zara hadn't minded that the return of All Out meant she couldn't attend. Fullerhill had never been her place, but she'd thought Newbeck, as they'd officially christened their home on the boundary, might be. Especially since the Trust had offered Lady Stansfield the job of caring for the grounds. Zara wasn't sure she'd ever seen Jill so happy. Naturally, they were still working out the kinks in their schedules—with Zara performing at night and Jill rising with the sun—but with forever in both their minds, nothing had seemed too difficult.

"You know," Zara said casually, thinking this might be a good time to mention something that had been bothering her. "I never read the last page of your letter."

"I know." Jill slipped on her robe as Zara sat up on the mattress.

"What do you mean?"

"Because the last page was the same in everyone's letter. It was my bequests." She looked away for a few seconds. "In case something happened to me."

"Oh shit, babe. Never mind, then." Zara suppressed a shiver.

"No, not never mind. I decided to go ahead with what I'd planned. To the extent I could, I took care of everyone else last night."

"What do you mean?"

Jill went to the wardrobe and tossed Zara a T-shirt and shorts. "Get dressed while I tell you."

When Lady Stansfield got that commanding tone in her voice, Zara knew better than to argue. She liked it best when they were in bed, but Jill was dressing as well. "I gave Constance my mother's gemstone comb and brooch. It's really beautiful and unusual, like she is." Zara grinned. "For Nelson, my father's three volume set of David Roberts's *The Holy Land: Syria, Idumea, Arabia, Egypt, and Nubia.* It's a rare special edition, just like he is."

"I'm sensing a trend here," Zara teased.

"Indeed." Jill smiled. "And for Clive, something that expresses my fondest wish for him. My father's partner's desk."

"That's a beautiful piece," Zara said. Jill had walked her through every room before they'd moved into Newbeck, pointing out various pieces and telling stories of her past. "And a beautiful wish. I think we all have those same hopes for Clive.

Jill nodded. "Father never used the partner side of it, but perhaps Clive will, someday." Her expression turned solemn. "My darling Zara, I wanted you to have the Blüthner."

Zara felt a pang of loss. She'd taken Jill on a trip to the beach at St Ives, South Cornwall, during the week of the sale, not wanting her to have to watch so many of her childhood remembrances going out the door in the hands of strangers. Clive had told her the offer on the Blüthner grand had been too good to pass up, and she'd readily agreed. It was an amazing instrument, but her playing wasn't up to that level anymore. "Jill, it doesn't matter. I already have everything I could ever want."

Jill took her hands. "But as it happens, Mrs. Livingstone bought her great nephew a used piano several years ago, hoping he would take it up, but he never did." Zara heard the sound of a truck rumbling down their driveway, and Jill gestured toward it. "I was telling her what had happened with the Blüthner, and she said she wanted you to have his."

"Wait. Mrs. Livingstone hates me. Why would she want me to have anything other than a boot out the door?"

"She doesn't hate you. She was just trying to protect me. She didn't understand. We had a long talk and—" There was a knock on the door, and Jill went to open it. "Wonderful. Bring it in and put it over there, please."

Two burly men carried a large upright into the only empty corner of the room. Jill had always been vague about what they might put there. One of the men tipped his hat. "Lady said to tell you the tuner will be by in an hour."

Jill thanked them and closed the door. Zara was standing dumbstruck, so Jill went over and lifted the cover off the keys. When Zara saw the Steinway name, she covered her face with her hands. "Oh my God. This is…this is…."

When she didn't go on, Jill put her arms around Zara's neck. "Is it not all right?"

Zara took a shuddering breath and lifted her face to meet Jill's eyes. "This is exactly the model Mrs. Minton had. The one I learned to play on. The one I—"

"Deserved to have?" Jill finished.

Zara held Jill as tightly as she could, feeling like her life had somehow come full circle. The home, the family, and all the love she'd ever lost had come back to her in Jillian Stansfield.

About the Author

Jaycie Morrison traded the heat of her lifetime big city home of Dallas, Texas, for the cool beauty of the mountains in a small Colorado town and hasn't regretted a moment of it. After beginning her writing career with the historical Love and Courage series, she wrote her first contemporary romance, *The Found Jar*, which was a Goldie finalist. *A Perfect Fifth* steps back into the 1970s and brings in Jaycie's love of music. When not writing, Jaycie may be hiking, dreaming about traveling, or experimenting with gluten-free cooking. Catch Jaycie's doings at www.jayciemorrison.com or reach her at jaycie.morrison @yahoo.com. She is also on Facebook at https://www.facebook.com /jaycie.morrison

Books Available from Bold Strokes Books

A Good Chance by Ali Vali. Harry, Desi, and Desi's sister Rachel are so close to getting everything they've ever wanted, but Desi's ex-husband is coming back to get his revenge and rip apart their chance at happiness. (978-1-63679-023-7)

A Perfect Fifth by Jaycie Morrison. Streetwise pianist Zara Keller and Lady Jillian Stansfield couldn't be more different; yet their connection brings a new awareness of who they are and what they truly want in their lives—including each other. (978-1-63679-132-6)

Catching Feelings by Ana Hartnett Reichardt. Andrea Foster expected to catch a lot of pitches from the Alder Lion's star pitcher, Maya, but she didn't expect to catch feelings. (978-1-63679-227-9)

Defiant Hearts by Lee Lynch. In these stories, you'll find your lovers, friends, and lesbians you wish you knew—maybe even yourself. (978-1-63679-237-8)

Love and Duty by Catherine Young. All Princess Roseli wants is to marry her three lovers, but with war looming, she must instead marry Princess Lucia to establish a military alliance between their planets. (978-1-63679-256-9)

Murder at Union Station by David S. Pederson. Private Detective Mason Adler struggles to determine who killed a woman found in a trunk without getting himself killed in the process. (978-1-63679-269-9)

Serendipity by Kris Bryant. Serendipity brings jingle writer Annie Foster and celebrity pop star Bristol Baines together, and their undeniable attraction keeps them close, but will their different paths drive them apart? (978-1-63679-224-8)

The Haunted Heart by Jane Kolven. A ghost, a ring, and a quest to find a missing psychic—it's a spell for love. (978-1-63679-245-3)

The Rules of Forever by Nan Campbell. After reconnecting at their high school reunion, Cara and Lauren agree to embark on a textbook definition friends-with-benefits relationship, but trying to keep it uncomplicated is harder than it seems. (978-1-63679-248-4)

Vision of Virtue by Brey Willows. When virtue and desire come together, be prepared for sparks in this next installment of the Memory's Muses series. (978-1-63679-118-0)

Cherry on Top by Georgia Beers. A chance meeting leaves Cherry and Ellis longing for a different life, but when Ellis's search for truth crashes into Cherry's insta-filter world, do they have any hope at all of a happily ever after? (978-1-63679-158-6)

Love and Other Rare Birds by Angie Williams. Ornithologist Dr. Jamie Martin and park ranger Rowan Fleming are searching the Alaskan wilderness for a bird thought to be extinct and they're about to discover opposites really do attract. (978-1-63679-108-1)

Parallel Paradise by Mayapee Chowdhury. When their love affair is put to the test by the homophobia of their family, community, and culture, Bindi and Rimli will need to fight for a chance at love. (978-1-63679-204-0)

Perfectly Matched by Toni Logan. A beautiful Cupid named Hannah, a runaway arrow, and just seventy-two hours to fix a mishap that could be the best mistake she has ever made. (978-1-63679-120-3)

Royal Exposé by Jenny Frame. When they're grouped together for a class assignment, Poppy's enthusiasm for life and love may just save Casey's soul, but will she ever forgive Casey for using her to expose royal secrets? (978-1-63679-165-4)

Slow Burn by Missouri Vaun. A wounded wildland firefighter from California and a struggling artist find solace and love in a small southern town. (978-1-63679-098-5)

The Artist by Sheri Lewis Wohl. Detective Casey Wilson and reclusive artist Tula Crane are drawn together in a web of passion, intrigue, and art that might just hold the key to stopping a killer. (978-1-63679-150-0)

The Inconvenient Heiress by Jane Walsh. An unlikely heiress and a spinster evade the Marriage Mart only to discover true love together. (978-1-63679-173-9)

A Champion for Tinker Creek by D.C. Robeline. Lyle James has rescued his dad's auto repair business, but when city hall condemns his neighborhood, Lyle learns only trusting will save his life and help him find love. (978-1-63679-213-2)

Closed-Door Policy by Erin Zak. Going back to college is never easy, but Caroline Stevens is prepared to work hard and change her life for the better. What she's not prepared for is Dr. Atlanta Morris, her gorgeous new professor. (978-1-63679-181-4)

Homeworld by Gun Brooke. Headed by Captain Holly Crowe, the spaceship Velocity's crew journeys toward their alien ancestors' homeworld, and what they find is completely unexpected—and they're not safe. (978-1-63679-177-7)

Outland by Kristin Keppler & Allisa Bahney. Danielle Clark and Katelyn Turner can't seem to stay away from one another even as the war for the wastelands tests their loyalty to each other and to their people. (978-1-63679-154-8)

Secret Sanctuary by Nance Sparks. US Deputy Marshal Alex Trenton specializes in protecting those awaiting trial, but when danger threatens the woman she's falling for, Alex is in for the fight of her life. (978-1-63679-148-7)

Stranded Hearts by Kris Bryant, Amanda Radley, Emily Smith. In these novellas from award winning authors, fate intervenes on behalf of love when characters are unexpectedly stuck together. With too much time and an irresistible attraction, anything could happen. (978-1-63679-182-1)

The Last Lavender Sister by Melissa Brayden. Aster Lavender sells her gourmet doughnuts and keeps a low profile; she never plans on the town's temporary veterinarian swooping in and making her feel like anything but a wallflower. (978-1-63679-130-2)

The Probability of Love by Dena Blake. As Blair and Rachel keep ending up in the same place despite the odds, can a one-night stand turn into forever? Or will the bet Blair never intended to make ruin their happily ever after? (978-1-63679-188-3)

Worth a Fortune by Sam Ledel. After placing a want ad for a personal secretary, a New York heiress is surprised when the woman who got away is the one interested in the position. (978-1-63679-175-3)

A Fox in Shadow by Jane Fletcher. Cassie's mission is to add new territory to the Kavillian empire—murder, betrayal, war, and the clash of cultures ensue. (978-1-63679-142-5)

Embracing the Moon by Jeannie Levig. Just as Gwen and Taylor are exploring the new love they've found, the present and past collide, threatening the future they long to share. (978-1-63555-462-5)

Forever Comes in Threes by D. Jackson Leigh. Efficiency expert Perry Chandler's ordered life is upended when she inherits three busy terriers, and the woman she's referred to for help turns out to be her bitter podcast rival, the very sexy Dr. Ming Lee. (978-1-63679-169-2)

Heckin' Lewd: Trans and Nonbinary Erotica by Mx. Nillin Lore. If you want smutty, fearless, gender diverse erotica written by affirming own-voices folks who get it, then this is the book you've been looking for! (978-1-63679-240-8)

Missed Conception by Joy Argento. Maggie Walsh wants a relationship with Cassidy, the daughter she's only just discovered she has due to an in vitro mix-up. Heat kindles between Maggie and Cassidy's mother in a way neither expects. (978-1-63679-146-3)

Private Equity by Elle Spencer. Cassidy Bennett spends an unexpected evening at a lesbian nightclub with her notoriously reserved and demanding boss, Julia. After seeing a different side of Julia, Cassidy can't seem to shake her desire to know more. (978-1-63679-180-7)

Racing the Dawn by Sandra Barrett. After narrowly escaping a house fire, vampire Jade Murphy is unexpectedly intrigued by gorgeous firefighter Beth Jenssen, and her undead existence might just be perking up a bit. (978-1-63679-271-2)

Reclaiming Love by Amanda Radley. Sarah's tiny white lie means somehow convincing Pippa to pretend to be her girlfriend. Only the more time they spend faking it, the more real it feels. (978-1-63679-144-9)

Sol Cycle by Kimberly Cooper Griffin. An encounter in a park brings Ang and Krista together, but when Ang's attempts to help Krista go spectacularly wrong, their passion for each other might not be enough. (978-1-63679-137-1)

Trial and Error by Carsen Taite. Attorney Franco Rossi and Judge Nina Aguilar's reunion is fraught with courtroom conflict, undeniable chemistry, and danger. (978-1-63555-863-0)

A Long Way to Fall by Elle Spencer. A ski lodge, two strong-willed women, and a family feud that brings them together, but will it also tear them apart? (978-1-63679-005-3)

Barnabas Bopwright Saves the City by J. Marshall Freeman. When he uncovers a terror plot to destroy the city he loves, 15-year-old Barnabas Bopwright realizes it's up to him to save his home and bring deadly secrets into the light before it's too late. (978-1-63679-152-4)

Forever by Kris Bryant. When Savannah Edwards is invited to be the next bachelorette on the dating show When Sparks Fly, she'll show the world that finding true love on television can happen. (978-1-63679-029-9)

Ice on Wheels by Aurora Rey. All's fair in love and roller derby. That's Riley Fauchet's motto, until a new job lands her at the same company—and on the same team—as her rival Brooke Landry, the frosty jammer for the Big Easy Bruisers. (978-1-63679-179-1)

Inherit the Lightning by Bud Gundy. Darcy O'Brien and his sisters learn they are about to inherit an immense fortune, but a family mystery about to unravel after seventy years threatens to destroy everything. (978-1-63679-199-9)

Perfect Rivalry by Radclyffe. Two women set out to win the same career-making goal, but it's love that may turn out to be the final prize. (978-1-63679-216-3)

Something to Talk About by Ronica Black. Can quiet ranch owner Corey Durand give up her peaceful life and allow her feisty new neighbor into her heart? Or will past loss, present suitors, and town gossip ruin a long-awaited chance at love? (978-1-63679-114-2)

With a Minor in Murder by Karis Walsh. In the world of academia, police officer Clare Sawyer and professor Libby Hart team up to solve a murder. (978-1-63679-186-9)

Writer's Block by Ali Vali. Wyatt and Hayley might be made for each other if only they can get through nosy neighbors, the historic society, at-odds future plans, and all the secrets hidden in Wyatt's walls. (978-1-63679-021-3)

BOLDSTROKESBOOKS.COM

Looking for your next great read?

Visit BOLDSTROKESBOOKS.COM
to browse our entire catalog of paperbacks, ebooks,
and audiobooks.

Want the first word on what's new?
Visit our website for event info,
author interviews, and blogs.

Subscribe to our free newsletter for sneak peeks,
new releases, plus first notice of promos
and daily bargains.

SIGN UP AT
BOLDSTROKESBOOKS.COM/signup

Bold Strokes Books
Quality and Diversity in LGBTQ Literature

*Bold Strokes Books is an award-winning publisher
committed to quality and diversity in LGBTQ fiction.*